THE DEEP END

Books by Joy Fielding

THE BEST OF FRIENDS

TRANCE

THE TRANSFORMATION

KISS MOMMY GOODBYE

THE OTHER WOMAN

LIFE PENALTY

THE DEEP END

THE
DEEP END

Joy Fielding

Doubleday & Company, Inc.
Garden City, New York

Doubleday Canada Limited
Toronto, Ontario

1986

Canadian Cataloguing in Publication Data
Fielding, Joy.
    The deep end
ISBN 0-385-19847-7
I. Title.
PS8561.I44D44   C813'.54   C86-093047-5
PR9199.3.F542D44 1986

Library of Congress Cataloging-in-Publication Data
Fielding, Joy.
    The deep end.
    I. Title.
PR9199.3.F518D44 1986   813'.54   85-16281
ISBN 0-385-19847-7

Designed by Virginia M. Soulé

For Shannon and Annie

THE DEEP END

Chapter 1

The phone is ringing.

Joanne Hunter stares at it from her seat at the kitchen table. She makes no move to answer it, already knowing who it is and what he will say. She has heard it before, has no desire to hear it again.

The phone continues to ring. Joanne, sitting alone at her kitchen table, closes her eyes, trying to conjure up images of happier times.

"Mom . . ."

Joanne hears her younger daughter's voice as if through a tunnel. Her eyes open slowly. She smiles toward the young girl in the doorway.

"Mom," her daughter repeats, "the phone's ringing." She looks at the white wall phone. "Should I answer it?" she asks, clearly disconcerted by her mother's zombielike state.

"No," Joanne tells her.

"It might be Daddy."

"Lulu, please . . ." But it is too late. Lulu's hand is already on the phone, lifting the receiver to her ear. "Hello? Hello?" She makes a face. "Is someone there?"

"Hang up, Lulu," her mother instructs sharply, then instantly softens her tone. "Hang up, sweetie."

"Why would someone call if they're not going to say anything?" the child pouts.

Joanne smiles at her daughter, named Lana on her birth certificate, called Lulu by everyone except her sixth-grade teacher. The child has the remarkable ability to look both younger and older than her eleven years.

"Are you all right?" Lulu asks.

"Fine," Joanne responds, her mouth a smile, her voice steady and reassuring.

"Why would someone do that?"

"I don't know," Joanne says truthfully, then lies, "maybe it was a wrong number." What else can she tell her daughter? That death is on the line? That he is merely "on hold"? "Are you ready to go?" she asks, changing the subject.

"I hate this dumb uniform," Lulu announces, looking down at herself. "Why couldn't they pick something pretty?"

Joanne checks her daughter's sturdy frame. Lulu is built more like her father, whereas Robin, her older daughter, is built more like herself, though both girls have their father's face. She thinks the dark green shorts and lemon yellow T-shirt are, in fact, flattering and well suited to her daughter's fair complexion and long, light brown hair. "Camp uniforms are always yucky," she tells the child, knowing it would be pointless to try to persuade her otherwise. "You look very sweet," she adds, unable to help herself.

"I look fat!" Lulu argues, an idea Robin has recently put into her head.

"You don't look fat." Joanne's inflection indicates the end of that particular topic of conversation. "Is Robin ready?" Lulu nods. "Is she still angry?"

"She's always angry."

Joanne laughs, knowing this to be true, but wishing it were not.

"What time is Daddy picking us up?"

Joanne checks her watch. "Soon," she realizes aloud. "I'd better get ready."

"Why?" Lulu asks as her mother stands up. "Are you coming with us?"

"No," Joanne acknowledges, remembering that they have already decided that it will be better if only Paul drives the girls to the bus. "I just thought I'd change . . ."

"What for?"

Joanne runs a nervous hand down the length of her orange T-shirt and white shorts. Orange is Paul's least favorite color, she recalls; the shorts are old; there is a stain on one cuff she hasn't noticed before. She would like to look nice for Paul, she thinks. She looks down at her bare feet. Her two big toenails are discolored a deep purple from playing tennis in shoes a half-size too small. She thinks of slipping on some sandals but decides against it. If Paul notices her toes, it will give them something to talk about. It has been several weeks since they talked about anything but the children.

The doorbell rings. Joanne's hand flies skittishly to her hair. She hasn't combed it yet this morning. Perhaps she could run quickly upstairs while Lulu is opening the door, pull a brush through her hair, change into the turquoise sundress that Paul always liked, and appear in the front hallway just as Paul and the girls are leaving, affording him only the briefest of glimpses, enough to whet his appetite, to make him think twice about what he has done.

It's already too late. Lulu is at the front door, leaving Joanne no room to run. Hand on the door handle, Lulu turns back to her mother, whose lips automatically flex upward into a smile. "You look fine, Mom," Lulu reassures her. She pulls open the front door.

The stranger who greets them is Paul Hunter, Joanne's husband of almost twenty years. He is of average height and build, though Joanne notices new muscles beginning to bulge from under his blue short-sleeved shirt, undoubtedly the result of his recently implemented weight-lifting regimen. She thinks in that instant that she prefers his arms the way she has always known them—on the thin side, not so carefully delineated. She has always had great difficulty adjusting to change. This is probably one of the things that drove Paul away in the first place.

"Hello, Joanne," he says warmly, his arm around their younger child. "You look well."

Joanne tries to speak but is unable to find her voice. She feels her knees go weak, is afraid that she is about to fall, or burst into tears, or both. She doesn't want to do this. It will make Paul uncomfortable, and that is the last thing she wants. Above all else, she wants her husband of almost twenty years to feel comfortable in his own home because she is still hoping that he will decide to come back. After all, nothing has been decided yet. It's only been two months. He is still "thinking things through." She is still in limbo, her future the direction in which his thoughts ultimately lead them.

"How have you been?" he asks, his presence filling the front hall.

"Fine," Joanne lies, knowing that he will believe her because this is what he wants to believe. He will not see the longing in her eyes, nor hear the quiver in her voice, not because he is a cruel man but because he is frightened. He is afraid that he will be pulled back into a life he no longer wants. And he is afraid because he doesn't know what he wants to replace it.

"What happened to your toes?" he asks.

"Mom's been playing tennis in shoes that were too tight," Lulu answers for her.

"They look very sore," Paul observes as Joanne notices for the first time how tanned he is, how well rested he appears.

"Actually," Joanne tells him truthfully, "they don't hurt. They did before they turned purple," she continues, "but now I guess they're kind of numb." Joanne thinks this is probably a good way to describe her life but doesn't say so. Instead she smiles, wondering whether she should invite him into the living room to sit down.

Paul checks his watch. "We should get going pretty soon," he says, his voice casual, as if he is really not concerned about leaving. "Where's Robin?"

"I'll get her," Lulu volunteers and disappears up the stairs, leaving her parents to walk their invisible tightrope without the safety net her presence provides.

"Would you like a cup of coffee?" Joanne asks as she follows Paul into the large, bright kitchen off the center hall.

"I'd better not." He walks directly to the sliding glass door that makes up the kitchen's south wall and stares into the backyard. "Quite a mess," he comments, shaking his head.

"You get used to it," Joanne tells him, realizing that she has.

The mess to which he refers and to which Joanne has adjusted herself is a large, empty, concrete-lined, boomerang-shaped hole that was supposed to have been their new swimming pool. Designed by Paul (though he is a lawyer by profession) to provide the optimum swimming area in the given space, it was intended originally to be their equivalent of a summer vacation, or as the man from Rogers Pools described it only days before his company went belly-up, their "summer cottage without the traffic."

"I'm doing all I can to get things moving again," Paul tells her.

"I'm sure you are." Joanne smiles to convince him that she understands he is not at fault. "What can you do?" She shrugs.

"It was my idea."

"I don't swim anyway," she reminds him.

He turns from the window. "How's your grandfather?"

"The same."

"And Eve?"

"The same." They laugh.

"Any more phone calls?" he continues after a slight pause.

"No," she lies, recognizing that to say otherwise would only make him edgy. He would then be forced to repeat what he has already told her: that everyone gets crank calls, that she is in no danger, that if she is really worried, she should call the police again, or better yet, call Eve's husband, Brian. He's a police sergeant and he lives right next door. These are the things he has already told her. He has also told her—as gently as he could—that he feels she is over-reacting and probably exaggerating, although this may not be inten-tional, that it is her way of keeping him tied to her, making him feel responsible for her when he has abdicated that responsibility, at least temporarily. He has not suggested, as her friend Eve has suggested, that the calls might be a product of her imagination, her way of dealing with her present situation. Joanne doesn't understand this theory of Eve's but then Eve is a psychologist as well as her best friend. And Joanne is what? Joanne is separated.

Separated, Joanne repeats silently, following Paul back into the hall. An especially apt description. Almost schizophrenic. Separated, she thinks, like an egg.

The girls are waiting for them at the foot of the stairs. "Got everything?" their father asks.

Joanne stares hard at her daughters, looking for hints of the children they once were in the young women they are now. Lulu has changed the least since infancy, she thinks, her enormous brown eyes —a gift from her father—still the focal point of her face, her other features existing merely as backdrop. If the baby jowls have thinned and shaped themselves into adolescence, if the lips have acquired an almost sultry pout, and the nose is now clearly a nose and not just a tiny bit of upturned flesh in the middle of her face, the eyes have remained the same. She has grown up around them.

Robin is different, although she, too, has her father's upturned nose and square-set jaw. At age fifteen, she is only now starting to peck her way out of the awkward shell that puberty imposes, one that Lulu has yet to enter. As a result, nothing quite matches, the legs too long, the body too short, her head too big. In another year or two, Joanne thinks, Robin will be beautiful, the elegant swan emerging from the ugly duckling. Surprisingly, however, and unlike Joanne at her daughter's age, Robin's looks are very "in." She dresses accord-ingly. Even now she has obliterated the bland statement of her camp uniform by defiantly lacing a shocking pink chiffon scarf through her short, overly permed hair. Her eyes—ordinary hazel eyes like her mother's—stare resolutely at the floor.

"I'll wait in the car," Paul tells them, opening the front door and stepping outside into the bright sunlight.

Joanne smiles at her daughters, feeling her heart beginning to pound against her chest. This is the first time, she realizes, that she will be completely on her own. Her entire life has been spent living with—living *for*—other people. Yet for the next two months, there will be no one but herself to look after.

"Don't worry, Mom," Lulu begins before Joanne has a chance to speak. "I know the speech by heart: I'll be careful; I won't take any silly chances; I'll write at least once a week; and I won't forget to eat. Did I leave anything out?"

"How about having a good time?" Joanne asks.

"I'll have a good time," Lulu agrees and throws her arms around her mother's neck. "Will you be all right?"

"Me?" Joanne asks, smoothing a few stray hairs out of her daughter's eyes. "I'll have a ball."

"Promise?"

"I promise."

"Things have a way of working out," Lulu intones so seriously that Joanne has to bring her hand to her mouth to hide a budding smile.

"Who told you that?"

"You do," Lulu informs her. "All the time."

This time, Joanne's smile spreads beyond her fingers into the corners of her face. "You mean you actually listen to what I say? No wonder you're so smart." She kisses Lulu as many times as the child will allow, then watches her run down the stairs to Paul's car. Robin is immediately at the door behind her. "Will you at least *try* to have a good time?" Joanne asks.

"Sure, I'll have a ball," Robin responds pointedly, using Joanne's words.

"I think you'll see that we made the right decision . . ."

"*You* made the decision," Robin corrects. "Not me."

"I meant your father and me," Joanne continues, aware that she has never made a major decision entirely on her own in her life. "We all need time to cool off and think things through . . ."

"The way you and Daddy are doing?" Robin asks with just enough politeness for Joanne to wonder if the implicit cruelty of the remark was intentional.

"I guess so. Anyway," she stammers, "try to make the best of things. You may even find that you enjoy the summer." In spite of yourself, she thinks.

"Sure," Robin grunts.

"Can I kiss you goodbye?" Joanne waits for her daughter's permission and interprets her silent shrug as a go-ahead, enveloping the girl in her arms and kissing her heavily rouged cheek. Robin's hand moves to smooth the makeup her mother may have disturbed. Or is she erasing my kiss? Joanne wonders, seeing Robin as a child, stubbornly wiping unwanted kisses away. "Take care of yourself," she calls after her older daughter, watching her skip down the front stairs and disappear into the back seat of her father's car.

Paul climbs out of the front seat and looks toward the house. "I'll call you." He waves to his wife before driving away.

The phone is ringing as Joanne steps back into the house. She ignores it as she proceeds past it through the kitchen, bending down to unlock the Charley-bar at the bottom of the sliding glass door, flipping open the additional lock at its side, and sliding the door open. She steps onto the newly erected back porch, still awaiting a final coat of varnish, and walks down the newly constructed steps that lead to the pool. Slowly, the phone still ringing behind her, she lowers herself onto one of the rose-colored slabs of flagstone that surround the concrete-lined hole and dangles her feet into what was supposed to have been the pool's deep end. It's hard to feel too sorry for a woman with a swimming pool, she thinks, looking up at the house next door and catching sight of her best friend, Eve, staring down at her from the bedroom window.

Joanne raises her hand and waves, but the shadowy figure in the window suddenly backs away and is gone. Joanne brings her hand up to her eyes, shielding them from the sun, as she tries to relocate her friend. But Eve is no longer there, and Joanne wonders if, in fact, she ever was. Lately, her mind has been playing tricks . . .

("I'm not saying that someone isn't phoning you," she hears Eve say.

"What *are* you saying?"

"Sometimes the mind plays tricks . . ."

"Did you talk to Brian?"

"Of course," Eve tells her, suddenly defensive. "You asked me to, didn't you? He says that everyone gets obscene calls and that you should just hang up on the guy."

"I'm not even sure it *is* a man! It's such a strange voice. I don't know if it's young or old, male or female . . ."

"Well, of course it's a man," Eve states flatly. "Women don't make obscene phone calls to other women."

"These are more than just obscene calls," Joanne corrects her. "He says he's going to kill me. He says I'm next. Why are you looking at me like that?"

Eve is about to protest but changes her mind. "I was just wondering," she admits, trying to soften the harshness of her suspicions with an understanding smile, "whether the phone calls started before or after Paul left.")

Joanne is wondering the same thing, trying very hard to assign some order to the events of the last several months. But like a child caught up with the eternal riddle of the chicken and the egg, she is unable to determine exactly what came before what.

She knows only that in the last several months, everything in her life has been turned upside down, that she is hanging by her heels from the ceiling, watching as familiar objects fall away from her, seeing them suddenly distorted and strange. There is nothing for her to grab onto, no arms to pull her to safety. Things have a way of working out, she hears Lulu repeating, purposely using the very phrase Joanne has used so often in the past, the same words she remembers her own mother repeating to her.

Joanne pulls herself to her feet, aware that the phone has stopped ringing. She walks around to the shallow end of the aborted swimming pool, and climbs down the three steps into the empty pit. Maybe I am crazy, she thinks, deciding that this is probably the easiest solution to her problems.

Joanne Hunter watches the world recede as she progresses farther into the deep end of the empty concrete hole. She pushes her back against the rough cement at the corner from which the boomerang veers, and slowly slides down along its harsh surface to the bottom. Sitting with her knees drawn up against her chest, she hears the phone on her kitchen wall once again begin its persistent ring. It's just you and me now, he is telling her. Joanne nods her head in silent acknowledgement of the unstated fact and tries to conjure up images of happier times.

Chapter 2

As Joanne recalls, the phone had been ringing just before Eve arrived at her front door almost two months earlier. "Hello?" Joanne said into the receiver, more a question than a statement. "Hello. Hello?" She shrugged her shoulders and replaced the receiver. "Kids," she pronounced, still shaking her head with dismay as she ushered Eve inside several minutes later.

"You ready?" Eve asked.

"I just have to find my racquet." Joanne opened the closet in the front hall. "I think I buried it back here somewhere."

"Well, hurry up and find it. I understand that the new pro is quite delicious, and I wouldn't want to miss a minute of our lesson."

"I don't know why I let you talk me into these things."

"Because you've always let me talk you into everything. It's part of your charm."

Joanne stopped searching for a minute, squatting under the family's assorted spring coats, and turned to face her friend of almost thirty years. "Do you remember what my mother always used to say?" Eve's quizzical expression indicated that she didn't. "She used to ask me, 'If Eve told you to jump off the Brooklyn Bridge, would you do it?' "

Eve laughed. "At least she didn't call all your friends at two o'clock in the morning to find out where you were, or come downstairs to 'fix the plumbing' when you were entertaining a boy in the rec room."

"I never entertained boys in the rec room," Joanne reminded her, resuming her search.

"Yes, I know. You were always so disgustingly pure." She looked toward the kitchen. "The pool seems to be coming along great guns. I keep tabs from my bedroom window."

"Well, the man said ten days to two weeks, tops, so it looks like they may finish on schedule. Found it," she said, triumphantly retrieving her racquet from the back of the closet. "I'll just tell the men I'm leaving."

"Hurry, we'll be late."

"You're always in such a hurry," Joanne laughed as she ran back into the kitchen and opened the sliding door to inform the workers she would be gone for several hours.

"And you're always so slow," Eve countered after Joanne returned. "It takes a stick of dynamite to get you moving."

"That's why we've been friends for so long. If we were both like me, we'd never get anywhere. If we were both like you, we'd blow each other up."

It was true, Joanne thought in the car on the drive to Fresh Meadows Country Club, reflecting on her long-standing relationship with her oldest and best friend. They had met in seventh grade at the awkward age of twelve. Even then, Eve had been something of a standout, a tall, gangly redhead with an infectious giggle and a commanding tone to her voice.

"I need a partner for science," Eve had announced one morning in class, indicating to Joanne that she was it. Joanne had said nothing, feeling tongue-tied and overwhelmed that the most popular girl in the class had actually selected her for a partner. "Are you always this quiet?" Eve had demanded later, as their teacher was passing around dead frogs for dissection.

"I'm scared," Joanne had whispered, hoping she wouldn't be sick as the plump, lifeless body of a frog was dropped onto the table before her.

"Scared of a dead frog?" Eve flipped it over with casual fingers.

"I don't think I can do this."

"You don't have to," Eve had assured her, obviously delighted. "I'll do it. I love stuff like this. Blood and guts. It's great. If I were a boy, I'd be a doctor when I grow up." She paused briefly, studying her new partner as closely as if she, and not the frog, were the specimen to be dissected. "Why don't you ever say anything in class? Nobody knows you're here."

"Why did you pick me for a partner?" Joanne asked instead of answering.

"Because you never say anything in class and nobody knows you're here," Eve smiled slyly. "I like to be the center of attention."

They became inseparable friends, one rarely seen without the other. Mutt and Jeff, Joanne's mother used to tease, not without affection. If Eve asked you to jump off the Brooklyn Bridge, would you do it?

Probably, Joanne thought now as Eve pulled the car into the crowded parking lot. "There's a space over there. To your right."

Eve automatically turned left.

Joanne laughed, recalling that it had taken her friend three tries to pass her driver's test. "Isn't that Karen Palmer?"

"Where?" Eve narrowly missed the car beside them as she backed into a vacant space and bumped into the rear fender of a new Mercedes.

"There. Going inside. It looks like her, but something's different."

"My God, she's got boobs!"

"What?"

"She had a boob job to go with her face-lift. When did you ever know Karen Palmer to have tits that bounced?."

"Why would she do something like that?" Joanne asked as the two women proceeded toward the clubhouse.

"Her husband's always been a boob man," Eve confided. "Haven't you noticed the way he always looks at your chest when he talks to you?"

They deposited their bags in their lockers and headed directly for the courts.

"Is it that important?" Joanne wondered out loud.

Eve shrugged. "To some men. Brian, for example, is an ass man. Did I tell you what he did the other night?"

"Spare me," Joanne interrupted. "I don't want to know."

"You're no fun. You never let me tell you anything."

"I would just feel uncomfortable looking Brian in the face if I knew too many details about your sex life."

"Trust me, his face is not his best feature."

"Eve!"

"Joanne!" Eve mimicked.

"Eve and Joanne?" the tall, muscular blond asked. "I'm Steve Henry, the new tennis pro."

"There really is a God," Eve whispered as she and Joanne took up their positions in front of the net.

"So, what do you think?"

"Seems like a good instructor."

"That's not exactly what I was talking about," Eve informed her friend with a mischievous twinkle.

"I don't look at men that way," Joanne told her, her expression midway between a scowl and a smile.

"Well, he was sure looking at you," Eve teased.

"Looking at my rotten backhand, you mean. If I hear the words 'follow through' one more time, I will scream."

"It was your back*side,* not you backhand, he was looking at, and you know it."

"He's a natural flirt, that's all. Besides, he thinks coming on to middle-aged women is part of his job."

"He didn't come on to me."

"Your rear end doesn't droop enough."

"No, I don't have your legs."

"And I don't have your mouth. Shut up, you're making me self-conscious."

"Why do you always put yourself down?" Eve demanded, her voice suddenly serious.

"I don't."

"Yes, you do. You have ever since I've known you."

"I just have a realistic understanding of my own limitations."

"Is that supposed to mean something?" Eve asked. "Look at you. There's absolutely nothing wrong with you that a little self-confidence and a few blond streaks wouldn't fix."

Joanne ran an embarrassed hand through her light brown hair. "And losing five pounds, and getting rid of the bags under my eyes, and getting my teeth straightened."

"Talk to Karen Palmer. Her husband's a dentist. And while you're at it, ask her who did her boobs."

"Ask her yourself; she's right behind you."

"Hi," a woman with a perpetually surprised expression greeted them. "Did you hear about the latest grisly Great Neck killing?"

"Third one this year," Eve elaborated. "Same M.O.—that's modus operandi—as my husband would say. I thought we all moved to Long Island to be safe!"

"That poor woman—strangled, then hacked all to pieces!" Karen Palmer further embellished, her voice assuming an almost eery lilt as she warmed to her subject. "Can you imagine what must have been going on in her mind during those last horror-filled moments? The terror she must have felt?" Karen Palmer's eyes grew even wider, as if she were watching the scene in her mind. "Jim got hold of a porno movie once. It was supposed to be one of those 'snuff' films—you know, where they actually murder some poor girl on camera, and I swear you could almost *taste* her fear . . ."

"Do we have to talk about this?" Joanne interrupted.

"She's no fun." Eve smiled at the obviously deflated Karen Palmer. "She never lets you talk about any of the good stuff."

Karen Palmer shrugged. "Did you just have a lesson?" she asked, seeking safer ground.

"The tennis pro has the hots for Joanne." Eve laughed, removing her purse from her locker and slamming the locker door shut.

"Oh, I'd follow through on that one if I were you," Karen advised with obvious relish.

"That's exactly her problem," Eve stated. "She doesn't 'follow through.' "

"Very funny," Joanne told them, feeling her face redden.

"She's blushing," Eve teased triumphantly, always pleased when she could draw color to her friend's cheeks. "Where there's smoke . . ."

"He's barely out of his teens . . ."

"At his peak."

"He's twenty-nine," Karen told them.

"Past his peak," Eve lamented. "But not bad, nonetheless."

"You're both crazy," Joanne admonished them playfully as they left the clubhouse and walked toward the parking lot. "You both have perfectly nice husbands."

"Nice, yes," Eve corrected. "Far from perfect." She turned directly toward Karen, who looked surprised to see her. "Where are you getting your hair done these days?" she asked, trying, but not quite succeeding, to keep her eyes away from the woman's newly expanded upper torso.

Karen Palmer smiled. "Rudolph's. I've been going there for years."

"I have to find a new hairdresser," Eve deadpanned. "I'm tired of homosexual hairdressers. You tell them to make you look sexy, they make you look like a boy." All eyes moved immediately to Karen's chest. "Well, nice seeing you again." They watched the other woman maneuver herself into her Corvette, hitting her breasts against the door as she tried to lower herself inside. "I still haven't quite got the hang of them." She smiled self-consciously. "But it's worth it," she added, starting the engine, "if only to see the smile on Jim's face every morning."

"Let me tell you what makes Brian smile," Eve began as they reached her car.

"Excuse me, Mrs. Hunter!" a masculine voice called from across the lot. Joanne looked up to see the new tennis pro running with long, careless strides toward them.

"A vision in white," quipped Eve.

"You left these on the court," he said as he reached the two women, producing from his back pocket a set of keys dangling on a chain.

"Oh my God, thank you. I'm forever leaving these things somewhere." Joanne felt the blush spread across her cheeks and into her scalp as she took her house keys from the tennis instructor's outstretched hand.

"See you next week." He smiled and was gone.

"Mrs. Hunter is red all over," Eve laughed as they got into the car.

"Mrs. Hunter is going home to take a shower."

"Think you can wash your shame away?" Eve joked.

"You really enjoy embarrassing me, don't you?" Joanne asked, good-naturedly.

"Yeah, I do," Eve admitted and both women laughed. "I really do."

The phone was ringing as Joanne stepped out of the shower. "Damn," she muttered, throwing a towel around her wet body and running toward the bedside phone. "Hello?" There was no response. "Hello . . . hello?" She watched the drops of water make a trail down the length of her left leg and disappear into the soft beige carpet under her feet. "One last chance . . . hello?" She returned the receiver to its cradle in disgust. "Goodbye," she said, catching a glimpse of one of the workers in the backyard as he passed under her window to confer with one of his colleagues. He looked up, staring directly at her though he gave no acknowledgment of her presence. Immediately, Joanne ducked beneath the windowsill. Had he seen her? No, she thought, crawling back to the bathroom on her hands and knees. She could see him, but he couldn't see her.

The thought of watching someone unaware of being watched gave Joanne a momentary shudder. She reached the bathroom, checked to make sure the blinds were tightly closed, and only then stood up, the towel falling from her body to the tile floor.

She caught her nude image in the full-length mirror, and instinctively turned away. She'd never liked confronting her naked body, even before time and the bearing of children had rendered it something less—or something more, depending on where you looked— than it once was. She thought of Karen Palmer, a few years younger than herself, who had subjected her body, and her psyche, to the repeated nips and tucks of the surgeon's knife. For what? For her husband? For the sake of her own vanity? How did the woman feel when she surprised herself in the mirror each day, every year bringing forth a new model, like a line of new cars.

Joanne felt herself being drawn toward the bathroom's full-length mirror, her eyes focused on her face. Aging was such an amazing process, she thought, her fingers reaching up to smooth out the small lines around her eyes. When had they first appeared? She touched the contours of her face, moving her hands along her neck, studying the natural creases of time. How noticeably we get older, she thought, and yet how invisibly. Her eyes, while they reflected no great wisdom, certainly reflected the passage of the years. They were more knowing, less trustful. The bags beneath them, which used to evaporate with a good night's sleep, were now a permanent part of her features. How long had it been since someone had stared into them and told her how beautiful she was? A long time, she thought.

Her eyes fell reluctantly to her breasts, breasts which in her youth had been high and firm, but which were now less clearly defined. They dipped in slightly just before the nipples, giving them the somewhat exotic look of Aladdin's pointed-toed shoes. Her stomach, once concave, now rounded noticeably, and her waist was creeping inexorably into the area of her still-narrow hips. Only her legs, always her proudest attribute, showed no signs of betrayal, no little purple veins sprouting behind her knees such as the ones Eve had started complaining about. At forty-one, she still had no worries about saddlebags or cellulite, and if her rear end was a few inches lower now, well, at least Paul had never complained. Maybe he wasn't an ass man, she thought, remembering Eve's earlier remark. She hoped he was a leg man, she decided, realizing that he had never stated any particular preference, reaching into the cabinet under the sink for the hairdryer.

It wasn't in the usual place. "Oh great, where did Paul put it?"

she asked her reflection, opening another cabinet. It wasn't there. But something else was, a magazine of some sort, pushed to the very back of the shelf. Joanne reached in and pulled it out. "Oh my," she gasped, flipping it over to discover a smiling and full-bosomed young woman staring back at her as if she were an old and dear friend. While there was a certain innocence to the girl's expression, there was nothing innocent about her pose, which showed her nude and unquestionably voluptuous body reclining against a large and equally well-equipped stereo system, a microphone thrust none-too-discreetly between her legs. "And what are we going to sing today?" Joanne asked, hearing Eve's voice filtering through her words. She began turning the pages, her eyes widening with each successive photograph. "My God," she gasped, trying to look away, her eyes riveted to the boldly colored pictures. "Since when did Paul start going out with the likes of you?" she asked, recalling that Paul had seemed preoccupied of late, that his usually quick smile came slower these days, that he often appeared distracted, even depressed. She had assumed it had something to do with whatever was going on at work—Paul had always preferred not to bring the office home with him—and so she had chosen to ignore what she assumed was a temporary malaise. All couples, she concluded, especially ones who had been married as long as she and Paul, went through periods of decreased ardor. When his workload lessened, she reasoned, he would return to his normally gregarious self, his interest in her would pick up again. Could it be, she wondered now, that he had ceased to find her attractive? Had their sex life become so routine that he no longer required her active participation? Had her body lost the appeal it had once so effortlessly held for him? "Is that why you're here?" she asked the smiling photograph. What does he see when he looks at you? What does he see, she amended the question further, studying herself in the mirror, when he looks at me?

Slowly, self-consciously, Joanne shifted her body into a position similar to that of one of the women in the photographs, her arms back, chest thrust forward, knees up, legs well apart. "How do they get them so pink?" she asked aloud, standing up abruptly, embarrassed though she was alone. She had never subjected her body to such intense scrutiny before, never before tried to see herself through Paul's eyes. Suddenly she bent over and grabbed her toes, echoing another pose in the magazine. "Beautiful," she said sarcastically, staring at herself upside down from between her legs.

"Oh, Mom—gross!"

Joanne scrambled to straighten up, throwing the magazine inside the cabinet and kicking the door closed with her foot. At the same time, she grabbed one of the towels off the floor and wrapped it around her, feeling her damp skin grow warm with the heat of her embarrassment.

"What were you doing?" Lulu asked.

"I was looking at my toe."

"You were looking at your toe?"

"I hurt it playing tennis," Joanne told her, her voice noticeably shrill. "What are you doing home so early?"

"The teachers had a meeting or something. You know how they always have meetings on Friday afternoons." She rolled her eyes. "Is it all right if I go to Susannah's house? Her dad got a new pinball machine."

"Sure, go on. But don't be late for supper," she called after Lulu, who was already halfway down the stairs. "Good God," she sighed with a combination of discomfort and relief as she heard the front door open and close.

The phone rang.

She moved quickly to answer it, careful not to walk too close to the window. "Hello?" As before, there was no response. "Oh no, not again." She waited a second, listening to the ominous silence at the other end, feeling invisible eyes upon her, as if the phone were a camera, and she dropped the receiver back onto its carriage as if she had just received a sudden charge of electricity. "Go bother someone else," she admonished it, falling back across her bed, feeling exposed though she wasn't sure why.

That stupid magazine, she thought, renewed embarrassment creeping across her bare arms and legs as she contemplated her daughter's startled expression at catching her mother with her head down between her thighs. Not that she was a prude about her body, Joanne thought. It was just that she had never made a point of parading around without her clothes in front of her daughters. She had never seen her own mother nude, she realized, until the woman had become too weak and sick to dress herself. What was Paul doing buying magazines like that? And why?

"Hello? Is anybody home?" the masculine voice called as, once more, Joanne heard her front door open and shut.

"Paul?" Joanne sat up, startled, quickly retrieving a robe from her walkin closet and wrapping it around her before her husband appeared in the doorway. "What are you doing home in the middle of the afternoon? Are you feeling all right?"

He didn't look well, she thought, kissing him gently on the cheek. "I wanted to talk to Mr. Rogers," he said, looking out the window. "Has he been around today?"

"Just the workers. Although he might have been here—I was gone for a few hours. Eve and I had a tennis lesson at the club. A new instructor. He seems to feel that I have a certain natural ability, but I don't know. It's been so long since I played . . ." What was she rattling on about? Why was she so nervous?

She looked at her husband's back as he stared out the window. There was something about his stance, something about the tilt of his head, the visible tension in his shoulders, that made her uncomfortable. He turned toward her, and she didn't like the expression on his face.

"What is it?" she asked, wishing she could get that damn magazine out of her mind. "Is something wrong? Something the matter with the pool?" she questioned, though she knew instinctively that the pool was not the issue.

He shook his head. "No. I just thought that if Rogers was around, I'd speak to him for a few minutes. That's not it," he continued almost in the same breath. "That's not why I'm home early. It's not the pool. It's me."

"You? What's wrong?" She felt herself begin to panic. "Have you been having pains in your chest?"

"No, no," he quickly reassured her. "No, it's nothing like that." There was a long, uncomfortable pause. "I have to talk to you," he said finally.

Joanne sank into the blue well-stuffed chair at the foot of their bed. She nodded her readiness to listen. He looked at her with the same trepidation that she had seen in his face on that afternoon three years earlier when he had rushed home in the middle of the day to tell her that her father had suffered a heart attack and had been rushed to the hospital. She didn't know what he was going to say. She knew only that she wasn't going to like it.

Chapter 3

Later that night, after her husband had packed some things in a small suitcase and left to spend the night in a hotel, Joanne ran the scene in her mind as Eve would have played it.

She pictured her friend in her place, leaning forward on the blue chair, her red hair falling in attractive waves down the sides of her slender face, her narrow chin resting on the palm of her hand. Now standing with his back to the window, Paul, unaware of the substitution, views Eve as if she were his wife, talks to her as if she were Joanne.

"What is it?" Joanne hears Eve's image ask. But the tone of Eve's voice is entirely her own, more casual, less fearful. Curious, almost challenging. "Something happen at work?"

Joanne laid her head back against her pillow and closed her eyes, watching the scene unfold with her best friend in her place, catching the hesitation in her husband's eyes, feeling the twitch of his lips as they struggle to spit out the words. "I've been rehearsing this in my mind for weeks," he says. "I thought I knew just how to say it . . ."

"Oh, for God's sake, Paul," Eve interrupts, impatience mixed with intrigue, "just say it."

Paul turns back toward the window, unable to confront his wife directly. "I think we should separate," he says finally.

"What?" Eve's gasp carries traces of a laugh. She knows this is a joke, a prelude to an announcement that will undoubtedly please her.

Paul turns slowly back in her direction, his voice steadier, gaining confidence through repetition. "I think we should separate, live apart for a while . . ."

"All this because I refused to go skiing last winter?" Eve teases. "Don't you think you're overreacting just a tad?"

"I'm serious, Joanne," Paul tells her.

Eve sees that he is. Her back sinks into the softness of the blue chair. For an instant, but only an instant, her eyes cloud over with the hint of tears, and then, almost imperceptibly, her face changes, the set of her jaw hardens, and the clouds are gone, the would-be tears evaporate. Eve stares at Paul with cold, clear eyes, and when she finally speaks, her voice is hard, her words angry. "Do you mind telling me why?"

"I'm not sure that I can."

"I think you'd better try."

"I don't know why," Paul admits after a lengthy pause.

"You don't know why," Eve repeats, nodding as if she understands, which only serves to underline the absurdity of what Paul has just said. "You're a lawyer, Paul," she prods. "Come on, you're usually so good with words. Surely you can think of something, some little reason that might help explain why you'd walk out on a marriage of almost twenty years, not to mention the two daughters of that marriage. I don't think I'm making an unreasonable request."

"Please, Joanne," he urges, "don't make this any harder for me than it already is."

Eve is on her feet now, furiously pacing back and forth. "Yes— heaven forbid we make this any harder for you." She bites off each word abruptly.

"Believe me," he tries lamely, "I don't want to hurt you."

"Then why are you?"

"Because I'd be hurting you more if I stayed."

The look on Eve's face is a mixture of scorn and bewilderment. "How could you possibly be hurting me more if you stayed?" she demands, and when he says nothing, demands further, "How?" She stops her pacing, stands directly in front of him, carefully measuring out the force of her words. "Don't think you're doing this for me, Paul. You're not doing this for me. At least be honest. The only person you are doing this for is yourself."

"All right," he admits, his own voice rising in anger for the first time. "I'm doing it for myself. Don't I count for anything?"

"Not a whole lot," Eve shoots back, seeking to wound, succeeding.

"I'm sorry. What else can I say?"

"You can tell me why," Eve persists, unwilling to let him off the hook with a simple apology, no matter how sincere the delivery.

His face searches the room for answers, his ears catching the laughter of the outside workers around their intended swimming pool. "I'm just not happy," he says finally. "I realize how trite that sounds . . ."

"But do you realize how trite it *is?*" Eve counters quickly. Thrust and parry. "Does this have anything to do with Barry Kellerman?" (Barry Kellerman is one of Paul's law partners. About a year ago, he walked out on his wife of eighteen years, leaving her with four small children under the age of ten. After eight months of dating a succession of adorable and adoring young women, he became engaged to a former Miss Erie County, who, at age twenty, is the same age as the first Mrs. Kellerman when he married her.)

Paul seems genuinely puzzled. "What has Barry Kellerman got to do with anything?"

"With the fact that maybe you're jealous?" Eve offers. "With the fact that maybe you feel you're missing something?"

"I'm not jealous," Paul answers too quickly. Eve waits for him to continue. "I *do* feel I'm missing something," he finally admits. "I'm forty-two years old, Joanne. We got married when I was still in school."

"My parents helped to support us," she reminds him.

"You were only the third girl I'd ever seriously dated."

"You were my first," she says, knowing it is unnecessary to add "and only."

"Haven't you ever wanted another man?" he demands suddenly, surprising her. "Haven't you ever wondered what it would be like with someone else?"

"You bet your sweet ass I have," Eve retorts angrily. "Everyone has thoughts like those from time to time. But you don't break up a marriage, you don't walk out on two daughters who need their father, you don't break up a family just because you're 'not happy'! Who promised you that you were always going to be happy?"

"I want more," he offers weakly.

"You want *less!*" she corrects. "One less wife, two less children . . ."

"I'm still the girls' father."

"The way Barry Kellerman is still a father? Whenever it's convenient to be one? Whenever he can sweep in with some expensive presents and a few shallow words of affection, and take his kids out for a couple of fun-filled hours before bringing them back to Mommy when they start getting on his nerves? He's not the one who has to deal with the chaos he leaves behind after he's gotten into his new

sportscar and driven off to his new life! It's Mommy who's left to deal
with all the anger and the confusion that his super little fatherly visits
have created."

"I am not Barry Kellerman!"

"Sorry," Eve says quickly. "It's rather hard at this moment for
me to tell the difference."

"I have never cheated on you, Joanne. Not in twenty years," he
tells her.

"Is that supposed to make me feel better?" Eve asks. "When
they serve me with my divorce papers, am I supposed to shrug and
say, 'well, at least he never cheated on me'?"

"I never said anything about a divorce."

Eve stares at Joanne's husband. "I must have missed something.
What are we talking about?"

"We're talking about a separation," he explains. "Six months,
maybe a year. We could still see each other . . . maybe go to a movie
. . . have dinner . . ."

"You want to date?" Eve asks incredulously. "Is that what you're
saying?" He nods, his face reflecting optimism. "You want to go
backward? You want me to start dating the man I've been married to
for half a lifetime?" Eve's confusion is genuine. For the first time
during this confrontation, she is unsure of what to say. "I wouldn't
know what to do. I wouldn't know who to be."

"Just be yourself."

"You don't want *me!*"

"Please, Joanne, I'm just asking for a little time to think things
through. I don't want to rush into a divorce. I just need time to decide
what it is I *do* want, whether or not I want to stay in law, whether or
not I want to stay married . . . I just don't know anymore. I need
time to be alone, to be by myself. I'm hoping that in a few months I
can see my way clear to making some concrete decisions, that maybe
this separation will be good for us, that we'll find a way to get back
together."

"People don't separate to get back together. They separate to
get divorced."

"Not necessarily."

"Paul, don't be naive. You've seen what's happened to other
people. You saw what happened to Barry and Mona Kellerman. A
separation takes on a life of its own. Then you're not only dealing
with whatever problems you started out with, you've also got the

separation to contend with. If we have problems, then you have to stay and try to work them out. You have to start talking to me, telling me what's bothering you instead of trying to insulate me all the time. My parents did that to me, and they were wrong. Because they spent their lives trying to protect me, and then all of a sudden they were gone, and now you're doing the same thing, and it isn't fair."

"You'll be fine," Paul interjects quickly, feeling her growing panic transferring to him. He rushes to reassure them both. "You're strong, stronger than you think. You'll cope the way you always do—beautifully. In fact, you'll probably start having the time of your life. I'll have to wait in line . . . ."

Eve's voice goes suddenly flat. "Please don't tell me how I'll be."

There is silence while each contemplates what is left to say.

"I thought I'd find an apartment close to the office," Paul announces as a loud argument erupts outside between two of the workers. "You and the girls will stay put, of course. I'll continue to pay for everything. Anything that you need or want, just let me know. There won't be any problems about money, I promise you that."

"Until you meet someone else," she informs him caustically. "The world is full of women struggling with the 'no money' problems their ex-husbands have left them after they've gotten over their initial guilt." She shakes her head. "Guilt is an amazing thing." There is another long, uncomfortable pause while each waits for the other to speak. "Who will tell the girls?" Eve asks, hearing Robin arrive home.

"I will," Paul concedes.

"When?"

"Whenever you like."

"We're doing what *you* like this afternoon," she reminds him.

His voice is suddenly as cold as hers. "Now, then," he says, hearing their daughter moving around in the kitchen directly underneath them.

"Lulu's over at Susannah's," Eve tells him.

"Would you mind calling her for me?" he asks.

"You're the one who wants to speak to her," Eve replies flatly. "You call her."

Paul nods.

This image remained as Joanne opened her eyes to stare into the darkness of the night-filled room.

None of it had happened that way.

She had said nothing. Nothing at all. She had simply sat there and listened as Paul tried to explain himself, tripping over his confusion, apologizing, trying to force some sense into his words. She hadn't opened her mouth, hadn't moved except to swipe at unwanted tears. She had sat immobile, unable to look into his eyes. She had made no protest, launched no soft-spoken appeal or blistering counterattack. She had simply listened, and in the end, she had phoned Lulu at Susannah's house as Paul had requested and asked her to come home. She had remained in their room while Paul had repeated to their two children his intention to leave home, and when they had reacted later, after he had gone, their anger had been directed at her, not at the man who had left, just as she had known it would be.

"It's not my fault," she had wanted to tell them, but she didn't, feeling somehow that it was.

Joanne pulled herself out of bed, feeling smothered by the empty space beside her. She stood by the window and stared down into her backyard, the blackness of the starless night mercifully hiding the empty pit the workers had left her. She shifted in the direction of Eve's house next door, the lights surrounding Eve's patio bright and accusing. Pulling the curtains tightly closed, she picked up the telephone and dialed, hanging up when Eve failed to answer after eight rings. It was late, she realized, remembering that Eve had told her that she and Brian were attending some police function that night. She wondered what time they would be home, saw by the clock on the bedside table that it was almost midnight already.

Lulu was asleep, or at least she had pretended to be asleep when Joanne looked in on her earlier. Robin was at a party.

Moving like an automaton, Joanne crawled back under the covers of the king-size bed she and Paul had purchased shortly after moving to this house some twelve years ago, after almost eight years of sleeping on a mattress on the floor in their older, smaller home in Roslyn. Up the ladder of success, she thought, feeling her life reduced to an unpleasant statistic.

Her parents had lied to her, she thought, trying not to see their faces behind her closed lids. They had promised knowledge and stability with the coming of age, if not in so many words, then by their very presence as adults. She would grow up, their smiles had silently promised, and the world would be hers. She would have control over her actions, over her fate. She would make decisions; she would vote; she would be secure in a world that was fixed and permanent.

And for a while they had been right: she had grown up essentially as planned, had married, the way it had been predicted, and had borne children of her own, children who had then looked to her as the established adult and keeper of wisdom. And she had become part of the secret conspiracy, which, while it never overtly lied, never really told the truth. Hearing a key turn in the lock, aware of Robin's footsteps on the stairs, Joanne fell asleep with the memory of the smell of her mother's perfume.

In her dream she saw the sun shining, unimpeded by clouds, causing the concrete squares of the narrow path before her to sparkle like bright diamonds, warm against her bare feet as she walked toward the small white cottage ahead. She was perhaps five years old. Her brother, two years her junior, was taking his afternoon nap. She could hear laughter coming from inside, knew that her mother and grandmother were already in the kitchen preparing supper for when their men returned from the city, as they did every Friday afternoon during the two months of summer that the extended family shared this cottage in the country. The child Joanne skipped toward the front door, glancing sideways at the driveway, projecting ahead an hour or two when, one after the other, the two cars would pull into the driveway, and first her grandfather, a huge, robust man, and then her father, smaller but with a strong, hearty laugh, would appear, their arms loaded with fresh breads and blueberry buns and cherry danishes, enough to tide them over until the following weekend. Her father would bend forward to kiss her before disappearing inside the cottage, but her grandfather would linger, throwing down the paper bags of baked goods, and scooping her up into his mammoth arms, twirling her around again and again. When you're older, he would tell her, I'll teach you how to play gin rummy. And each week, Joanne would wonder if she was older yet. She reached the front door of the cottage, eager to embrace the warm darkness of the interior rooms, hearing her mother's high, girlish giggle ringing through the heavy wooden door.

The phone was ringing. Joanne groped for it in a daze, her eyes unwilling to open, her mind clinging to her child's body, her mother's laughter luring her back to sleep. "Hello," she said, not sure for the moment who she was, only that she was no longer a little girl.

There was no one there. Not even silence, she realized slowly, coming fully awake. A busy signal only. Had the phone rung at all? She lay back down, her heart thumping wildly. Joanne spent the rest of the night trapped somewhere between sleep and wakefulness, wondering whether the ring that had awakened her had been the telephone or her mother's laughter, finally telling her the truth.

Chapter 4

The girls were still asleep—or pretending to be—when Joanne left the house at just before noon the next morning. She was tired, her eyes swollen from a combination of tears and lack of sleep. She rubbed them, hearing her mother tell her that would only make them worse. What would you say to me now, Mom? she asked the cloudless sky as she crossed from her front lawn over to Eve's. Shoulders back, stomach in! she heard her mother answer and she smiled. Her mother's answer to everything.

You always liked Paul, Joanne continued silently, feeling her mother's presence beside her as she mounted the steps to Eve's front door. What wasn't there to like? her mother responded simply. A smart, good-looking boy from a nice family, he wanted to be a lawyer, he loved my daughter . . .

Loved, Joanne repeated in her mind. What do you do, Mom, she questioned, knocking on Eve's door, when someone suddenly stops loving you?

No one came to the door. Joanne knocked again, then rang the bell. The sound of the chime reminded her of the phone ringing in the middle of the night. Had it rung or had she dreamt it? And what kind of sick mind got its kicks from phoning other people in the early morning hours and frightening them half to death? She had tossed and turned for the rest of the night, unable to find a comfortable position without Paul's body to act as a guide. She was going to need all the sleep she could get if she was going to make it through the next little while without falling apart, if she was to maintain a calm exterior in front of her daughters. Don't worry, darlings, everything will work out.

In the meantime, she needed to talk to Eve. Eve would put everything in its proper perspective. She would help Joanne understand Paul's point of view. "There are always two sides to every story," she could hear Eve declare. "Yours—and the shithead's!" Eve would make her laugh, and if not, at least they could cry together. Where was she? Why wasn't she answering the door?

Eve's husband, Brian, appeared just as Joanne was about to give up and go back home. A tall man who had always seemed vaguely uncomfortable with the strong, imposing image he naturally projected, he had surprisingly gentle eyes which betrayed nothing of the daily horrors to which his job regularly exposed him. The perfect policeman's face, Joanne thought as Brian Stanley, looking exactly his age at forty-five, ushered Joanne inside, smiling but obviously preoccupied. Normally a man of few words, today he said even less. "You talk some sense into her," he said, indicating that his wife was in the kitchen.

Joanne walked through the front hall of the house, which was the mirror image of her own. She found Eve sitting at her kitchen table nursing a cup of coffee. Something was out of place, Joanne felt as soon as she saw her friend. (What's wrong with this picture? she heard echoing in the back of her head.) "What's up?" Joanne asked, realizing that her friend was still in her bathrobe and that her usually perfect hair was uncombed.

"Nothing," Eve told her, making no effort to disguise her annoyance. "It's a lot of fuss over nothing."

"Sure, it's nothing," Eve's mother chastised, appearing seemingly from out of nowhere to stick a thermometer into her daughter's reluctant mouth.

"Hello, Mrs. Cameron," Joanne said, surprised to see the woman, whose strawberry blond hair was several shades lighter than Joanne last remembered. She wondered what Eve's mother was doing here. "What's going on?"

"What's going on," the woman repeated, "is that my daughter collapsed last night and had to be rushed to the hospital."

"What!"

Eve whipped the thermometer out of her mouth. "I did not collapse. I am perfectly fine."

"Put the thermometer back in your mouth," her mother instructed as if Eve were a child of four. Eve looked imploringly toward the ceiling but she did as her mother said. "You didn't have pains last night and have to leave the party? Brian didn't take you to the emergency ward at North Shore University Hospital? He didn't call me first thing this morning and ask me to look after you because he has to go out?"

"I had a few pains," Eve corrected, once again removing the thermometer from beneath her tongue, "and everyone over-reacted."

"What kind of pains?" Joanne asked, temporarily forgetting her own problems.

"Just a few small pains in my chest." Eve indicated the precise area with the tip of the thermometer. "I've been having them for a few weeks."

"Just a few small pains," her mother repeated incredulously. "Did she tell you that the pains were so bad she couldn't stand up?" she asked Joanne.

"Were you there?" Eve demanded.

"Would somebody please tell me what is going on?" Joanne implored, remembering countless such scenes she had witnessed between these two throughout her girlhood. She felt transported back in time, and despite the fact that Eve now towered over her mother's squat, plump frame, they remained as they had always been, the overbearing mother confronting her rebellious daughter.

Brian spoke from the doorway. "We were at a party being hosted by someone from my division . . ."

"I told you about it," Eve interrupted.

"She tells you everything," her mother added immediately. "Do you think she tells me anything?"

"Mother!"

"Look, ladies, I have to go. I'm late already." Brian's voice was past the point of exasperation. "The facts are that Eve started experiencing some pains in her chest at around midnight and that she had trouble standing up, so I took her to the hospital."

"Where they gave me some tests and decided that everything was all right," Eve stated.

"Where they gave her an EKG and whatever else they give you if they think you might be having a heart attack . . ." Brian tried to continue.

"And they found out that I wasn't."

"And they recommended that she have further tests later in the week."

"For what?" Joanne asked, concerned.

"Ulcer, gall bladder, that sort of thing," Brian answered. "But she's refusing to go."

"It was a little indigestion, for God's sake. I am not going to put myself through a battery of unpleasant tests just so some doctor can get some admittedly much-needed experience at my expense. I have seen all I want to see of hospitals, thank you very much."

"Talk some sense into her," Brian repeated. "I have to go." He kissed his wife reassuringly on the top of her head, a gesture which brought a small stab of pain to the vicinity of Joanne's own chest and the threat of tears to her eyes. Before they could form, Joanne turned and quickly swiped at her face with the palm of her hand. Now was obviously not the time to announce Paul's sudden departure.

The three women listened in silence as Brian closed the front door behind him. When Eve opened her mouth to speak, her mother automatically thrust the thermometer back inside it.

"For God's sake, will you stop doing that!" Eve exclaimed, angrily hurling the thermometer to the floor and watching it break neatly into two pieces, mercury spilling out onto the tile, immediately forming into groups of small gray clusters.

"You never listen to anyone." Her mother picked up the broken glass and expertly scooped the balls of mercury into a tissue. "That's always been your problem, and where does it get you?" She waved the broken thermometer in front of her daughter's face.

"Mother, go home," Eve said gently, the chuckle in her voice becoming a sudden gasp of pain, her body caving inward against the kitchen table.

"What's the matter?" Joanne and Eve's mother asked together, the two women instantly at her side.

"Where does it hurt?" Eve's mother demanded, though her voice was weak and her hands shook.

"It's all right now. The pain's gone." Eve straightened her shoulders and sat back in her chair. "Stop worrying—it wasn't that bad."

"It *was* that bad. Look at you—you're as white as a ghost."

"I'm always as white as a ghost. You're the one who keeps telling me to wear more makeup."

"Maybe you *should* see the doctor," Joanne urged, trying to sound casual. "What can it hurt to have a few more tests?"

Eve's eyes moved from her mother to her oldest and closest friend.

"All right," she agreed after a lengthy pause.

"Sure," her mother pounced. "For her, you'll go. When I ask you, what kind of answer do I get?"

"I said I'd go, Mother. Isn't that what you want?"

Mrs. Cameron immediately turned her attention to Joanne. "How are your daughters?" she asked, abruptly changing the subject and almost managing to sound interested.

"They're good kids," Joanne smiled. "Like Eve."

Eve laughed. Her mother did not. "Sure, stick together like you always have. You tell me—am I wrong to be concerned because my daughter has to be rushed to the hospital by her husband, who we all know is not exactly an alarmist? If anything, he doesn't pay *enough* attention to Eve."

"Mother . . ."

"Yes, I know, it's none of my business. Do your daughters tell you that things that concern them are none of your business?"

"Mrs. Cameron," Joanne began, "if it'll make you feel any better, I'll take Eve to the doctor myself." She turned back to Eve. "When's your appointment?"

"Friday morning." She winked. "So we don't miss our tennis lesson."

"Tennis," her mother scoffed. "It's too soon after the miscarriage to be playing tennis. That's probably what brought on the pains in the first place."

"Oh, let's not start that again," Eve pleaded. "The miscarriage was six months ago, and I had one tennis lesson yesterday afternoon. Not even a private lesson, for heaven's sake. I don't think I have been exactly overexerting myself."

"You work too hard, you take too many extra classes, you do too much."

"I'm a teacher, Mother."

"A professor," her mother corrected, looking at Joanne to check that the distinction was not lost. "A psychologist."

"A psychology professor, okay? A teacher. I don't work too hard. I have Fridays off. I'm taking a few extra courses at night."

"What do you need more courses for? You're forty years old. You need children, not Ph.D.'s. Am I wrong to want grandchildren?"

"I don't want to talk about this," Eve said, banging down hard on the table. "You are making me crazy, Mother."

"Sure, blame the mother for everything. Tell me, Joanne, do your daughters say such things to you?"

Joanne thought back to the previous afternoon, after Paul had packed his small suitcase and left her to confront her daughters'

confusion alone. "I'm sure we all say things to our mothers occasionally that we regret."

"Tell me," Mrs. Cameron continued, "how's your grandfather?"

"He's okay. I'm going to visit him this afternoon."

"Now, you see?" Eve's mother asked. "This is a responsible girl.
Nobody has to remind her to show proper respect for her elders."

Joanne rolled her eyes in her friend's direction, and Eve stuck
out her tongue in return.

"Sure, make a joke. I'm going to watch television. Call me if you
need anything. Nice seeing you, Joanne." She was almost at the
kitchen door when she turned back. "Talk to her, will you? Remind
her that I won't be around forever."

"Just long enough to drive me crazy," Eve called after her as the
woman disappeared into the other room. "Who's she kidding? She's
already buried three husbands. She'll outlive us all."

"She hasn't changed a bit," Joanne marveled. "You should be
used to her by now."

"Some things you never get used to," Eve told her, and Joanne
knew instantly that would be true of Paul's departure. "You look
tired," Eve remarked suddenly.

"Some idiot phoned in the middle of the night and hung up,"
Joanne told her. "Eve . . ."

"You don't think these pains really could have anything to do
with the miscarriage, do you?" Eve interrupted, looking very fragile.

"How do you mean?"

Eve tried to laugh. "Well, you know, maybe they left something
in there after they cleaned me out. I did lose a lot of blood."

"I'm positive they didn't leave anything inside you," Joanne
assured her, watching a hint of color return slowly to her friend's
cheeks. "You'd be dead by now if they had," she added, and both
women laughed in earnest.

"Thanks," Eve smiled. "You always did know how to cheer me
up."

Baycrest Nursing Home was located on South Drive, a block and
a half from Great Neck Hospital. It was an old brick structure that
had survived several renovations without noticeable change to its
appearance. Outside, the windows had been replaced by more modern Thermopane glass; inside, though the walls had recently been
repainted in shades of trendy peach, the corridors still looked as sad

and abandoned as most of the residents who walked them. No amount of bright colors or modern art could disguise the forced joviality of the institutionalized setting. Death row with flowers, Joanne thought as she moved toward her grandfather's room at the end of the hall.

She could hear the commotion even before the nurse appeared in the doorway. "Honest to God, that man!" the very fat, very black nurse exclaimed, smoothing her uniform as she struggled to calm herself. "Oh, not your granddaddy, honey," she said to Joanne, recognizing her and smiling. "Your granddaddy is no trouble at all, sleeps like a baby all the time. And he looks so cute in his little hat."

"Is Mr. Hensley giving you more problems?" Joanne asked. Sam Hensley was notorious among the nurses at the Baycrest Nursing Home. He had been shuffled between the various floors ever since his arrival six months before.

"I went in to ask whether he needed help in relieving himself, and you know what he did? He threw the bedpan at me. Thank God it was empty! Honestly, I don't know what happens to some people when they get old." The woman stopped abruptly. "I don't mean any disrespect, Mrs. Hunter," she stammered. "Your granddaddy is such a sweet little man. He never gives anybody any trouble."

"My grandfather doesn't know where he is most of the time," Joanne said softly, thinking how strange it sounded to hear the massive man her grandfather had once been described as sweet and little.

He had started shrinking, she recalled, in the year following the death of his wife of almost sixty years. Little by little, his weight fell away; his shoulders sank; his long neck withered. She felt lately that he resembled not so much a man as an ancient snapping turtle.

He had begun spinning his cocoon soon after he checked himself into the Baycrest Nursing Home five years ago, and he had sealed himself inside it forever around the same time that Joanne's mother had discovered a lump in her left breast. He had never asked why his daughter's visits became less frequent, and when she had succumbed to the disease three years ago—three years ago already? Joanne marveled as she pushed open the door to her grandfather's room— Joanne and her brother had decided not to tell him. Instead, she had stepped in to fill the vacant role, visiting the old man every week, less from a sense of duty, as Eve's mother had earlier suggested, than because he provided her with her only tangible link to the past.

This was the man who had sat with her on rainy afternoons at the cottage and patiently explained the intricacies of gin rummy, who had boiled her perfect five-minute eggs, covering them with little hand-crocheted hats to keep them warm, watching while she ate them, talking to her animatedly about his week in the city, never condescending or patronizing, always exuberant and bursting with life.

"Linda?" her grandfather asked as Joanne approached his bedside and took his hand in hers, his voice almost a parody of what it had once been.

"Yes, Pa," Joanne answered, unconsciously assuming her mother's voice as she pulled up a chair. "I'm here." When was the last time he had called her by her rightful name? she wondered. It's Joanne, she wanted to tell him, but he was already snoring, and Joanne was left clutching his hand through the bars at the side of the bed, wondering whether she would ever get used to being called by her mother's name.

"Amazing how they can just drop off like that," the voice said from somewhere beside her. Joanne looked over at the other bed, where old Sam Hensley was currently sleeping peacefully. "A minute ago," the woman standing at the foot of the bed continued, "he was a raving lunatic. You should have seen him. He threw a bedpan at the nurse! I don't know what I'm going to do. If they kick him off this floor, I don't know where they'll put him. This is the third home I've had to move him to. I'm going out for a cigarette." She spun around and for the first time since Joanne had entered the room, she was aware that the woman's son was also present, leaning his straight-backed wooden chair against the wall, his head resting against his right shoulder, his eyes closed. "Can you believe this?" the woman demanded. "If either one of these sleeping beauties wakes up, tell them I've gone down the hall for a cigarette."

Joanne watched the woman leave, trying to connect a name to the curious combination of defeated face and defiant strut. They had been introduced about a month ago when the woman's father had been transferred to this room. Marg something-or-other, Joanne recalled, feeling her grandfather's hand stir inside her own. Crosby, she remembered with some satisfaction. Marg Crosby and her son, Alan, a boy of about eighteen. Maybe a bit older. Or younger. It was so hard to tell these days, her grandfather would have said.

"Linda," her grandfather murmured.

"Yes, Pa," Joanne answered, almost by rote, "I'm here."

Again, the old man fell quiet. Where are you? Joanne asked him silently. Where do you go? Her eyes moved slowly across his pale, thin face, his cheeks less than half their former size, rough with the leftover stubble of a poor morning shave, administered daily by one of the orderlies. His once wide mouth now puckered inward, and his expansive forehead was completely hidden by the worn-out Sherlock Holmes cap that someone had perched atop his head, a gift from her on his eighty-fifth birthday ten years ago.

The decade had brought decimation: her grandmother passed away and her grandfather began his retreat; her mother discovered a cancer in her left breast which spread to every part of her body and ultimately killed her in eighteen months, while her father succumbed to a massive coronary only nine days after they had buried her mother. And now Paul was gone. He had deserted her too.

"Paul's left me, Grampa," she whispered, knowing that he didn't hear her. "He doesn't want to be married anymore. I don't know what I'm going to do," she cried softly as the old man opened his eyes and stared directly into hers, as if he suddenly understood exactly who she was and what she had said. "Grampa?" she asked, seeing a flicker of the man she remembered from her childhood pass across his features.

His face relaxed into a slow smile. "Do you work here, dear?" he asked.

Old Sam Hensley suddenly bolted upright in his bed and burst into song. "It's a long way to Tipperary," he bellowed with surprisingly accurate pitch. "It's a long way to go!"

Beside him, young Alan Crosby almost fell off his chair with the sudden sound. "Granddad," he whispered hurriedly, jumping to his feet and looking nervously toward the door. "Sh."

"Ssh yourself if you don't like it," the old man shot back loudly, returning to his song.

"It's his military period." Alan smiled meekly at Joanne as his mother and the nurse ran back into the room.

"Oh for God's sake, Dad, shut up," Marg Crosby barked as the nurse tried to gently push Sam Hensley back against his pillow.

"There, there, Mr. Hensley," the nurse was saying, "the concert's been canceled."

"Get the hell away from me," Sam Hensley shouted, taking aim at the woman's vast girth with a box of tissues from the side table.

"Dad, for God's sake . . ."

"Why don't you just let him sing?" Alan Crosby asked, leaning back against the wall, trying to suppress a smile.

"Oh, Alan," his mother exclaimed impatiently, "don't you start, too."

"Linda," a frightened voice cried, "what's all the commotion?"

"It's all right, Pa," Joanne whispered, patting her grandfather's shaking hand reassuringly. "I'm here."

Chapter 5

The phone woke her up at not quite seven o'clock the next morning. "Hello," Joanne said groggily, wiping her eyes and straining to make out the time on the bedside clock. "Hello? Who is this?"

There was no reply.

Joanne sat fully up in bed, resting the phone in her lap before reaching over and dropping the receiver back onto its cradle. "Damn kids," she muttered, looking down at the old cotton nightgown she always wore to bed. "No wonder your husband left you." She pulled the blankets up around her neck, trying to block out the early morning light coming through the bedroom curtains. But as soon as she buried her nose into the soft down of the king-size pillow, she smelled traces of Paul, his absence filtering up through her nostrils. She felt his arm fall carelessly across the raised curve of her hip, his knees burrow in against the backs of her own, pressing her rear end into the arch of his groin.

Her eyes drifted open; Paul was inside her head now and he would stay there for the rest of the day. No matter what she did or where she went, Paul would be right beside her. She would take him with her even as she struggled to leave him behind. Her only escape had been a few hours of sleep after she was too exhausted for further recriminations, too worn out for additional regrets. The new day would produce fresh lists of items for which she could berate herself: if only she hadn't done this; if only she *had* done that. If only Paul would come back, she would be more *this* way, less *that.*

She had fallen into bed at one o'clock in the morning, having stayed up to watch a movie she had no desire to see. She was still awake to hear the front door open at just past three, to listen as Robin snuck past her mother's bedroom, the door to her room closing softly behind her.

It must have been 5 A.M. before Joanne finally succumbed to sleep. Two whole hours, she thought now, trying to will herself sev-

eral more. It would be hard to look twenty years old on only two
hours of sleep a night, and she had concluded just before drifting off
to sleep early that morning that her appearance had a great deal to
do with Paul's departure. The woman he married had been twenty-
one years old. He hadn't counted on her getting so noticeably older.
Perhaps she should talk to Karen Palmer, ask her who did her
eyes . . .

Joanne was still trying to force herself back to sleep a half hour
later when the phone rang again. "Hello?" she whispered, hoping it
might be Paul telling her that he couldn't sleep either, that he
wanted to come home. There was no response. "Hello? Hello? Is
someone there? Why are you doing this?" she pleaded, about to hang
up when she heard something. "Did you say something?" she asked,
returning the phone to her ear.

There was a brief pause. Then, "Mrs. Hunter?"

"Yes?" Joanne tried quickly to place the somewhat raspy sound,
but while there was a quality to it that was vaguely familiar, she was
unable to determine what precisely it was. Certainly no one who
knew her well, or he would have addressed her by her first name.

"Mrs. Hunter," the voice repeated.

"Who is this?" Joanne asked, afraid of the voice though she
wasn't sure why. It defied categorization, she realized, neither young
nor old, and curiously sexless.

"Have you read the New York *Times* this morning, Mrs.
Hunter?"

"Who is this?"

"Read the morning paper, Mrs. Hunter. There's something in it
that concerns you. Page thirteen of the first section."

The line went dead in her hands.

"Hello?" Joanne repeated, though the caller had already hung
up. She sat motionless in bed for several minutes, listening to her
heart thumping, her senses heightened, like an animal when it instinctively feels the presence of danger. Whose voice had she heard
and why the intrigue? What could there possibly be on page thirteen
of the morning paper that would concern her? Something about
Paul? she wondered, getting out of bed.

Pulling her arms through the sleeves of her housecoat, Joanne
quietly tiptoed down the stairs to the front door. The girls were still
asleep. She wasn't even sure the *Times* would be there this early.

It was, she found, lifting the heavy Sunday paper and carrying it

into the kitchen, dropping it onto the round pinewood table. The
weatherman was calling for rain, she read, checking the increasingly
cloudy sky through the sliding glass doors that made up the kitchen's
south wall. She hoped the rain would stop by tomorrow or the men
wouldn't be able to continue work on the pool, and Joanne was eager
to have it completed and the strangers who paraded back and forth
under her bedroom window out of her life. Especially now that Paul
was gone.

She flipped quickly to page thirteen and took a cursory glance
down the various columns, seeing nothing that concerned her. Normally she avoided the front pages of the paper, the information
therein usually too depressing and no way to start the day. She
reasoned that news that was important for her to know would eventually filter down to her, and she had a definite, if not specific, sense
of what was going on in the world. Maybe that hadn't been enough
for Paul, she realized now. He was a lawyer, after all, an educated
man, and while she herself was university educated, it was true that
in recent years she had insulated herself from as much unpleasant
news as possible. Since the death of her parents three years ago,
Joanne had regularly read only the entertainment and family sec-
tions of the newspaper. It made life easier, she rationalized, as slowly,
more carefully, her eyes perused the designated page.

There was nothing about Paul or his law firm, nothing about
anyone she knew. There were just continuations of articles from
other pages, something about a union dispute within the garment
industry, a report of a roominghouse fire that left four people dead,
and some further details about the woman who had been hacked to
pieces in her home in Saddle Rock Estates. Joanne shrugged, closed
the paper, then quickly reopened it to check out the page beside it.
But there was nothing of note on that page either. What had the
caller wanted her to see? She pushed the first section of the paper
away and ferreted out the entertainment section, deciding that
maybe she'd take the girls into Manhattan later in the week to see a
Broadway play.

The last play she had seen had been a revival of *Come Blow Your
Horn* at the Burt Reynolds Dinner Theater in Jupiter, Florida, where
she and Paul had vacationed briefly the previous year. Perhaps what
Paul wanted was a woman more interested in the cultural scene, a
wife who made it a point to acquire tickets to all the latest theatrical
events. Yet if that were the case, he had only to say so.

She thought of the evening they had spent at the theater in Florida. Paul seemed happy enough then, relaxed, as he always appeared when he had a tan. They had enjoyed both the production and a pleasant dinner, and at the evening's conclusion, Paul had bought her a T-shirt as a souvenir. It was red with bold white letters across its front proclaiming I SPENT THE NIGHT WITH BURT REYNOLDS . . . Only when the T-shirt was turned onto its back did it continue . . . AT THE BURT REYNOLDS DINNER THEATER.

She had never worn it, Joanne realized. She should have worn it. Paul had bought it for her; he must have intended that she wear it.

She was on her third cup of coffee when Lulu shuffled sleepily into the kitchen in her babydoll pajamas and floppy slippers. "It's raining," she announced as if it were somehow her mother's fault.

"Maybe it won't last," Joanne replied hopefully. "What do you want for breakfast?"

"French toast?" Lulu asked, plopping down into one of the kitchen chairs as her mother poured her a large glass of orange juice. With one hand Joanne cracked some eggs into a bowl, quickly adding milk, vanilla, and a sprinkle of cinnamon.

"Did you sleep well?" she asked. Lulu only shrugged, flipping absently through the morning paper. "I thought maybe we could see a play this week," Joanne offered. "Is there anything that you want to see?" Lulu shook her head indifferently. "What about that new Neil Simon play?"

"That would be nice," Lulu agreed, a smile creeping into her half-closed eyes. She stared into the backyard. "When are they going to be finished out there?"

"Soon, I hope." Joanne flipped two slices of soggy bread into the frying pan.

"Will Daddy come to the play with us?"

Joanne's hand began to tremble. "I don't think so," she answered, struggling to keep the tremble out of her voice.

"Can we ask him?"

Joanne hesitated. "I thought it was something the three of us could do. You know, kind of a girls' night out."

"I'd like to ask Daddy," Lulu persisted. "Can I?"

"Sure," Joanne agreed, hoping this would end the conversation. "If you'd like."

"Why did Daddy leave?" the child asked abruptly.

Joanne aimed another piece of bread at the frying pan but it

missed and landed on the counter, splattering its sticky coating across
the front of Joanne's housecoat. Joanne picked the errant slice up
again, watching as it came apart against the sharp prongs of the fork.
"I'm not sure," she said, trying to keep her voice even as she maneuvered the crumbling piece of bread into the pan and flipped over the
other two. "Didn't he tell you?"

"He said he needed time alone."

"That's about what he said to me."

"To think things through. What things? Why can't he think at
home?" Lulu continued accusingly.

"I don't know, sweetie," Joanne told her honestly, flipping the
browned toast onto a plate and bringing it to her daughter at the
table. "Those are questions you'll have to ask your dad."

She watched as Lulu scooped a great glob of butter onto each
piece of French toast before drowning her plate in maple syrup.
"Good?" Joanne asked as Lulu began stuffing the pieces into her
mouth with almost manic determination, careful to avoid her mother's eyes.

"Is it because of me?" the child asked finally, unable any longer
to keep the tears out of her voice or away from Joanne. "Because I'm
not doing very well in school?"

It took a minute for Joanne to connect this thought to Paul's
departure. "Oh no, sweetheart," she rushed to assure her. "Daddy's
leaving has nothing to do with you." And everything to do with me,
she almost added. "Besides," she said instead, smoothing Lulu's hair
away from her face, "you're doing fine in school. There's nothing
wrong with your marks."

"They're not as good as Robin's."

"Who told you that?"

"Robin."

"Figures."

"Robin's been acting very peculiar lately," Lulu sidestepped.
"Have you noticed?"

"More peculiar than usual?" Joanne asked and Lulu smiled.
"Anyway, I wouldn't worry about your marks. Robin is a different
type of student. She never has any trouble memorizing facts. She's a
bit like Eve, who still doesn't know her left hand from her right, but
she can memorize anything you put in front of her. It doesn't mean
that Robin is any smarter than you are. You just have different ways of
showing how smart you are."

"I didn't ask for a lecture," Lulu sulked and left the room.

The phone rang as Joanne was rinsing the syrup off Lulu's plate. Warily, she checked the time. It was exactly eleven o'clock. "Hello," she answered, glancing toward the New York *Times* on the kitchen table.

"You'll never guess who's going to be a movie star!" came the excited exclamation from the other end of the line.

"Warren?" Joanne exclaimed, barely recognizing her brother's voice. "What are you talking about? What's going on?"

"They want to make your baby brother a star. Steven Spielberg, no less. Wait—Gloria will tell you all about it."

"Gloria, what's happened to my brother?" Joanne laughed as her brother's wife came on the phone.

"It's true," Gloria announced, her deep voice sounding even huskier than usual. "Can you imagine? I slave in this business for years and where do I get? Your brother delivers some star's baby and gets introduced to Steven Spielberg, who's been looking for a gyne-cologist to act as a consultant for his new picture. He takes one look at Warren's baby blues and decides to give him a small part. They shoot in August. I'm so jealous, I could kill."

In the background, Joanne could hear high-pitched yelling.

"What's that?"

"The girls are fighting, as usual," Gloria told her. "It never stops. Kate hates Laurie. She really hates her."

"I'm sure she doesn't."

"Yes, she does. But it's all right. I understand. I hate her too. How's everything on the East Coast, and when are you all going to come to your senses and join us here in Fantasyland?"

"Everything's fine here," Joanne lied, understanding that reality had no place in the world of fantasies. Besides, why upset her brother and his wife? What could they do from three thousand miles away? "I'll let you talk to your brother," Gloria was saying.

Joanne and Warren spent the next five minutes in pleasant, if essentially mundane, conversation, Warren filling his sister in on the more important events of the past week, Joanne leaving them out.

"You're sure everything's all right?" her brother asked as the conversation wound to a close.

"What could be wrong?" Joanne asked before she hung up.

Robin was standing in the doorway.

"Uncle Warren sends his love," Joanne told her as Robin flopped

into the chair her sister had previously occupied and yawned loudly.
"I'm surprised you're up this early. You were out very late last night."
She watched her daughter's shoulders stiffen exactly the way Paul's
always did when faced with something he didn't wish to discuss.
"After three, wasn't it?" She placed a glass of orange juice on the
table. Robin immediately drank it down.

"I didn't notice the time."

"Well, I did, and I don't want you coming in that late again,"
Joanne stated simply, without harshness. "Is that clear?"

Robin nodded.

"Was it a good party?" Joanne continued gently.

"Not very."

"So why'd you stay so late?" Joanne was aware that her question
skirted the delicate balance between interest and interference.

"We didn't."

"Who's we?"

"Scott and me."

"Who's this Scott?"

"Just a guy." Robin regarded her mother shyly. "He's real nice.
You'd like him."

"I'd like to meet him. The next time you go out with him, why
don't you bring him around to say hello?"

"Sure," Robin agreed quickly.

"You've never mentioned Scott before," Joanne persisted. "Is he
in your class?"

"No," Robin said, aware her mother was waiting for further
elaboration. "He doesn't go to school."

"He doesn't go to school? What *does* he do?"

"He plays guitar in a rock group." Robin shifted uneasily in her
chair.

"He plays guitar in a rock group," Joanne repeated, hearing
traces of Eve's mother in her voice. "How old is he?"

Robin shrugged. "Nineteen, maybe twenty."

"That's too old for you," Joanne stated flatly.

"He is not too old for me," Robin argued. "Boys my age are
babies."

"So are you."

Robin's eyes glared instant daggers.

"I'm sorry," Joanne apologized. "You're not a baby. But twenty is still too old for you. What else does he do but . . . rock?" she asked. Again her daughter only shrugged.

"It takes time to build a career," Robin explained.

"I take it he doesn't go to college?"

"They don't give degrees in rock groups at college."

"No, but they do give degrees in music," Joanne reminded her.

"Scott says he doesn't need a degree."

"Everybody needs an education."

"Mo . . . ther!"

Joanne bit down on her lower lip. "Where did you meet this Scott?"

"A party at somebody's house."

"When?"

"I don't know. A month ago maybe."

"You're very vague."

"I don't mean to be. Look, I said I'd bring him around the next time I saw him. What more do you want?"

Joanne stared hard at the wood grain of the kitchen table as if it could provide her with a suitable reply. "Would you like some breakfast?" she asked instead.

Robin shook her head. "I promised I'd help Lulu study for her history test."

Joanne nodded wordlessly as Robin departed.

The phone rang just as a loud fight between the sisters erupted upstairs. "Girls, please," Joanne shouted up at them as she reached for the phone. If they heard her at all, which she doubted, they ignored her. "Hello," she said, closing the kitchen door to block out the sound of their squabbling.

"Mrs. Hunter . . ."

Joanne recognized the strange voice immediately. "Yes?" she asked, afraid again though she wasn't sure why.

"Did you read page thirteen of the morning paper?"

"Yes I did," she replied, feeling foolish. Why was she talking to someone she didn't know? "But I think you've made a mistake, or you've got the wrong Mrs. Hunter . . ."

"You're next," the voice said simply and then was gone.

"Hello? Hello," Joanne repeated. "Really, I think you've made a mistake." She hung up the phone, her eyes returning slowly to the kitchen table. The morning paper was lying across it in roughly the same position that she had discarded it earlier. Slowly, the strange voice, like an invisible magnet, pulled her back across the room until her fingers were brushing against the rough edges of the newspaper. Nervously, but with increasing determination, she flipped through the pages until she once again found page thirteen. With growing uneasiness, her eyes retraced the columns, skimming over the possible strike by garment workers, reading more carefully the report of the roominghouse fire, finally coming to rest on the story of the housewife who had been hacked to pieces in her home in nearby Saddle Rock Estates. Without warning, Joanne felt an invisible presence standing beside her, bending close to whisper in her ear.

"You're next," he said.

Chapter 6

"For God's sake, why didn't you tell me?" Eve Stanley was pacing back and forth across Joanne's living room.

Joanne was sitting in one of two cream-colored swivel chairs situated on either side of the black marble fireplace at the far end of the oblong room. "I tried last weekend," she said softly, feeling vaguely guilty and not sure why, except that she was feeling guilty about everything these days. "But you weren't feeling very well, and your mother was there . . . The rest of the week kind of got away from me."

"Yeah, well, I can understand that," Eve admitted, falling into the other cream-colored chair and twisting it nervously back and forth. "Actually, it was Brian who mentioned that he hadn't seen Paul's car all week. I didn't even notice, I've been so busy with my aches and pains. Include my mother on that list. Anyway," she continued in one breath, as if to erase the earlier remark, "when I came home this afternoon, I saw Lulu sitting outside. She didn't look very happy, by the way . . ."

"She failed her history test."

". . . and I asked her if Paul was out of town, and she told me the news. Needless to say, I almost fainted dead away."

"I'm sorry. I should have called. I'm not functioning very well lately."

"And no wonder. I can't believe Paul would do such a thing, the bastard, may he rot in hell."

Joanne smiled. "I knew you'd cheer me up."

"What exactly did the asshole have to say?"

"He said he wasn't happy," Joanne laughed, biting down hard on her lower lip to keep the laugh from becoming the cry it was aching to be.

"He has no right to be happy. I hope he gets a toothache every time he smiles. Did he give you any examples?"

Joanne took a moment to collect her thoughts. "I think it was a general malaise more than anything specific."

"Malaise," Eve repeated, savoring the sound. "It should only have been malaria. Do you think he has somebody else?"

Joanne shook her head. "He says no. He says he's never been unfaithful to me."

"Do you believe him?"

"I always have."

"You believe everyone," Eve stated flatly.

"Do *you* think he has someone else?" Joanne asked.

"No," Eve replied truthfully.

"I think he just stopped loving me," Joanne said simply.

"I think he's an asshole," Eve repeated. "Come on, it can't be that vague. People don't just stop loving other people for no reason. It *has* to be something more specific. How was your sex life?"

"What?"

"I know you don't like to talk about these things, but we have to get to the bottom of this."

"Our sex life was fine," Joanne told her, feeling her face redden. "Maybe not like yours and Brian's . . ."

"Whose is?" Eve deadpanned, and both women laughed. "How often did you make love?"

Joanne squirmed in her seat. She noticed that Eve's chair was absolutely still, her friend leaning forward to rest her elbows on her knees. "I don't know. I never kept track. Once, twice a week, I don't know. As much as either of us wanted."

"Are you sure?"

"Are you kidding? I'm not sure of anything anymore."

"How adventurous were you?"

"What do you mean, adventurous?"

"You know, did you try new things, did you . . . ?"

"Eve, I really don't want to talk about this. I don't see any point. I've gone over every possible reason Paul could have had for leaving. Maybe it *was* our sex life, I don't know. He never complained, but maybe I wasn't . . . adventurous enough. Maybe I wasn't a lot of things. In fact, I'm *sure* I wasn't a lot of things. I'm sure it was all my fault."

"Hold on a minute," Eve insisted, standing up abruptly and sending the small chair spinning in circles. "Who said anything was all your fault?"

"Nobody has to say it. Obviously it was. Why else would he have left? I didn't do *anything* right."

"Oh, I see. In twenty years? You didn't do anything right?"

Joanne nodded.

"What about Robin? What about Lulu?"

"They don't count. They're separate people."

"Who made them separate people? Don't tell me you didn't do anything right. You have two beautiful daughters . . ."

"I have two beautiful, *obnoxious* daughters," Joanne corrected and looked guiltily around her in case one of them had crept, unnoticed, into the room. "I mean, I love them more than anything else in the world, but I don't know what happens to girls when they get to a certain age. Were *we* like that?"

"According to my mother, I still am." Eve shook her head. "Maybe it's a good thing I had that miscarriage," she continued matter-of-factly, sitting down again, this time on the blue-and-beige-striped velvet sofa facing the two cream-colored chairs. "She's always wished on me a daughter like the one I was. That's the only reason she wants grandchildren, you know. So she can watch me suffer. Anyway . . ." She clapped her hands on her knees. "We are not talking about my mother, we are talking about you, about how you haven't done anything right in twenty years and probably your whole life for that matter." Joanne tried to smile but failed. "You're not a great cook? Is there anyone on earth who makes better pies and cakes than you do?"

"That doesn't count either."

"What do you mean it doesn't count?"

"It would only count if I had a full-time job." Joanne stood up, moving her hands in front of her body as if she were physically collecting her thoughts. "I've been baking a *lot* of pies and cakes this week," she explained, nodding as she spoke, "and while I've been baking all these stupid pies and cakes, I've been thinking about the last twenty years, and how I've spent them . . . what I've been doing and what everyone else has been doing . . . and can't you see, Eve? I'm an anachronism. Everything I was brought up to be went out of style."

"Being a loyal wife went out of style? Being a good mother went out of style? Being a terrific friend doesn't count anymore? Says who? Show me who says it and I'll beat him up right now, the bastard, may he rot in hell." She stopped. "Anyway, I better not say anything else

because if I do, and you and Paul get back together—which you will
—you'll hate me and I'll have lost my only friend in the world."

"You'll never lose me," Joanne smiled. "You're the one constant
in my life. I can't imagine a time that we wouldn't be friends."

"I love you," Eve said simply, walking toward her.

"I love you too," Joanne repeated. The two women drew together in a long, comforting embrace. "What time is your doctor's
appointment tomorrow?" she asked, the first to pull away.

"Oh, forget it, you don't have to take me."

"Don't be silly. Why should you go alone? Besides, if I stay home,
it just means I'll bake more of those dumb pies and cakes."

"Okay, you talked me into it. I'm supposed to be there at nine-
thirty. And I can't eat anything after midnight, so don't mention
those pies and cakes again." She caught sight of her reflection in the
glass of one of the many paintings that lined the walls. "Oh God, who
is that woman? Look at me! I look awful." She pushed some stray
hairs away from her forehead. "Look at this." She rubbed the skin
around her eyebrows so that it produced small flakes which fluttered
into her lashes. "I'm falling apart."

"It's called dry skin," Joanne told her.

Eve laughed. "Terminally dry skin. I don't know, I always used to
have oily skin."

"The joys of middle age."

"I suppose. Anyway, I'd better go. I have a million papers to
mark."

"Eve . . ." Joanne's voice stopped her friend as she reached the
front hall. "What do you know about that woman in Saddle Rock
Estates?" Eve regarded her quizzically. "You know, the one who was
murdered."

Eve shrugged. "Not much," she said. "Just what I read in the
papers. She was raped and beaten and strangled and stabbed. Anything that he could do to her, he did."

"And you said she's the third one this year?"

"According to Brian, it's the same guy. Why?"

Joanne told her about the phone call. "He says I'm next."

Much to Joanne's surprise, Eve burst out laughing. "I'm sorry,"
she said quickly. "Really, I didn't mean to laugh. It's just that you look
so worried."

"Well, I *am* worried. Paul's gone and . . ."

"And some crazy phones you and tells you you're next on his list.

I know, I shouldn't laugh. But do you know how many women he probably called? Half of Long Island, I'll bet. He's harmless, Joanne. Guys who get their kicks long distance rarely have the guts to do anything in person. This is some loony who gets his rocks off terrifying women over the phone. Do you have any idea how many sickies there are like that in a city like New York? Probably half the male population. Listen, I'm sure it's nothing, but if it'll make you feel better, I'll tell Brian about it, okay?"

"I'd appreciate it," Joanne told her.

"You don't have to appreciate it," Eve smiled, hugging her friend close. "Just don't worry about it. You have enough to worry about right now. And tell Lulu not to worry about failing that test. Remind her that I failed everything in high school and that I never would have graduated at all if my mother hadn't gone to the principal and threatened to send me back the following year if he didn't pass me." She laughed, opening the front door. "The power that woman yields! Don't forget about our tennis lesson tomorrow afternoon," she called from halfway down the front steps.

"Meet you in the driveway at nine." Joanne waved as Eve disappeared inside the house next door.

"You'll just have to study harder," Joanne was saying only minutes later as Lulu helped herself to a second piece of freshly baked cake. "That's enough, Lulu, we're eating supper in an hour."

"Why'd you make it if we're not supposed to eat it?" Lulu shoved the corner of the moist lemon cake into her mouth, making no move to wipe up the crumbs that spilled from her bottom lip onto the floor.

"I made it for dessert."

"So, I'll have some for dessert too."

Joanne decided against pursuing the subject. "Maybe we could work out some sort of system that would help you to remember dates." Lulu's eyebrows narrowed together, accentuating her enormous brown eyes. "I always remembered the date of the Battle of New Orleans because there was a song about it when I was in high school. 'In 1814, we took a little trip . . . ,' she began, then stopped. "Well, I don't remember all the words, but I always remembered the date. 1814—I bet every kid in school knew it."

"Maybe we could ask Michael Jackson to write a song about the Civil War," Lulu suggested jokingly.

"That's not such a bad idea."

"Life isn't Sesame Street, Mother," Lulu reminded her, finishing off the piece of cake.

An eleven year old is telling me about life, Joanne thought. There was a sudden knock on the sliding glass door. Joanne turned in its direction.

One of the workers from the pool was smiling at her from the other side of the glass. Joanne rose slowly from her seat and unlocked the door to slide it open.

"We're finished for today," the man (tall, skinny, with wind-blown brown hair) informed her. "I was wondering if I could use your phone."

Joanne backed out of the way to let him in. As she pulled the door shut behind him, she noticed the trail of dirty fingerprints he had left along the glass and the moist earth caked around his shoes that he was now scattering carelessly across the kitchen floor. "It's on the wall," she indicated, pointing to the white phone.

"Thank you," he said, smiling at Lulu. When he turned toward the wall to speak, Lulu made a face in her mother's direction indicative of displeasure. The man suddenly swiveled around again, his back slumped against the wall. "Got me on hold," he muttered, and Joanne nodded understanding. "Your husband home?" he asked.

Joanne shook her head. "Do you need to speak to him?"

"Nothing that can't wait." His attention was rediverted to the phone. "Hello, yes, can I . . ." He snickered impatiently. "Got me on hold again." He looked down at his boots self-consciously.

"Dad phoned," Lulu said softly, newly reminded.

"When?" Joanne felt her hands start to shake and steadied them between her knees. "Why didn't you call me?"

"You were in the bathroom. And I didn't call you because he didn't ask to speak to you. Just to me."

Joanne felt the saliva stick in her throat. "What did he want?"

"To know how I made out in my test. To make plans for the weekend."

"The weekend?" Joanne hadn't given any thought to the coming weekend.

"He wants me to spend it with him in the city. I told him it was okay."

"Don't you think you should have checked with me first?"

"No," Lulu answered defiantly. "He's my father. I can see him if I want to."

"Nobody said you couldn't see him."

The man at the phone cleared his throat as if to remind them he was there and then shifted back to the wall, speaking in a voice that was low enough to be a whisper. Joanne lowered her own voice accordingly.

"What about Robin?" she asked.

"Robin has a date Saturday night."

"Okay," Joanne gave in. "You can spend the weekend with your father. Just make sure he has you back early on Sunday night. You have school Monday."

"I know I have school Monday. So does Dad," Lulu informed her mother with no small degree of annoyance.

"Lulu, can you please watch the way you talk to me."

"What's wrong with the way I talk to you?"

"Excuse me," the man at the phone interrupted. "I'm finished. Thank you." He moved away from the wall. Joanne noticed the marks from his dirty fingers along the white face of the phone. "How do you like it?" he asked as he stepped outside, his large hands making a sweep toward the freshly laid stone slabs.

"Pretty color," Joanne said.

"See you tomorrow."

Joanne closed the door and snapped the lock shut after him.

"He gives me the creeps," Lulu whispered, watching as, seconds later, the tall, skinny worker laughed easily with one of the other workmen by the deep end of the pool.

"Why?" Joanne asked. "He seems nice enough."

"I don't like the way he stares at people. He drills holes in you like he's working on one of those pieces of stone."

"You've been watching too much television," Joanne said, feeling uncomfortable with the analogy. "Anyway, he won't be here much longer. They should be finished soon."

"I hope so. It'd be nice to use the pool before we leave for camp. What's for supper?"

"Chicken."

"Chicken again?"

"We haven't had chicken in a long time."

"Why don't you make one of your lemon meringue pies?"

"Because I don't want to!" Joanne snapped, surprising them both with her fury.

Paul had asked her to bake him a lemon meringue pie. His favorite, he told her. His mother always made them and he'd never found anyone else whose pies could match hers.

"I bet mine could," Joanne told him, taking up the challenge and rushing home to ask her mother how it was done.

"He must be special, this Paul," Joanne could hear her mother saying as she gathered together the ingredients she would need.

"He is," Joanne heard herself agree.

"Okay." Her mother smiled. "We'll make him a lemon pie that'll knock his mother's oven mitts off. You watch carefully now. This is how it's done." She bent forward conspiratorially. "The secret is in the meringue."

Joanne watched her mother mix together the various ingredients that went into the making of the filling and the meringue topping. "How come you're using a frozen pie shell?" she asked, surprised when she realized that her mother wasn't rolling her own.

"Pie shells are a pain in the neck to make. Besides, nobody ever notices the difference between a shell that's precooked and one that you spend half the day slaving over. Trust me, darling, he'll never know the difference."

He knew the difference. Biting into the generous helping, the meringue a high, perfect arc, Paul chewed with deliberate slowness, then lowered the piece of pie to his plate while Joanne gazed on expectantly. "That's the best meringue I've ever tasted," he pronounced and Joanne inhaled a deep sigh of appreciative relief. "But I can't understand it," he continued, shaking his head.

"Can't understand what?"

"I can't understand how hands that could make this incredible meringue could also make this awful pie crust," he told her, waiting for her response.

Her response was to go home and make him another. And another. Rolling her own dough until she got it right. Until making pie shells was as ingrained in her as all the other baking skills her mother had taught her. Until he was forced to admit that his mother's pies couldn't hold a candle to hers and that he would love her forever and had he ever told her about his mother's incredible peach cobbler?

Now whenever she baked, he complained that he was getting too heavy. Rich foods weren't good for him, he told her, they needed to cut down their fat intake. High fiber, low fat, he informed her. They needed to rethink the way they ate. More chicken, less red meat. More fruit and vegetables, less pastries and fancy sauces. Bran, he repeated often, as if the word itself were sacred.

And so she had stopped baking and started buying chicken and fish instead of lamb chops and steaks, and the fridge was filled to bursting with apples and grapefruits and cauliflowers and squash, and plastic bags of bran from health food stores lined the kitchen counters, and everybody went to the bathroom with alarming regularity and complained that there was never anything in the house to eat.

And still he had left, Joanne thought, conjuring up the look of utter contentment that had flooded across Paul's features when she had finally produced the perfect lemon meringue pie. It was an image Joanne fought to keep before her eyes when she finally closed them later that night and tried, unsuccessfully, to sleep.

Chapter 7

"So, how'd it go?"

"Please, let's just get out of here, then we'll talk."

Joanne had to walk quickly to catch up to her friend, who was already half a corridor ahead of her. "Can't we take the elevator this time?" she pleaded as Eve reached the stairway marked Exit.

"You know what hospital elevators are like," Eve stated, pushing open the stairwell door and starting down the steps. "You wait half an hour for one and then thousands of people appear and you have to wait for another one. Then they stop at every floor. Come on, we'll be out much faster this way and I'm starving. I haven't eaten anything since last night, remember. Except for that awful barium they made me drink this morning."

"So what kind of tests did they give you?"

But Eve was already a full flight ahead and didn't answer the question. By the time they reached the bottom of the seventh flight, both women were audibly out of breath. "At least it was better going down," Eve smiled.

"My calves will never forgive me," Joanne told her.

"In years to come, they'll thank you. It's good exercise. I always take the stairs. Elevators are a Communist plot."

"Are you going to tell me what they did to you in there or not?" Joanne asked again as the two women pushed open the heavy hospital door and emerged into the steady drizzle outside.

"Oh hell, it's still raining."

"Where do you feel like eating?" Joanne asked.

"Let's go to The Ultimate. It's always nice, and it's close."

It was also crowded and they had to wait fifteen minutes for a table. When they were finally seated, Eve ordered a bottle of white wine to go along with their Caesar salads.

"Should you be drinking?" Joanne asked as Eve gulped down

one glass as if it were ginger ale and then poured herself another.
"What did the doctor say?"

"Nothing that any normal human being can understand. They
speak the language of the gods they think they are."

Joanne laughed. "You used to want to be a doctor," she reminded
her.

"Lucky for all of us I was born a decade too early." Eve took a
stab at her salad. "Aren't you going to try the wine?"

"I don't think I should. You know how dizzy wine makes me.
Especially in the afternoon."

"You're dizzy all the time. Come on, don't be so timid," Eve
admonished, watching as Joanne gingerly sipped at the top of her
glass. "Wine at lunch isn't nearly as decadent as it used to be. We're
liberated now, you know."

"Could have fooled me," Joanne sighed, allowing herself a
healthy drink. The wine *was* good, she thought, holding it in her
mouth for several seconds before swallowing, then immediately taking another, longer sip. "So," she said, reluctantly returning her glass
to the table, "do you or don't you have ulcers or gallstones?"

"After strapping me on this dumb table and turning me virtually
on my head, the doctor said he couldn't see a thing on the X-rays,"
Eve answered seriously, "and it'll be a while before they get the
results of the blood tests."

"Why'd they do blood tests?"

"Why do they do anything? They love sticking little needles into
people. It gives them an enormous sense of power. How's your
salad?"

"Not as good as the wine." Joanne emptied her glass. "So what
happens now?"

"Life goes on. We finish our lunch, then play some tennis . . ."

"It's raining," Joanne reminded her.

"Then we sit here and drink," Eve replied without missing a
beat.

Things have a way of working out, Joanne thought.

In the end, they decided to go to a movie.

"I don't believe I let you talk me into seeing this film," Joanne
giggled. Her head felt as though it were balanced precariously on her
shoulders.

"Film is too good a word," Eve laughed, "for what we are about to see." She grabbed for a handful of the popcorn in Joanne's lap and watched as half the box spilled onto the floor.

"Thanks a lot," Joanne told her. "I thought you said you never ate popcorn."

"I thought you said you never go to horror movies."

"I'm only here because you dragged me."

"You were in no condition to drive. I probably saved your life."

"Is there anyone else here?" Joanne looked around slowly, her eyes having difficulty focusing on the few scattered figures she could make out just before the lights dimmed. "Is it getting dark?"

"No dear," Eve replied seriously, "you've got the dreaded Bette Davis *Dark Victory* syndrome. Prepare yourself, you have only thirty seconds to live."

The two women dissolved into drunken giggles as the theater was plunged into total darkness and the curtains parted.

COMING ATTRACTIONS! the screen blazed. The following sixty seconds consisted entirely of the sound of gunfire and the sight of falling bodies. "They did him wrong," a disembodied voice narrated professorially. "Now he's coming back to do them in!"

"My kind of movie," Eve squealed.

Joanne was aware of a slight movement behind them. She swiveled around in her seat as a young man carrying a motorcycle helmet seated himself directly behind them, despite the fact that most of the other chairs in the theater were vacant. He seemed to be smiling, a row of bright, white teeth cutting through the darkness as he lowered the helmet to his lap, his hands remaining underneath. Joanne turned quickly toward the screen, feeling her head struggling to catch up. "Let's move," she whispered to Eve.

"Why? I'm comfortable."

"I'd rather sit in the middle," Joanne told her, her body midway between a crouch and a stand.

Eve pulled her back down. "You know I like an aisle seat."

"Okay." Joanne pointed to the aisle several rows ahead. "We'll sit down there."

"Too close."

"Eve, there's this funny guy behind us. I don't like the looks of him."

Eve executed an abrupt turnaround to stare at the young man behind them. "He looks okay to me," she whispered. "Kind of cute from what I could make out."

"Why does he have to sit so close? Why's he got that helmet on his lap?"

"Why don't you stop worrying and watch the picture?" Eve chastised, and Joanne understood that Eve wasn't about to move anywhere. "Relax, this is going to be great," Eve continued as a pretty young ingenue with long, straight blond hair ran in obvious terror across the screen. Joanne watched the helpless girl fall straight into the arms of a deformed madman with a knife, who wrenched the girl's head back violently and proceeded to slit her throat. Her bright red blood assumed an almost three-dimensional quality as it dripped from her neck and gathered in pools at the bottom of the screen, only to rise again seconds later in the form of large, undulating capital letters—SWAMP MONSTER OF DOOM. Joanne felt her stomach turn over. "Great stuff," Eve muttered.

"You're a very sick person," Joanne whispered, staring into her lap, feeling the back of her seat vibrate, trying not to think about what the boy behind them might be doing. Without raising her head, she lifted her eyes to the screen to see another young woman, not noticeably different in appearance from the first, sneaking around an old house in which she clearly did not belong. The music warned her loudly to leave the premises immediately, but since the girl couldn't hear the music, Joanne decided, perhaps it was the audience that was being warned to get out. Why do they always snoop where they're not supposed to? Joanne wondered as the girl neared an old red tassled curtain and pulled it open. A young man fell forward, a dagger thrust into his chest clean through to his back. The girl shrieked as the boy fell into her arms and burst into howls of insane laughter. Joanne watched in horror as the boy removed the fake dagger from his chest, and the young couple, both blond California-style teenagers with perfect tans, proceeded to make love on the creaking hardwood floor, unaware that they were being watched from the doorway by the deformed monster from the swamp, his knife poised and eager to strike.

What was she doing here? Joanne pondered, turning her eyes resolutely away from the screen. What was she doing in the middle of a Friday afternoon, in the middle of a life that was disintegrating around her, watching a gore-filled horror flick with a friend who might or might not have ulcers and a boy who might or might not be masturbating into his motorcycle helmet in the seat behind her? Did she need this aggravation in her life? Wasn't it enough that her husband had walked out on her and some lunatic with a phone fetish was threatening to hack her into little pieces? Did she also need the Swamp Monster of Doom in her life at this moment?

No, she should have run when she saw the marquee: "This movie will give you nightmares for the rest of your life!" Who needs nightmares for the rest of their lives? she had been about to ask, but Eve was already at the wicket buying their tickets. Recognizing that it was Eve's way of dealing with the morning's frustrations and sensing that she was too tipsy to drive, Joanne had gone along with her. Who was she kidding? She'd made going along a lifelong occupation. Whatever anybody wanted to do, wherever anyone wanted to go, Joanne Hunter was always ready to oblige.

"Are you crying?" Eve asked her suddenly.

"I don't think so," Joanne replied honestly.

"Are you going to be sick?"

"Not that I know of."

"Then why is your head in your lap? Why aren't you watching the movie?"

Joanne lifted her head just in time to see another young woman, this one with a long, angular face and no visible bosom, glancing with a mixture of envy and disdain at yet another California-style couple grappling with each other's clothing on the same creaking hardwood floor. The phone rang. "I'll get it," the flat-chested rectangle declared, unaware of the danger lurking just out of the camera's range. No one paid her any attention, and the girl left the room to the strident accompaniment of the musical score. The camera followed her into the kitchen, where she picked up the phone. "Hello?" she said, eyes wide, voice soft, and then repeated it when she received no response.

Joanne squirmed uneasily in her seat, glancing over at her friend, whose eyes were riveted to the screen. Why had Eve brought her here?

"Don't be so nervous," Eve reassured her. "She's the survivor. You can tell because she has no boobs and no boyfriend. The only ones that get killed are the ones who are always making out. The minute you see sex, you know they're as good as dead. The wages of sin and all that. Don't worry about this one; she'll be fine."

"Hello?" the girl on the screen repeated into the telephone.

"Mrs. Hunter," the voice whispered menacingly in Joanne's ear.

"What!" Joanne gasped, feeling the warm breath on the back of her neck and jumping from her seat as she spun around.

There was no one there. Even the boy with the motorcycle helmet had disappeared.

"What the hell are you doing?" Eve cried. "You scared me half to death, for heaven's sake!"

"I thought I heard something. Did you hear someone call my name?" She lowered her voice to a whisper. "Mrs. Hunter," she repeated, trying to catch the exact intonation.

"I know what your name is," Eve replied testily, "and no, I didn't hear anybody call you. Never scare a woman who's had too much to drink. Now I have to go to the bathroom." She stood up, about to make her way up the aisle.

"Wait, I'll come with you."

"You certainly will not. Somebody has to stay and fill me in on what I miss."

Joanne watched Eve disappear up the aisle, catching sight of a young man sitting alone near the back of the theater. The boy with the helmet? she wondered, straining through the darkness for a better look. But the young man raised his hand to his face—to scratch? to block out the screen? to hide?—and Joanne could discern nothing. She turned back toward the front of the theater.

The young couple were still rolling on the floor, but this time in the throes of agony, not passion. Above them, the hideously deformed creature was slicing the unhappy duo into new tassles for his curtains with a butcher knife the size of Long Island. What was she doing here? Joanne thought again, stealing another surreptitious look around the dark theater. The boy in the back row was gone. Had he been there at all? She looked toward the ceiling. When do we start acting like grown-ups? she questioned silently as Eve bounced back down into the seat beside her. They watched the remainder of the movie in uneasy silence.

"At least it's stopped raining," Eve said as they emerged from the movie theater and began walking down the street toward Joanne's car.

"Don't ever do that to me again," Joanne warned. "Getting me drunk and then dragging me to a movie like that. My head is pounding."

"Go home and take a nap."

"Maybe I will," Joanne agreed, trying to shake the heaviness out of her head. "I don't understand why they make films like that."

"Because people like you and me pay good money to see them," Eve told her.

"And why do we do that?" Joanne asked, genuinely interested in Eve's response.

"Because we know we're not in any real danger," Eve explained as they crossed the street. "I think we're going the wrong way," she announced after they had walked for several blocks.

"Really?" Joanne suddenly had no idea where she'd left the car.

"Didn't you park on Manhasset?"

"Did I?"

"I think so." The two women did an immediate about-face and started walking the other way. "Is that it?" Eve pointed to a maroon Chevrolet parked at the far end of the street.

"I think so. What's that on the windshield?"

"Shit—a ticket." They drew nearer to the car. "No, it's too big to be a ticket. It's a piece of newspaper. Looks like the wind blew it across your windshield. Yeah, that's all it is." Eve reached the car before Joanne and pulled the piece of newspaper free of the windshield wipers. She took a brief glance across it, then tossed it onto the road. "Too bad about that roominghouse fire," she said matter-of-factly as she and Joanne climbed into their respective seats.

"What are you talking about? What roominghouse fire?" Joanne asked, faint traces of the movie's musical score wafting through her memory as she started the engine and pulled the car away from the curb.

"It happened last week sometime, I guess," Eve said. "I don't know, I noticed it on that newspaper I took off your window."

Joanne slammed down hard on the brakes, violently thrusting both women forward in their seats despite their seat belts.

"Jesus Christ, what are you doing?!" Eve exclaimed.

"The newspaper!" Joanne demanded. "Where is it?"

"You saw me—I threw it away. Why? What are you doing?"

But Joanne had already opened her door and run around to the other side of the car.

"For God's sake, Joanne, where are you going?" Eve shouted as Joanne scooped up the newspaper from the curbside just as it was about to blow away. "Is there a sale at Bloomingdale's or something?"

Joanne said nothing. She stood motionless at the side of the road, clutching the piece of damp newsprint firmly between her fingers. Half the page had been torn away, and the rain had rendered most of what remained virtually illegible. Still, it was unmistakable.

Last Sunday's New York *Times*. Page thirteen.

Chapter 8

"It could be a coincidence," Eve was repeating, as much to herself as to Joanne as the two women waited in Joanne's living room for Paul to arrive.

"You keep saying that," Joanne reminded her. "Do you really believe it?"

"I don't know."

"Could you try Brian again?"

"I've already left two messages."

"Well, maybe I should speak to someone else."

"Go ahead." Eve followed Joanne into the kitchen. "You don't think you should wait till Paul gets here?"

"Who knows when that will be? You know the traffic on a Friday afternoon." Joanne picked up the phone and held it against her chest. "He didn't sound very happy about having to drive out here. He's taking Lulu for the weekend, and this means he has to make an extra trip."

"Tough," Eve said simply. "Some crazy threatens the mother of his children, I think the least he can do is drive out here and give you some support. Are you going to use that or do you just enjoy holding it?" Eve pointed to the receiver in Joanne's hand.

"I don't know the number."

"555-5212." She picked up Joanne's telephone address book, which rested on the counter underneath the phone. "Here, I'll write it down for you."

Joanne's fingers pressed down on the appropriate buttons, missing one and having to push them again, then pressing down on a three instead of the final two and having to repeat the procedure yet another time.

"Let me do that," Eve said, taking the phone. She pressed the buttons quickly and accurately. "I might as well do the talking. Sit down. You look like you're going to faint." Joanne lowered herself into one of the kitchen chairs without any recollection of having crossed the room. Her eyes watched Eve, who smiled as if to reassure her that everything would be all right, she was in control. "Yes, hello. My name is Joanne Hunter," Eve said confidently, making a face in Joanne's direction. "I'd like to speak to somebody about some threatening phone calls I've been getting. Thank you." She pushed the hair out of her face and waited. "Hello. Yes, this is Joanne Hunter. I live at 163 Laurel Drive. I'd like to report some threatening phone calls I've been getting. Who am I speaking to, please?" Joanne leaned back in her chair in admiration. She would never have thought to ask for the man's name. "Sergeant Ein," Eve repeated, then copied it down on a piece of scrap paper. "Yes, I've been getting these calls lately. They started . . . ?" She looked at Joanne for the necessary answer.

Joanne shrugged. "He spoke to me for the first time last Sunday, but I've been getting weird calls for a few weeks now, maybe more," she whispered quickly.

"Yes, I'm still here. I've been getting them for a few weeks now," she said, paraphrasing Joanne's reply. "Some guy . . ." Joanne lifted her palms into the air to indicate doubt. "At least I *think* it's a guy," Eve corrected, "has been calling at all hours, early in the morning, the middle of the night, that sort of thing, and then on Sunday, he threatened me. Yes, threatened. What exactly did he say?" she repeated.

"He says I'm next," Joanne whispered.

"Well, when he called last Sunday," Eve embellished, "he told me to look at page thirteen of the New York *Times.*" Joanne nodded approval. "And I did and there was that article about the woman who was murdered in Saddle Rock Estates, which is just near here. And then he called back later and told me that I'm next." There was a pause. "Yes, that's all he said. No, he didn't come right out and say he was going to kill me . . . but today I found a piece of newspaper on my car window, and it was the same page thirteen of last Sunday's *Times.* The same page, so this guy is obviously following me and I'm afraid that if he's the one who killed that other woman . . . yes, I know that. Yes, I'm sure there are. Yes, I realize that but . . . well, I hate to do that. Isn't there anything else you can do?" There was a long pause. "Yes, I understand. Thank you very much." She hung up the phone in obvious disgust. "New York's finest," she said sarcastically.

"What did he say?"

"What I knew he'd say."

"Which was?"

"That 'you're next' isn't exactly the worst threat he's ever heard, and have I any idea how many phone calls the police have received in the last few weeks from women who are convinced that they're the Suburban Strangler's—that's what they're calling him—next victim? He said some women have even pointed a finger at their husbands and boyfriends, and that if they had to investigate every crank call people received, they wouldn't have time for anything else. So, he advises me—or rather, he advises you—to change your phone number because there's really nothing else he *can* advise you to do, and there's nothing else that he can physically do unless the guy actually makes a move."

"At which point I could well be dead."

"Come on, cheer up. Brian wouldn't let anything happen to you. That's one of the benefits of living next door to a cop. I'll tell Brian about the calls tonight. That's if he gets home before I'm asleep, which is unlikely given the way his week has been running."

"What did the policeman say when you told him about the newspaper on the windshield?"

Eve shrugged. "Not much. Said it could be a prank . . . or a coincidence. Listen, it's a sad state of affairs, I'll grant you, but looking at the situation objectively, what can the police do?"

"Couldn't they put a tracer on my phone?"

"Only if this were the movies. Basically, it's like the man said— they have to wait for this kook to make a move . . . which he won't," Eve said quickly. "What about installing a burglar alarm? Now that Paul's gone . . ." She broke off abruptly. "I mean, even if, even *when* Paul comes back . . ."

"That's a good idea," Joanne agreed. "It would make me feel a lot safer. I'll ask Paul when he gets here."

"Why don't you just *tell* him?"

"I'll ask him," Joanne repeated as the doorbell rang.

"I'll get it," Eve volunteered, walking to the front door. Joanne hoped that Eve would excuse herself immediately and leave, but after greeting Joanne's husband with surprising warmth, she followed Paul into the kitchen and leaned against the counter, watching them carefully and obviously going nowhere.

Joanne felt a dull ache at the sight of him. He looked so handsome, so concerned.

"Now what's this about some guy threatening you?" Paul asked, coming directly to the point.

Joanne haltingly explained the phone calls and the piece of newspaper that had been left on her car window.

"Have you called the police?" he asked.

"Eve just spoke to them."

"And?"

"And there's nothing they can do unless the guy actually makes a move," Eve told him. "I'll talk to Brian about it later and see if he can persuade them to do a little more."

"Where's this piece of paper?"

Joanne couldn't remember. What had she done with it?

"It's on the coffee table in the living room," Eve reminded her, leading the way.

Paul took the piece of newsprint from Eve's hand and quickly looked it over. "There's nothing here about a murder," he said.

"That part is missing," Joanne explained, feeling a sudden hollowness in her chest.

"There isn't even a page number," Paul continued, a slight impatience creeping into his voice.

"It's page thirteen," Joanne told him. "I know because I read every article on that page several times and there was that story about the roominghouse fire and that other one below it about the garment workers . . ."

"This page could have come from anywhere."

"And the articles on the other side are the same."

"Joanne, I can see that you're scared, and I'm not trying to minimize your fear, but don't you think you're letting your imagination run away with you just a little bit?"

"No, she doesn't," Eve said.

"I don't know," Joanne said, sinking into one of the swivel chairs. Was she?

"Look," Paul continued gently, "some crackpot calls you on the phone and scares you half to death. It's only natural that you'd be a little spooked, especially now that I'm not . . ." He broke off, looking toward Eve.

"I'd better go," Eve said quickly. "Nice seeing you, Paul. Don't forget to tell him about the alarm," she added before she closed the door behind her.

"What alarm?" Paul asked.

"Eve thought it might be a good idea if I put in a burglar alarm system. Of course, if you think it's too expensive . . ."

"No, it wouldn't be too expensive. The house is already wired for one. If it would make you feel better . . ."

"It would."

"Fine. Then do it."

"What do I do?" Joanne asked, feeling foolish.

"I'll do it," he said, "and call you Monday."

"Thank you." They stood in the center of the living room as awkwardly as if they were unwilling participants in a blind date that had confirmed each other's worst fears. "Would you like to sit down? I could make some coffee . . ."

"No, thank you," he responded quickly. "I have to get back into the city. Where are the girls?"

"At a track meet."

"How have they been?" He paused. "Have they been giving you any problems?"

"Not really. They miss their father."

"I know," Paul said softly. "I miss them too. It's very quiet without them."

"Lulu's looking forward to tomorrow," Joanne said, forcing herself to sound cheerful. "Can't wait to see her dad's new apartment."

"It's not much," Paul explained. "It's very cramped, very impersonal. Did Lulu give you my phone number?"

"Yes."

"If you need anything, don't hesitate to call."

"I won't."

"If it's important, you can always reach me at the office."

"Thank you. That's good to know." There was an awkward pause. "Have you had time to think yet?" she asked finally.

Paul looked across the room. "Not really. I've been so busy with the move, trying to get organized. It's only been a week . . ."

"I baked a nice lemon cake yesterday," Joanne said, quickly changing the subject. "I think there's still some left."

"I better not." He patted his stomach. "I'm trying to watch it."

"You look well."

"Thank you."

"I must look awful."

"You look fine. A little tired maybe. Those phone calls haven't helped your sleep, I'm sure."

"I was scared."

"I'm sure you were."

"You were gone . . ."

"Try not to worry about it," Paul said, sidestepping her remark. "Just hang up the next time the jerk calls."

"What if he did kill that woman?"

"He didn't."

Joanne stared at her husband. "I miss you," she said simply.

"Joanne, don't . . ."

"I don't think I can manage without you."

"You can. You're strong."

"I don't want to."

"You have to." There was silence. "I'm sorry, I didn't mean to sound so harsh. Joanne, you know I'm always here if you need me."

"I need you."

"But you can't come running to me every time you have a little problem. It isn't good for you, and it isn't good for me."

"This isn't just a little problem."

"What is it?" he asked, holding up the piece of newspaper. "Let's look at it realistically. Some guy calls and tells you to look in the paper and that you're next. A week later you find half a piece of paper on your car window and overreact . . ."

"I'm not overreacting."

"Maybe not. But I see this sort of thing all the time, people jumping to conclusions . . ."

"I'm not jumping to conclusions."

"Has he called again?"

"What?"

"Has he called again?" Paul repeated though he knew she had heard him the first time.

Joanne shook her head.

"There, you see."

"No. What should I see?"

"That there's nothing to be afraid of. Joanne, if I were home, you wouldn't give this matter a second thought."

"But you're not home."

"No," he said, the softness of his voice undercutting the harshness of his words, "and this isn't going to bring me home either. Can't you see what you're doing?"

"What am I doing?"

"I don't think you mean to," he explained awkwardly, "at least not on a conscious level."

"What don't I mean to?"

"I think that subconsciously," he emphasized, "it's your way of binding me to you."

"No."

"Joanne, if our marriage has any hope of surviving, you have to give me this chance to be by myself to think things through. You can't keep finding excuses to bring me back here."

Joanne said nothing. Was he right? Was she trying to bind him to her? Was she overreacting? The newspaper had been wet and torn; it was true the page number was missing . . .

"I have to go now. I have clients waiting."

Joanne nodded, following Paul to the front door.

"I didn't mean to sound so cold."

"You didn't."

"I think it's best."

"Of course. You're right."

The phone rang.

"Do you want me to wait?" he asked.

Joanne nodded and ran to the kitchen, picking up the phone before it could ring again. "Hello?"

"Mrs. Hunter."

Joanne froze at the sound of the familiar voice, her eyes frantically summoning Paul from his position in the front hall. Paul walked quickly toward her and took the phone from her outstretched hand. Joanne held her breath as all around her normal household squeaks grew ominous.

"Hello," Paul said forcefully. "Who is this?" Joanne waited. Thank God he was here. "Who?" she heard him ask. "Oh yes, yes, she's right here. I'm sorry, she must have misunderstood." He handed the phone back to Joanne. What was going on? "I have to go," he said quietly. "Tell Lulu I'll pick her up at ten o'clock tomorrow morning. I'll call you Monday about the alarm."

"Hello?" Joanne asked into the receiver, hearing the front door close.

"Mrs. Hunter?" the voice said again, this time more of a question. "Mrs. Hunter, it's Steve Henry, the tennis pro at Fresh Meadows. Mrs. Hunter, are you there?"

"Yes," she whispered, recalling the look that had passed across

Paul's eyes moments earlier. The phone call had only confirmed his suspicions. "I'm sorry. I didn't recognize your voice."

He laughed. "No reason that you should. Not yet anyway." Joanne wondered what he meant but didn't ask. "I thought you might like to arrange for another lesson to make up for the one you missed today. I have some free time over the weekend . . ."

"No, that's impossible."

"All right," he said quickly. "Is everything okay?" He seemed genuinely concerned. "You sound a little strange."

"I'm fine. A bit of a cold coming on, I think."

"Drink lots of orange juice and load up on vitamin C. It always works for me. Well," he continued when she said nothing, "I guess we'll just leave your lesson until next Friday."

"That's fine." She hung up without further comment.

How could she have made such a dumb mistake? Especially when Paul was there. She'd been so sure. When she picked up the receiver, when she heard the sound of his voice. "Mrs. Hunter," he had said in that same way.

The phone rang again. Joanne reached over automatically, thinking that it was probably Eve, who'd no doubt been watching for Paul's car to leave and was anxious to know the outcome.

"Mrs. Hunter," the voice said before Joanne had a chance to say hello. "Did you get my message, Mrs. Hunter?"

This time there could be no mistake.

"What message?" Joanne asked, knowing the answer. She sank slowly to the mustard-colored tile beneath her feet, her breathing almost still.

"The one I left on your car, Mrs. Hunter. You couldn't miss it. I left it right across your windshield where you'd be sure to find it. Did you enjoy the movie, Mrs. Hunter?"

"Listen," Joanne pleaded, trying to be forceful but sounding only desperate. "Listen," she repeated, "I think you better stop this little joke right now. My husband doesn't think it's very funny."

"Your husband's gone, Mrs. Hunter," the voice informed her casually. "In fact, he's gone for good. Isn't that so, Mrs. Hunter? And I know how horny women get when their husbands aren't around to take care of them, and I intend to see that you don't have that problem. Yes ma'am, you don't have to worry about that—before I kill you, I'm going to show you a real good time."

Joanne let the phone drop, hearing it hit the floor with a sharp crack. She remained in this position, her back against the wall, her knees drawn up into her chest, with the phone buzzing an unpleasantly insistent signal from somewhere beside her, until she heard a key turn in the front door and her daughters burst into the house demanding to know what was for dinner.

Chapter 9

The two men from Ace Alarms Incorporated arrived promptly at ten o'clock the following Thursday morning to begin installation of the new alarm system for Joanne's home. Paul had arranged everything; all that was required of Joanne was her presence.

"I guess I should show you around," Joanne told the two men, both brown-haired and muscular, divided by perhaps a generation. Possibly they were father and son, Joanne thought, remembering that Paul had been disappointed when their second child had been another girl. Maybe if she had given him a son . . .

Stop this at once, she scolded herself, smiling at the men and fighting the urge to flee to the sanctuary of her bedroom. Masking a growing uneasiness, she tried unsuccessfully to recall exactly what Paul had told her she was supposed to do. He said so many things when he had telephoned late Monday to inform her of the arrangements he had made: that conversations with various friends, acquaintances, and partners over the weekend had convinced him that Ace Alarms was the best, if not the cheapest, way to go; that his own discussions with representatives from various firms had confirmed this impression; and that he had already worked out with the men who would be coming the type of system that would best suit their home. Anything else he had said had been lost on Joanne, who remembered clearly only the reference to their home as if it were somewhere that he still lived, or to which he was some day planning to return.

"Your husband didn't think it was necessary to install wires around all the windows," the more senior of the two men—Harry, he'd said his name was—informed her as she led the way into the kitchen. "Just the ones downstairs and around the front door, and the sliding glass doors. There's another one downstairs like this one, right?" Harry knelt at the base of the sliding kitchen door, examining its construction. "That's quite a mess you've got out there," he added, his eyes directed at her backyard.

"They're pouring the concrete today," Joanne told him. "I'm hoping that means they're almost finished."

"They're never finished," Harry said matter-of-factly. "Once you start with a pool, there's always something. More trouble than they're worth, if you ask me. But I guess if you like to swim . . ."

"I don't swim," Joanne told him. "I never learned."

"Well," the man continued, undaunted, "I guess it's one way of insuring that you'll see more of your kids this summer."

"The girls are going to camp," Joanne said, growing giddy. "My husband swims." Of course, my husband doesn't live here anymore, she wanted to confide, but didn't.

"You gonna show us the door downstairs?" Harry asked.

"Oh, certainly," Joanne answered, hearing her suddenly high-pitched voice. The men followed her into the hall. "You saw the front door," she squeaked, clutching her hands together to keep them from shaking. Why was she so nervous?

"When we came in," Harry said drolly.

"Yes, of course." She led the two men down the stairs to the bottom level of the three-story house, constructed so that all three floors were above ground.

"We'll replace the locks," Harry told her as they entered the family room at the back of the house beneath the kitchen. "The ones you've got are strictly Mickey Mouse. It's a wonder you haven't been broken into already. All it would take to open that front door is a good, swift kick." Once again he bent down to examine the sliding glass door that led to the backyard.

Joanne caught a glimpse of the dark-haired skinny worker who Lulu said gave her the creeps. He was staring at her from the side of the pool, but quickly looked away as their eyes connected. Joanne likewise turned around, only to find herself confronting the dark, almost black eyes of Harry's son, who, as far as she could remember, hadn't said a word since he had walked through the front door. She felt a shortness of breath and told herself to breathe deeply. She wanted to sit down on the gray corduroy sofa but her feet wouldn't budge, sharp needles plunging like knives through her toes and heels to nail her to the dark wood floor. What was happening to her?

"We'll put Charley-bars across these sliding doors," Harry informed her, "and a deadbolt on the front one. That won't necessarily keep anyone out, but it'll sure make them work a lot harder to get in. Most crooks don't like to work that hard. Where's your fuse box?"

"I don't know," Joanne said, realizing that she didn't. "Where are they usually?" This brought a laugh from Harry's son. He thinks I'm a dumb housewife, Joanne thought. And he's right. I *am* a dumb housewife. Why don't I know where the fuse box is? Eve would know where her fuse box is.

"Where's your furnace room?" Harry smiled indulgently. "You know where your furnace room is, don't you?" He said it as a joke, but as with many jokes, it came attached to a sharp undercurrent of truth, which gave his words a bitter coating. Still, his face was gentle, almost playful, and Joanne ignored the implicit condescension of his remark.

Joanne led the men toward the furnace room. The large metallic fuse box, located prominently on the wall facing the doorway, mocked her with silent menace. "Can I get you a cup of coffee?" Joanne offered as father and son set about examining the assorted fuses.

"That would be real nice," Harry agreed. "Leon, how about you?" Leon nodded but said nothing. "Cream and sugar for me. Black for my brother."

So they were brothers, Joanne thought, returning to the kitchen to prepare the two cups of coffee. There was quite an age difference, she calculated, her mind conjuring up a plausible history for the two men: the family had split up; probably the father had left Harry's mother for a younger woman when Harry was a boy—yes, that was the most likely story—and after a few years, Harry's dad had started a new family, and Leon was the result; at first there was much for Harry to adjust to, but as they matured, the two brothers, same father, different mothers, learned to love one another and eventually went into business together. So in the end, everybody was happy. Except Harry's mother, the wife who went along only to be left behind, who would always remain an ex and a hyphen away from the respectable new family unit.

Joanne watched as the coffee dripped one slow drop at a time from the filter into the glass pot of the Mr. Coffee machine. If Paul were to remarry in the next year, she further calculated (allowing time for their divorce), and if he started another family (add on another year), well then, in less than two years, Robin, who would be going on eighteen, and Lulu, who would be thirteen, could have a new baby brother, because of course the baby would be a boy . . .

There was a knock on the sliding door. Joanne swung toward it as if she had been struck. The tall worker with the dark hair who gave Lulu the creeps was smiling at her from the other side of the glass. "I need to use your phone," he mouthed.

Joanne walked hesitantly to the door and pulled it open. The man, in his late twenties or early thirties, she estimated, stepped in immediately, his eyes falling across the pink cotton shift she wore as if it were a flimsy negligee. "It's there," Joanne said, realizing as she spoke that he already knew where it was.

"Thank you." He smiled out of the side of his mouth, his eyes seeming to take in each detail of the room as he ambled across the floor and picked up the phone. Leaning back against the white-and-yellow flowered wallpaper, the fingers of his hands leaving another trail of dirt across the recently cleaned face of the white phone, he pushed down on the appropriate buttons. "Got a new number, huh?" He indicated the new number printed in the center of the phone.

Joanne nodded, trying not to listen to his conversation, noisily removing several mugs from the cupboard, retrieving the cream from the fridge and the sugar from its shelf, uncomfortably aware that his voice carried familiar traces of a slight rasp.

Her eyes locked on the back of his head at the same instant that the man turned away from the wall, so that they found themselves staring directly at one another. Casually he replaced the receiver and almost provocatively relaxed his posture, making no effort to leave. "Your husband home?" he asked. The same words he had used the previous week, a different tone.

"He's at work," Joanne answered, realizing he had probably overheard at least part of her conversation with Lulu and had already figured the situation out for himself.

There was a sudden loud knock on the front door and Joanne jumped. "Busy day," the man said, his lips twisting into a knowing smirk. Joanne squirmed uneasily, the tingles in her feet that had immobilized her downstairs returning to root her to the spot. She wanted to move but couldn't. The man's smirk broadened into a grin. "Aren't you going to answer it?"

Don't be silly, Joanne silently admonished herself, finding her feet and moving toward the front door. Just because the man looks creepy, that doesn't necessarily mean he *is* creepy. How many times had she warned her daughters when they were little that bad people didn't always look bad, that appearances could be deceiving? Many people's voices were vaguely hoarse. It didn't mean anything. She was being ridiculous, letting her imagination run away with her. Everyone sounded raspy. Everyone appeared sinister.

She opened the front door.

"Mrs. Hunter," the short, pear-shaped man standing before her said.

"Mr. Rogers," Joanne greeted him in return, recognizing the man who owned and operated Rogers Pools.

"I was wondering if you could move the truck in your driveway. My men need to get in so they can start spraying the concrete."

"Oh yes, just a minute." Joanne raced into the hall to the top of the stairs. "Mr. . . . Harry," she called, not sure whether he had given her his last name. "Harry . . . Leon, could one of you move your truck?"

Leon took the stairs two at a time, saying nothing as he nodded to Mr. Rogers and skipped down the front steps. Maybe he *couldn't* speak, Joanne pondered. An accident at birth perhaps . . .

"Having some work done?" Mr. Rogers asked, interrupting her thoughts.

"We're installing a burglar alarm."

"Good idea. What system are you going with?"

"I don't know," Joanne told him, feeling stupid again. Why didn't she know? "My husband worked it out . . ."

But Mr. Rogers had already walked past her into the kitchen as if he took it for granted he had been invited inside. "How do you like it?" he asked, staring out the sliding glass door to the backyard.

"Well, it's kind of a mess," Joanne said meekly, following behind him and relieved to see that the creepy man was gone from her kitchen, though she noticed that he'd left a trail of muddy footprints. She saw her purse on the floor beside the phone. Had it been lying on its side that way when she ran to answer the door, or had it been moved?

"It'll be beautiful. You'll see. You'll love it. All you'll have to do is walk into your backyard and you'll be on vacation. Just like a summer cottage. Better. No traffic."

"When do you think you'll be finished?" Joanne ventured.

"Another few days, tops. It depends on the weather. We would have been finished by now except for all the rain. We'll get the concrete in today. After that it's just a matter of the finishing touches."

"Seems like there's quite a bit of work left."

"No, nothing really, once the concrete's in. Which, by the way, means another payment. You think you could have a check ready for me by the end of the day? Just give it to Rick there."

"Rick?" Joanne glanced over at the pool, half-expecting the tall, skinny worker who had been inside her home to acknowledge the casual introduction with a wave of his dirty fingers. But Mr. Rogers pointed past him at another skinny worker with dark hair, who smiled and nodded his head. "That's Rick," Mr. Rogers said. "Just give him the check."

"How much?" Joanne asked as Mr. Rogers, whom Joanne realized also had a slight rasp to his voice, handed her an invoice.

"See you later," Mr. Rogers told her as he and Leon passed each other at the front door.

"Your coffee's ready," Joanne called after Leon, but he said nothing and continued down the stairs as if he hadn't heard her. Why doesn't he speak? she wondered, returning to the kitchen and pouring coffee into the waiting mugs. Maybe he was just shy. Or maybe he was afraid that she might recognize his voice . . .

She froze, feeling her hands shake and the newly poured coffee slosh about dangerously close to the rims of the mugs. She lowered the mugs to the counter. If she wasn't careful, she'd scald herself. And for what? Because every man who spoke to her, or for that matter, who *didn't* speak to her, might be the mysterious caller? Someone who everyone kept assuring her was just some harmless crackpot. Someone who hadn't even phoned in the few days since she'd had the number changed.

"Okay," Harry said, appearing behind her without warning.

"My God!" Joanne gasped, spinning around and knocking over one of the mugs. She watched in helpless frustration as the dark brown liquid—like blood, she thought—dripped steadily to the floor by her bare feet.

"You got some paper towels?" Harry asked when Joanne made no move to wipe up the mess.

His words had the effect of a sharp jab to the ribs, and Joanne was instantly on the floor wiping up the spilled coffee and then pouring him another cup. "I'm so sorry."

"Careful," Harry cautioned, taking both mugs from Joanne's

unsteady hands and setting them down on the kitchen table. "We're ready to start now," he informed her, and Joanne realized that Leon had quietly entered the room at some point during the confusion of the last several minutes and had been observing her, his face a study of bemused indifference. He thinks I'm an idiot, Joanne thought.

"How long will it take?" she asked, careful to keep her eyes on Harry, with whom she felt more comfortable.

"A couple of days. We got a lot to do."

"What exactly?" Joanne asked, wanting to sit down.

"Don't you worry about it," the man said, having obviously decided it was beyond her comprehension. "We got it worked out with the man of the house. I'll explain how everything works after we get it installed. You decided yet where you want the intercom?"

"The intercom?" Now that she heard the word, Joanne vaguely remembered Paul saying something about . . .

"Your husband told us to install an intercom system. The house is already wired for one. You gotta have a main terminal. Most people like it in the kitchen." He looked around the room. "There, beside the phone. That's probably the best place for it." He looked to Joanne for approval. She nodded silently, hearing a faint buzz in her ears. Probably all those butterflies flapping around in her stomach, she thought, trying to concentrate on what Harry was saying. But the harder she tried to listen, the more difficult the task became. Something about intercoms in all the rooms, about being able to listen in, and to speak to one another without having to yell. The man was obviously not a father of daughters. Joanne smiled, aware that he had finished speaking and had taken her smile for agreement. After all, he had already discussed everything important with the "man of the house." Of course, the man of the house had neglected to mention that he was no longer "of the house" these days. Did that mean he was planning to come back?

The phone rang.

"It's Paul, Joanne," the voice said, businesslike, polite, as if she were a pleasant but distant relation. "Did the men get there?"

"From the alarm company? Yes, they're right here." It was only then that she remembered she was supposed to have phoned him after their arrival. "I'm sorry, I forgot . . ."

"Let me speak to Harry."

Silently, she handed the phone to the older of the two men and listened while he conferred with her husband. She smiled nervously at Leon, who smiled back easily without speaking, slowly sipping his coffee, lost somewhere in thoughts of his own.

"Let's get to work," Harry announced suddenly. Leon quickly followed his brother out of the room.

"Didn't my husband want to speak to me?" Joanne called after them.

"Didn't say so," Harry called back, disappearing down the steps.

Without prior thought as to what she was going to say, knowing that Paul would consider whatever she said another invasion of his time but unable to stop herself, Joanne picked up the phone and dialed her husband's Manhattan office. "Paul Hunter," she said to the receptionist of the large firm. Did the young woman know that Paul had moved out? The receptionist connected her immediately to Paul's office. "Can I speak to Paul?" Joanne asked his secretary, Kathy. Did she know?

"He's in a meeting," Kathy answered, her voice resolutely non-descript. "Can he call you back?"

"I'm returning his call," Joanne persisted. "It's important."

"Just a minute. I'll see if I can interrupt him."

Paul came on the phone a few seconds later. "Is there a problem, Joanne? Four guys just walked into my office."

Joanne told him about Mr. Rogers' request for more money, and Paul responded that the checks were in the drawer underneath the phone where they always were. Though he kept his voice even, he was clearly annoyed at what he felt was an unnecessary interruption.

The rest of the afternoon had the feel of an out-of-focus photograph, the house full of men scurrying about like mice. Several of the pool workers needed access to a pipe they could reach only through the furnace room and so they joined the two men from Ace Alarms, who were already inside, busy connecting wires and hooking up little boxes. At various intervals, a shrill bell would sound—"We're testing the system," Harry informed her—and each time Joanne would jump. Eve phoned when she returned from work to ask what all the trucks were doing on the street and to say that, on top of everything else, she thought she might be coming down with a sore throat; Robin and Lulu shot through the front door in the middle of a heated argument, which continued even after both girls were in their separate bedrooms supposedly doing their homework; Rick came to the door to collect the check promptly at five o'clock, just as Harry was asking Joanne what combination of numbers she had selected for the alarm.

"Numbers?" Joanne asked after Rick had departed with the money, suddenly aware that Leon, who always seemed to appear from out of nowhere when she thought she was alone with Harry, was watching her. He's trying to decide whether I'm always this scatterbrained, she thought.

"Your husband said the numbers were up to you." Joanne stared at Harry. "You're supposed to pick four numbers, Mrs. Hunter," Harry continued gently, sensing that something was the matter but unwilling to risk asking what it was. "Whatever combination you want." He led her to the small box that they had installed just inside and to the left of the front door. It contained a series of push buttons identical to the face of a telephone. "Whenever you're going to leave the house, you push the four numbers. A green light will go on. Then you have thirty seconds to get out and close the front door behind you. The same thing when you come back. You come inside, and you have thirty seconds to press the numbers to turn the system off. The green light will go off. If you don't, the alarm goes off. Understand?"

Joanne nodded. The butterflies in her stomach had scrambled up into her chest, and were currently trapped inside the maze of her ribcage.

"So, pick four numbers."

"Any numbers?"

"Whatever numbers your little heart desires."

Leon suppressed a chuckle, disguising it as a cough, as from upstairs there came a barrage of loud accusations and the sound of doors slamming. "Girls," Joanne called, secretly glad for the distraction. "Cut it out!"

"She called me a liar!" Lulu shrieked.

"She *is* a liar!" Robin yelled after her. "She says she wasn't in my room."

"I only went in there to get a book that belongs to me."

"Liar!" Robin shouted.

"Thief!" came the instant retort.

Again the hall shook with the sound of doors slamming.

"The numbers?" Harry asked patiently.

"When was the start of the Civil War?" Joanne asked, her mind upstairs with her daughters.

"I beg your pardon?" Harry asked. "The Civil War?" He looked toward his brother.

"1861," Leon said evenly. A perfectly nice voice, Joanne thought, but one he obviously didn't exercise more than was minimally required.

"Can I use that?" Joanne asked.

"You can use the start of the Boer War, if you want," Harry told her. "1-8-6-1 it is."

"My younger daughter is weak in history . . . in remembering dates. Maybe this will help her," Joanne confided, but the two men were already halfway down the stairs.

Joanne turned back toward the kitchen. The tall, creepy workman was standing in the doorway. How long had he been there?

"I knocked on the kitchen door," he explained. "Guess you didn't hear me. Is your husband home yet?" Joanne shook her head, unable to speak for the butterflies trying to push their way out of her throat. "He said that he wanted to talk to me before we went ahead with the grouting for the tile. We'll be doing that tomorrow."

"I'll call him," Joanne said, finding her voice and her feet at the same time and returning to the kitchen. She thought, as she listened to the man talking quietly to her husband over the phone seconds later, that his voice had lost any trace of the raspiness she had heard in it earlier. In fact, if she were being objective, she'd have to admit that his voice was rather pleasant. There was nothing especially creepy about the way he looked, either, she knew, observing him closely and clearing her throat to rid herself of the scrofulous sensation that seemed to have lodged there.

The tall, skinny worker who gave Lulu the creeps (not Joanne, now that she was being so objective) replaced the receiver and swiveled on his heels to face Joanne. "Thank you," he smiled, his eyes burrowing into hers as if he knew something that she didn't. All her misgivings instantly returned. Had he been in her purse earlier? How long had he been standing in the doorway? Had he heard the numbers she and Harry had discussed? Did he understand what they were for? She couldn't take a chance that he did—she'd have to change the combination.

"Harry," Joanne called down the stairs seconds after the tall, skinny worker had departed and she had securely fastened the lock on the sliding glass door behind him.

"Yes, Mrs. Hunter?" Harry's voice echoed with benign impatience, as if he already knew what she was about to say.

"When was the start of the Boer War?" she asked, hearing Leon break into unrestrained laughter. He thinks I'm an idiot, she thought.

Chapter 10

"How *are* you?" Karen Palmer asked with a touch more solicitousness than the question normally required. She knows, Joanne thought, feeling suddenly sick to her stomach. She pushed her purse inside her locker and tried to smile. She had held together this long—she was not about to fall apart in the women's locker room of the Fresh Meadows Country Club. Especially in front of this woman, who was a casual friend at best.

"Fine," Joanne answered simply, hearing her voice quiver. She bit down hard on her bottom lip, feeling it slide away from her toothy grip, and promptly burst into tears. The silent tears quickly grew into loud wails she was unable to control. Helplessly watching herself dissolve, Joanne stood in the middle of the gray carpeted floor and howled like a wounded animal.

"Oh my God, you poor dear," Karen Palmer exclaimed, immediately wrapping her arms around Joanne. "Come on, let's sit down." Joanne allowed herself to be led to a row of comfortable chairs against one pale pink wall of the women's locker room. "Go ahead, cry it out," Karen Palmer advised as Joanne buried her head in the woman's huge bosom. It was like lying on a foam rubber pillow, Joanne thought between sobs, unable to stop shaking, her arms and legs tingling, a queasy feeling building in her gut. She hoped she wouldn't throw up. Eve would be very upset with her if they missed another lesson. Where was Eve? Why wasn't she here yet? "Do you want to talk about it?" Karen asked gently.

Joanne wiped her eyes, her sobs shuddering to a halt as she regained control, and lifted her head. "My God, what did you do to your hair?" she asked, really looking at the other woman for the first time that afternoon.

Karen Palmer's hand flew immediately to the top of her head, her fingers picking through the remains of what had once been a luxurious crop of auburn hair. "It's punk," Karen explained. "Jim was getting tired of the old style. I'd been wearing it the same way for so long." She tried to laugh. "He said I looked like I'd been frozen in the fifties. And he was right. Rudolph agreed. Couldn't wait to get his scissors at it. Of course, now Jim claims he never meant he wanted it *this* short. Oh hell—men! They don't know what they want half the time . . ." She broke off. "I heard about you and Paul. I'm so sorry."

"It's just temporary. We're trying to work things out." Joanne heard her words as if they came from someone else's mouth.

"I'm sure you will," Karen agreed, and Joanne wondered how anyone could be sure of anything, especially things that didn't concern them, although she realized she would probably have said the same thing had their situations been reversed. "I don't know what comes over men when they get to a certain age," Karen continued. "It's like the books say—they go kind of crazy. How are you managing?" she asked.

"All right," Joanne said. What was the point in saying more? "I'm installing a burglar alarm system," she went on when she saw that more was expected.

"You mean you don't already have one?"

Joanne shook her head.

"Not that they do much good," Karen continued. "They're always going off at the wrong times, and the police never show up anyway."

"What do you mean?"

"The police are too busy to answer every false alarm they hear."

"But how do they know they're false?"

"Most of them are. And even if they're not, the police are just too busy. Have you ever tried calling Emergency? 911?" Joanne shook her head. "Try it sometime. See what happens. Nothing happens, that's what. You listen to a recorded message tell you that all the lines are busy. If you're still alive after the twenty minutes it takes for someone who isn't a machine to come on the line, the police *may* decide to investigate the problem . . . if you're lucky." She laughed. "Of course, if you were lucky, you wouldn't be calling them in the first place. But it's still a good idea to have one," she added illogically. "I mean it's better than nothing. Are you installing panic buttons?"

"Panic buttons?" Panic, Joanne repeated silently, a word she could understand.

"You should get a few of those, just in case someone breaks into the house when you're home. Then all you have to do is press the button and the alarm goes off. Assuming you can get to the button, of course." She smiled.

Joanne wondered why she was talking to this woman. She was worse than the horror movie Eve had dragged her to. She checked her wristwatch. "I wonder where Eve is," she said out loud. "She's usually so prompt."

"You're having another tennis lesson?"

"In five minutes," Joanne told her, lifting herself up and edging her way to the door.

"She'll be here," Karen Palmer stated with the same authority with which she had earlier assured Joanne that her marriage would work out. Where does she get such omniscience? Joanne wondered. She excused herself and escaped the warm pink and gray of the locker room for the cool green and white of the lobby.

"We've been paging you," a woman she barely recognized informed her seconds later. "There's a message for you at the front desk."

Joanne approached a crisp blond young woman behind the reception desk, deciding that in her next life this was the woman she was going to be, and was handed a note informing her to call Eve Stanley at home.

"What are you doing at home?" she asked as soon as she heard Eve's voice. "Are you okay?"

There was a slight pause. "Well, I'm not sure. I have this dumb sore throat and these stupid pains in my chest. I didn't go to school today. My mother's here."

"So why'd you tell me to meet you here?" Joanne asked.

"Because I knew you wouldn't go if you thought I wasn't going."

Joanne said nothing; Eve was right.

"Anyway, it's probably nothing, but I thought—or, more accurately, my mother thought—that if I stayed in bed for a couple of days, I might get rid of this thing, whatever it is."

"Did you get the results of the blood tests?"

"Yes. Negative. Everything checked out."

"Well, that's a relief anyway."

"My mother's not satisfied. She's making another appointment for me with her cardiologist."

"Let me know when it is. I'll take you."

"Thanks. I'd better get back to bed. Mommy is making faces at me."

"Okay. I'll call you when I get home."

"Have a good lesson."

"Thanks a lot."

"You have a strong, natural backhand, Mrs. Hunter," Steve
Henry was explaining enthusiastically. "You just have to learn to be
more aggressive. You're waiting too long to hit the ball. You should be
hitting the ball when it's out here"—he indicated where—"not back
here." He smiled. "You have to use your body more. You're relying
too much on your arm. Now, it's a nice, strong arm, but it doesn't
have to work that hard. Lean into the ball more. Here, like this." He
positioned himself behind her to guide her right arm, pulling it back
across the left side of her body, then pushing it forward to confront
the imaginary ball. "Move into it. That's right. When you see the ball
coming at you, swivel . . . that's right . . . back foot firmly on the
ground . . . now lean into the ball and hit it when the little bugger is
out here." He indicated where. "Don't wait till it's back here. You've
lost half your power that way. Okay? Let's try some more like that.
You're doing very well, Mrs. Hunter. Just relax. You're supposed to be
having a good time."

Joanne smiled, stealing a surreptitious glance at her watch to
figure out how much time remained in her lesson. She was tired; her
legs ached; her arm hurt; the sun was in her eyes; she was perspiring
into her new white tennis dress. Can't he see that I'm an old lady? she
wondered, slapping at the sudden appearance of the lime green ball
as if it were a pesky fly.

"Follow through, Mrs. Hunter," the voice across the net urged.
"Follow through."

What was he talking about? Joanne asked herself, swinging
wildly at the next ball and then accidentally lobbing the one that
immediately followed high into the air. What does this man want
from me? What am I doing here? Tennis lessons were Eve's idea,
damnit! Why does she get to stay at home in bed sick, while I have to
run around this dumb court chasing fluorescent balls? Don't you
realize that I have more important things to do? Joanne shouted
wordlessly at the young man on the far side of the court. Like what?
she heard him demand as he effortlessly returned the ball she had
somehow managed to get over the net. Lots of things, she pouted,
running backward to reach a low, baseline shot. Like waiting for my
daughters to come home from school! Like waiting for my husband to

make up his mind! Like baking a bunch of goddamn lemon meringue pies while I'm doing all this waiting! She slammed the next ball straight into the net.

"Follow through, Mrs. Hunter," Steve Henry called out, his body sweeping forward to underline his words.

You can't understand, Joanne realized, you're too young. Yours is the generation that thinks they can have it all. And maybe you can. Good luck to you. But I'm from the generation that just missed. When I was growing up, it wasn't fashionable for girls to be too bright or too independent. Girls were encouraged to encourage their men. We were taught to be clever, but never cleverer than, to be bright but dependent nonetheless, and to want only what a man would be able to provide. And I was good at that! I passed with honors! And then you come along and rob me of my degree. Is that fair? I'm too old to learn a new set of rules. She swung ferociously at an oncoming ball, missed it entirely, and landed hard on her behind.

Steve Henry was instantly at her side. "Are you all right?" His voice was solicitous as his arms reached under hers to help her up. "Well, you followed through all right," he smiled. "But you took your eye off the ball."

"I'll never get the hang of it," she told him, dusting off her white tennis dress, now ribboned with streaks of green clay.

"It might help if you got yourself a new, oversized racquet. It would improve your game tremendously."

"I didn't mean tennis," she explained. "I meant life."

He laughed. "Want to rest a few minutes?"

"You mean the lesson isn't over yet?" This time they both checked their watches.

"We still have ten minutes."

"I think I've had it," Joanne said. "I'm too old for this."

"Too old? You have the best legs of any woman at this club." The remark was casual, delivered as if it were a simple, inarguable statement of fact. Joanne felt her face flush. "Sorry, I didn't mean to offend you," he covered quickly, though his smile remained.

"You didn't," she told him, walking briskly off the court.

"How old *are* you?" he asked, suddenly at her side.

Joanne took a deep breath and let it out slowly. "Forty-one," she replied honestly, remembering that, even on her deathbed, her mother had refused to reveal her true age to her doctors.

"You look ten years younger."

"That's not young enough, I'm afraid."

"For whom? Afraid of what?"

Joanne bit down on her bottom lip. Was he coming on to her? She dismissed the unsettling idea, deciding that she probably wouldn't recognize a come-on if it climbed on top of her. No, he was just a natural flirt. Tennis instructors were supposed to make their students feel good about themselves. It was part of their technique.

"Your husband's a lucky man," Steve Henry said as he opened the door to the court and stepped back to let her pass through before him.

"He isn't a leg man," Joanne heard herself respond, not quite believing her ears. Why had she said that? It was something Eve would say.

"Then he's a fool," Steve Henry told her, ending the discussion. "You left these on the court," he said, pulling her dark blue sunglasses out of his back pocket and handing them to her. "See you next week."

Who was he kidding? Joanne thought as she sudsed herself in the club shower after her lesson; she looked every one of her forty-one years, maybe more. The strange thing was that she really didn't feel any older than she had twenty years ago. Inside, she was still the same insecure little girl she had always been, trying to be the perfect realization of whatever everyone wanted her to be, afraid to laugh too loud or say too much, to run too fast or want too much, to say something she might later regret, to fail at something she should never have tried. She found herself laughing into a harsh spray of hot water. She had failed anyway. But why? She had been a good girl. The perfect daughter who had grown into the perfect wife and mother, projecting an air of cheerful invincibility. You're strong, her husband had told her as he was leaving her, and again a week ago. I am woman, Joanne sang silently as she submerged her head under the full blast of the shower spray.

So, what now? she pondered, stepping out of the shower and wrapping herself in one of the club's luxurious pink towels. Pink for girls, she thought. What do you do, she asked herself again, when somebody suddenly stops loving you?

When had he stopped? On her fortieth birthday? On her thirtieth? Had he stopped little by little or all at once? Had it been a gradual decline or something that struck him suddenly one morning when he turned over in bed and saw her lying beside him, her mouth open in sleep, her hair askew across the pillow? When had he tired of the things he once found so reassuring? When had he stopped loving her? *Had* he stopped loving her?

He said he wasn't happy. Who was happy? Nobody could be happy all the time, or even most of the time. Usually, people occupied a neutral middle ground. The only thing that prevented people from being happy twenty-four hours a day, Joanne thought with a sharp cackle, was life.

A short, surprisingly muscular woman weighing herself on a nearby scale shot Joanne a strange look. One didn't laugh out loud when walking alone in the women's locker room of an expensive country club in Long Island. Joanne plopped down in front of one of the vanities provided for drying one's hair, plugged in the hairdryer lying on its side on the little table, and aimed the gun-shaped blower at her head. Blowjob anyone? she heard Eve ask playfully, and looked in the mirror to see herself blushing.

What did Paul mean, he wasn't happy? And was she the one who should be held accountable for his happiness? Yet hadn't she handed Paul the responsibility for her own happiness many years ago? She stared with mild shock at the middle-aged woman in the mirror. "What on earth have I done to my hair?" she asked out loud, staring at the tangled mess of curls at the top of her head. It's punk, she heard Karen Palmer say, deciding against wetting it and starting over. Nobody would be seeing it. She was going straight home, where she and Lulu would probably spend the evening watching television; Robin had a date. Would Scott be picking her up so that she could finally introduce him to her mother? "I'm not ready for daughters who date," Joanne whispered at her reflection, then stuck out her tongue.

The short, muscular woman from the scales sat down at the table beside Joanne and threw her another worried look. She thinks I'm crazy, Joanne thought. Welcome to the club! She stood up, knocking over the chair on which she had been sitting. So what if I talk to myself? she demanded as she stooped to right it. As my mother always said, Whenever I want to talk to an intelligent person . . .

Things will be different for my daughters, she thought, picking up the thread of her earlier musings as she located her locker and started roughly pulling on her clothes. They were being raised in a different world, being taught to stand on their own two feet, not to depend on anyone else for their happiness. She stopped abruptly as she was stretching her purple T-shirt over her head, her elbows in the air, her face completely hidden under the soft jersey.

How different would things be for her daughters? What kind of example did Robin and Lulu have? A woman who had moved from her parents' home to her husband's apartment without ever having gotten to know herself? A wife who had married young and had dedicated her life to running errands and making lemon meringue pies? A mother who spent her days picking up after everyone and mouthing dull platitudes like "I want whatever makes you happy," just as her mother had assured her? A woman who had never made an important decision—a decision that was hers alone—in her entire adult life? A daughter who had disguised her grief after her parents died so that her own daughters wouldn't be needlessly upset; who mourned the loss of her husband in the same silent way, protecting her children the way she had always been protected as a child, trying to spare them. From what? Life spares no one, she thought.

I want whatever makes you happy, she heard her mother whisper against the soft inside of her jersey. "Well, I'm not happy," Joanne cried out loud angrily, tugging the T-shirt across her face and pushing her arms through the short sleeves. "I'm not happy! Can you hear me? I'm not happy!" She sank down onto the floor, the rest of her clothes in a pile around her bare knees.

"Are you all right?" the woman from the scales asked Joanne—was she following her?—as she bent down and supported her weight on muscular calves. "Are you all right?" she repeated when Joanne failed to answer.

Joanne stared into the other woman's eyes and saw that she was vaguely frightened. She allowed the woman to help her to her feet. "My husband walked out on me and there's some lunatic phoning me all the time who says he's going to kill me," Joanne replied simply. The woman's face went totally blank.

Well, Joanne thought as she put on the rest of her clothes and left the woman standing alone in the middle of the locker room, she asked!

Chapter 11

"I had a phone call when I got home this afternoon," Joanne announced, looking across the dinner table at her older daughter. Robin, a mouthful of bright orange spaghetti dangling from between her pursed lips, regarded her mother with a mixture of curiosity and ennui. "You know why, I take it."

Robin inhaled a long breath of air, as if she were taking a deep drag on a cigarette, and slowly sucked up the straggly strings of spaghetti. She then chewed indifferently for several seconds, saying nothing, staring resolutely into her plate as if spaghetti were her life and refusing to acknowledge her mother.

"Robin . . . are you going to answer me?"

Robin said nothing.

"Robin . . ."

"Why should I answer you?" Robin demanded. "You already know the answer. You always do this. You always ask questions when you know the answers. Why?"

Joanne wasn't sure how to respond. "I don't know," she said finally. "I guess I want to hear the answer from you."

"What's going on?" Lulu asked, her eyes traveling back and forth between her mother and her sister as if she were an observer at a tennis match.

"Shut up," Robin snapped in her sister's direction.

"Robin . . ." her mother warned.

"*You* shut up!" Lulu shot back.

"Girls, please . . ."

"Why don't you go crawl into a hole somewhere," Robin continued. "You're such a worm."

"Robin, that is quite enough."

"At least it's better than being a snake," Lulu yelled. This time it was Joanne's eyes that darted back and forth across the kitchen table.

"Worms are the lowest," Robin sneered, "especially *fat* ones."

"That's enough, Robin." Joanne fought to keep her own voice down. "Can't we get through one meal without this bickering?" It was more plea than question. "You girls are sisters; you're all you've got . . ."

"I wish I didn't have anything." Robin angrily shoved another forkful of spaghetti into her mouth.

"Yeah, well I wish *you* were dead," Lulu cried.

"Stop it!" Joanne shouted, momentarily losing control. "Stop it," she repeated quietly, regaining it. "Now, let's sit here quietly and finish our meal. I don't want to hear another word from either one of you." She tried to twirl some noodles around her fork and failed, lowering the utensil to her plate and taking a deep breath. She felt her eyes well up with tears and hastily moved to wipe them away. "You're going to have to help me, girls," she told them, struggling to keep her voice even. "This is a very hard time for me. I know it's a hard time for you, too, but it's even harder for me. I'm not asking you to tiptoe around me. I am just asking you to go easy on each other. At least at mealtimes. I would love to get through at least one meal without a bunch of knots in my stomach."

"I'm not fat," Lulu said.

"Are too," came the immediate response.

"She is not fat," Joanne snapped. "And I'm warning *both* of you that if you say another word until I give you permission, you'll be grounded for the weekend." Robin glared at her mother. "I mean it," Joanne said, hearing Lulu fidget in her chair. The remainder of the meal—fresh pasta which Joanne had made herself—was passed in taut silence, the taste of the spicy, homemade tomato sauce lost, the fine texture of the angel's hair noodles unnoticed. "I want to talk to you," Joanne said to Robin as she was clearing away the plates and both girls were preparing to leave the table.

"I have to get ready for my date," Robin protested.

"That'll have to wait," Joanne told her firmly. Robin let out an impatient sigh. "You can go," Joanne said to Lulu.

"I want to listen," Lulu protested.

"Would you get out of here," Robin yelled.

"Try and make me."

"Lulu, go to your room and keep yourself occupied for a few minutes," Joanne ordered.

"Doing what?"

"I don't know. Do your homework."

"I already did it."

"Then take a bath."

"Now?"

"Lulu, I don't care what you do, just do it somewhere else."

"My name is Lana! From now on, I want to be called by my real name . . . Lana."

"A worm by any other name . . ."

"Robin, I'm warning you, one more word and you can forget about your date tonight."

"What did I do?"

Joanne marveled at the altogether innocent face before her and almost laughed. Instead, she took several deep breaths, silently counted to ten, and turned back to her younger daughter. "Lulu, please, I'll talk to you later."

"Lana!"

"Lana," Joanne repeated, watching her younger daughter walk slowly—as slowly as she had ever seen her move—from the room. She heard the name echo in her head, and tried to fit it around her tongue. The name had been Paul's idea; she had preferred Lulu, which he thought was better suited to a nickname. So they had compromised and named her Lana but called her Lulu. And now Paul was gone and she was stuck with a Lana, Joanne thought, pulling up the chair beside her older daughter and wondering what it was that she had started out to say. "I had a phone call from your math teacher this afternoon," she began. Robin said nothing, staring down at the table as intensely as she had earlier studied her dinner. "Mr. Avery isn't very happy about your work lately. He says that you've been skipping classes."

"I haven't . . ." Robin protested, then broke off. "They're so boring, Mom."

"I don't care how boring they are. You have no choice in this." Joanne carefully chose her next words. "He said you didn't do very well in your last math test."

"I *failed* my last test."

"Yes, that's what he said."

"Then why didn't *you* say it? Why don't you ever say what you mean?"

"I thought I did."

"You *never* do."

"Robin, we are not here to discuss my shortcomings. We can do that on another occasion when we have lots of time. We are talking about *you* at the moment. I want to know why you've been skipping classes."

"I told you. They're boring."

"That's not a good enough reason." Joanne looked around the room, half hoping that someone with a cue card would miraculously appear to feed her her next lines. "You were always very good in math. If you're having any trouble understanding anything, you should speak to Mr. Avery. He seems like a nice man."

"He's a jerk."

"You'll have to do better than that, Robin." Joanne grabbed at some hair that had fallen into her eyes and scrunched it into a tight ball. "Robin . . ."

"What'd you do to your hair?" the girl asked, suddenly aware of her mother in much the same way that Joanne had earlier noticed Karen Palmer at the club.

Joanne released the hair in her fist and stared upward in defeat. "I don't know," she responded wearily. "I was in a hurry after my tennis lesson. I wasn't paying attention."

"I like it," Robin told her, obviously sincere.

"Thank you," Joanne said, marveling at how quickly the young were able to shift gears. "About Mr. Avery . . ."

"Oh Mom, do we have to?"

"Yes, we have to."

"I won't skip any more classes. Okay? I promise."

"He said that there was no reason for you to have failed that test because you're a very bright girl. He also said that you haven't been very attentive in class lately even when you do show up."

"I've had a lot on my mind."

Joanne said nothing, feeling responsible for her daughter's state of mind and quietly accepting the blame. They were all of them going through a very bad time, she realized. "It's only another month and then school's over. You can hold on that long, can't you? I'd hate for you to mess up a good year because . . ." Because we've messed up your life, she thought but didn't say.

"I'll be a good girl," Robin told her, and Joanne felt an unpleasant twinge. Would she be the good girl Joanne had always been? Is that what she was bringing Robin up to be? "Can I get ready now? Scott will be here in an hour."

Joanne nodded, remaining in her seat as she heard Robin scramble up the stairs. She was almost on her feet when she heard Robin's voice reverberate through the household. "Fatty!" the voice cried shrilly.

"Fucking asshole!" came the quick, bitter response. Joanne lowered her forehead to the table, her arms lifelessly at her sides, as from upstairs came the sound of two doors slamming.

When he finally appeared at the front door, Scott Peterson was a distinct anticlimax. As lean as a sharpened pencil and not very tall, in the manner of many current rock stars, he cut a distinctly unimposing figure. His hair was short and dark blond. There were no purple or orange streaks—was that passé?—and no earrings or eyeshadow. He wore tight white jeans and a bright, oversized red shirt. His face, while thin and pale, wasn't any more emaciated than the currently acceptable social norm. He looked more like a local garage mechanic than he did a future Elvis Presley, but then he was barely old enough to remember Elvis Presley.

Joanne tried to imagine a world of young people to whom the name Elvis would be simply another icon from the past, a shadowy curiosity from a time that didn't concern them, the way Glenn Miller had been for most of her generation.

Turn off that noise, she remembered her father yelling, and Joanne would grumble but do as she was told, silently reassuring herself that she would never get too old to appreciate the genius of Little Richard and Dion and the Belmonts. But at least that was music! That was rock and roll! The kids still listened to some of the oldtimers of her day—Mick Jagger and Elton John. My God, Joanne thought as she stepped forward to be introduced, I'm older than Elton John!

"Scott, this is my mother," she heard Robin say.

"Hi," Joanne and the boy said together.

Scott Peterson stared directly at her, but she recognized that he didn't—couldn't—see her. What he saw was Robin's *mother*, not a person at all. He looked through Joanne as if she were invisible, the way young people often look at their elders, the way she, herself, she realized with a slight shock, continued to see those of the previous generation. The image of Eve's mother—unannounced and uninvited, the way she often appeared in life—suddenly came before Joanne's eyes.

Scott Peterson continued to stare at her as if he were blind. I'm not really any older than you are, Joanne tried to communicate with her expression. Inside I'm the same age as you. The difference isn't with me; it's in the way you *perceive* me. Again, Eve's mother bullied her way into the forefront of Joanne's imagination. How hard it must be for her, Joanne suddenly understood, to be thought of as old, to be categorized and restricted, ultimately discarded. Is that how she would end up? Joanne wondered, the image of Eve's mother superseded by that of her grandfather, asleep in his bed. Old and alone, in a home or in the way?

"Ahem," came the loud coughing noise from the foot of the stairs. Lulu stood twirling her long brown hair between nervous fingers.

"This is my sister," Robin said reluctantly, and then pointedly, *"Lulu."*

"Lana," came the immediate correction.

"I kind of like Lulu," Scott said, smiling. "Little Lulu and the Lunettes. Great name for a group."

Lulu said nothing, her face frozen in admiration.

"We'd better go," Robin announced, putting a preemptive hand across Scott's arm.

"I'll have her home by one, Mrs. Hunter," Scott assured Joanne without the need for prompting. "Nice meeting you. You too, Lana."

"Lulu," the child said quickly.

"You liked him?" Joanne asked her younger daughter after the front door closed. Why was she asking that? As Robin informed her earlier, she already knew the answer.

"He's neat," Lulu said, floating through the hall. "Robin doesn't deserve him."

"Can't you ever say anything nice about your sister?"

"She called me a worm."

"And you called her a f . . . you know what you called her."

"There's a good movie on TV tonight. You want to watch it with me?" Lulu asked, changing the subject.

Joanne followed her daughter downstairs to the family room. Lulu plopped down into the gray leather chair, her feet pushing the matching ottoman a comfortable distance away as Joanne hastily adjusted the vertical blinds on the windows and sliding glass door. It was still light out and would stay that way for perhaps another hour. Still, Joanne didn't like the idea of people being able to see into the room, to know that she and her daughter were alone in the house.

"What's the movie?" she asked, sitting down on one of the two gray corduroy sofas that stood at right angles to each other in the center of the large room.

"Invasion of the Body Snatchers," Lulu answered.

"Tell me you're joking."

"It's supposed to be real good."

"I'm sure it's wonderful. It's just that I don't think I'm up for that kind of movie tonight. Isn't there something else that we could watch?"

"Mom . . ." The word contained at least three more syllables than necessary and Joanne understood that to argue would be to waste one's time and breath.

"What did *you* think of Scott?" Lulu asked while they waited for the program to begin.

"He seems like a nice boy," Joanne replied truthfully. "I just wish he were a few years younger and still in school."

"Then you wish he was someone else," Lulu said simply.

I guess I do, Joanne agreed silently, thinking that Scott did seem like a nice enough young man. He was polite; he'd been sweet to Lulu; he acknowledged Joanne's rules if not her presence.

"Oh no," Lulu cried suddenly. "It's in black and white."

"It must be the original."

"I don't want to see the original," Lulu wailed. "I want to see the one that's in color."

"I hear the original's better," Joanne told her, trying to recall where she had heard that. From Eve, of course. Joanne peered through the bookshelves on the far wall as if she could see into the house next door, wondering how her friend was feeling.

Eve and Brian had purchased the house as soon as it had gone on the market, shortly after their marriage seven years ago. Actually, it had been Eve's mother who had given them the money for the down payment and who was continually slipping them extra dollars even now to keep them in comfortable extras. Eve had confided all this to Joanne and sworn her to confidentiality. Brian would be mortified, she explained unnecessarily, if he knew anyone else knew that he was being virtually supported by his mother-in-law. Joanne never told anyone, not even Paul, who would have pronounced Brian a fool to make himself so indebted to a woman he could barely tolerate. Joanne wondered which came first—the debt or the dislike.

"I don't want to see some old movie," Lulu stated flatly, returning Joanne to the present. Lulu pressed the remote control unit and began flipping mechanically through the various channels. Joanne was about to protest when she remembered that she didn't especially want to watch either version. *Was I like that?* she wondered as her daughter impatiently sifted through the different offerings. *So quick to turn off the past?*

Joanne squirmed in her seat, hypnotized by the visual assault of quick flashes and blurred impressions that sprang from the television screen. "Can you please stop doing that?" she implored her younger daughter, whose thumb seemed stuck to the remote control unit.

"I can't find anything that I want to watch."

"So turn it off."

Lulu stared at her mother as if the woman had gone mad. "All right, we'll watch this." Lulu returned the dial to its original channel.

They watched the movie in silence, Joanne's initial reservations disappearing as the simple tale chillingly unfolded. She watched, mesmerized, as a young Kevin McCarthy struggled valiantly against an alien evil dropped into the small California town in the form of giant pods which had the ability to assume human form while their potential victims slept. Come morning the takeover would be complete, the body intact but the emotions vanished. *I don't want to live in a world without love, without feeling,* a distraught but lovely Dana Wynter cries into young McCarthy's arms as the film nears conclusion. *Don't fall asleep,* he cautions her, leaving her side momentarily to check their surroundings. But of course she does fall asleep, and when he returns, she is a different person than the warm, loving woman he left. *I fell asleep,* she tells him, then shouts, *He's in here!* He flees—"Run!" Lulu urged from beside her, and Joanne wondered at what point in the proceedings her daughter had joined her on the sofa—and is eventually picked up on the highway and driven to a hospital in a nearby town, where he tells his story to a disbelieving medical staff. "Why won't they believe him?" Lulu wailed. *Sure,* Joanne thought, an unwanted image of her own mangled corpse suddenly flashing before her eyes, *ask people to believe their lives are being threatened by a bunch of giant egg rolls!*

"That was fantastic," Lulu enthused as she and Joanne lifted their weary bodies off the sofa and headed up the stairs to bed.

"Could you just check under the bed for me?" Lulu asked timidly as Joanne tucked the covers under her daughter's chin. Joanne lifted the white dust ruffle to peer under the bed.

"No egg rolls." She smiled, kissing Lulu's forehead. "Good night, sweetie. Sleep well."

Joanne began undressing even before she reached her bedroom, discarding the last of her clothing as she opened the middle drawer of her dresser, then searching through it for her white cotton nightgown, remembering it was in the wash. Her hand stumbled across an old T-shirt of Paul's that lay scrunched at the rear of the drawer. She pulled it out and put it on, feeling it hug her body loosely, reassuringly. She turned back toward her bed and screamed.

Lulu, standing alone in the doorway, screamed loudly in return and jumped into her mother's arms. "It's all right," Joanne laughed and cried simultaneously. "You just scared me. I didn't expect you."

"Could I sleep with you tonight?" the child asked plaintively, and Joanne nodded. "Did you check under the bed?"

"Not yet," Joanne smiled, doing just that.

"No egg rolls?"

"Not even a cracker."

As they cuddled together in the king-size bed, Joanne was struck anew at how empty the bed had felt these last several weeks. It felt good to have someone beside her. She leaned over and kissed her daughter's forehead. "Good night, darling."

"Mom," came the small voice in the darkness, "do you think I'm fat?"

"Fat? Are you kidding me?"

"Robin says I'm fat."

"Robin says a lot of things. You don't have to believe all of them."

"But . . ."

"No buts. We'll talk about this another time. Now go to sleep—you're not fat."

Within minutes, Joanne became aware of her daughter's soft, steady breathing beside her, while she herself could only drift in and out of sleep until she heard Robin come through the front door at ten minutes to one. Only then was she able to give in to her fatigue. Quickly, she fell into a deep, dreamless sleep, her arm stretched comfortably across her younger daughter's back.

The phone rang.

Joanne jumped up immediately and grabbed the phone, pressing it to her ear before she was either fully awake or knew what she was doing. Lulu stirred and rolled onto her back, but did not wake up. "Hello," Joanne whispered, the thumping of her heart sounding louder than her voice.

"Mrs. Hunter," the voice teased, jolting Joanne into full consciousness. "Did you think I wouldn't find out your new number?" An unpleasant chill, like a trail of cold water, ran down the length of Joanne's spine.

"Stop bothering me," Joanne replied forcefully, glancing at the luminous face of the bedside clock and seeing it was 4 A.M.

"Your new locks won't keep me out." Joanne felt an involuntary loosening of her bowels. "Sweet dreams, Mrs. Hunter."

Joanne jumped from her bed and raced down the stairs. Moving like a woman possessed, she checked the locks on the front door and the sliding glass door in the kitchen. Then she hurried down the steps to the family room. Everything was secure. She peered through the vertical blinds into the darkness, the quarter moon only barely illuminating the outline of the pool. Was her tormentor somewhere out there hiding? She returned to the front hall, glaring at the numbered buttons of the alarm system on the wall. There was a way of turning on the system while you were in the house without setting off the alarm, she remembered, trying desperately to recall what Harry had told her. There was another button she could push. Her eyes darted frantically across the small box. "The bottom button," she said aloud, hearing Harry's voice gently against her ear. The one without a number. Simply press it and the alarm would be set. It would go off if someone subsequently opened one of the doors or downstairs windows. Slowly, Joanne's trembling finger moved toward it. She pressed down, watching the small green light flicker on. Holding her breath, she waited for the unwanted shriek of the alarm. But none came. I did it right, she sighed, releasing the air in her lungs, her legs shaking their way back up the stairs to check on Robin before crawling into bed. At least now they would have some warning if he tried to break in.

Was it a he? she asked herself as her head sank into the soft pillow. The voice was such an obvious disguise, and there was something so . . . neutered . . . about it. What was the current word? Androgynous? That was the term she kept hearing with regard to the current fashion scene, to hairdos, to rock singers . . .

The image of a boy as thin as a sharpened pencil greeted her newly closed lids. He looked past her as if she weren't really there, then promptly disappeared. Joanne remained awake for the balance of the night, watching a young Kevin McCarthy embrace a beautiful Dana Wynter for the last time and warning her not to fall asleep.

Chapter 12

"You should have seen us," Joanne was saying. "Robin didn't know the alarm was set, and poor thing, I think it's the first time she's woken up before ten in her entire life"—Robin groaned loudly from somewhere beside her—"and she opened the front door to get the paper and the alarm went off, you had to hear those damn sirens, and she started screaming, and Lulu and I were blasted out of bed and, of course, *we* started screaming and everybody was running around like inmates of a lunatic asylum, and naturally I couldn't remember how to turn the damn thing off, so it rang for over half an hour and finally, *finally*, the police came, and I had to explain to them what happened, and, needless to say, they weren't exactly thrilled."

"Mom," Robin said wearily, "he doesn't hear you."

"He hears me," Joanne replied stubbornly. "Don't you, Pa?" Joanne stared into her grandfather's soft blue eyes, eyes that managed to stare just past her no matter where she placed her body. "Anyway, I had to call Paul and explain what happened and ask him how to shut the alarm off because I couldn't find the phone number for the alarm company—I don't know where I put it—and so he had to do all the telephoning and call me back, and the alarm people came over and explained the whole thing to me again—that only cost sixty-five dollars—and now Paul is mad at me and the police are mad at me and Robin is mad at me . . . ."

"Who said I was mad?" Robin demanded angrily.

"Anyway," Joanne continued, trying to laugh, "at least we know the alarm works."

"And I'll never forget the date of the start of the Boer War," Lulu piped up from beside the window. Joanne smiled, grateful that at least one of her children was trying to take part in the conversation. She glanced to the other side of the room, where old Sam Hensley sat berating his daughter and grandson, then back at her grandfather, who lay still under a mountain of covers. Where had his fight gone?

she wondered, thinking she might have preferred a little of Sam Hensley's feistiness. Come on, Pa, she pleaded silently, hearing her mother's voice, let's see some of that old team spirit.

"Mom," Robin whined, "can't we go now?"

"No, we can't," Joanne said sharply. She immediately softened her voice. "Look, you don't come here very often. It's not going to kill you to sit still for a few minutes."

"He doesn't know who I am," Robin protested.

"You don't know that."

"Linda . . ." the weak voice called out, the old face all but swallowed up by the stiff white sheets that crept up past the once sturdy chin, the blue Chairman Mao hat that someone had perched on his head falling low across his layered forehead. Who had given him that hat? Joanne wondered now.

"Yes Pa, I'm here," she replied automatically.

"Who are all these people?" His eyes were unable to focus on anyone in particular though his voice was instinctively wary.

"You see," Robin muttered, not quite under her breath.

"These are my daughters, Pa," Joanne said proudly. "You remember Robin and Lulu." She reached out her hands in their direction, drawing them to her. "You probably don't recognize them, they've gotten so big. This is Robin . . ." Robin smiled meekly, as if she were confronting a mythical troll and was afraid to get too close. Or perhaps it was his age she was afraid to get close to, Joanne postulated, afraid in some vague way that it might be contagious. It is, Joanne thought. Aloud she said, "And this is Lulu, my baby."

"Mom!" Lulu protested. "Hi, Grampa," she whispered, not sure how she should address this man she barely knew, this ancient artifact who had already lived through eighty-four years by the time she was born.

If only you could have seen him thirty years ago, Joanne thought as her daughters withdrew quickly into their previous positions.

"Nice, very nice," her grandfather murmured, his eyes clicking into focus. He suddenly pushed himself up on his elbows to stare at the bewildered girls. "Do you children play cards?" he asked clearly.

Joanne felt a smile spring to her lips, a sudden giddiness seize her spirits—how many rainy afternoons at the cottage had she and her grandfather passed playing gin rummy?

But before her mind could formulate an answer, Joanne was aware it was no longer relevant. Her grandfather, his old eyes vacant once again, his unsteady head returned to the safety of his pillows, had slipped back into the only world with which his frail body was currently able to cope. The room was suddenly silent.

Joanne looked over at the other bed, saw old Sam Hensley propped up by several pillows, his visitors gone, his eyes clouded with tears. "Mr. Hensley," Joanne said softly, slipping her hand out of her grandfather's and crossing to the other bed. "Are you all right? Are you in any pain?" Slowly, Sam Hensley brought his head around. "Do you want me to call the nurse?"

Sam Hensley said nothing. But as he continued to stare at Joanne, his emaciated, hawklike features underwent a subtle though swift and thorough metamorphosis, curiosity becoming indifference, indifference disappearing into animosity, animosity ultimately being swallowed whole by a palpable hatred so intense that Joanne actually felt herself stumbling backward, as if she had been physically pushed away. Large, bony hands reached up toward her as if eager to encircle her throat, and a low wail, which seemed to start at the floor, began to fill the room, forcing those standing to flee the area for lack of space.

"My God, he's worse than the alarm," Robin exclaimed nervously from the doorway. "What set him off?"

"What did you say to him, Mom?" Lulu demanded.

"I just asked him if he was all right."

The low wail continued building in intensity as, all the while, Sam Hensley lay motionless in his bed, his arms outstretched, his eyes open wide and fierce. In the next instant, the room was filled with nurses. Joanne saw the flash of a syringe. She looked over at her grandfather, his eyes closed in sleep, completely unaware of the commotion that raged around him. "Let's go, Mom," Robin whispered, pulling on her arm.

"Perhaps you could step outside for a few minutes," one of the nurses suggested, pulling a curtain abruptly around Sam Hensley's bed. "He gets like this occasionally. It'll only take a few minutes to calm him down, then you can come back in."

Joanne nodded wordlessly and led her daughters out of the room, each one understanding the visit was over. They walked silently down the corridor, catching sight of Sam Hensley's daughter and grandson in the visitor's lounge across from the elevators. Marg Crosby was smoking a cigarette. Her son was staring at the black-and-

white television set against the pale peach wall. Joanne approached
the woman and explained gently what had happened.

Marg Crosby shrugged and finished her cigarette. "It's hap-
pened before," she said, reluctantly getting to her feet. "You coming,
Alan?" she called to her son, whose eyes remained riveted on the TV.
"Alan?" she repeated.

He turned in his mother's direction as if surprised she was there,
but his eyes quickly continued past her, past Joanne, to somewhere
behind them, a small smile gradually creeping into the corners of his
mouth. Both Joanne and Marg Crosby turned slowly around curiously, only to find Robin, her eyes shyly downcast, with the same
small smile on her overly glossed lips.

"Down, Rover," the woman chuckled knowingly, and Joanne
thought, as she had the previous night with regard to Robin's friend
Scott, he doesn't even see me.

"Time to go home," Joanne stated, placing her hands on each of
her daughters' shoulders and maneuvering them in the direction of
the elevator.

"Ma'am?" the voice called after her.

Joanne looked around for a woman who suited that form of
address, realized it was intended for herself, and stopped.

The boy came to an abrupt halt several paces behind her. "Are
these yours?" he asked, referring to a set of keys in his outstretched
palm.

Joanne immediately recognized the key chain as her own. She
felt the sudden weight of the keys as the boy dropped them into her
hand. "Where did I leave them this time?" she asked, a feeling of
helplessness surrounding her.

"On a table in the visitor's lounge," Alan Crosby said and smiled,
again just past her to where Robin stood waiting.

"Thank you," Joanne told him, and watched him walk away. She
turned to face her daughters. "Home, James," she said.

"I really don't feel any older than they are," Joanne was telling
Eve, who sat at her kitchen table drinking a large glass of milk and
clutching nervously at her blue terrycloth robe. "I look at Robin and
Lulu and I can feel what they're thinking—that we're worlds apart—
and I want to tell them that it's not people who change, *we* don't
change, it's *time* that changes." She paused, not sure whether or not

she was making any sense. "I just wish they'd had the chance to see him as I did, to have known what he was like."

"You expect youth to understand what it's like to grow old?" Eve chortled. "How can they? Do you? No, if old people can't understand young people, and they've *been* young, how can you expect young people, who have absolutely no basis for comparison, to understand what growing old is all about. As far as they're concerned, growing up means falling apart, and as far as I'm concerned, they're absolutely right."

Joanne laughed, though underneath the laugh there was concern, concern for her friend's depressed state, for her almost alarming appearance. Eve had always taken great pains to look, if not spectacular, at least dramatic. The only thing dramatic about the woman sitting across from her at this minute was the fact that she was drinking milk, something Joanne hadn't seen Eve do in years. She looked like the stereotype of a suburban housewife: feet in slippers, hair unwashed and in need of a strong brushing, tatty old blue bathrobe, inexpressibly weary eyes. Eve had never been one to complain, never one to let sickness get or slow her down. Now she seemed, if not stopped, then stuck. It disturbed Joanne, threatened her already shaky frame of reference, to see her friend, always the stronger of the two, so overwhelmed by her discomfort. She prayed the doctors would discover exactly what Eve's problem was and fix it quickly. Joanne noticed a strange look suddenly cross Eve's face. "Eve? Is something wrong? Are you having more pains?"

"It's not a question of more pains," Eve admitted, a sense of defeat clinging to each word. "It's just one, steady ache. I keep expecting it to disappear. I go to bed hoping that when I wake up, everything will be okay. But it never is. If anything, it's getting worse. It seems to be spreading. You know when you feel on the verge of a sore throat? That's how my throat feels, kind of constricted, like I've got something caught, like I'm going to choke. I was up the whole night. I finally took my temperature at six o'clock this morning."

"And?"

"Up half a degree."

"Maybe you're coming down with the flu."

"I weighed myself too. I was two pounds lighter than I was at midnight."

"People usually weigh less in the morning than they do at night,"

Joanne said quickly. "Paul once told me," she continued, feeling the breath tighten in her lungs, "that we all go up and down within a four-pound spread, depending on the time of day and how much water we're retaining, that sort of thing."

"And I'm constipated," Eve continued, as if Joanne hadn't spoken. "I swear I'm falling apart. It's like my whole body has decided it doesn't want anything more to do with me. Look at my stomach—I'm so bloated, I look like I did when I was pregnant."

"Are you?" Joanne asked hopefully.

"Are you kidding?" Eve asked in return. "I have my period." Her eyes suddenly shot to Joanne's. "You don't think I have toxic shock syndrome, do you?"

"I don't think your symptoms are anything like the ones you get with toxic shock," Joanne replied thoughtfully, momentarily sharing her friend's concern. "But if you're worried, don't wear tampons."

"And do what instead?"

"Wear a pad."

"Good God," Eve replied, horrified. "I'd rather have toxic shock!"

Joanne laughed. "That's more like the Eve I know and love. When's your next doctor's appointment?"

"Tuesday morning at the cardiologist, Friday morning at the gynecologist. A few others, I can't remember when. You don't have to go with me."

"Of course I'll go with you." There was a moment's silence. "Maybe you could convince Brian to take you to a horror movie, get your mind off everything."

"I can't sit up straight for that long. Besides, when was the last time you saw Brian?"

"He's still working all that overtime?"

"The man loves his work. What can I tell you?" Eve suddenly caved forward, pressing her chest against the curve of her white kitchen table, her eyes closing as she sucked in her breath.

"Another pain?"

"Let's call it a spasm," Eve whispered, reopening her eyes and releasing the air in her lungs. "It doesn't sound quite so threatening that way." She straightened her back and tried to smile.

"Let's play some cards," Joanne said forcefully, looking toward the shelf against the wall where Eve usually kept such miscellaneous items. "Come on, we'll play gin rummy." Joanne found a deck of

playing cards and quickly slid them from their package, feeling a
rush of childhood exhilaration pushing through her fingers.

"I can never beat you at gin," Eve grimaced.

"Too late, I'm already shuffling." Joanne expertly shuffled the
cards in the manner her grandfather had taught her when she was
barely a decade old, and began dealing. "Ten cards," she said. "No
going down."

"Please," Eve teased, "I'm a respectable girl."

Joanne blushed.

"You dealt . . . that means I go first," Eve said after Joanne had
lowered the deck to the table. Eve looked at the upturned queen of
diamonds. "I don't need that," she said, her lips a pout.

"Neither do I," Joanne agreed.

"Then I pick," Eve said triumphantly, as if this were a small
victory in itself, and pulled the first card from the top of the overturned deck. "Don't need that one either." She tossed the unwanted
card unceremoniously on top of the upturned queen.

"I can use that one," Joanne told her, lifting Eve's discarded ten
of spades into her own hand, throwing off a two of hearts.

"Naturally," Eve said. "What was that you took?"

"The ten of spades."

"The ten of spades, huh? Okay, I'll remember that." She studied
the two of hearts for several seconds before lifting it to her hand, then
subsequently throwing it back and drawing another card, which she
also threw down.

Joanne automatically picked it up.

"What did I give you that time?"

"Six of clubs."

"Six of clubs, don't let me forget. Uh huh!" she exclaimed as
Joanne discarded a nine of hearts, which she picked up. "Shouldn't
have let me have that one."

"Gin?"

"Not yet. But close."

They continued their ritual for several seconds without speaking. "Has Brian said anything recently about . . ." Joanne began,
then broke off.

"About what?" Eve looked up from her hand, her eyebrows
lifting.

"About the guy who murdered those women," Joanne muttered,
trying to sound casual, as if the thought were unimportant.

"Your secret admirer?"

"Thanks."

"Sorry, didn't mean to upset you." She laughed and threw off the jack of spades, which Joanne picked up. "What was that?" Joanne showed her. "No, nothing new. Did you tell the police about last night's phone call?"

Joanne nodded. "They said there was nothing they could do. I told them that he knew about my new phone number, my new locks. They said there was still nothing they could do. I said, all right then, what can *I* do? They said to change my phone number again and keep turning on my alarm every night. But to *please* remember to turn it off the next time." She smiled. "It was almost like they were put out that I was still alive. Gin," she added, laying down her cards, trying to disguise the trembling in her hands.

"Shit! You caught me with a mittful." Eve laid down her cards. "Don't look so scared, Joanne. It's just some dumb kid playing a sick prank. Come on, deal! You won't beat me again." Joanne reshuffled the cards and dealt them out. "It's probably one of Lulu's or Robin's friends. You know how dumb teenagers are."

"I don't think any of the girls' friends are *that* dumb." Joanne picked up a five of clubs and threw off the queen of spades, hesitant to let go of the card, seeing Scott Peterson's smile on the lips of the discarded queen.

"You putting down that card or not?"

Joanne released her fingers from the queen's throat.

"It could be anybody," Eve continued. "That truck was parked in your driveway for days. Anybody passing by would have seen it. Does he sound like anybody you know?"

"That's the problem—he sounds like *everybody* I know."

"Wait a minute, what's that card? I'll take that card."

Eve pulled the card from the top of the deck and triumphantly tucked it into her hand.

"So, are you going to do it?" Eve asked.

"Do what?"

"Change your phone number again."

"I don't know," Joanne admitted. "It's such a nuisance. Think of all the people I'd have to call again. Whoever it is found out the first time. He'll probably find out whatever number I change it to this time too, and we'll be back where we started."

"Or he'll get tired and that'll be the end of it. Unless that's not what you want . . ."

"What do you mean?"

"Nothing," Eve stated, tossing her head. "Play a card. You have nothing to worry about except my superior playing."

Joanne threw off a king of diamonds, which Eve appropriated, discarding a three of clubs. "That's gin," Joanne said, nervously spreading her cards across the table, unconvinced she had nothing to worry about and puzzling over Eve's earlier remark.

"I give up. Your granddaddy taught you too well. I'd better stick to solitaire." She took the deck and began laying the cards down flat across the table in the proper fashion for solitaire, stopping when she had seven neat little piles. "At least this way I can cheat."

"People who cheat at solitaire are insecure," Joanne said, smiling as she recalled her grandfather's words.

"You know I'm a sore loser," Eve pronounced truthfully. "Give me victory or give me death," she declared, then doubled over in pain, sending the cards flying and knocking over the glass in front of her, spilling what was left of the milk to the floor. "Shit!"

"I'll get it." Joanne grabbed a dishcloth from the sink and quickly mopped up the spilled milk, then returned to the sink, rinsed out the cloth and rewiped the floor with fresh water so that it wouldn't be sticky. She deposited the now empty glass in the sink. "Are you all right? Maybe I should take you to the hospital."

Eve waved away the suggestion with an impatient hand. "I've been that route, remember? It's okay. I'm sure I'll survive till Tuesday morning."

"Why don't you go lie down for a while?"

Eve agreed to the suggestion with surprisingly little argument. "I just thought of that accident we were in when your grandfather was driving us to school one afternoon. Remember?" she asked as Joanne was guiding her up the stairs to her bedroom. "Your grandfather was straddling the middle line and some guy wanted to pass him and he ended up smashing into the side of our car, and they started fighting in the street, until your grandfather said he couldn't waste any more time arguing with an idiot because his granddaughter would be late for school! And he drove off, leaving that guy screaming in the middle of the road, and the police came later and charged your grandfather with leaving the scene of an accident. Do you remember that?" She smiled. "Nothing was more important than his granddaughter."

Joanne pulled down the covers of Eve's large four-poster bed. "You're leaving out the best part," she smiled, watching as Eve crawled under the blankets without removing her housecoat. "The part where we met with my grandfather's lawyer, and he asked you a few questions, and you couldn't get your left hand straight from your right, and the lawyer finally exclaimed, 'If you want to win this case, keep that girl *out* of court.'" Joanne laughed. Eve closed her eyes. "Can I get you anything before I go?"

Eve opened one eye. "There's a *People* magazine somewhere," she said. "You can just lay it on the bed."

Joanne looked around but saw nothing. "You have a new cleaning lady or something?" she asked. "I've never seen this place so neat."

"My mother's been 'fixing,'" Eve said. "Maybe Brian took it. Look in his office."

It was always a strange experience, being in Eve's house, Joanne thought now, as she walked along the hallway to the front of the house. Everything was the reverse of what it was in her own home, a disconcerting mirror image to which she had never been able to adjust. Brian's office, located to the right of the hallway, was the larger of the two front rooms. In her own home, the larger of the two rooms was located on the left and was occupied by Robin. Joanne took a brief glimpse around the study, curious but reluctant to snoop. She wondered when Brian worked in here—he was so rarely home. Her eyes fell casually across the top of the large cluttered desk. There were lots of papers, a police manual, and a few books, but no *People* magazine. For a second, Joanne debated leaving Brian a note asking him to call her, but decided against it. Eve had said she would tell Brian about the threatening calls she'd been receiving and she probably already had. Obviously, he didn't think there was anything for her to be concerned about or he would have contacted her. As Eve kept saying, *everybody* got obscene phone calls. She had *nothing* to worry about. She walked out of the room, worried nonetheless.

Across the hall was the smaller of the two front rooms, the room that Eve and Brian had been reserving for a nursery. Joanne approached the doorway and looked inside. Six months ago the room had been a pink-and-white dream, decorated for the little girl the amniocentesis had revealed was due at the beginning of May. After years of frustration, a baby was finally expected, her name selected, the appropriate merchandise assembled. Now the room lay empty, the white crib dismantled, the ruffled curtains removed, the musical mobile stuffed back in its box, only the delicate pink-and-white-striped wallpaper giving any indication for what purpose this room had been intended. Joanne was about to turn away when she saw the *People* magazine lying overturned on the floor by the curtainless windows. Quickly, she tiptoed across the pale pink carpet to retrieve it, then immediately returned to the hall. What was the magazine doing in here? Did Eve come here to brood? If so, it was time to do something else with the room, Joanne thought, deciding she would mention it to Eve in as gentle a way as possible. But when she approached Eve's bed, she saw that Eve was already asleep, and so she laid the magazine gingerly at the foot of the bed and as silently as she could, left the house.

Chapter 13

"What do they think is wrong with you?" the short, wiry woman with auburn streaks in her already dark hair asked Joanne shakily. Joanne estimated the woman's age at thirty, though it was hard to tell as she had one of those faces that was old before its time and perversely young after it. She took note of the plain gold band on the appropriate finger of the woman's trembling left hand, and lowered her magazine to her lap.

"I'm waiting for a friend." Joanne smiled amicably, eager to return to her magazine, though, in truth, she was too restless to read.

"What's wrong with her?" the other woman pressed, obviously eager to talk despite the slight tremor in her voice.

"They don't know," Joanne replied. "She's in X-ray."

"I'm waiting to go for X-rays," the young woman nodded. She seemed unbearably fragile. "Something's wrong with my stomach," the woman continued almost under her breath. "I'm a little scared."

"I'm sure everything will be all right," Joanne said, uncomfortably conscious of the platitude, hearing Karen Palmer's voice through her words.

"I don't know," the woman continued. "I have this . . . kind of a . . . lump."

Joanne returned her magazine to the cluttered Formica table beside the green vinyl sofa on which she was sitting, her thoughts on Eve. "I'm sure you have nothing to worry about," she heard herself say. The woman tried to smile but Joanne could see that she was close to tears. "What's your name?" Joanne asked, more as a means of delaying that eventuality than through genuine interest. She shifted her legs, bare beneath a simple blue cotton dress, prying her thighs away from the sticky vinyl.

"Lesley. Lesley Fraser. Yours?"

"Joanne Hunter."

Once again Lesley Fraser nodded, rubbing her hands together

anxiously in her lap. "I've got three little kids, that's why I'm so frightened. They're so little, you know, to be left without a mother . . ."

"Hey, hey, slow down," Joanne interrupted quickly, "who said anybody's going to be left without a mother? Even if worse does come to worst, and they do find something there that shouldn't be, that doesn't mean you're going to die." The image of her own mother flashed before Joanne's eyes. "They'll just take whatever it is out, and you'll be fine again. Haven't you been reading about all the incredible advances that medical science has made in the last few years? It's in all the magazines." She pulled a *Time* magazine from the top of the Formica table and casually flipped it open. She couldn't remember whether there had been anything in it about the wonders of medical science or not.

"Pretty scary, huh?" Lesley Fraser said, nodding toward the magazine.

"Scary?" Joanne asked, not sure what they were talking about until she actually glanced at the opened page of the magazine in her hands. "Crime," the headline read. "Long Island's Suburban Strangler." Joanne quickly closed the magazine and dropped it back onto the table.

"Oh well," Lesley Fraser said, trying to laugh, "I guess if one thing doesn't get you, something else will. It just goes to show you how little control we actually have over our lives."

Joanne didn't feel up to dealing with the implications of this remark. Instead, she looked nervously around at the anxious faces surrounding her in the crowded waiting room. "The odds are with you," she said to the young woman beside her.

"I know the odds," Lesley Fraser told her. "My mother died of cancer."

"So did mine," Joanne replied automatically before thinking that it was probably not the most comforting thing to say. "The odds are with you," she repeated with quiet strength.

"Well, if it doesn't kill me physically, it'll sure slaughter us financially," Lesley Fraser went on. "We don't have a lot of money. How can you save anything with three kids? My husband works two jobs as it is. I don't know how we're going to cover all the medical bills."

"Worry about one thing at a time," Joanne told her, and a slight laugh managed to escape the woman's mouth before her eyes suddenly spilled over with the long-threatened tears.

"I'm so scared," the woman whispered.

Joanne reached over and took Lesley Fraser's hand, saying nothing.

"Lesley Fraser," a young woman wearing a green lab coat over a white uniform called from the doorway, her eyes squinting at the chart she held at arm's length in front of her.

"Here," Lesley answered, raising her hand as if she were in a classroom.

"This way," the nurse instructed, pushing open the door.

Lesley Fraser jumped quickly to her feet, though once there she seemed unable to move.

"Good luck," Joanne said.

Lesley Fraser nodded. "I hope everything goes well with your friend," she said. In the next instant she disappeared through the door to X-ray.

Joanne stared at the empty doorway, her mind curiously blank. What do you think about all day? she had once worked up the courage to ask her dying mother, and the woman, who spent every day lying on her back staring at the ceiling, had stared back at her through once vibrant eyes and answered, Nothing. It's strange, isn't it? she had said, to lie here day after day and think about absolutely nothing.

Snapping back into the present, Joanne realized she was staring at the elderly woman across from her. The woman shifted in her seat uncomfortably, turning her head away from the intense scrutiny to which she felt she was being subjected. Joanne lowered her eyes, searching for something to do with her hands. Absently, she began rifling through the magazines on the table beside her, careful to avoid the latest issue of *Time*, and finally selecting a copy of *Newsweek* that she had already glanced through and knew to be safe. She flipped through the pages, noting that there *was* an article on several recent medical breakthroughs. She tried to read it, but she wasn't really interested in any such medical miracles. They had come too late to help the people she had cared about. Much as she wanted to be optimistic, the image of her mother, ever hopeful herself and protective of her daughter until the end—don't you worry, baby, everything will be all right—kept intervening. Joanne dropped the magazine unceremoniously back on top of the pile and retrieved yet another, her hand passing across the top of the *Time* magazine, feeling it pull against her palm like a magnet.

After several seconds, Joanne's arm—acting as if it had a life of its own—reached over and picked it up. Carefully avoiding the Crime section, Joanne turned to the Cinema page, read through three caustic reviews of movies she would never see, then flipped to the Books section and did the same. She noted the plays reviewed in the Theater section, wondering absently if Robin and Lulu might be interested in either of them, and then checked the People page for the latest carryings-on of the rich and famous, before finally checking in on Milestones to see who had married, given birth, divorced, or died. As usual, most people listed occupied the final category. Joanne then deliberately closed the magazine, checked her watch, and wondered what was keeping Eve. The last time Eve had undergone these tests, she had been finished much faster. Had they discovered something? Joanne reopened the magazine. She knew, even without looking, what she would find. "Crime," the headline read. "Long Island's Suburban Strangler."

Joanne gasped loudly despite herself, attracting the unwanted attention of the elderly woman across from her, who regarded her with ill-concealed annoyance. Feeling almost guilty, Joanne's gaze fell back across the column, feeling the woman's eyes on her now, as if she were waiting for further interruptions.

Joanne forced herself to calmly read through the collection of dispassionate facts: the three murdered women were all residents of Long Island; they were middle-aged and married, all with families; one worked outside the home, the other two did not. There was no rational motive for the murders, none but the most superficial of connections between the victims. All had been sexually molested before being killed.

Joanne's eyes reached the bottom of the page and she once again gasped. The woman across from her got up and moved to the other side of the room. Photographs. Three little squares at the bottom of the page containing the faces of the murdered women.

Joanne studied the pictures carefully. There was nothing particularly memorable about any of the women, she realized quickly. They looked like the suburban housewives and mothers they were: pleasant, attractive, but not beautiful; two blond, one brunette; ordinary women who led ordinary lives. The only extraordinary thing about them had been the manner of their demise.

Police were issuing the usual warnings for women in Long Island to be extra careful, not to open their doors to strangers, to report any prowlers seen lurking in the neighborhood to the police. Other than that, a frustrated police force admitted there was little they could do. The responsibility, they stressed, rested with women to take all necessary precautions. The police, virtually clueless, the article concluded, were despairing of catching the Suburban Strangler before he caught his next victim.

Joanne's eyes returned to the photographs at the bottom of the page. She felt ashamed of her objective appraisal, seeing her own picture—which one would they use?—squeezing its way onto the page to take its place beside the others. Would people be so quick to dismiss her as pleasant, attractive, ordinary? And wasn't it interesting, she found herself thinking, that the police considered the matter to be women's responsibility and not their own?

"Let's get out of here," the voice announced firmly from somewhere beside her.

"What's the matter?" Joanne asked, springing to her feet, the vinyl reluctantly releasing her thighs with a loud sucking sound, the *Time* magazine bouncing off her knees to the floor, as she hurried to chase after Eve.

"The bastard," Eve was muttering as she found the exit stairs and began her quick descent. Joanne chased after her, feeling an almost overwhelming sense of déjà vu. Hadn't they been through this same scene weeks earlier?

"What happened?" she cried, hearing only the clacking of Eve's heels in response. "For God's sake, Eve, you'll fall and break your neck if you don't slow down. Wait a minute. What happened?"

"Where's the car?" Eve demanded as soon as they reached the street.

"In the parking lot where we left it. Will you tell me what happened in there?"

Eve marched toward the parking lot, stopped abruptly, and turned to face a startled, worried Joanne. "That bastard," she muttered again, about to turn away.

Joanne grabbed the sleeve of Eve's white linen jacket. "Would you please stop running and swearing long enough to tell me what went on in there?"

Eve took several deep breaths in a conscious effort to calm herself down. "Do you know what that asshole had the nerve to say to me?" Joanne shook her head, eager for Eve to continue. "He had the nerve to tell me that my pains are all in my head."

"What?"

"He said that there's nothing wrong with me physically, at least as far as *he* can determine, so obviously, there can't be anything wrong with me as far as anyone else might be able to determine . . ."

"Eve, slow down, you're losing me."

Eve began pacing the hot pavement, an imposingly distraught figure against the impassive backdrop of parked cars. "He did the same battery of tests as the doctor at Northwest General. Of course I didn't tell him I'd already had those tests, but I did tell him about the cardiologist and the gynecologist, and that guy who specializes in exotic parasites, which was probably my mistake, I shouldn't have told him anything, the bastard . . ."

"Eve, calm down . . ."

"And he said that as far as he could determine, there wasn't anything wrong with me, that the X-rays showed everything was fine. I'm in perfect health! So I said, what about the pain? And he said that my body had undergone a recent trauma, meaning the miscarriage, of course, and he thinks that what I'm experiencing is a typical example of postpartum depression. I told him that I'm not depressed, but he said that clinical depression is different from what we mere mortals think of as depression, and I told him I didn't need him to define clinical depression to me, that I'm a professor of psychology, and he said, and I quote, 'A little knowledge is a dangerous thing.' Can you imagine the nerve of that man?" She spun around in a full circle. "I told him that I know the difference between physical pain and mental anguish, and that pompous son of a bitch smiled patiently like he was talking to a two year old and said, Sometimes the mind plays tricks. The mind plays tricks," she repeated incredulously. "He actually wrote me out a prescription for Valium!"

"Did he think you should have further tests?"

"As far as he's concerned, I've had more than enough tests already. I said, what about those things they stick down your throat to get a look at your stomach? He said, what do you want to put yourself through that for? I said, I want to get to the bottom of this pain. He said, it'll go away by itself and getting hysterical about it won't help anything. I said the only thing that was making me hysterical was his attitude and he said I could always find another doctor. Frankly, I don't remember what I said to him after that. But whatever it was, I don't think he'll forget me in a hurry."

"Let's go home," Joanne said, unable to think of anything else, leading her friend to her car.

"Can you imagine the nerve of that guy?" Eve was still repeating as Joanne pulled her car out of the parking lot and into the street. "*He* can't figure out what's wrong with me, so of course, it has to be all in *my* head. I said, how do you explain the weight loss and low-grade fever? He said my weight is fine for my age and height and I don't *have* a fever. I said how do you explain that my bowels aren't functioning normally? You know how regular I've always been about my bowels." Joanne nodded, though in fact, she had no idea about the state of Eve's bowels. "He said to take the Valium, my bowels would sort themselves out."

"So maybe you should . . ."

"What?"

"Maybe it will . . . relax your bowels, I don't know . . ."

"No, you sure don't. Valium is a tranquilizer, not a cure for cancer."

"Who said anything about cancer?"

There was an uncomfortable pause, heavy with unspoken implications. "Well, what do you think I have?" Eve asked quietly.

"I don't know," Joanne said, alarmed by her friend's surprising assertion, though the thought was one that had crossed her own mind several times. "I'm not a doctor," she said weakly.

"You think they know anything more than you do? How many have I been to in the past five weeks? What . . . one a week? More? Ten altogether?"

"Not that many."

"But enough. And not *one* of them can tell me anything. All these big-shot specialists and they don't know any more than my poor little family doctor who knows bugger-all. Meanwhile, I've missed the entire last month of school; I didn't complete the courses I'm taking or get my essays handed in; I'll have to take the damn courses again next year." She suddenly burst into a torrent of angry tears. Joanne quickly pulled the car to the side of the road. She had never seen Eve cry before. She had seen her happy, sad, excited, frustrated, and furious, but she had never seen Eve cry. Even after she had lost the baby, she had allowed herself no room for self-pity, plunging right back into her hectic schedule with a curt "That's life."

"Eve . . ."

"Why can't somebody tell me what's the matter with me?" she

pleaded. "You know me better than anyone, for God's sake. You know that I'm not a hypochondriac. You know that if I say something hurts me, then something really hurts me. I was the one who initially insisted that nothing was wrong. I was convinced that Brian and my mother were overreacting."

"I remember . . ."

"So now when the pain is really bad, when, I swear, there is *nothing* in my body that is functioning properly, why *now* is every-one telling me that there's nothing wrong?"

"Who else has told you there's nothing wrong?"

"Well, none of the other doctors has been as direct as this jerk, but they've all hinted. You know how subtle doctors are. I've had all the blood tests; I've seen all the specialists. Everything's negative. So now Brian . . ."

"What about Brian?"

"You know Brian, he's very offhand. He says that if the doctors can't find anything, then it can't be anything very serious, so to ignore it. Ignore something that won't let me eat properly or sleep properly or shit properly . . . ignore pain that won't let me stand up straight for more than five minutes at a time. Go out and get my hair done. Buy some new clothes. If I were a man, and it was my precious little penis that was bothering me, I wouldn't be dismissed this easily. They wouldn't tell me to go out and get my hair done then!" She looked around, startled and disoriented. "Why are we stopped?"

Joanne immediately started the car up again and pulled back into the street. "We'll just keep going to doctors until we find out what it is," she said steadily. "I know you. I know that if you complain, it's because there's something wrong. We'll keep checking until we find out what it is."

"At which point I might well be dead," Eve told her, and Joanne suddenly laughed out loud. "You find something funny in that thought, do you?" Eve asked, wiping away the last trace of her tears.

"No," Joanne smiled. "Of course not. It's just that we had this conversation in reverse the afternoon I took you to the hospital the first time. When I found the newspaper on my car and you called the police and they said there was nothing they could do until the guy actually made a move and I said, 'By which point I might be dead,' or something like that. Don't you remember?"

Eve shook her head. "Have you had any more calls lately?" she asked, reluctant, Joanne realized, to change the subject, to shift the focus of attention away from herself.

"Twice," Joanne said. "I hung up as soon as I heard his voice."

"That's good," Eve replied distractedly.

"I don't think he's a harmless crank," Joanne ventured slowly, voicing her deepest fears aloud for the first time, seeing the magazine photographs of the murdered women appear in the reflection of the car's rear view mirror. "I really think he's . . . the one who killed those other women. I think he's biding his time, watching me, playing with me . . . you know, like a cat plays with a mouse before he kills it."

"Come on, Joanne," Eve laughed. "Don't you think you're being just a touch melodramatic?"

Joanne shrugged, feeling vaguely hurt—she had indulged Eve her moment of high drama, was it expecting too much for her to be afforded the same privilege?—but she said nothing.

"Tell me, Joanne," Eve said, her voice assuming a flat, clinical air, "is there ever anybody else at home when you get these calls?"

"What do you mean?"

"Are you alone when the calls come or is there ever anybody with you?"

Joanne had to think for a minute. "I guess I'm usually alone, at least alone in the room, when he calls. Except for the night he called when Lulu was asleep beside me."

"But she didn't hear anything." It was a statement, not a question.

"Well, she didn't wake up," Joanne demurred. "Why? What are you getting at?"

Eve shook her head. "Nothing," she said, looking out her side window.

"What are you trying to say? That I'm imagining things?"

"That's not what I'm saying."

"What are you saying?"

"Sometimes the mind plays tricks," Eve said, invisible quotes around the words the doctor had earlier used with regard to herself. Joanne wondered if the choice of those words was intentional and if Eve had meant them to sound so cruel.

"Did you talk to Brian?" Joanne asked, deciding to ignore the many implications of Eve's assertion.

Eve's tone became defensive. "Of course I talked to Brian," she told Joanne. "You asked me to, didn't you? He says the same thing we've all told you, that if you're getting obscene calls, to hang up on the guy."

"I'm not even sure it *is* a man," Joanne reminded her. "It's such a strange voice."

"Well, of course it's a man," Eve stated, leaving no room for argument. "Women don't make obscene phone calls to other women."

"These are more than just obscene calls!" Joanne corrected her angrily. "He says he's going to kill me. He says I'm next. Why are you looking at me like that?"

Joanne caught a moment of indecision in Eve's eyes. "I was just wondering," Eve admitted, her face relaxing into a kind smile, "whether the phone calls started before or after Paul left."

Joanne said nothing, feeling her shoulders slump and her back collapse against the soft leather upholstery of the car seat, too confused and defeated to challenge her friend.

"I'm not saying someone isn't phoning you," Eve repeated apologetically as Joanne pulled into the driveway of her home. "Hell, I don't know what I'm saying. Joanne, look at me. Please. I'm sorry. Look at me." Joanne turned off the engine and pulled the key out of the ignition. She turned slowly around to face her friend of almost thirty years. "Please forget everything I said. I didn't mean it. I was mad at that stupid doctor and frustrated because nobody can figure out what's wrong with me, so I took it out on you. The doctor tells me that my problems are all in my head, so I tell you the same thing. What are friends for? Very mature, right? Give the little psychologist a gold star in adult behavior. Please forgive me, Joanne. I didn't mean it." Joanne nodded. "You know that I love you," Eve continued. "I'm just so frustrated."

"I know. And I understand, really I do."

"And *I* know that you have nothing to worry about," Eve said. "If anyone's going to die around here, it's going to be me, so don't you dare steal my thunder, you understand?"

Joanne saw that Eve was serious, that she was genuinely frightened. "You're not going to die," she repeated. "I promise," she added when she saw that Eve was waiting for just those words.

Eve pulled her friend to her, hugging her so tightly that Joanne found it difficult to breathe. "Please don't be mad at me," she whispered.

"I'm not," Joanne responded earnestly, smoothing Eve's hair. "Our first fight," she smiled.

"I guess it was." Eve's hand patted the hair that Joanne had stroked. "It's so dry," she said, trying to sound casual. "Remember, I always used to have such oily hair."

"You'll be fine," Joanne told her.

"So will you," Eve replied.

Both women got out of the car, their doors slamming in unison.

Chapter 14

Joanne stood naked in the middle of her walk-in closet with a frown on her face and a pile of discarded clothes on the floor around her bare feet. There was simply nothing in here that she wanted to wear. Everything that her hands touched felt foreign and unfamiliar, as if each item had been purchased by someone else. Someone with absolutely no taste or sense of style, Joanne thought now as she pulled a navy-and-white dress from its hanger and held it up against her sweaty breasts.

Why was she perspiring? She never perspired. The house was air-conditioned; why was she so hot? She dropped the dress to the floor—it wasn't right. It made her look like a middle-aged matron. Never mind that's what she was, she told herself, it was the last thing she wanted to resemble. It was too severe, too rigid, too old-fashioned, with its neat little Peter Pan collar and crisp blue leather belt. She hated this dress. What had ever possessed her to buy it in the first place? If she had a photograph of herself wearing this dress, she decided, it would undoubtedly be the picture they'd use in all the newspapers after her mutilated corpse had been discovered. Victim number four, she saw written above her smilingly nondescript face. Attractive, people would say (as she herself had observed of the strangler's other victims). Pleasant. Ordinary.

Perhaps she should run out now, she thought almost giddily, and have her picture taken in one of those little booths that give you four snapshots for a dollar, or whatever it cost these days, only pin a little note to the white Peter Pan collar that said, "I told you so" in bold black letters. No, she corrected, kicking the dress aside, *navy* letters. To match. Heaven forbid the note didn't match the dress.

She grabbed another outfit from its hanger, a white linen number the saleslady at Bergdorf Goodman's had cajoled her into purchasing against her better judgment. What better judgment? she wondered as she held it against her. It was unquestionably the most stylish thing she owned, but it was almost transparent and that meant she'd have to wear a slip and it was too hot to wear a slip, and linen wrinkled too fast anyway, even though the saleslady had assured her that it was supposed to look wrinkled, that was the look, but Joanne had always felt uncomfortable with wrinkles—she continually wanted to reach for an iron—and it was bad enough that she felt uncomfortable, she didn't want to *look* uncomfortable. She wanted to look beautiful. She wanted Paul to take one look at her and throw his arms around her and tell her how sorry he was, what a stupid fool he'd been, and if she would just forgive him please and take him back, he'd spend the rest of his life making it up to her, and all that in front of Robin's math teacher, Mr. Avery, who would smile and say that he was sure the problems he was experiencing with Robin would straighten themselves out now, he was sorry to have troubled them. And they would smile at him, tears of gratitude streaming down their happy faces, and tell him not to be sorry, after all he was the one who had brought them back together.

Joanne dropped the white linen dress to the floor and felt a tear fall the length of her cheek. That would never happen, she thought. It would never happen because she had nothing to wear! She would meet Paul in Mr. Avery's office an hour from now—my God, an hour from now!—and she would be wearing the same old clothes as the woman he had left, and Paul would look at her and smile—her dowdiness reinforcing his decision to leave—and they would sit side by side without touching, concerned parents still, if nothing else, and listen to whatever Mr. Avery had to say, and then they would go out for lunch—Paul had agreed to her suggestion of lunch, perhaps that was a sign that he missed her?—and they would discuss Mr. Avery's concerns and try to determine the best way to deal with Robin's problems in a civilized fashion. Civilized! That was the exact problem with all her clothes. They were so civilized. She could be comfortably buried in any of them.

The phone rang.

Joanne stood naked in the middle of her walk-in closet and stared in its direction without moving. He knew she was in here, she thought, feeling a fresh outbreak of sweat covering her body. Somehow he could see into this small windowless room; he knew that she was nude; even now his eyes were examining her, his fingers poking at her flesh, prodding the all-too-obvious flaws. Joanne stood motionless, holding her breath lest the sound of her breathing betray her,

until the phone stopped ringing. Then she resumed rifling through
her closet, her shaking hands selecting a turquoise sundress that had
at least a spark of youth about it, then running to the chest of drawers
in the bedroom, careful to duck out of sight of the window, although
there was no one presently working in her backyard. She opened the
top drawer and retrieved a pair of plain white panties and a matching bra—why didn't she have anything sexier?—and slipped them
on, her fingers fumbling with the hook of the white cotton brassiere.
Why didn't she possess any of those skimpy little lace undies that Eve
was always purchasing? She made a mental note to buy some in the
near future. Perhaps if there was enough time she could stop at a
store on the way to Robin's school and pick something up. She
checked her wrist, realized that she wasn't wearing her watch, and
looked over at the bedside clock beside the phone. Ten minutes to
ten already—she'd never have time.

What was she thinking about anyway? She laughed, the kind of
sharp staccato laugh that sticks in the throat. She stepped into the
turquoise dress. Paul wasn't interested in her underwear. He wasn't
going to see it. They were meeting with Robin's teacher in forty
minutes to discuss their older daughter, and they were having lunch
afterward—at *her* suggestion to *further* discuss their older daughter.
There would be no romantic trysts in a nearby hotel room for dessert.

Joanne marched into the bathroom and appraised herself in the
full-length mirror, one quick glance convincing her that her husband
of almost twenty years would not be so overcome with passion that
he would be in any hurry to see what kind of underwear she had
selected for the occasion.

She pulled spitefully at her hair, thinking that the problem
wasn't with her clothes at all but with her face. All she needed was a
new head, she thought, growling at her reflection. She looked so
pasty. Returning to the bedroom window and slipping a pair of old
sandals on her feet—what was happening to her big toenails?—she
stared into the mess that had once been a well-tended lawn and
garden. My summer cottage without the traffic, she thought ruefully,
staring into the empty concrete hole that had once been her backyard.

It had been ten days since any of the workers had been around,
seven days since she had been curtly informed that Rogers Pools had
gone into receivership, five days since Paul had told her he was trying
to straighten everything out.

Makeup, she thought suddenly, a little makeup. She hurried to the bathroom, flung open her medicine cabinet, and pulled out the rows of expensive tubes that Eve had once persuaded her to buy, though she couldn't remember the last time she had used any of this stuff. Pretty is as pretty does, her mother had always preached, and Paul had told her repeatedly that he disliked artificiality of any sort. Still, a little makeup couldn't hurt. Not enough to notice; just enough to make a difference. She rubbed a hint of color into her cheeks, decided it wasn't enough, then rubbed in some more. Now it was too much. She quickly washed it off and tried again. After four such tries she was still not satisfied. She'd have to ask Eve how it was done. Giving up on her cheeks and reaching for her mascara, she began gently rolling the curved applicator upward in a series of slow, careful gestures.

The phone rang. At the sudden sound, her hand jerked roughly into her eye, her eyelashes blinking furiously with the unexpectedly sharp pain. Joanne pressed her hand to her right eye to stop the harsh stinging, and when she looked at herself seconds later, she saw that she had smeared the mascara all over the side of her face. "Terrific," she said out loud, her voice trembling, her eyes filling with tears of self-pity. "Just great. The closer she gets . . . ," she uttered, recalling the old Clairol commercial of a beautiful young woman running in slow motion through a field of flowers to embrace her eager young lover.

The phone was still ringing. "Goddamn you," Joanne yelled in its direction. "Look at what you made me do. It's not enough you're going to kill me, you have to ruin my makeup!" She stomped angrily over to the phone and jerked it off its carriage. "Hello," she barked, bracing her body for the strange rasp that would instantly reduce her flesh to jelly.

"Joanne?"

"Warren?" She was momentarily disoriented. Why was her brother calling her—it was barely 7 A.M. in California—unless something terrible had happened? "What's the matter? Is everyone okay?"

"Everyone's fine on this end," he responded curtly. "You're the one I'm calling about."

"Me?"

"For Christ's sake, Joanne, why didn't you tell me?"

It took Joanne a moment to sort through her confusion and to understand what Warren was talking about. "You mean about me and Paul?" she asked.

"Among other things. Why didn't you tell me?"

"I didn't want to upset you. I was hoping it would all be worked out by now," she explained, thinking that she did not need this phone call at this moment in her life.

"But it's not."

"No," she admitted. "At least not yet. But I'm having lunch with Paul today and . . ."

"I spoke to Paul yesterday."

"You did?" Silly question, Joanne thought after she had asked it. How else would he have found out about their separation? "What did he say?"

"Well, you can imagine what kind of idiot I felt like," Warren began, avoiding her question. "I phone your number only to be told it's been disconnected, so I call Paul's office and I ask what's going on, and there's this awkward silence, and he says finally, you mean Joanne hasn't told you? And I say, told me what? And so he tells me."

"What?"

"What?" he repeated. "That the two of you have separated, that he has his own apartment in the city, that you were getting some obscene phone calls—Joanne, are you all right?"

Of course I'm not all right, Joanne thought. "Of course I'm all right," she said. "Paul just needs time to . . . to think things through. He's confused, that's all."

"Would you like some company? Gloria could fly over for a few days . . ."

"No, I'm fine, really." If she admitted the need for Gloria's company, it would only alarm her brother further. What was the point in doing that?

"Gloria wants to say a few words to you."

"Hello, Joanne." Gloria always sounded as if her nose had just caught a whiff of something unpleasant. "How are you holding out?"

Joanne told her that she was fine. She didn't tell her that she had mascara all over the right side of her cheek, that she had nothing decent to wear, that her closet floor was a mess of discarded clothing, that her backyard was a mess of abandoned concrete, that her best friend was falling apart, and that she was increasingly convinced she was to be the Suburban Strangler's next victim. She said she was fine because she knew that was what Gloria wanted to hear.

"Well, that's good. I mean, I know it's your life and everything," Gloria continued, "but try not to take it too seriously. You know what I mean?"

"I thought we were going to have lunch," Joanne was saying.

"I know and I'm sorry," Paul explained, a slight edge in his voice. "I tried to call you this morning when this thing came up, but nobody answered." Joanne saw herself standing in the middle of her walk-in closet, the phone ringing shrilly from the bedside table. "I'm really sorry, Joanne. There was nothing I could do. This is an important client and when he suggests lunch, it's more than a casual suggestion, if you know what I mean." Joanne looked toward the floor. (You know what I mean? her sister-in-law asked again from three thousand miles away.) "Look, I do have time for a quick coffee," he said, his voice softening.

"Where?" Joanne asked, her eyes skimming the empty high school corridor.

"There's a cafeteria, isn't there?"

"Here? In the school?"

"What better place to discuss Robin's problems?"

You had to admire his skill, Joanne thought as her husband took her arm and guided her down the wide stairs to the cafeteria. In one simple sentence, he had said everything: they were here to discuss their daughter's problems, not their own; he was prepared to go no further; to try for something more would be singularly inappropriate, given the time and place; keep things casual, he was warning, simple, and above all, unemotional.

Joanne gripped the banister for support as Paul released her arm. Feeling her knees knocking against each other, she slowed her steps, afraid she would fall, embarrass him further. The smell of food began mingling with other familiar smells, the odor of old socks and gymnasiums, of chalk and blackboards, of exasperation and enthusiasm. Of youth, she realized, seeing herself and Eve when she looked at two teenage girls giggling together beside their open lockers, lined with pictures of the latest teen idols.

"Here we are," Paul said, pushing open the double doors to the cafeteria and standing back to let Joanne pass through.

("Over here!" Eve called to her immediately, jumping up and down in her seat. "You can have the sandwich my mother made me—baloney again, if you can believe it. We must have shares in a baloney factory—what did your mother make you? Tuna fish, great, we'll trade.")

"What would you like?" Paul grabbed a tray from the stack and slid it along the steel bars toward the cash register.

"Just coffee," Joanne said, snapping back into the present, seeing Eve as she watched a tall, slender girl of perhaps fifteen, her thick red hair pulled back into an unruly ponytail and secured by a dark green ribbon.

There were only a handful of students in the large room, the tables arranged precisely in long rows. Several of the students looked in her direction as she followed Paul to a table by the window, which was located above their heads so that all one saw of the outside schoolyard was feet. Paul removed the two mugs from the stained orange tray and slid the tray over to the adjoining table, studying his coffee as if he expected to be quizzed on it at any minute, reminding Joanne strongly of the daughter they were here to discuss. "So, what did you think of what Avery had to say?" he asked finally.

"I think he's very concerned about Robin."

"You don't think he's overreacting?"

Not everyone is overreacting these days, Joanne wanted to tell him, but said instead, "I don't think so."

"I just meant that it's June, for Pete's sake, the kids are restless, school's over this afternoon except for the final exams, and he even admitted that Robin was sure to pass."

"He's concerned about next year, her attitude . . ."

"She'll be fine by the fall."

"Will she? Why?" Joanne was as startled by her own question as her husband. "Will things be any different in the fall?" she pressed.

"Joanne . . ."

Joanne looked at the dotted squares of the soft ceiling tile. "Sorry," she said quickly. "I just don't think we can afford to be too cavalier about this."

"Nobody's being cavalier. There's no question we'll have to talk to Robin, make her understand the seriousness of her actions, that she can't afford to start the next year the same way she finished this one, that she'll have to attend all her classes, that skipping any of them is totally unacceptable behavior."

"When are *we* going to tell her all this?"

Paul said nothing, taking a long sip of his coffee. "I'll speak to her on the weekend," he said finally, pointedly checking his watch.

"Paul, we need to talk." Joanne heard the tremble in her voice, hating herself for it.

"We *are* talking," he said, deliberately missing the point, refusing to look at her, taking another long sip from his mug.

"I miss you," she whispered.

Paul looked from side to side with obvious discomfort. "If there's anything you need . . ."

"I need you."

"This isn't the place."

"What is? You keep saying you'll call but you never do. I was hoping we could talk at lunch."

"I explained about lunch."

"That's not the point."

"The point is that I haven't had enough time," he told her as he had told her once before. "I'm just starting to get used to being on my own." He lifted his head from the table to stare directly into her eyes, his voice low now, barely audible. "You have to get used to it too."

"I don't want to get used to it," she told him, surprised by her own assertiveness.

"You have to," he repeated. "You have to stop calling me at the office over every little problem."

"This wasn't a little problem. Mr. Avery . . ."

"I'm not talking about Mr. Avery. I'm talking about things like the gas bill . . ."

"There was a mistake on the invoice. I couldn't figure it out."

"I'm talking about *Sports Illustrated* . . ."

"I didn't know if you wanted to renew your subscription."

"You could have made the choice."

"I didn't want to make the wrong one!" She promptly burst into tears. "I'm sorry," she cried softly, grabbing a paper napkin from its aluminum container and blowing her nose. "I didn't mean to cry."

"No," he said gently, suddenly reaching across the table and taking her hand in his. "I'm the one who's sorry." Joanne stared across the table hopefully. This is the part where he tells me what a stupid fool he's been and begs my forgiveness, if I'll only take him back he'll spend the rest of his life making it up to me. "I shouldn't have said anything," he said instead. "I knew this wasn't the time or place. Jesus, Joanne, you make me feel like such a bastard."

Joanne covered her eyes with her free hand, biting down so hard on her lower lip that she tasted blood. "Are my eyes smeared?" she asked as he withdrew his hand. She pushed at her hair absently and fumbled with the neckline of her dress.

"No," Paul said, his eyes soft, his voice tender. "You look lovely. You know I've always liked that dress."

Joanne smiled. "I love you," she said, not looking at him, her lips quivering despite all efforts to control them.

"I love you too," he said simply.

"Then what are we doing?"

He shook his head. "I don't know," he admitted.

"Come home."

He looked toward the door to the cafeteria as a young couple bounded in noisily, laughing and gaily hurling mock insults at one another. "I can't," he said, and although his words were lost in the sudden swirl of activity around them, Joanne had only to stare at his eyes, which were focused resolutely on his now empty mug, to understand what he had said.

"Mrs. Hunter," the voice called to her from across the lobby.

Joanne swung around abruptly, almost knocking into a woman in tennis clothes who was passing in front of her.

"Sorry, I didn't mean to startle you," Steve Henry said, crossing the green-and-white lobby of the country club.

"Did I leave something on the court?" Joanne asked, automatically feeling in her purse for her keys.

"No," he laughed, a dimple creasing his left cheek. "I had a cancellation, so I was wondering if you'd like to join me for a cup of coffee. We could talk about how much your game has improved over the last couple of weeks," he added.

"I don't think so," Joanne answered hastily.

"You don't think your game has improved or you don't think you'd like to join me for a cup of coffee?"

"Both, I'm afraid." She'd had enough talks over coffee for one day. "I'm running kind of late."

"Sure," he said easily, walking beside her toward the door. "What about your friend, the redhead . . ."

"Eve?"

"Yes, Eve, the one with the weak forehand and the wicked laugh." Joanne smiled agreement. Eve's laugh *was* wicked, as if she knew something the rest of the world didn't but might be persuaded to tell. "Will we ever be seeing her again?"

"Oh, I'm sure she'll resume the lessons as soon as she starts feeling better."

"I hope so," he said, "although she'll have to work hard to catch up to you."

"I don't think so."

"Who's the teacher here?" Joanne tried to return his smile, but there was something about Steve Henry's blond, effortless good looks that made her uneasy. "You were hitting some very nice shots there," he continued. "I had you running all over the court, and you were getting to all of them."

"And sending them right into the net."

"You're still not following through all the way," he agreed. "But, I don't know, I sensed a new aggressiveness out there this afternoon." Joanne laughed despite herself. "There, you know what I'm talking about, don't you?"

"Look at my toes," she wailed, not sure what else to say, looking down at the blue-tinted large toenails poking out from under the straps of her sandals. "They look like they're about to fall off."

"You probably will lose the nails," he told her matter-of-factly. "Your shoes must be too small. To play tennis, you need a half size larger. What's happening is your toes keep jamming into the top of your sneakers because they don't have enough room to move around."

"They're such a lovely shade of blue," she smiled as they reached the front door.

"Like your eyes," he told her.

Oh, Joanne thought, surprised and instantly speechless, we're not talking about tennis.

Chapter 15

"Yes, so then what did you say?"

"What do you mean, what did I say? I didn't say anything."

"Joanne, for God's sake," Eve exclaimed impatiently, "the man was obviously making a pitch, he tells you your toenails are the same color as your eyes . . ." Both women suddenly burst out laughing. "All right, so it's not the most romantic thing he could have said, but it is kind of cute."

"My eyes aren't blue, they're hazel."

"Picky, picky. That's not the point. The point is that he was telling you that you have beautiful eyes. When was the last time anyone told you that?" Joanne smiled, remembering that she had asked herself that same question not too long ago. "The point is," Eve continued, "that he's obviously interested."

"In me," Joanne stated, though it was unmistakably a question.

"Why not in you?" Eve demanded. The two women were standing beside the built-in stovetop in Eve's kitchen looking over the Saturday-night dinner Eve had prepared. "Loosen up a bit, put a few blond streaks in your hair, and you're a very beautiful woman."

"I think all those X-rays have affected your brain," Joanne told her friend playfully, though she was grateful for the compliment.

"You're the one who's crazy if you don't take advantage of what Steve Henry is offering you."

"Which is?"

"One of the nicest twenty-nine-year-old bodies I've ever seen. Come on, Joanne, if for no other reason, do it for me."

Joanne laughed out loud. "I can't," she said finally.

"Why the hell not?"

"Because I'm a married woman."

There was a long pause before Eve spoke again. "You think Paul is sitting home nights telling everybody he's a married man?"

"What do you mean?" Almost before the question was out of her mouth, Joanne was sorry she had asked it.

"Look, I'm not saying that he has anything serious going . . ."

"What are you trying to tell me?"

"I don't know anything for sure," Eve backtracked.

"What have you heard?"

"A few people have seen him around."

"With whom?" The question was pushed out of her throat by the sudden rapid beating of her heart.

"Some girl. Judy somebody-or-other. Nobody anybody knows." She shrugged, her face registering proper disdain. "A blonde, naturally."

"Young?"

"Mid to late twenties."

Joanne braced herself against Eve's kitchen counter for support.

"Listen," Eve said quickly, "I did not tell you about this blond Judy whatever-her-name-is to upset you. I told you about her to get you off your ass. This is opportunity knocking, for God's sake. How many chances like this do you think you're going to get? Steve Henry is a certifiable hunk. Do you know the stamina that twenty-nine-year-old men have? Think about it, Joanne. That's all I'm asking you to do."

"What the hell's going on in there?" a masculine voice called from the dining room. "I thought we were going to have some dinner around here."

"Coming," Eve called out, noisily maneuvering the various pots on the top of the stove without actually doing anything. "The point is, Joanne," she continued in a whisper, "that Paul isn't spending all his nights alone in his new apartment thinking things through; he's also going out and . . . not thinking." Eve gathered a large casserole dish and a few side plates around her and began organizing the dinner she had prepared. "Brian's in a rotten mood," she informed Joanne as they neared the connecting door to the dining room, their hands loaded with the various delicacies. "Try not to talk about his work, okay?"

Joanne nodded, feeling numb from the top of her messy brown hair to the bottom of her bright blue toenails. She was no longer hungry, despite the delicious smells, and she doubted she'd be able to say anything at all to Brian with the huge lump that was blocking her throat.

"So, how are the girls?" Brian was asking, his large mouth full of food.

"They're fine," Joanne replied automatically. "Well, actually, no, they're not fine," she corrected, looking up from her untouched plate of Chinese-style beef on a bed of rice, which Eve had no doubt spent the entire day preparing. "I mean, healthwise, they're okay, I guess. But Lulu's driving me nuts about her final exams, she's convinced she's going to fail everything, and Robin is driving me nuts because she's convinced she's going to pass everything without having to do any work. She's out tonight because God forbid she should stay home on a Saturday night! And Lulu, who *is* home studying, is crying because her history exam is Monday and the only date she can remember is the start of the Boer War, and naturally they didn't study the Boer War this year."

Brian laughed. "Why the Boer War?"

"Oh, it's the combination for the numbers on our burglar alarm system."

"I understand you had another false alarm this morning," Brian said, helping himself to more salad.

Joanne nodded. "After lecturing the kids a million times about checking to make sure the alarm is off before they open the door in the morning, guess who forgot and did just that? Oh well," Joanne smiled sadly, "it gives me something to talk to my grandfather about."

"How is he?"

"Not good." Joanne lifted her fork to her lips, then lowered it without having taken any food into her mouth. "He's starting to look a little gray around the edges."

"You keep the alarm on even when you're in the house?" Brian asked, his professional instincts returning them to the original conversation.

Joanne nodded. "I feel safer since the phone calls."

"What phone calls?" Brian asked.

A sudden loud noise—Eve's fork cracking against the side of her plate as it fell from her hand—transferred the focus of attention back to Eve's end of the table. Eve jumped to her feet clumsily, knocking over her wine glass, spilling what was left of the expensive burgundy into her salad. "Oh God," she exclaimed, "I seem to be having a sharp pain."

"Where?" Joanne asked, immediately at Eve's side.

"The usual places," she gasped, trying to laugh. "My heart, my lungs, my stomach, my groin . . ."

"What should we do?" Joanne asked Brian who remained in his chair.

"There's some Valium in the medicine cabinet in our bathroom," he began.

"I don't need Valium," Eve shouted. "I need a doctor who knows what he's talking about. Shit, look at this tablecloth." Joanne glanced down at the bright bloodlike stain that was shaping itself almost like a placemat around Eve's plate.

"It's all right, I'll wash it out," Joanne offered. "Maybe you should go upstairs and lie down."

Eve glared at her husband, who sat impassively across the table, not moving. "Okay," she agreed.

"I'll help you."

"No, I can manage." She wiggled out of Joanne's protective grasp, her body doubled forward. "I'll be down again soon," she promised. "You finish eating."

"You sure you don't want me to come up with you?"

"I want you to rinse out the damn tablecloth before it's ruined completely," she answered, trying to smile. "And I want you to follow through with Steve Henry, damnit." She disappeared up the steps with proper dramatic flair.

"What was that all about?" Brian asked as Joanne began soaking up the spilt wine with her napkin.

Joanne started clearing away the dishes. "I was about to ask you the same question," she said without looking at him.

"Sit down," he told her casually, but with an unmistakable air of authority. "I'm not finished with my meal yet. And you haven't even touched yours. Come on, Eve's mother will be only too happy to buy us another tablecloth. It'll give her something useful to do and it'll keep her off my back for ten minutes. Eat."

Joanne reluctantly returned to her seat and stared coldly at Eve's husband, whose face was surprisingly soft despite the gruffness of his voice. She made no effort to hide her displeasure.

"You think I'm a cold-hearted son of a bitch, right?" he said.

"I probably wouldn't have put it that way," Joanne admitted, "but yes, that's an essentially accurate description." She was surprised at her own directness. Normally she would have found some way to soften her words, so as not to risk hurting his feelings. But at this moment she doubted Brian Stanley had any feelings.

"You don't know the whole story, Joanne," he told her simply, his deep-set eyes revealing nothing. A policeman's eyes, she found herself thinking.

"I know that my best friend is in terrible pain and that her husband looks like he couldn't give a damn."

Brian Stanley tapped his fingers impatiently on the table. "I repeat," he said, his voice steady, "you don't know the whole story."

"I may not know the whole story," Joanne began, using his words, "but I do know Eve. This is not a woman who gets hysterical about a few small aches and pains. She's always been very much in control. Even after she lost the baby, she just picked herself up and carried on with her life."

"You didn't think that was just a little bit strange?"

His question caught Joanne off guard. "What do you mean?"

"A woman tries for seven years to have a child and she finally conceives at the age of forty, finds out that the baby is a girl, selects a name, Jaclyn, immediately—over her mother's loud objections I might add—then loses the baby and goes right back on with her life as if nothing happened. Doesn't shed a tear. Christ, Joanne, *I* cried!"

"Eve was never one to show her emotions in public."

"I'm not the public—I'm her husband!" Brian realized he had raised his voice and took a long, deep breath, looking toward the stairs. "There are other things."

"Like what?"

"Individually they don't amount to much," he admitted, "but when you put them all together . . . it's a little like solving a crime."

"It's not a crime to be sick."

"I'm not saying that it is."

"Then why aren't you helping her?"

"I'm trying. She won't accept the kind of help I'm offering."

"Which is?"

"I want her to see a psychiatrist."

"Why? Because one doctor suggested her problems were psychosomatic."

"Not just *one* doctor. Joanne, please hear me out. You may be the only one who can convince her to get the help she needs. You're the only one she listens to." He waited as if he expected Joanne to say something, but she said nothing, only waited for him to continue. "Like I said," he began again, "it's a combination of things."

"Like what?"

"Like whenever we go to the theater, she has to have an aisle seat."

"What!" Joanne was incredulous. What was this man talking about? "What's the matter with that? Lots of people like to sit on the aisle."

"But do they refuse to go to the theater if they can't?" He paused. "Do they walk out of a movie they've stood in line for an hour to see because they can't get the seat they want? She won't use an elevator," he continued in the same breath, as if fearful Joanne might interrupt again. "She'll walk up and down twenty flights of stairs rather than set foot in a goddamn elevator." Joanne was about to object. "And don't tell me that lots of people have phobias about elevators. I know that. I'm not crazy about them myself. But that doesn't mean I won't accept dinner invitations because the people live in a high-rise, or that I won't go somewhere where an elevator can't be avoided."

"I'm sure Eve wouldn't let those things stop her."

"You don't live with her, Joanne. I do. I know exactly what 'those things' have stopped her from doing. We hardly go anywhere anymore. It's gotten worse over the years. When was the last time you remember Eve and me going away on vacation?"

"You can't blame that on Eve. You're the one who's always working."

"Is that what she told you?" He stood up, running an oversized hand through his curly brown hair, peppered increasingly these days with gray. "Look, it's true, I work hard and I work a lot. Why not? To be very frank, there's not a whole lot to come home to these days." He paused, looking down at the table. Joanne was surprised at how vulnerable this very large, very tough man seemed just now. His next words were an obvious struggle to formulate, more painful still to voice. "Eve doesn't love me," he said slowly, as if admitting this fact to himself for the first time. "If I'm being completely honest with myself, I'd have to say that I don't think she ever really did. I think she married me because she knew it would enrage her mother, if you really want to know what I think," he went on, wound up now. "But that's beside the point. The point is that we have no relationship to speak of. As far as Eve is concerned, she made a bad mistake seven years ago, and now she wants as little to do with me and my world as possible."

"Brian, how can that be true? She was going to have your baby, for God's sake!"

"For her mother's sake, you mean!" He held up his hands. "Okay, okay, maybe I'm going overboard a bit, maybe I'm wrong, maybe she *does* love me . . ."

"I'm sure she does. She's always talking about you. She's very proud of you, I know she is."

"How do you know? What does she say?"

Joanne fought hard to remember anything positive Eve had ever told her about Brian. She stared into Brian's surprisingly kind face. ("Trust me, his face is not his best feature," she heard Eve say.) "Well, of course she never went into any details," Joanne stammered with some embarrassment, "but I know she . . . found your work very interesting," she said, unable to bring herself to discuss their sex life.

"My work?" he hooted. "Eve likes blood and guts! Most of my work is boring as hell. She couldn't care less about my work. What has she told you about our sex life?" he asked, as if he could read her mind.

"Just that it's a good deal more than satisfactory," Joanne said quietly, then quickly added, "Terrific, actually."

"Our sex life is nonexistent," he spat out.

"Well, I guess since the miscarriage . . ." Joanne stumbled, once again caught off guard.

"It has nothing to do with the miscarriage. We haven't had a good sex life in years!" He spun around, allowing himself to fall back wearily into his chair. There was a long silence. "Look, I don't know how or why I got into all this. As I said, it's beside the point." He laughed bitterly. "My life is beside the point." Joanne felt tears springing to her eyes. For the first time since he had started speaking, she understood exactly what he was saying. ("I mean, I know it's your life and everything," her sister-in-law had stated, "but try not to take it too seriously.")

"I was telling you about the fact that Eve and I haven't taken a vacation together in years. And not because I'm too busy. Because she won't fly."

"Lots of people don't like to fly," Joanne maintained stubbornly.

"They don't like it, but they do it. I only get two weeks, Joanne. I don't have time to take a boat to Europe. But okay, forget about flying, I'll give you flying, but the fact is that even if I suggest we drive somewhere, Boston, for Christ's sake, or Toronto, *anywhere,* the answer's no. And do you want to know why?" Joanne was quite convinced she didn't want to know but equally convinced he was going to tell her. "Because she won't leave her mother!"

"What? Brian, that's ridiculous. Eve can barely stand being in the same room with her mother for more than two minutes."

"I know that. I also know that, for some reason, she feels responsible for her and that she won't leave her. It's a very complex relationship. There's a lot of guilt involved. Hell, I'm a cop, not a psychiatrist. But I'm telling you that there's a lot going on in Eve's head that you don't know about, and that her mother has a great deal to do with it."

"Okay," Joanne said, trying to sift through the confused layers of her thoughts. "Maybe Eve has some problems. I admit that I wasn't aware of the depth of some of her phobias, but I still don't think they mean that the pains she's been having . . ."

"I've spoken to all the doctors, some more than once. They all say the same thing—that there is nothing physically wrong with Eve, that the tests indicate nothing out of the ordinary. Joanne, nobody falls apart all over their whole body. Eve has pains everywhere. Take her to one doctor, it's pains in her chest. Take her to another, they're in her groin. Her stomach isn't working properly, she complains, her weight's down, her temperature is up. We're talking half a pound, half a degree! I threw away the damn scale; she bought another one. I tell her to stop taking her damn temperature, she just glares at me. She's obsessed."

"She's in pain!"

"I don't doubt that. Believe me, I don't doubt that for a minute. What can I say?" He looked around the room helplessly. "I spoke to the police psychiatrist. I asked her what she thought."

"And?"

"She said that it sounded to her like a fairly typical case of postpartum depression brought on by the miscarriage, the same thing that the other doctors have concluded. She said that I shouldn't allow myself to be manipulated, that I shouldn't cater to Eve's illness because I'd only be reinforcing it, that I should suggest strongly that Eve talk to someone on a professional basis, but, of course, Eve won't hear of it. She says she knows enough about pyschiatrists to know that she wants nothing to do with them. She says that she shouldn't have to defend herself to me or apologize because she's having pains. She's furious with me for even suggesting she see someone. Joanne, is it so wrong? This has been going on for almost two months now. She's already seen half the specialists in New York; she has appointments with the other half. She'll see all those doctors, why won't she see a psychiatrist? I mean, even if I'm wrong and it *is* something physical, something that all the tests have missed, what harm could it do to talk to somebody about it, to learn to cope with it? If you were in horrendous pain, wouldn't you do everything you could to get rid of it, even if it meant talking to a shrink?" Joanne stared into his eyes but said nothing. "I'm sorry. I didn't mean to dump this all on you."

"Eve is my closest friend. I want to help her if I can."

"Then convince her to see a psychiatrist," Brian urged. "Sorry, there I go again. Police training, I guess. I'm sorry, you obviously have enough to worry about right now. What was that about some phone calls you've been getting?"

The sudden switch in gears took Joanne by surprise. "What?"

"Before Eve had her attack, you were saying something about feeling safer with the alarm on since the phone calls."

"Yes," Joanne agreed, her adrenaline level rising, her mind furiously backtracking. "I've been getting these threatening calls. Eve didn't tell you about them?" she asked, watching him shake his head from side to side. "Well, maybe she said they were obscene calls."

"She never said anything about any calls, period."

"Are you sure?" Joanne felt suddenly queasy. "She promised me that she was going to. She said she had."

"The only thing that Eve and I have discussed over the past few months are her assorted aches and pains. What kind of threatening calls?"

Joanne told him about the series of phone calls, the late-night threats, the newspaper left on her car window, the fact that she had changed her number and still the calls continued. "Eve never mentioned any of this?" she asked again though she already knew the answer.

He shook his head. "Would you like a drink?" he offered, moving to the liquor cabinet.

"No, thank you." She watched while he poured himself a healthy snifter of brandy. "Paul thinks I'm overreacting," she said. "So does Eve," she added. "That's probably why she didn't say anything."

Brian laughed out loud, taking a quick sip of his drink. "Eve's a fine one to talk about overreacting." He took another, longer swallow. "But she's probably right about there not being anything to worry about. Loonies like the Suburban Strangler bring all the other nuts out of the woodwork. We must have seen a thousand guys who've already confessed to the killings." He downed the remaining contents of his glass. "And I couldn't begin to count the number of women who have reported calls like the ones you've been getting, although . . ."

"Although what?"

"Do you still have the newspaper that was left on your car?" Joanne shook her head. She'd thrown it away long ago. Brian shrugged. "We probably wouldn't have gotten anything from it anyway." His hand reached for the bottle of brandy and then moved away. "I'm sure you have nothing to worry about, Joanne," he was quick to assure her again, noting the look of concern in her eyes. "It's probably some stupid prank, and unfortunately, as the police have already told you, our hands are tied. The best advice I can give you is what Eve has already told you—be extra cautious, change your number again, and in the meantime, keep hanging up on the guy."

"I'm not even sure it *is* a guy," Joanne heard herself reply, almost a reflex action, she realized, wondering why she bothered.

Brian regarded her with a subtle yet unmistakable interest. "What makes you say that?"

"Some quality in the voice. Neither here nor there. Although," she added, trying to laugh, not quite sure what he was getting at, "the Suburban Strangler could hardly be a woman."

"You know something we don't?" he asked, and Joanne wondered if he was serious.

"I don't understand," Joanne stammered. "I read that the Suburban Strangler's victims were raped."

"You read that they were sexually assaulted. There's a difference."

"I don't understand," Joanne repeated.

"I'm afraid I can't be more explicit."

"You're saying that the killer could be a woman?"

"It's a very remote possibility, I grant you; she'd have to be exceptionally strong. But a lot of women are into body building and weight training these days. Who knows? Anything's possible. Besides, whoever's phoning you isn't necessarily the killer. It's probably just some sickie who's gone off the deep end and could very possibly be a woman."

"Eve says women don't make obscene calls to other women."

"Eve says a lot of things," Brian replied cryptically, coming up behind her and putting his arms around her shoulders in what was intended as a comforting gesture. "Look, try not to worry. I'll talk to my lieutenant about it, see if we can't get someone to drive by your house on a regular basis. And of course, I'll keep an eye out."

"Thank you," Joanne said gratefully, feeling she should probably go home but liking the security of masculine arms around her. She patted the hairy tops of his hands. "I'd appreciate that."

"Just be careful," he told her moments later as he walked her to the front door.

"Tell Eve that dinner was lovely and that I'll call her tomorrow."

"Will do," he said, watching her as she cut across his front lawn to her own and ran up her front steps.

She waved goodbye, fishing in her purse for her keys. "Where are they?" she muttered out loud, unable to find them. "Damn it, I must have left them at Eve's." She looked back to where Brian had been standing, but he'd already retreated inside his house and closed the front door. She debated running back. "Oh hell, I'll get them tomorrow," she decided, ringing her doorbell and waiting, her eyes carefully searching up and down the dark street. "Some eye he's keeping out," she muttered, looking back at Eve's house, catching sight of a quick movement in the window of the smaller front bedroom. "Come on, Lulu, where are you?" She pressed the doorbell again, hearing it chime.

A loud voice suddenly blasted into the darkness. "Who is it?" the voice boomed and Joanne felt the muscles in her neck painfully contract as she recoiled in fright.

"My God!" she cried, realizing that the voice was Lulu's and that it was coming from the small box next to the doorbell, part of the new intercom system that had been installed.

"It's Mommy," she answered, her heart pounding wildly.

"Where's your key?" the child asked as she pulled open the door and backed away, her eyes resolutely downcast.

Joanne had only to look at her to know that something was wrong.

Chapter 16

"What's the matter?" Joanne asked immediately.

Lulu shook her head, turning away. "Nothing," she mumbled.

Joanne reached out and touched her daughter's shoulder, slowly spinning the reluctant girl around and lifting her chin with gentle fingers. "Tell me," she said. Lulu began shuffling from one foot to the other, looking from side to side and avoiding her mother's penetrating gaze. "What is it, Lulu? What happened?" Lulu's eyes focused briefly on her mother's before retreating to the safety of the surrounding walls. She opened her mouth as if she were about to speak, then said nothing. "Did someone phone?" Joanne asked, holding her breath.

"No," Lulu told her, obviously surprised by the question. "Who would phone?" Once again, her body began swaying rhythmically back and forth.

"Lulu, something's wrong. I could see it the minute I walked in the door. Did you have another fight with Robin before she went out?" Lulu shook her head vehemently. Too vehemently, Joanne thought. "What happened, Lulu?" she asked patiently, her fear subsiding.

"I don't want to tell you."

"That's obvious. It's also obvious that it has something to do with Robin." Lulu raised her head, opening her mouth to protest, then quickly lowering it again, saying nothing. "Did she say something that hurt your feelings?" Lulu shook her head. "Does whatever happened have anything to do with Scott Peterson?"

"No," Lulu said, a touch too adamantly. "Yes," she whispered.

"Did he . . . did he do anything to upset you?" Joanne asked gently. She saw Lulu's eyes fill with tears. "Lulu, did he touch you in a way that made you uncomfortable?" Lulu stared at the floor, her right hand wiping away a loose tear. "Lulu, tell me. This is not the time for twenty questions."

"He didn't touch me!" Lulu cried. She turned from her mother and ran quickly up the stairs to her room.

Joanne stood in the front hallway trying to decide what to do: she could follow her daughter upstairs and continue peppering her with questions until she received some satisfactory answers; she could wait and confront Robin when she came home; she could go to bed and do nothing, which, in truth, was what she really wanted to do, and hope that the problem would go away by itself. Things have a way of working out, she tried to tell herself, turning to the stairs.

Lulu was standing at the top of the landing. "Robin and Scott were smoking marijuana," she said quietly.

Joanne felt her body go numb. "What?"

Lulu said nothing, knowing her mother had heard what she said.

"Please don't tell me that," Joanne whispered, more to herself than to her daughter. She walked over to the staircase and sank down on the bottom step. From behind her, she felt Lulu approaching, the child's arm falling protectively across her mother's shoulder as she placed herself on the step behind her. "What happened?" Joanne asked, wishing that she didn't have to hear the answer.

"Scott came to pick her up a few minutes after you left. Robin was still getting ready. Scott said he'd go up and hurry her along. So he went into her room, and I was trying to study, but they were making so much noise, Robin was giggling like crazy. You know that cackle she gets when she's really laughing. Anyway, I went in there to tell them to please keep it down. I knocked first but they didn't hear me. So I opened the door, and there they were on the floor beside her bed . . . passing this joint back and forth."

"Doing what?"

"You know, passing a marijuana cigarette back and forth." Lulu pressed her chin down painfully into Joanne's shoulder.

"How do you know what it's called?"

"Mom," Lulu exclaimed with obvious exasperation, "everybody knows that."

Joanne maneuvered her body so that she could escape her daughter's killer chin and also watch the child's face while she spoke. "Then what happened? After they saw you."

"They offered me a drag."

"They offered you a drag," Joanne repeated, hating the expression almost as much as the fact. "That was very thoughtful of them."

"Robin looked kind of scared. I think she was afraid that I might tell you, but that if I smoked some too, then I wouldn't."

"Robin's a very clever girl," Joanne agreed. "She should only be that clever in school."

It all came clearly into focus: Robin's schoolwork; her change in attitude; the poor grades; the frequent absences from class. The classic signs of involvement with drugs Joanne kept hearing about on the radio and from various friends and acquaintances with regard to their teenagers. But not mine, Joanne had always thought, letting the warnings slip past her unheeded. Children of perfect mothers never smoked dope or did things they weren't supposed to do. How could I be so smug? she asked herself now. How could I be so stupid? Where the hell have I been all my life?

"What's the matter, Mom?"

"What?"

"Your whole body's shaking."

"What happened then?" Joanne asked.

"Nothing. I said no, I didn't want any, and I went back to my room. A few minutes later Robin came in and told me not to tell you, that it would only upset you and that you've been upset enough since Dad left."

"She's so considerate."

"That's why I was so worried. I didn't know what to do."

"You did the right thing," Joanne assured her, smoothing a few stray hairs away from Lulu's tear-stained face.

"What are you going to do?" the child asked sheepishly.

"I'm not sure. I'll have to speak to your father about it." She looked at her watch. It was almost eleven o'clock. Was it too late to call him? "You go to sleep, sweetie. It's late."

"I have to study."

"You'll study in the morning. Go on, I'll be up in a few minutes to tuck you in." She kissed her daughter's cheek, slightly sticky from her tears, and watched her run up the stairs. Try not to take it too seriously, she admonished herself silently, standing up, trying to decide what to do. "Remember, it's only your life," she said out loud. An hour later she was still standing in the same spot.

"Good night, sweet thing," she whispered, bending over to kiss her daughter's cheek although Lulu was already asleep. Joanne tiptoed from Lulu's room down the hall to her own, pulling off her

clothes and hurling them angrily across the carpet. It would be another hour before Robin returned home. That gave her sixty minutes
to decide what she was going to say and do. She debated getting into
the bathtub, letting the hot water soak away her anxieties, then
decided a bath would leave her not only anxious but wet. She fumbled inside her dresser for a T-shirt, pulling one out and over her
head in one continuing gesture, and headed for the bathroom. She'd
brush her teeth, throw a housecoat over the T-shirt—when had she
started wearing T-shirts to bed?—and wait calmly downstairs for
Scott to bring Robin home. But first she would phone Paul, she
decided, catching her reflection in the bathroom mirror. I SPENT THE
NIGHT WITH BURT REYNOLDS . . . her chest proudly proclaimed as
she squeezed the reluctant toothpaste out of its near-empty tube. She
squeezed too hard and the toothpaste ended up missing the bristles
of her brush entirely, plopping with a singular lack of grace into the
middle of her clean white sink. Joanne stared at the large blue glob
and made no move to wipe it up. "So I won't brush my teeth," she
said defiantly, and left the bathroom.

She sat on the bed, her hand on the phone for another ten
minutes. Would she be waking Paul up? Would he even be home?
Would he be impatient, tell her that this was precisely what he meant
when he said she should be handling things herself and not calling
him over every little problem? Could this be considered a little
problem? Would he be furious with her for disturbing him? Joanne
pulled the phone off its carriage and dialed Paul's number. Let him
be furious, she thought, listening to the phone ring. It rang once and
then was quickly picked up, as if he had been sitting right beside it, as
if he were expecting her call.

"Hello?" a strange voice answered. A woman's voice.

For an instant Joanne said nothing, convinced she must have
dialed the wrong number. She was about to hang up when the unfamiliar voice spoke again. "Did you want to speak to Paul?" it asked
pleasantly.

Joanne felt sick to her stomach. "Is he there?" she heard herself
ask.

"Well, he is," the girl giggled, "but he can't come to the phone at
the moment. Can I take a message?"

"Is this Judy?" Joanne heard her equally unfamiliar voice ask
after what felt like a very long time.

"Yes it is," the voice smiled broadly, obviously pleased to be recognized. "Who's this?"

Joanne let the receiver slide down her neck and drop gently into its carriage. "No!" she suddenly shouted, grabbing Paul's pillow off the bed and hurling it across the room before dropping on her knees to the floor, swaying her body back and forth, burying her outraged sobs in her bare thighs.

The phone rang.

Joanne jumped immediately to her feet. It was Paul. Judy had told him about the strange phone call and he had concluded that it could only be her. He would be angry. Well, so what if he was angry! she thought, bringing the phone to her ear. She was pretty angry herself.

"Mrs. Hunter," the voice teased unctuously, "you've been a naughty girl, haven't you, Mrs. Hunter? Playing around with your best friend's husband." The words held Joanne in an instant state of paralysis, the raspy voice so totally unexpected at this moment. He knew where she'd been! He was watching her! "You're going to have to be punished, Mrs. Hunter," the voice continued gleefully. "I'm going to have to punish you." There was a long, chilling pause.

"Oh God," Joanne moaned.

"I'm going to start by pulling down your panties and spanking you . . ."

"Go to hell!" Joanne shrieked and slammed the receiver down so hard that it bounced back up at her like a snake, and she was forced to slam it down a second time.

"Mom?" the frightened voice asked. Joanne spun around to see her younger daughter in the doorway watching her, eyes like saucers. "What's the matter? What are you doing?"

"I had an obscene call," Joanne answered quickly, her voice husky, her breathing rapid. "Didn't you hear the phone ring?" she asked, seeing the look of surprise that crossed Lulu's face.

Lulu shook her head. "I only heard you yelling."

Joanne sat for a minute on the floor, letting this statement sink in, before pushing herself to her feet.

"Sorry, I didn't mean to wake you up." Joanne escorted her sleepy, puzzled daughter back to her room. "Go back to sleep, sweetie. I'm sorry I woke you."

"Is Robin home yet?"

"Not yet."

"I thought at first you were yelling at her," Lulu explained, her eyes closing upon contact with her pillow. "It's so strange to hear you yell," she whispered.

Joanne returned to her bedroom, threw her bathrobe over her T-shirt, and clumped down the stairs to wait for her elder daughter to return home.

"Tell him to come in," Joanne said evenly as Robin was about to close the front door.

"You better come in," she heard Robin whisper to the young man behind her.

Scott Peterson shuffled inside and smiled innocently at Joanne. "Close the door," Joanne told him. She heard Robin take a deep breath. "Maybe we should go into the living room," she suggested and the silent couple reluctantly followed her inside. Joanne flipped on the light. "You can sit down if you'd like," she indicated, but no one moved. "I think you both know what this is about."

"The little tattle-tale," Robin immediately sneered, just loud enough to be clearly heard.

"Don't start blaming Lulu for this," Joanne cautioned.

"It wasn't anything . . ." Robin protested.

"And don't tell me it wasn't anything," her mother countered, her voice rising. What was she supposed to say next? She cleared her throat. Why wasn't Paul here to help her? "I don't want to argue with you," she said, her voice steady once again. "As far as I'm concerned there's nothing to argue about. I think I have a pretty clear picture of what happened. You can dispute me if anything I say is substantially wrong." That sounded fair, she decided, looking from her daughter to Scott Peterson, whose eyes were burning holes right through her. She wasn't invisible now, she thought, almost wishing she were. "Lulu said that you were in your room earlier this evening smoking . . . a joint . . . and that you offered her some." There, she congratulated herself, that was quite well done. Paul would be proud of the way she was handling this situation. She saw him nod his invisible approval from his place across the room.

"She had no business coming into my room," Robin was objecting loudly.

"I beg your pardon?" Joanne exclaimed, momentarily amazed at the sound of her own voice. "I beg your pardon?" she repeated as if to solidify it was in fact her own, watching the startled image of her husband rising in his best lawyerlike fashion to object. Keep it steady, he was telling her. Nobody wins any points in anger. "You don't think she had any business coming into your room?" Joanne repeated Robin's words with a sense of awe. The best defense is a good offense— her father's daughter, all right, she thought. Except where was her daughter's father now? Too damn busy with little blondes in their twenties to be available for such minor problems as this. Paul's image smiled sheepishly. A bosomy blonde appeared beside him. "You don't think she had any business coming into your room." Joanne's voice grew even louder.

"You don't have to say everything twice. We're not deaf."

"I'll say things as many times as I goddamn well please," Joanne heard someone shout—surely not herself! The blonde's arms went fearfully around Paul's waist. "And what's more you'll listen to every word till I'm damn well finished."

"Mom!"

"Mrs. Hunter, it's really not all that big a deal."

"You shut up!" Joanne shouted at the invisible blonde, though it was Robin's boyfriend who took a step back. "I'll decide what's a big deal around here. How dare you bring dope into this house!" How dare you bring this woman in here! "How dare you offer it to my children!" How dare she come before our children's welfare!

"Robin's not exactly a child, Mrs. Hunter. Nobody forced anything on her. She didn't have to take it."

"No," Joanne said with a sudden icy calmness, watching Paul's arm protectively circle the young blonde's shoulder, "and neither do I. Get the hell out of this house," she continued, her voice level rising steadily, "and don't you ever try to see my daughter again, because if you do and I find out about it, which I will, make no mistake, I'll have you arrested, do you understand me?" Paul turned his back to her question. "Have I made myself very clear?"

"Mom!"

"This is no idle threat," Joanne said, her voice steel as she watched her husband and his young friend disappear.

"Hell hath no fury like a mother hen," Scott Peterson quipped sarcastically, his body already angled toward the front door.

"Get out of my house," Joanne ordered, her body shaking with barely controlled rage.

"Gladly," the boy sneered, pushing past her, his bony shoulder catching the corner of hers. He opened the front door and walked out into the street without looking back.

"What have you done?" Robin shrieked. Joanne stared at her without speaking. She had nothing left to say. "You had no right to talk to him like that," Robin persisted.

"Please don't tell me my rights."

"Now he'll tell everyone I'm a kid!"

"That's what you are. And not a very bright one at that. What's the matter with you?" Joanne demanded, feeling her anger dissipate into helpless tears. "How could you be so stupid?"

"This is all Lulu's fault."

"This is all *your* fault."

"She didn't have to tell you."

"Really? What choice did you leave her? You didn't have to smoke the dope right under her nose. Were you looking to get caught?"

For once, Robin was silent. "So what happens now?" she asked after a long pause.

Joanne shrugged. "I'll have to talk to your father," she whispered, watching Judy reappear and wave to her from beside the fireplace.

"What? I didn't hear you."

"I said I'll have to talk to your father!" Joanne yelled, frightening the image away.

"All right, you don't have to bite my head off. I didn't hear you, that's all." Joanne lifted the palm of her hand to her forehead, closing her eyes against the feel of her flesh, trying to block out further unwanted visions. "Do you have to tell Daddy?"

Joanne nodded.

"Why do you have to?"

"Because he's your father and he has the right to know," Joanne answered simply, lowering her head.

"What rights does he have anymore?" Robin demanded.

"He's your father."

She heard Robin's sneer.

"We'll decide together the proper punishment," Joanne told her, watching Robin's eyes fill with tears. "In the meantime, until I can speak to him, you're grounded."

"What?"

"You heard me. No more dates, no more evenings out. When

you're not in school taking an exam, you're home studying for one. Do you understand?"

Robin said nothing, her body fidgeting nervously.

"Do you understand?"

"Yes," Robin snapped. "Can I go to bed now?"

"Go to bed," Joanne ordered simultaneously.

She stood in the middle of the now empty living room. "Well, I messed that one up pretty good," she said aloud to any ghosts that might still be listening. Then she walked to the front door, double-locked it, and pressed the bottom button of the alarm to trigger the system before retreating to the cold comfort of her empty bed.

She was dreaming.

She knew it was a dream because there were no conjunctions, no ands or buts or howevers to connect disparate thoughts. One minute she was standing outside her front door fumbling inside her purse for her keys, the next minute she was inside her kitchen breaking eggs into a large mixing bowl.

If you're making those for Paul, the blonde is telling her, don't bother. He hates lemon meringue pies, always has.

I'm not making them for Paul, Joanne says defiantly. I'm making them for me.

Selfish girl, you'll have to be punished, Eve's mother chastises, approaching and then disappearing, only her voice remaining, the Cheshire cat mistaking a middle-aged, brown-haired matron for Alice. Daughters are like that. You can never give them enough. Nothing you do is right for them. You try. You work your fingers to the bone, what do you get?

Bony fingers! the country-and-western singers on the radio respond in a burst of harmony.

Turn that down, Mom, I'm trying to study, Lulu wails from upstairs.

Sorry, sweetie, Joanne says quickly, these are noisy eggs.

In the next instant, she is swimming in the deep end of her pool. The water is warm; the day is sunny; her strokes are sure and swift. She is wearing a bathing suit she has never seen before, black with fluorescent orange suspenders, that hugs her barely pubescent body like a black elastic stocking. She has no breasts, narrow hips, and knees that knock together in adolescent awkwardness. When she smiles, she shows the braces on her teeth. She is smoking a strange cigarette that is making her dizzy, affecting her strokes. She wants to spit it out but it is caught in the wire of her braces. Besides, if she spits the dirty thing into the pool, Paul will be angry. They are paying good money for people to keep this pool clean. She looks up. One of the workers from Rogers Pools is standing above her, the skinny one with the dark hair who gives Lulu the creeps. You'll have to be punished, he tells her. I'm going to start by pulling down your panties and spanking you. He is bending over her, his hand reaching out to lift Joanne out of the blue water—blue, he says, like your eyes.

My eyes are hazel, she corrects him, feeling her child's body being pulled from the water, her knees scraping against the rough concrete as she is laid on her stomach against the rose-colored flag-stone. Actually, she continues, my toenails aren't really blue any-more. They're more purple now.

Picky, picky, Eve says, bending over Joanne, who is suddenly on her back. Eve's smile is wide, her eyes as sparkling as the chlorine of the water beside them.

Did I leave my keys at your house? Joanne asks. Eve says noth-ing, using a heavy pink towel to dry Joanne's legs. Why did you lie to me about your sex life? Joanne questions.

Who said I lied? Eve looks indignant.

Brian told me that you haven't made love in years.

Silly you, Eve admonishes, rubbing Joanne's legs forcefully. Don't you know that you can't believe a word Brian tells you? He's a terrible liar. She rubs so hard on Joanne's thigh that Joanne begins to bleed. Oh look, Eve laughs cruelly, you've got your period. Joanne stares down helplessly at the blood between her legs. Here's your key, Eve taunts, standing up and hurling the silver key chain into the deep end of the pool. Jump in, she laughs. The water's wonderful.

If Eve asked you to jump off the Brooklyn Bridge, she hears her mother ask, would you do it?

Joanne jumps.

From under the water, she hears the telephone ringing. She is drowning.

I'm going to start by pulling down your panties and spanking you, a voice calls to her from the other end of the pool. She turns to see someone swimming toward her, bubbles filling the distance be-tween them. She can't make out who it is. The blade of a long knife catches the reflection of the sun beneath the water. It blinds her. She no longer knows from which direction the swimmer is approaching.

Suddenly she feels arms surrounding her and the cold surface of the knife at her throat.

This is a dream, she reminds herself, forcing her eyes to open. This is a dream.

The telephone was still ringing when she opened her eyes. Joanne reached over, her body wet with sweat, and picked it up. What choice did she have? she thought dully. On Monday she would call the phone company and arrange for yet another number. In the meantime, she had no choice but to answer the damn thing. It could be the Baycrest Nursing Home, she reminded herself, knowing it wasn't. Or it could be Paul.

"I'm going to start," the dull raspy voice began as if it had never been interrupted, "by pulling down your panties and spanking you. And I'm going to stop," he continued, pausing for proper dramatic effect, "by killing you."

Joanne stood up, the phone still dangling from her hand, and walked to the bedroom window. She pulled back the curtains, and stared out at the empty concrete pool, struggling to make out the identity of the shadowy figure who was inexorably swimming toward her through the darkness.

Chapter 17

The phone is still ringing as Joanne Hunter picks herself up off the bottom of the deep end of her empty, aborted swimming pool and heads back inside the house. The girls have left for camp. For the first time in her life, she is completely alone. She has the house to herself. She is expecting no one. She glances at the phone. It's just you and me now, he is telling her.

Ignoring the persistent ringing, Joanne pours herself a large glass of skim milk. She has been drinking a lot of milk lately, ever since Eve told her that women require more calcium than men in order to keep their bones supple and prevent shrinkage in old age. She laughs and some of the milk escapes the sides of her mouth. The image of herself as a slaughtered corpse tossed across the rose-colored flagstone at the side of her pool returns. She won't have to worry about her old age, she thinks, finishing the last of the milk, catching the reflection of her grandfather in the pearl-gray coating the milk leaves at the bottom of her glass. At least her children will be spared her senility, she thinks, congratulating herself on always being able to see the bright side of any situation. Perhaps she should get an answering service, she thinks, then dismisses the consideration. She has told Paul that the phone calls have stopped. She doesn't want to arouse his suspicions by hiring a service. Besides, it would make no difference—he has already told her that. The phone stops ringing.

The house is now completely still, as quiet as it has ever felt, although Joanne has been alone in the house before. But that was different, she understands, because that was temporary. A few hours perhaps, never more than a day. There was always someone to answer to, something to answer for. Now there is no one. She has no schedule. She has nothing, she thinks, shuffling into the living room in her bare feet and plopping down on the large, comfortable sofa she and Paul purchased together only four years ago. Her body is immediately surrounded by the warm sunlight that streaks through the thin venetian blinds of the room's southerly bay windows. She has recently handwashed these slivers of white metal blinds, just as she has cleaned the various floor surfaces until they shine, dusted the wood furniture until her reflection appears, vacuumed the carpets until they look new, and polished the silverware until her hands were sore. Her freezer is stacked with baked goods—in case Paul decides to bring a few people home after her funeral, she laughs sardonically, wondering when she has developed this decidedly black sense of humor.

Karen Palmer has suggested to Joanne that she do some traveling; go to Europe, she has suggested. But Joanne has always dreamed of seeing Europe with Paul, and the idea of going off on her own does not appeal to her. She likes to share, to have someone to talk to at the end of the day, to laugh with over pizza or french fries, to help her see things she might have missed on her own. She believes that to try to escape her loneliness by escaping to a foreign country will only succeed in making her lonelier still.

She has mentioned the possibility of a trip to Eve. Not the entire summer, of course, two weeks only, the two of them, a girls' holiday, perhaps no farther than Washington or the mountains. But Eve has a string of doctors' appointments that take her through the end of August, and besides, she is in no shape to travel, she has told Joanne. It's all she can do to get out of bed.

There is no one else Joanne would like to travel with, no one she feels close to except her family and her oldest friend. Now that friend is sick and her family is gone. Joanne wonders how the girls will like camp this summer, how Robin, in particular, will get along. She worries whether or not the decision to send Robin to camp was the right one and decides that there is no point now in having second thoughts. What's done is done, she tells herself. Visitors' Day is in four weeks; she will have some idea then of the correctness of their choice. If she is still around, she thinks, pressing the back of her head against the sofa. "Who'd have thought?" she asks aloud, trying to decide what to do with the rest of the day.

She could go to the club, she thinks, but what is the point? She thinks of Steve Henry. She has canceled her last two lessons, unwilling or unable to deal with the suggestiveness of his recent remarks. What does he want with her anyway?

He has obviously heard that she has separated from her husband and perhaps decided she will be an easy mark. The lonely middle-aged divorcée. Easier to please than the young ones coming up. Grateful as opposed to judgmental, delighted instead of demanding.

The phone begins ringing again. Joanne jumps as she does every time she hears the once welcome sound. She has changed her number twice, and still he has found her. There was a brief, seven-day respite—one week when she felt her body relaxing, her fears subsiding—and then the calls started again, angrier and nastier, if such a thing were possible, than before. Does she think she can escape him so easily? he demands. Does she think she is dealing with such a fool? Change your number as often as you please, he taunts her, hire an answering service. I'll still find you.

Joanne returns to the kitchen, standing in front of the phone until it stops its shrill cry. Then she picks up the receiver and quickly dials Eve's number. Eve answers immediately, as if she has been expecting Joanne to call.

"How are you?" Joanne asks.

"The usual," Eve answers, her voice rife with annoyance at her condition. "Did the girls get off okay?"

"Paul drove them to the bus this morning. They're probably halfway to camp by now."

"Robin give you any trouble?"

"No." She pictures Robin on the stairs, bracing her body against her mother's kiss. "Actually, I think she's relieved to be going, although I don't think she would admit it. I just hope we're doing the right thing," she continues, aware that she has already decided not to have second thoughts.

"Sure you are," Eve says quickly, surprising Joanne, who sensed that Eve wasn't really listening. "A few months in the country, all that fresh air, lots of other kids, plenty of adult supervision . . ."

"I hope you're right."

"Have I ever been wrong?"

"Do you feel like going for a walk?" Joanne laughs. "I need to get out of the house."

"Are you kidding? I couldn't get as far as the corner."

"Come on," Joanne pleads. "It'll do you good. It'll do *me* good," she corrects immediately.

"My good deed for the day?"

"I'll meet you outside in five minutes," Joanne tells her and hangs up before Eve can change her mind.

"So, what tests are scheduled for this week?" Joanne and Eve are circling their block for the third time. They have already discussed the weather forecast—continuing sunny skies—and the current state of Joanne's toenails—continuing purple—which leads to talk of tennis which leads to talk of Steve Henry which leads to Joanne's question about which tests Eve is scheduled to undergo in the coming week.

"You're avoiding the issue," Eve tells her.

"There's nothing to say," Joanne answers. "What's the point of expensive tennis lessons when I have nobody to play with? When you get better, we'll start the lessons together again. I don't see what's the big deal."

"Steve Henry's the big deal. And he's yours for the taking. All you have to do is reach out and grab him."

"I don't want him."

"Wait a minute," Eve says, stopping dead in her tracks and hitting the palm of her hand against the side of her ear. "There must be something wrong with my hearing now too. I actually thought I heard you say that you didn't want Steve Henry." She laughs, then turns to face her friend, eyes wide, hands on Joanne's shoulders. "Please tell me that you didn't say that." Joanne laughs and shakes her head. "Why not, for God's sake? And please don't give me that depressing crap about your being a married woman."

"I love Paul," Joanne whispers. What else is there to say?

"So?"

"So, I don't love Steve Henry."

"Nobody's asking you to love the man. Who said anything about love, for God's sake? It's probably the last thing on Steve Henry's mind. Not that you aren't infinitely lovable, of course."

"Can we please talk about something else?"

Eve is silent.

"You still haven't told me what tests you're scheduled for this week." Joanne slows down when she notices that Eve's pace has slackened.

"Monday, there's the gynecologist . . ."

"You've already seen three gynecologists."

"This is another one."

"You think that's necessary?"

"Tuesday," Eve continues, ignoring Joanne's question, "is a series of tests at St. Francis cardiac hospital. And Thursday is an appointment with a dermatologist in Roslyn, Dr. Ronald Gold, I think his name is, no wait, that's next Thursday, this Thursday it's some X-rays at the Jewish Medical Center."

"You're being very ecumenical."

"I'm giving everybody a chance."

"Why a dermatologist?"

Eve stops, rolling back the hair from her face with the back of her hand. "For God's sake, Joanne, look at me. I'm green!"

"You never had a peaches-and-cream complexion," Joanne reminds her gently.

"No, but I never looked like moldy bread either."

"You still don't," Joanne laughs. "I think you look pretty good. A little pale maybe . . ."

"Love is blind." She rubs her forehead. "Look at this."

"Look at what?"

"This flaking! And look at this." She holds out her hands, palms down.

"What am I supposed to be looking at?"

"The veins, for God's sake!"

Joanne sees some perfectly ordinary blue veins protruding from beneath Eve's semitranslucent skin. "What's wrong with them?" Joanne asks, displaying her own hands.

Eve takes a long look. "Oh," she says, "your veins are bigger than mine."

"It's a very exotic condition," Joanne tells her. "It's called middle age."

"Can middle age also account for the way everything in my body is drying up on me?"

"Like what? What are you talking about?"

"I'm talking about the fact that there is no wax in my ears anymore, no mucus in my nose."

"What do you mean? How do you know?"

"What do *you* mean—how do I know? I checked. How else would I know?"

"What do you mean you checked?" Joanne asks. "You sit around picking your ears and your nose?"

"That's just the point. There's nothing to pick!"

"Eve, don't you think there's something faintly ridiculous about this conversation?"

"Look, Joanne," Eve pleads, her voice peppered with invisible italics, "I don't know *what's* the matter with me. Maybe I *am* acting a little peculiar. Maybe I'm grasping at some pretty far-out straws. But something is happening to me," she reiterates for what Joanne feels is the thousandth time. "Something is happening to my body. Nothing works properly. I'm in constant pain. And nobody can tell me what's the matter. I know my body, Joanne. I know what's normal for me and what isn't."

"Take it easy," Joanne advises, trying to calm Eve down, her arm encircling her friend's waist. "Somebody's going to figure all this out soon enough. I promise." Eve smiles, her body relaxing against Joanne's arm. "You said you're seeing a Dr. Ronald Gold?"

"A week from Thursday. Why?"

"We went to school with a boy named Ronald Gold, remember?" Eve shakes her head. "I wonder if he's the same one."

"He must have been short if I don't remember him," Eve quips. They have completed their fourth circle around the block and are back in front of their respective homes. "I think I'd better go inside now," Eve says.

"More pains?"

"Same ones. It feels like . . . like someone is tightening a belt around my ribs, like something . . . I don't know . . . is *sticking* to them. I can't explain it. The more I try, the crazier it sounds. Brian thinks I'm off my rocker. He wants me to see a psychiatrist."

"Maybe that's not such a bad idea," Joanne says, catching the look of animosity in Eve's eyes. "Just to help you deal with it," Joanne explains hastily.

"I don't want to deal with it," Eve informs her curtly. "I want to get rid of it." She looks toward her house. "Look, sorry. I didn't mean to snap at you. But this isn't exactly your area, and it's not the kind of advice I need from you. Believe me, if I thought I needed a psychiatrist, I would be the first person to go to one. Look, just stick with me, huh? Be my friend. Please."

"I *am* your friend."

"I know," Eve agrees. "Going to visit your grandfather this afternoon?"

Joanne nods.

"Give the old guy a kiss from me," Eve instructs as Joanne watches her friend slowly pull herself up the outside steps and disappear inside her front door. Then, taking a second glance at the large veins protruding from the back of her hands, Joanne heads for home.

The phone is ringing when she walks through her front door several hours later. "Oh, shit!" Joanne yells angrily in its direction, surprised by her easy use of the profanity. "Enough!" she states emphatically, marching toward it, watching it ring, not picking it up. Has he been following her? Is it a coincidence that he is calling at the precise moment that she has walked in the house, that he seems aware of her every move?

Joanne picks up the receiver on its fifth ring. "Why are you doing this?" she says instead of hello.

There is a slight pause, then, "Joanne?" the voice asks.

"Paul!"

"Who did you think it was?"

Joanne tries to laugh. "I don't know," she tells him, so glad to hear his voice.

"I thought you said you weren't getting any more of those funny calls."

Joanne isn't sure how to answer him. He hasn't phoned to discuss this particular problem. He has made it quite clear on previous occasions how he feels about this issue. For whatever reason he is calling —and Joanne is sure it is to tell her that the girls got away safely—it is not to be pulled into any unpleasantness. She doesn't want to put him off by telling him the truth, that nothing has changed, except possibly for the worse. She doesn't want him to think that she is appealing to his guilt, trying to bind him to her. Ironic, she thinks, that the only chance she has of getting him back is by proving to him that she doesn't need him back. Especially now, when she needs him more than ever.

"Joanne, are you still getting those threatening calls?" he asks again.

"No," she says quickly. "Just someone pestering me about some theater subscription."

He accepts the lie easily. "That's good. I called you earlier—you were out."

"I went for a walk. Then I went to see my grandfather. Did the girls get off okay?"

"Everything proceeded exactly on schedule, smooth as a whistle."

"Did Robin say anything?"

"Just goodbye. I have to tell you it was all I could do to keep from shaking her."

"That would have gone over big with the other parents in the parking lot."

"You'd be surprised," he laughs. "I got the feeling I wasn't the only father entertaining such thoughts." Joanne can feel him smiling. He says nothing, but Joanne senses a reluctance on his part to terminate the conversation. "They're really growing up," he finally exclaims, a sense of wonder in his words, and Joanne nods agreement. "You remember what it was like on your first day of camp?" he asks suddenly.

"I never went to camp," she reminds him. "We had the cottage."

"Oh yeah, that's right. Do you think the girls missed something by our not having a cottage?" he asks after a slight pause, and Joanne finds herself staring into their backyard, at their empty, unfinished "cottage without the traffic." Would it have made a difference?

"The girls have always enjoyed camp," she tells him, not sure what else to say, wondering where this conversation is headed. Is he feeling at loose ends the same way she is now that the girls have left?

"They better enjoy it for what it's costing!" he exclaims. "It's like going to an exclusive resort for two months. Not like when I went. We slept in sleeping bags in tents, for God's sake."

"You did not. I've seen the photographs of you at camp, of your beautiful log cabins, and I remember your mother's same complaints about what it cost to send you, and all the expensive equipment you needed."

He laughs loudly and easily. "I guess you're right. I must have been thinking about the canoe trips."

"Which you always hated because there were so many bugs . . ."

"Not to mention those damn canoes."

There is another long pause. "Paul . . . ?" Joanne asks, breaking the silence, then lapsing back into it.

"Yes?" he asks.

Is he waiting for her to make the first move? To be the one to suggest that they get together? Is that what he wants? It's what *she* wants, she realizes, wondering what would be the best way to phrase such a request. Would you like to come over and talk? she hears herself ask, though the question remains unvoiced. Do you want to come home? Is that what you want me to say? God knows I want to say it. Yet something stops her—the certain knowledge that should she do so, he will turn her down, as he has done in the past. Help me, please, she thinks, looking at the ceiling. Tell me what to say to this man to whom I have been married for twenty years and thought I could say anything to.

Her mind is a maze of confused thoughts and images. She sees her husband sitting at their kitchen table drinking his morning coffee and grumbling about office politics. She feels him beside her, his breath warm against the back of her neck, his arms encircling her waist. Then she feels another pair of arms around her throat, hears the familiar dull rasp at her ear.

"Joanne?" Paul is asking.

"Yes, sorry, did you say something?"

"No. You started to ask me something."

"Do I have any life insurance?" she asks, the question catching her by surprise probably as much as it does him.

There is a moment's silence. "No," he answers. "But *I* have plenty. Why?"

"I think I should have some."

"Sure," he agrees quickly, "if you'd like. I could make an appointment for you with Fred Normandy."

"I'd appreciate that, thank you. I guess I should let you go now."

"Joanne?" he asks.

"Yes?"

Silence, then, almost tentatively, "Are you busy tonight?"

She is more nervous than at any moment in her entire life, more nervous than when they had their first date, if this is possible. She has been getting ready for two hours. She has soaked herself raw in the bathtub, polished and repolished her nails, washed her hair, set it, then combed it out only to reset it again and wet it yet a third time. She is still trying to decide what to do with it as she checks her reflection in the bathroom mirror.

She looks frightened, she thinks, lifting her arms to apply some deodorant, flapping them up and down in the air like a crazed chicken in an effort to dry them, her breasts bobbing restlessly in her new white lace brassiere, the one she raced out this afternoon to buy, the kind that clasps in the front. So much easier, she thinks. Why hasn't she bought this kind before? And the panties, delicate silk bikinis with a soft pink ribbon lacing through the top elastic. They make her feel pretty, she realizes, deciding to buy more next week, despite their exorbitant price.

You've been a bad girl, she hears a cruel voice whispering in her ear, invisible eyes traveling the length of her body, unseen fingers snapping at her new purchases. You'll have to be punished. I'm going to start by pulling down your panties . . . "Well," she states, curtly dismissing the voice with the sound of her own, "at least these will give you something pretty to pull down."

She spins around, wondering if the men's magazine she came across several months ago is still in the cabinet or whether Paul took it with him, deciding not to look. Either way, it would only depress her. Not simply that she can't measure up, this goes without saying. Even twenty years ago, she would have provided these models with no serious competition. No, what depresses her about such magazines is the eagerness of grown men to purchase them and the seemingly endless supply of young women ready to pose for them.

She pictures Robin and Lulu several years from now, over eighteen, old enough legally to pose for such pictures without written parental consent. Would they? Would they consider it a debasement or a privilege to be asked? Once, Joanne thinks, studying her reflection, we were allowed to grow old. Now there is no excuse for age. There is no room for it.

"What the hell is that?" she asks suddenly, her nose pressing against the glass of the mirror. "A pimple?" She backs away from the reality of what she sees. "It can't be a pimple!" She stares at the center of her cheek in a kind of awe. *"Now* you have to come out?" she demands aloud, wondering if there is anything in all her makeup tubes that will disguise the unsightly blemish. Now she knows how Robin feels when pimples appear just minutes before a scheduled date, how empty her words of assurance—don't worry, darling, he won't notice—really are. Of course he'll notice! How could he help but notice?! "I can't believe I have a pimple," she mutters, and is still muttering the same thing when she hears the doorbell ring a half hour later and realizes that she is still in her underwear and has yet to do anything with her hair.

Chapter 18

"I like your hair."

"You're kidding!"

They are sitting by the window of a lovely, even romantic, restaurant in Long Beach, overlooking the Atlantic Ocean. The room is dimly lit, the ocean crashes rhythmically against the rocks below them—just like in the movies, she thinks—a flickering candle separates their nervous hands. The evening has been a quiet one. Joanne has taken great pains to let her husband initiate all conversation, to speak only when spoken to, to steer clear of any topics that might produce in him even vague feelings of anxiety. Show him you're interested in what he has to say, she remembers her mother advising her as a young girl, as she has advised her own daughters. Is it really such bad advice? she wonders. I *am* interested in what he has to say. He's saying he likes my hair, she realizes as he says it again.

"No, really, I think it's great. I meant to tell you that this morning when I picked up the girls." Joanne's hand moves automatically to smooth her hair down. "No, don't do that." Joanne immediately drops her hand to her lap. "It has a kind of . . . I don't know . . . carefree abandon . . . to it like that."

Joanne laughs. "That's me . . . carefree and abandoned." There is silence as the full weight of what she has just said hits her. "I honestly didn't mean to say that." Her voice disappears into a whisper, all her cautious dialogue destroyed by one careless phrase.

"That's okay," he is saying, and Joanne realizes he is on the verge of laughing. "Actually, it was a pretty funny remark." His voice is suddenly serious. "One I deserve, at any rate."

Joanne says nothing. What is he leading up to? I'm sorry? Forgive me? If you let me come home, I'll spend the rest of my life making things up to you?

"I'm not ready to come home yet," he says instead. "I had to say that now because I don't want to mislead you . . ."

"I understand."

"I want to be honest."

"I appreciate that."

"I love you, Joanne."

"I love you, too." Please don't cry, she tells herself. The man is telling you he loves you. Don't spoil it by crying.

"Please don't cry," he tells her.

"I'm sorry, I didn't mean to." Stop this damn crying.

"I know this is hard on you." She shakes her head, dislodging several tears. "I've been doing a lot of thinking about us, about our situation . . ."

The waiter approaches and inquires whether or not they would like to order dessert now. Joanne shakes her head, and stares resolutely into her lap. There is no way she can eat anything without risking the decidedly unromantic gesture of throwing up.

"Two coffees," Paul tells him as Joanne surreptitiously wipes her eyes with her napkin. "Did I tell you that I like your dress?" Paul asks suddenly, and Joanne has to look down to remind herself what she is wearing. "Is it new?"

"No," Joanne says, fidgeting with one of the front buttons. "I bought it last summer. I just never wore it because it's linen and it creases so easily."

"It's supposed to crease."

"Yes, that's what the saleslady told me."

"White's a good color for you. It shows off your tan."

Joanne's hand moves from the button to her face. "It's makeup," she tells him, feeling self-conscious. Should she have told him that? Paul is not a fan of makeup. There is another awkward silence. The waiter returns with two cups of coffee, placing them on the table and then discreetly disappearing.

"I need more time," he continues as if there had been no interruptions. "There's so much on my plate right now . . ."

"You mean at work?"

He nods. "I can't seem to get out from under."

"In what way?"

"I'm not sure I can explain it. It's not just the work load. I can handle the work load. I mean, I'm busy. I'm too damn busy. But then I've always been too damn busy. It's just that I'm so *tired* all the time. No matter how much sleep I get, it doesn't seem to make any difference."

Just how much sleep has little Judy been letting you get? Joanne wonders but doesn't ask. Instead she says, "Have you seen a doctor?"

"I had Phillips do a complete check, even took a stress test. Basically, I'm in pretty good shape for a man my age. My heart rate is good, my blood pressure is fine. I should exercise more, he told me, so I've started working out a bit."

"I noticed."

He checks his arms, now hidden under the light blue jacket he is wearing. "What do you think?" he asks shyly, a hint of pride in the edges of his voice.

Joanne shrugs and giggles, feeling like a silly schoolgirl. "You once told me that you could never develop muscles," she tells him, watching his smile grow.

"What? What are you talking about?"

"You once told me that the reason your arms were so thin was because when you were a boy, you fell and broke them a few times, and as a result, they never developed the way most boys' arms did."

"I didn't tell you that," he protests, the smile in his eyes betraying his words.

"Yes, you did."

"Well, I did break my arms a couple of times, that part's true, but that doesn't have anything to do with muscles." He takes a sip of his coffee. "I told you that, did I?"

"That's one of the things that made me fall in love with you," Joanne says quietly, not sure whether she has been too bold, gone too far. He regards her quizzically. "It was the one chink in the armor," she explains, deciding she might as well go all the way. He seems interested, even flattered by the unexpected admission. "You were always so sure of everything you did, everything you wanted to do. And you were so handsome . . . *are,*" she corrects, then returns immediately to the more comfortable past, "but you had no muscles, and I thought that was kind of strange. Most boys your age had *some* kind of muscles, and one day, I guess we must have been talking about it, because that's when you told me about your falling and breaking your arms several times when you were a youngster. And you suddenly seemed so vulnerable that I started to fall in love with you." She smiles widely. "And now you're telling me that it wasn't true!" Their eyes fasten on each other, each seeing a reflection of their youth in the other's eyes. Joanne quickly looks down into her coffee.

"So, I was always so sure of myself, was I?" he asks, not wanting to let go of their former selves.

"Always."

"Pretty obnoxious, I guess."

"I liked it. I was always the opposite."

"You never gave yourself enough credit. You still don't."

"That's what Eve's always telling me."

Paul finishes the coffee in his cup and signals to the waiter for a refill.

"What are you thinking about?" Joanne ventures, catching a look of fleeting bewilderment in his eyes.

"That I used to think I'd be the new Clarence Darrow," he admits with a laugh.

"And you've discovered you're not?"

He shakes his head. "Not even close."

"Is that such a bad thing?" He leans back in his chair, looking out at the ocean. "Do you remember what my mother always used to tell me?" Joanne asks, suddenly remembering. "She used to quote that phrase from *Hamlet*—'this above all, to thine own self be true.'" Joanne sinks back in her seat, wondering why, of all her mother's favorite sayings, this is the one phrase she has lost sight of. "What's wrong with being Paul Hunter? You're a good lawyer, Paul."

"I'm an excellent lawyer," he corrects her, managing not to sound boastful.

"Then what's the problem? A shortage of wrongs to right?"

He smiles. "Maybe that's it, I don't know." He seems to be searching the room for the right words, then returns his gaze to Joanne when he thinks he has found them. "They tell you in law school that not everyone you'll represent will be innocent. They also tell you that it isn't part of your job to determine innocence or guilt. A judge and jury do that. The lawyer's sole responsibility is to provide his or her client with the best possible defense. What they don't tell you, or maybe they do, maybe you just don't hear it with all that youthful idealism ringing in your ears, is that the practice you build up ultimately reflects your own personality, that you tend to attract clients who, in perhaps more ways than you care to admit, are very much like yourself. I'm not explaining this very well . . ."

"I think you are."

"A lot of the people that come into my office . . . I don't know," he stumbles, then starts again, "Sometimes you're really proud of the

things you do, I mean, there are things I've done in my career that
I'm proud of because I know that no one could have done them
better, but there are also times when you'll get a client who you know
is lying through his teeth, and you're supposed to get up there and
defend this jerk . . ."

"Even when you know he's lying."

"Well, yes and no," Paul backtracks. "If you're convinced he's
lying, then the answer is no, because there's no way you could be
providing him with the best possible defense he's entitled to under
the law. But it's easy enough to tell yourself that you could be wrong,
that you're not the judge and jury, that hell, the jerk *might* be telling
the truth, especially if there's a nice fat fee attached."

"Is that what you've been doing?"

"I don't know." He finishes his second cup of coffee. "That's one
of the things I've been trying to sort out."

"Maybe you could switch to some other area."

"Like what? Real estate? Divorce? Joanne, I'm a first-class litiga-
tion lawyer. I come to court better prepared than three-quarters of
the guys out there, which is why I usually win, and one of the reasons
I'm so busy. When I was a kid I actually thought that the greatest
thing in the world would be defending the American way in a court
of law."

"And it isn't?"

"It is. I just didn't realize how much other shit would be involved."

"What other . . . shit?" Joanne asks, taking a quick sip of her
coffee.

He shakes his head. "Let's talk about something else."

"Why?"

"Why?" he repeats. "Because this can't be very interesting for
you."

"But it is," Joanne tells him truthfully. "It's something we never
talked about before, and I think it's important."

"I never liked bringing my work home with me."

"Your work, no, but how you felt about it is important for me to
know. Please tell me. What . . . shit?"

Paul releases a deep breath of air. "We're having problems with a
couple of the partners . . . they don't like the way the firm is being
run, they want to get rid of McNamara."

"Why?"

"They say he's being too easy on some of the less successful partners."

"Is he?"

"Maybe. Look, we're talking about a major Wall Street legal firm, not some little law office in the middle of nowhere. This is the big leagues. You want to be successful, you have to produce. Of course it's high pressure. What else could it be?"

"Are you starting to feel that pressure?"

"I *thrive* on that pressure. At least, I used to." He laughs. "I guess this is what they refer to as a typical mid-life crisis. How come our parents never had mid-life crises?"

"They didn't know they were supposed to," Joanne says and they laugh. Joanne is aware that she has said two things tonight that have made him laugh. She also realizes that it is the first time that they have laughed together in a long while. "Do you remember the first time you took me to a Broadway play?" she asks, not sure what has put this thought into her head. "I'd always wanted to go on one of those horse and buggy rides through Central Park and I was going on about it after the play until you finally picked up the hint and offered to take me on one." He starts to laugh, obviously remembering. "I will never forget looking over at you halfway into that ride," she recalls, "and seeing the tears in your eyes, and thinking, my God, he's so sensitive, so romantic . . ."

"So allergic . . ." he interjects.

"And you ended up spending the rest of the weekend in bed. Why didn't you tell me you were allergic to horses?"

"I didn't want to spoil it for you."

"And then your mother bawled me out, told me I should take better care of you."

"She should have told you to run away as fast as you could."

"Too late. I was already in love."

"With my allergies and skinny arms," he says, and Joanne nods agreement. "And I always assumed it was my fine mind and good looks that did the trick."

"Funny the things we fall in love with," Joanne states, as Paul signals for the waiter that they are ready to leave.

"I don't think I should come in," he says at the doorway to their house. Joanne nods, though she has been just about to ask otherwise.

"Not that I don't want to," he adds quickly. "It's just that I don't think it would be a good idea."

"I agree," Joanne whispers softly.

"First night alone," he comments, as she fumbles in her purse for her keys.

"I have to get used to it sometime, I guess. I'm a big girl now." She triumphantly produces her set of keys.

"New key chain?"

"I lost my other set," she tells him, fitting the key into the lock. "Can you imagine? I have all the locks changed and then I go and lose the stupid things. I thought I left them at Eve's, but she swears I didn't. She says her mother searched the entire house and couldn't find them, so I don't know. I had a locksmith over but he said it would cost a fortune to change all the locks again, especially with the deadbolts, and since there's no way of telling whose keys they are, no address on them or anything, I decided not to bother. I have the alarm in case someone ever tried to get in," she adds reluctantly, pushing open the door and moving quickly to the alarm box in the front hallway, pressing down the appropriate buttons. The green light at the bottom of the box goes out, indicating the alarm has been turned off. "I'm nervous every time I do that," she tells him.

"You do it very well," he smiles. Joanne stares at him expectantly from the other side of the doorway. Was he going to kiss her good night? Should she let him? Is it all right to kiss on your first date when the date in question is your husband of twenty years? "I had a lovely evening, Joanne," he says, transporting her back through time, and Joanne can see that he means it, that he is not saying this simply to make her feel good.

"So did I."

"Thank you."

"For what?"

"For listening. It appears I really needed someone to talk to."

"I'm always here," she tells him as a little voice inside her chants, that's it, Joanne, play hard to get.

"I'd like to do it again," he tells her, and Joanne is about to ask when, but stops herself. "I'll call you." He leans forward to kiss her lightly on the cheek.

I love you, she mouths silently after him as she watches him climb into his car and pull away from the curb.

It is almost ten o'clock when Joanne opens her eyes the next morning. It takes her several seconds to come fully awake, to remember that she is alone, that the girls are away at camp. They have probably already finished their breakfast and are busy in their morning activity by now, she thinks, mildly curious as to what that activity is, wondering in the next instant what Paul is doing, whether he is awake yet. She has to stop herself from being too optimistic, from reading too much into the things he said last night. She must force herself to remember that Paul has told her he still isn't ready to come home, that although he has admitted he loves her, that he enjoyed being with her, he still needs more time.

She sits up in bed and stretches, despite her admonitions feeling good about the future for the first time in months. Paul will come home, she tells herself, pulling off her covers and swinging her feet off the side of the bed. It's just a question of time, and she will give him as much as he needs. In return, he has given her hope.

She walks to the bedroom window, aware of the slight stiffness in her joints as the sun beckons her from behind the curtains. Another nice day, she thinks, pulling back the curtain and staring into her back yard.

He is standing by the side of the pool. Tall, skinny, his curly dark hair reaching several inches past his shirt collar, his hands propped insolently on his waist, his back to her, he stands on the rose-colored flagstone he has helped to lay and stares down into the large empty pit he has helped to create. What is he doing here? she wonders, releasing her hold on the curtain and pulling her body back against the wall, feeling her breath heavy against her chest.

She runs immediately into her closet and pulls on a pair of baggy cotton pants, tucking the T-shirt she has slept in inside it, forgetting that she is braless until she is already halfway down the steps, seeing the outlines of her nipples bounce against the pale pink of her shirt. She debates running back up the stairs, decides against it, and continues down the steps and into the kitchen, realizing only as she approaches the sliding glass door that she has no idea what she is going to do once she gets there. What exactly is she hurrying toward? Is she planning to confront this man? Is this some sort of showdown? Hey you, in my backyard, have you been calling me? Are you here to kill me? What are you doing here? Better still, what am *I* doing here?

She takes several steps back from the sliding glass door but it is too late. He has already seen her. He smiles at her from his position beside the pool. He is waiting for her, she realizes, to come to him. Slowly, as if in a trance, Joanne unlocks the Charley-bar and releases the lock at the side of the door. She slides the door open, realizing only in that instant exactly what she has done, remembering that she has forgotten to turn off the alarm, knowing that it is already too late. The alarm has begun its shrill shriek, racing through the neighborhood on its way to the nearest police station.

Joanne doesn't know whether to feel angry or relieved. This is the third time she has set off a false alarm—this time she will be fined twenty-five dollars. But at least she'll be alive to pay it, she thinks, growing bolder, stepping out onto the back porch to face her grinning adversary. Surely he wouldn't be stupid enough to try anything now.

His grin widens as she approaches. "Forgot to shut it off?" he asks, though he obviously knows the answer.

"I turn it on every night before I go to bed," she tells him—warns him? "What are you doing here?"

"I was driving by," he answers easily, dropping his hands to his sides. "I thought I'd take a look and see if anything further had been done."

"Not a thing." Joanne wonders whether this conversation is really taking place. Possibly it is a dream. It has that quality, she thinks, the sirens wailing around her. She should go inside, she knows, and turn the alarm off. But it is her insurance and she decides to leave it on. The police will come now whether she shuts it off or not, and once again they will shake their heads at finding her alive.

"I feel real bad about that," the man says, ignoring the alarm, not in any hurry to leave. "We were doing such a good job. I was feeling real proud of this one." He looks around. "Don't always feel that way. Sometimes the pools we install aren't very interesting, the people got no imagination, but this one was a little different, with the boomerang and all at the deep end. I woulda liked to see it finished."

"I take it Rogers Pools is still bankrupt?" Even as she says this, Joanne feels the silliness of her words. Why is she out here talking to this man? Why is he here? Was he really just driving by? Did he really just want to check on the pool's condition?

"I don't know anything about Rogers Pools," he says. "I'm just a freelancer; I get contracted out to all sorts of different companies. Who knows, I might even be back here with some other outfit when you get around to finishing it. I hope so." He winks. "Doesn't look like you'll get much use out of it this summer." Once more, his eyes encompass his surroundings. Is he getting a better feel for the layout of the house? Joanne wonders. "Shame," he continues, "they say it's going to be a hot one." He smiles and shows a mouth of crowded teeth. Joanne shifts uneasily in her bare feet, unwittingly drawing attention to them. "What happened to your toes?" he asked.

"I played tennis in shoes that were too small," she tells him, almost convinced now that she is dreaming.

He looks at the sky and then shakes his head. "You should take better care of yourself," he tells her. Seconds later, he is gone. It is another fifty minutes before the police arrive.

Chapter 19

"You're late," Eve's mother tells her as Joanne steps inside the front door of Eve's house.

Joanne checks her watch. "Just five minutes," she says, determined not to feel guilty. "Where's Eve?"

"I sent her back upstairs to lie down." The implication is unavoidable—why should Eve have to suffer because her friend is irresponsible?—but Joanne says nothing, having learned long ago that this is the best way to deal with Eve's mother. "Eve," her mother calls up the stairs, "your friend finally got here."

"Really, Mother," Eve exclaims as she appears on the steps, "don't you think you're being just a touch heavy-handed?"

"Sure, stick up for each other," her mother says as Joanne and Eve exchange knowing glances. "And don't give me those smiles that you think I can't see," she further admonishes as the two women disappear out the front door. "Drive carefully," she calls after them.

"Oh, I forgot my *People* magazine," Eve says as they climb into Joanne's car. "You know how these doctors always make you wait with nothing to read but *Field and Stream.*"

"Do you want to go back and get it?"

Eve regards her mother standing in the doorway, her small, squat frame a formidable barrier to the inside of the house. "I don't think my poor frail body could take it."

"How long is she staying this time?" Joanne pulls the car out of the driveway.

"I think until I either get better or pass on." The two women laugh as Joanne pulls the car onto the street, seeing Eve's mother wince from the doorway. "There, did you see that?"

"See what?"

"That slight stiffening of her shoulders, the pulling back of her lips, the brave smile through it all even though she obviously thinks you're a terrible driver who'll likely kill her baby before we've even turned the corner. I tell you that woman missed her calling."

"She should have been an actress?"

"She should have been queen."

"If you find her so upsetting, why don't you just tell her to go back to her own apartment?"

Eve shrugs. "I don't have the strength to argue with her anymore. And frankly, since she moved her luggage in two weeks ago, the house has never looked so clean. She cooks, she does the laundry, she even does windows! Good help is hard to find these days. And you can't beat the price."

"I don't know," Joanne observes, thinking that the price might be too high. "How does Brian feel about having her around all the time?"

"I think he's relieved," Eve says. "He doesn't have to feel guilty about never being home himself. And when he does come home, there's always a hot meal waiting for him. I wouldn't be surprised if, after I die, he marries my mother. Stranger things have happened, you know."

"You're not going to die."

"That's what everybody keeps telling me."

"But you don't believe them?"

"I believe what my body is telling me." Joanne is about to say something reassuring when Eve stops her. "You remember Sylvia Resnick?" A vague image of a short blond girl smiles pleasantly at Joanne from the pages of their high school yearbook. "She was always a few pounds overweight and her blouses always looked like they hadn't been washed in months." Sylvia Resnick's grin—the corners of her lips always managed to turn down when she was smiling—comes into sharp focus, her stringy hair and gray-white blouse locking firmly into place. Joanne nods remembrance. "She died."

"What?"

"Yup. Thirty-nine years old. Four kids. Goes to a movie one night with her husband and suddenly keels over dead. Brain aneurysm."

"When was this?"

"Few months ago. I heard it from Karen Palmer. She loves talking about stuff like that. I swear, I could see her smiling through the phone wires. 'How are you feeling?' she chirps, and in the same breath informs me that Sylvia Resnick dropped dead!"

Joanne says nothing, feeling momentarily stunned by the news and trying to make a connection between what has happened to Sylvia Resnick and what is happening to Eve. "I think if you had a brain aneurysm, someone would have discovered it by now."

"I don't think I have a brain aneurysm," Eve says impatiently. "I'm just saying that you never know. I mean, one minute you're fine, the next minute you're dead. We're at the age, you know, where things start to go wrong."

"I'm sure you don't have a brain aneurysm," Joanne repeats, thinking she would like to talk about something else. It seems that all she and Eve talk about lately is the state of Eve's health, which is understandable but a trifle wearying. "Do you have life insurance?" Joanne asks her suddenly.

"What makes you ask that?" Eve regards her warily, as if Joanne knows something she doesn't.

"I took out a policy."

"You did? Why?"

"I thought it was a good idea. If something were to happen to me . . ."

"Nothing's going to happen to you," Eve says, simultaneously dismissing this possibility and the direction in which the conversation is likely headed. Joanne has noticed that Eve doesn't like to discuss the phone calls Joanne has been getting. She begins to fidget and her voice takes on an unpleasant edge. Joanne drops the topic, deciding not to tell Eve that she has included in her new insurance policy a clause for double indemnity. "The doctor who examined me for the policy said that I have a bit of blood in my urine," she tells her instead, bringing the conversation indirectly back to the subject of Eve's health. Blood in the urine is something that the doctors have also discovered in one of Eve's many tests. "She said it was nothing," Joanne elaborates. "She said that a lot of women have blood traces in the urine, depending on the time of month and everything."

"Sure," Eve replies cynically, "blame everything on the time of the month." Eve stares distractedly out the side window. "I was reading in *People* about this guy who lost one leg to cancer. He's running across North America . . ."

"Terry Fox?"

"No," Eve mutters, "Terry Fox died years ago. This is another one. Actually there are a lot of them doing it these days. I have a vision of all these one-legged runners colliding across the highways of America."

Joanne finds herself laughing at the rather grotesque image. "I guess some people cope better than others," she observes, thinking in general terms.

"What's that supposed to mean?" The tone of Eve's question is sharp.

"Nothing," Joanne answers honestly, taken aback by the sudden hostility in Eve's voice. "I didn't mean anything by it. It was just a comment."

"Yeah, well you can keep those kind of comments to yourself." Joanne feels tears spring to her eyes, as if Eve has slapped her across the face. "Sorry," Eve apologizes immediately. "Christ, there I go again. Joanne, I'm sorry. Please don't cry. I didn't mean it. You know I didn't mean it."

Joanne is shaking her head up and down, trying to tell Eve that she understands. But the truth is that she understands less and less every day about what is happening to her best friend.

"God, you've been so good to me. You drive me all over the place, you sit with me through one useless appointment after another, you're always there when I need you." She stops. "I guess it's true what they say about always hurting the one you love." Joanne manages a smile. "So," Eve says, changing the topic, "you really think this Dr. Ronald Gold is the same guy we went to school with?"

"I'll be with you as soon as I can," the dermatologist is saying as he comes out of his office into the crowded waiting room. He is about five feet seven inches tall, with a full head of reddish-blond hair and an engaging smile. There is no question that he is the same Ronald Gold they went to school with. Joanne watches as he fumbles with the appointment calendar on his cluttered desk, recalling similar gestures with his chemistry notebook. He hasn't aged a day, Joanne thinks, wondering whether he will feel the same way about her should he get the time to take sufficient notice of her presence. "I apologize," he says to his captive audience, composed mostly of teenagers, with a small sprinkling of adults. "I apologize for the chaos," he continues, obviously searching for a pen. "I know I put it down here somewhere," he mumbles. Joanne thinks that she sees a silver pen peeking out from underneath a stack of papers, but feels it is not her place to point it out. "My receptionist quit last week," he announces to no one in particular, "and I called an agency to send me a temporary but she never showed up. Actually, I'm probably lucky. Sometimes those temps are more trouble than they're worth. It takes you the whole day to explain things to them, and then they send somebody different the next day and you have to do it all again. I can't find the damn pen." He looks up from the table sheepishly. "Anybody here have a pen they can lend me?"

Joanne moves to his desk, extricates the lost silver pen from under its paper mountain, and hands it to the boy who used to crack his knuckles, along with a steady stream of jokes, behind her in chemistry class.

"You want a job?" he asks immediately, then, "Do I know you?"

"We went to school together. Joanne Mossman, well, that is, it *was* Mossman, now it's Hunter." Is it? she wonders.

His smile grows until it stretches into his ears. "Well, Joanne Mossman," he exclaims, "I wouldn't have recognized you—you look so much better now than you did as a kid." Joanne laughs, but the laugh is full of appreciation. "I'm serious. I'm not trying to snow you. I mean, you were always pretty, but you were always a little uptight, you know what I mean? Strictly the pearl necklace type. You look a lot looser now. I like what you've done to your hair." Joanne is aware she is blushing. "Hey, you still blush, I like that too." He puts his arm around her waist and motions with his other arm for the attention of the rest of the room. "Everybody, this is little Joanne Mossman. What's your married name again?"

"Hunter."

"Little Joanne Hunter. Same husband you started out with?" Joanne nods, not sure what else to do. "We went to school together. She had a clear complexion even then." He studies her face. "What's this? A pimple?" His expert fingers move across her face. "Nothing serious," he says. "We'll take care of you in a few minutes."

"I'm not here to see you," Joanne says quickly, aware that everyone is still listening to their conversation. "I'm here with a friend." She points to Eve, who is sitting in a chair against the wall, a stack of old magazines on her lap and a disgruntled expression on her lips.

"Is that little Evie Pringle?" Dr. Ronald Gold asks as Eve stands up, towering a good three inches above him. "Still together, you two, huh?"

"It's Eve Stanley now," Eve tells him. "We have an appointment twenty minutes ago."

If he is aware of the intended sarcasm, he ignores it. "Yeah, well, I'm sorry about the delay, but my receptionist quit on me and my nurse is out with a cold." The phone rings. "And the phone keeps ringing." He reaches over and grabs it. "For you," he says to Joanne. Her eyes widen. "Just kidding," he says quickly, catching the look of concern. "What? You gave somebody my number? Yes, this is Dr. Ronald Gold," he announces into the phone. "Certainly, I can see you, Mrs. Gottlieb. For you, anytime. Drop by this afternoon, I'll take a look. Don't worry, the offending blemish will be gone before the bar mitzvah on Saturday." He hangs up the phone and looks back at Eve. "I'll be with you as fast as I can. Michael," he calls to a young boy whose face is all but hidden by a raging mask of pubescent acne. He looks back at Joanne. "And after your friend, I want to take a look at you."

"So when did you start getting these?" he is asking as Joanne lies on the examining table, her face cold after the treatment of dry ice the doctor has applied. Ronald Gold's fingers press down hard on her chin.

"Just in the last month," Joanne tells him. "I couldn't believe it. Women my age aren't supposed to get pimples."

"Show me where it's written that women your age—*our* age—aren't supposed to get pimples. Women your age get pimples, believe me. I have lots of women coming in here in their forties, even their fifties."

"Great. Something to look forward to."

He pokes her cheek with a needle, causing a slight sting. "I'm just going to inject a little cortisone into this one. Tell me, what have you been doing to your skin lately?"

"What do you mean?"

"Anything different?"

"I've been using a new moisturizer that Eve recommended . . ."

"Eve's a dermatologist?"

"No, but she said that I should start taking better care of my skin."

"You still do everything Eve tells you? Just like the old days?"

Joanne tries to smile but his forearm is resting on her mouth as he presses down on another potential blemish. "Well, it's just that I never did anything with my skin before, to take care of it, I mean . . ."

"And you never had problems before, did you?"

"No."

"Doesn't that tell you something?" He backs away. "You've been plugging up your pores, little Joanne Mossman Hunter. All those fancy, expensive creams and moisturizers are giving you pimples. Stop using them."

"And do what?"

"And wash your face once a day—once—at night, that's all you need, with a mild soap—I'll give you a list. You don't need any moisturizers. I'll give you some vitamin A cream to apply before you go to bed. If you're going to wear makeup, use one with a water base, and use a powder blush, not a cream. Cream clogs the pores. And stop reading those fashion magazines. They know as much about proper skin care as your nutty friend Eve. What's her problem anyway?" he asks in the same breath.

"We were hoping you'd tell us."

"I'm a skin doctor. That's for the outside of the head, not the inside."

"You're saying it's an emotional problem?"

He shrugs. "Psychiatry is the dumping ground of the medical profession. A doctor can't find something physical, he assumes it's emotional. I couldn't tell you what Eve's problem is except that there's nothing wrong with her skin. It's a little dry, that's all. More than that, I can't tell you." He backs away and studies her face as if he were planning to paint her portrait. "That should do it," he says. "So you want a job?"

Joanne laughs, then realizes he is serious. "Are you kidding?" she asks.

He shakes his head. "You found my pen, you can do anything. Go ahead, name your price."

"I can't."

"Why not? Babies at home? A husband who doesn't want his wife to work? Tell him that times have changed. Hell, my wife's a dentist. She works harder than I do."

"That's not it," Joanne says, not sure exactly what it is.

"What then? Not challenging enough?"

"Are you really serious about this?"

"Do I look like a man who's joking? I look like a man in desperate need of a good receptionist."

"What would I have to do?"

"Answer the phone, greet the multitudes, keep my appointments straight, laugh at my jokes. If you're a really good girl, I might even let you squeeze a few pimples. What do you say? Is that or isn't that an offer you can't refuse?"

"Can I think about it?" Joanne asks, surprising herself. What is there to think about? She can't seriously be considering working for this man. Why not? she asks herself, the thoughts colliding in her head like so many one-legged runners across the highways of America.

"Sure. Think about it, talk it over with your husband, and call me Monday. Not that I'm trying to pressure you, you understand." He smiles.

"Why do you want *me* to work for you?"

"Why not you?" he asks. "Something wrong with you?" His boyish grin relaxes, his gray-blue eyes clear and warm. "I like you," he says simply. "You remind me of my youth. Hey, I read this somewhere—you want to know what's the really scary thing about middle age?" She nods. "It's waking up one morning," he tells her, "and realizing that your high school class is running the country."

Eve's mother is waiting in the doorway—has she been there the whole time?—as Joanne pulls her car into her driveway. "That's not really my mother," Eve states as she opens the car door. "It's Godzilla."

"Eve," Joanne urges, "if she's making you so miserable, just ask her to leave."

"I can't do that." Eve walks up her front steps with Joanne trailing after her.

"You were a long time," Eve's mother greets them, her voice vaguely accusing. "What took so long?"

"We had to wait almost an hour," Eve says, walking past her mother and into the house. "The good doctor was very disorganized."

"His receptionist quit and his nurse is out with a cold," Joanne further explains, although Mrs. Cameron is no longer paying attention.

"My God! What did you do with the furniture?" Eve exclaims, walking into the suddenly unfamiliar living room and restlessly pacing back and forth.

"I moved a few things around."

"A few things! Is there anything that you *didn't* touch?"

"Well, you were gone so long. I was nervous; I had nothing to do."

"You ever think of reading?" Eve asks as she and Joanne circle the newly arranged room, the lilac print sofa where the chairs were only hours ago, the mauve chairs consigned to opposite corners of the room, the coffee tables and lamps uprooted and relocated. "How did you move that sofa all by yourself, for God's sake? Who are you, the Bionic Woman?"

"Godzilla," Joanne mouths in Eve's direction when Mrs. Cameron is looking the other way.

"This is too much for me," Eve says incredulously, her voice somewhere between laughter and tears. "I can't cope."

"Go up and lie down," Mrs. Cameron says to her daughter, who is already out of the room and halfway up the stairs. "Stay," she whispers under her breath to Joanne. "I want to talk to you."

"Thanks, Joanne," Eve calls down the stairs. "I'll talk to you later."

"So what happened?" Eve's mother asks immediately.

"Nothing much," Joanne states, following the older woman into the kitchen and sitting across from her at the kitchen table. "Apparently the doctor gave her a pretty thorough examination. As far as he's concerned, there's nothing wrong with her skin except that it's a little dry."

"She told him she always used to have oily skin?"

"He said that skin changes, just like everything else. He said it could be her hormones, the pregnancy, the miscarriage. I'm not sure. Eve can tell you exactly what he said."

"But there's nothing serious?"

"Mrs. Cameron," Joanne says patiently, "how serious can dry skin be?"

"Did you tell Eve that?"

"I tried."

"And?"

"She says that the dry skin is only a symptom of the larger problem."

Eve's mother drums her fingers anxiously on the table, her face downcast. Joanne is suddenly aware of how much older Eve's mother seems these days, for the first time her features betraying their almost seven decades. The bags underneath her eyes are heavy and sagging. There is a slight twitch at the sides of her colorless lips. Joanne realizes that Arlene Pringle Hopper Cameron, who has buried three husbands, whom Joanne's mother always referred to affectionately as Mighty Mouse (though this is something she has never confided to Eve), is on the brink of tears. "I don't know what to do," she cries softly, lowering her head into her hands.

"Why don't you go home?" Joanne suggests gently, seizing the opportunity. "You look tired. You need some rest."

"I can't go home," the woman says, looking up at Joanne. "Eve needs me here."

"Eve can manage on her own, Mrs. Cameron," Joanne urges. "She has a cleaning lady twice a week, and I'm right next door. I'll talk to Brian, he'll just have to spend more time at home. It might even be good for Eve if she has to do more around the house. It might take her mind off her pains."

"Don't you think I've suggested that to Eve?" Mrs. Cameron asks, catching Joanne by surprise. Truthfully, this thought hasn't occurred to her. "I have my own heart problems, you know. You think this is easy for me? I have my own life, my bridge club, my mah-jongg ladies. I know that sounds pretty trivial, but what can you do? Some lives aren't as important as others. I'm too old to play nursemaid. But every time I suggest to Eve that I go home, that she try to help herself more, she gets angry. She yells, 'What kind of a mother are you that you'd abandon your own daughter when she needs you the most?' What am I supposed to do? If I even suggest going out for an afternoon, she gets hysterical. She says if I were any kind of a mother, I'd want to be here, to take care of her." She shakes her head. "I'm not perfect, Joanne, God knows. I've made a lot of mistakes. But I've tried the best I know how, and I don't know what else to do. You're the only one she listens to—you tell me, what should I do? She's my daughter and I love her. I don't want to see her unhappy. I don't know how to help her." She dries her eyes with a tissue. "She's forty years old but she's still my child. You don't stop being a mother just because your children get older. Well, I don't have to tell you that. How are your girls?" she asks, trying to smile.

"Fine," Joanne answers, a presumption since she has yet to receive any mail from them. She stands up and puts her hand on the older woman's shoulder. "Look, why don't you lie down for a while yourself? You moved all that furniture around; you must be exhausted."

"Will Eve be all right?" Eve's mother asks quietly at the front door.

"I'm sure she will," Joanne answers, surprised at how reassuring her voice sounds when, in fact, she isn't sure at all.

Chapter 20

"I don't know how I let you talk me into this."

"Hey, that's my line."

"The last thing I feel like seeing is some glitzy Broadway musical," Eve pouts, staring out the front of the car window at the early evening sky.

"It's supposed to be wonderful," Joanne tells her. "They say that the costumes are unbelievable, the dancing is glorious, and the songs are actually hummable."

"Who's this 'they'? The good doctor again?"

Joanne feels her shoulders slump and readjusts them, trying to force a smile. "As a matter of fact, yes," she answers, hoping to avoid an argument, giving up on the smile. Every time she and Eve get on the topic of Joanne's new boss, they invariably begin to bicker. "Ron and his wife saw the show last week and he hasn't stopped raving about it."

"If it's so good, how come we were able to get tickets?"

"I told you, his brother . . ."

"Oh yes," Eve cuts her off, "his brother is laying the production assistant."

Joanne winces. "He's *dating* the production assistant."

"Same thing—don't be so naive." Eve stares glumly out her side window.

"Look, if this is really such an ordeal for you, I'll turn the car around and we'll just go home."

"Now? We're almost there, for God's sake. You made me get all dressed and everything. Who said anything about wanting to go home? God, you're so touchy!"

"I just don't feel like driving into Manhattan in Friday night traffic if you're going to do nothing but complain all the way there and all the way back."

"Who's complaining?" Eve fidgets in her seat, pulling her silver shawl across her bare shoulders. "Geez, you're in a funny mood tonight."

"I was in a great mood," Joanne tells her.

"Was? As in 'not anymore?' "

Joanne feels her shoulders relax. "I'll be fine. Highway driving always makes me a little nervous," she lies.

"You don't think this job might be too much for you?" Eve asks after a slight pause.

"How do you mean?"

"Well, you know, you're not used to working. I mean, you haven't worked outside of the home, ever, have you?" Joanne shakes her head, not sure where Eve is headed. "And suddenly you're working every day from nine to five, and it must be quite a switch. You're bound to be tired."

"I'm not tired."

"You look tired."

Joanne glances across the front seat at her friend who pretends to be carefully studying the road ahead. "I do?" Joanne finds herself staring at her reflection in the rearview mirror. The lines around her eyes seem no more pronounced than usual. If anything, she is looking —and feeling—much better than she has in months. "I don't feel tired," she says. "In fact, I feel pretty good. I love the job . . ."

"How can you love a job that has you staring into faces full of zits every day?"

Joanne tries to laugh but the resulting sound is more of a grunt. "The people behind the pimples are very nice. Everybody's friendly. Ron couldn't be a nicer person to work for . . ."

"So you keep saying. Anything happening there that I should know about?"

"Like what?" Joanne begins to feel uncomfortable. This is not the first time that Eve has hinted that something distinctly unprofessional might be going on between Joanne and her new employer.

"I saw the way he looked at you that day in his office. Little Ronnie Gold and little Joanne Mossman, together again for the very first time!"

"Joanne *Hunter*," Joanne corrects sharply, "and I'm starting to resent this conversation."

Eve is clearly startled by Joanne's sudden assertion, as is Joanne herself. "Take it easy. I was only teasing."

"Ron is a happily married man, and I am a married woman,"

Joanne says, aware of the not-so-subtle distinction between the two. "He is my boss and I like him and respect him. That is all there is to it; that is all there will ever be to it."

"Methinks the lady doth protest too much," Eve mutters, almost under her breath. Before Joanne can object, Eve continues, "So, you think you'll keep working after the girls get home from camp?"

"I don't think so," she says, suppressing her annoyance. "I only agreed to take the job for the summer. By then Ron will have found someone else he likes, I'm sure, and hopefully, Paul and I . . ." She breaks off in mid-sentence. It has been two weeks since she last saw her husband.

"Hopefully Paul and you . . . ?"

"Who knows?" Joanne shrugs, not wanting to pursue the subject of a possible reconciliation. There is silence as Joanne realizes that there are increasingly few subjects she feels comfortable discussing with her oldest and closest friend.

Eve squirms in her seat and fidgets with her shawl. "You made sure we got an aisle seat, didn't you?" she demands.

"You already asked me that."

"And what was your answer?"

"Yes, I made sure we got an aisle seat."

"Good."

The conversation lapses into silence.

They have to park approximately six blocks away from the theater and, as a result, must run to make the eight o'clock curtain. The crowd outside the Barrymore Theater is moving slowly inside as Joanne and Eve arrive breathless and laughing at the doors. "I don't know what's so damn funny," Eve gasps, clutching at her throat. "I haven't run like that since I came first in the track and field day race at the end of our junior year. Remember that? I beat out everybody else by a good ten yards."

"Well, you certainly beat me," Joanne acknowledges, gasping for air. "I'd say that you were in pretty good shape!"

Eve's body goes suddenly rigid. "What's that supposed to mean?"

As has been happening with increasing frequency lately when she is with Eve, Joanne is unsure how to respond. Her hands move awkwardly in the air, her mouth refusing to open.

From inside the theater, a persistent bell is calling them to their seats. "I guess we should go inside," Eve says, her voice softening. "Isn't that Paul?" she asks suddenly.

"What? Where?"

"He just went inside. At least, I think it was Paul. I just saw him from the side. It might have been someone else."

Joanne feels her heart starting to thump wildly, understanding it has nothing to do with her recent exertion. She feels like a teenager, one of the pimply multitude she reassures daily. How does she look? she wonders, trying to catch her reflection in the glass doors. Eve said she looks tired. Does she? She is wearing a new red-and-white-striped cotton dress, scooped rather daringly in the front, ruffles at the bottom flouncing playfully around her knees. It is unlike anything she has ever owned and it was purchased with most of the money from her first paycheck. Her skin is clear once again, but her hair is a mess from running the six blocks to the theater. But then it is always a mess lately, and everyone keeps telling her how much they like it this way, including Paul. She looks a little thinner, she thinks, feeling herself being pushed through the lobby doors. She hands her ticket to the usher and is immediately pushed along the back wall toward the appropriate aisle. That she looks thinner is probably just the effect of the vertical stripes, she decides, although it is true that she has dropped a few pounds since she began working. New diet? Eve has asked. Yes, Joanne recalls thinking, the anxiety diet, though in truth, she feels less anxious each day.

They find their seats and sit down, Eve craning her tall, elegant neck to get a view of who is sitting where. With her red hair artfully framing her pale complexion, Eve resembles, for the moment, a humanized giraffe. "I can't see him," she says, obviously referring to Paul, stretching to look behind her.

"It probably wasn't him," Joanne says, knowing instinctively that it was. "Paul was never big on plays . . ."

"I couldn't see who he was with," Eve states as the lights go down and the orchestra starts up.

The music is loud, the beat thumping and vibrant. The audience seems to sway collectively in the darkness, anticipation mounting. Joanne is aware of the increasingly insistent sound; her feet catch the hum of the orchestra; she sees the curtains part, a set that instantly dazzles, costumes that startle and almost take one's breath away; she hears voices rising in clear, joyful confidence. Yet all she hears, sees and thinks is, I couldn't see who he was with.

Why hasn't this occurred to her? That if Paul is here, he is here with someone. Who? Possibly a client. Please let it be a client. Maybe a friend. Let it be a male friend. More likely a date. Most likely young and attractive. Possibly little Judy whatever-the-rest-of-her-name-is.

I couldn't see who he was with.

Joanne focuses hard on the spectacularly lit stage, now bathed in bright swatches of color, like a decorator's paint samples. In the center is a man cloaked all in black; he is singing to three women dressed in identical layers of multicolored chiffon, their hair dyed to match these layers, their faces similarly made up. Suddenly the lights go blue, then deep indigo, the women seeming to disappear into their surroundings, their faces reemerging as gold and silver masks. Joanne feels disoriented, at loose ends. She wonders what all this harsh stage makeup and strong lighting will do to the actresses' complexions. She glances over at Eve. Her face reflects the same silver and gold, her hair the icy blue of the stage lights, her eyes black and empty.

Once again, Joanne hears nothing, feels nothing.

I couldn't see who he was with.

Suddenly the women return and the stage is a bright, pulsating, lemon yellow, the man in black disappearing into what appears to be a great glob of blinding sunlight. Joanne closes her eyes against its persistent glare. She feels the heat of the round yellow ball. Turning back toward Eve, she notices that Eve's face looks especially cold in the warm sunlight, somewhat skeletal in the sun's harsh delineation of her features, almost cruel. Yellow was never my color, she can hear Eve say, though, in fact, Eve says nothing. The sun is now burning Joanne's skin, causing her forehead to break into a sweat. The sun is too hot, she thinks, wishing to escape into the outside air. Somebody please turn off the sun. Fighting her growing anxiety, Joanne focuses her attention on the stage, realizes that the women are now nude—have they been so all along?—clothed only in the iridescent layers of light.

The curtain suddenly goes down on the first act. The house lights come up. The theater bursts into a prolonged period of applause. All around her, people are rising to stretch their legs. "I can't believe it went so fast," Joanne hears herself say, aware her mind was else-where for much of the time.

"Are you kidding?" Eve asks. "That was the longest damn first act I've ever sat through. Don't tell me you actually liked that? So much for the good doctor's recommendations. Let's go outside."

"I think I'd rather stay put," Joanne tells Eve, thinking that only minutes ago, she felt desperate for some air.

"Let's go outside," Eve repeats, indicating that the discussion is closed.

On the way up the aisle, Joanne hears words like innovative and original, breathtaking and wonderful. Only Eve's lips are fixed in a permanent scowl. "It's a terrible show," she says, loud enough to be heard by everyone they are passing. "The worst thing I've seen in years." They reach the lobby, Joanne's eyes resolutely downcast. "There he is," Eve says immediately. "It *is* Paul," she continues. Joanne looks up. Paul is standing by himself along the side of the deep red wall. "Aren't you going to say hello?" Before Joanne can answer or object, Eve raises her arm to wave, catching Paul's eye and signaling for him to come over. "Here he comes."

Joanne takes a deep breath, feeling vaguely sick to her stomach. She feels the people beside her adjust to accommodate the newcomer, knows that Paul is now standing beside her. She reluctantly turns in his direction.

He is wearing a gray suit with a pale pink shirt and a maroon striped tie, and though he is smiling, he looks uncomfortable. "Hello, Joanne," he says softly. "How are you, Eve?"

Joanne nods as Eve replies. "Dying slowly," she says, her voice flat and humorless.

"You look fine," he tells her, and Eve grunts.

"You can write that on my tombstone," she says.

"How are *you?*" he asks, turning back to Joanne.

"Good," she tells him, realizing that she means it. "I have a job."

"A job? What kind of job?" He is surprised, interested.

"I'm . . . sort of a receptionist . . . for a skin doctor . . . for the summer . . . till the girls get back from camp."

"Sounds great."

"I'm enjoying it a lot," she tells him.

There is a moment's silence. "I've been meaning to call you," he says awkwardly, aware that Eve is closely monitoring the conversation.

"That's all right . . ."

"I've been very busy . . ."

"No problem," Joanne tells him.

"I thought that maybe we could drive out to the camp together on visitors' day. That is, if you haven't already made other plans."

"I'd like that," she agrees quickly. "I think the girls would too."

"Have you heard from them?"

"Not yet. You?"

"Not a line. Typical, I guess." He looks around. Why does he seem so uncomfortable? "Great show," he enthuses, taking a step backward as Eve sneers. "You don't agree?"

"Can't say that I do," Eve tells him, about to say more when she is interrupted by the appearance of a young, attractive—if overly made up—blonde who has materialized from out of nowhere to take a firm grip on Paul's arm.

Paul smiles in her direction; Eve smiles in her direction; Joanne smiles in her direction. The young blonde smiles back. They are all standing in the middle of the lobby smiling at each other like a bunch of idiots. Joanne feels the house lights bathe them in alternate shades of blue, yellow, and purple. She feels that they have suddenly been transported center stage and stripped bare. She feels her knees go weak and her stomach turn over. She now knows why Paul looks so uncomfortable. She wonders whether he will introduce them and how. Judy (for surely this must be little Judy), I'd like you to meet my wife; Joanne, this is little Judy.

The bell begins calling them back into the theater. Saved by the bell, Joanne thinks, knowing that she is past saving.

"I'll call you," Paul says quietly (so that his little Judy cannot hear?), leading the young blonde away without awkward introductions. Hasn't he told little Judy how much he dislikes artificiality? Hasn't he cautioned her about overapplying the blusher? Is it cream or powder? Joanne wonders, hoping it is cream.

"Are you all right?" Eve asks as the lobby slowly empties of people.

Joanne shakes her head.

"Do you want to leave?"

Joanne nods. If she tries to speak, she will break down. Stupid, stupid, stupid! she berates herself as Eve guides her outside into the night air.

"I never realized that Paul had such conventional tastes," Eve says as they begin walking in the direction of the car, Eve's arm through Joanne's.

"She's very pretty," Joanne manages to squeak out.

"She's very ordinary," Eve corrects impatiently. "Wash her face, take away the blond hair and the big boobs, and what have you got? Actually," Eve continues analytically, "you've got you, twenty years ago."

Joanne stops walking, trying to digest what Eve has just said, deciding she can't. "Was that an insult or a compliment?" she asks, genuinely puzzled by Eve's comment.

Eve dismisses the question with a sudden burst of speed. "I'm just saying that you married an idiot."

"I don't think so," Joanne tells her, stopping again.

"Will you quit stopping?! This is New York, for God's sake. You can get mugged standing around on street corners arguing."

"Paul is not an idiot," Joanne repeats.

"Suit yourself. He's your husband."

"Yes, he is, and I feel funny having to defend him to you."

"Then don't," Eve says simply. "I'm on your side, remember?"

"Are you?"

It is Eve's turn to stop. "What's that supposed to mean?"

"We keep asking each other that lately."

"So, what are you saying?"

Joanne resumes walking. "I'm not sure."

"Look," Eve tells her on the drive back to Long Island, "let's not blow this thing out of proportion, okay? You saw your husband out with another woman. That's bound to be a bit upsetting . . ."

"A *bit* upsetting?"

"Just don't take it out on me," Eve continues, ignoring the interruption. "It wasn't my idea to go to the dumb play. You're the one who insisted, who dragged me out of bed . . ."

"Eve, let's please drop it."

"I'm only trying to tell you not to let it get to you."

"Why not?" Joanne demands, pulling the car over to the side of the road and slamming down on the brakes. "Why shouldn't I let it get to me? I love my husband. We'll be married twenty years in October. I'm desperately hoping we'll get back together. Why shouldn't I go to pieces when I see him out with another woman? Why is everything that happens to me so damn inconsequential and everything that happens to you so earth-shatteringly important? Why is my pain somehow less valid than yours?"

"Joanne, let's not get silly. Your life is not at stake."

"Neither is yours!"

"Oh, really? You know that, do you?"

Joanne takes a deep breath. Somehow, she thinks, the conversation always reverts to Eve. "Yes," Joanne says emphatically. "Yes, I do. Eve, how many doctors have you seen? Thirty? Forty?" Eve refuses to look at her. "You have seen every specialist in New York; you have had every test known to man. The only thing left for you to do is to check yourself into the Mayo Clinic and let them do all the tests over again. How many times do you need to be told that there is nothing wrong with you?"

"Don't you dare tell me that there's nothing wrong with me! I have pains all over my body!"

"That's precisely the point. Nobody can pin any of your pains down. You have everything. Your ribs, your chest, your groin, your veins, your weight, your bowels, your skin, your hair, the mucus in your eyes and nose, your temperature, your eyes, your throat. Forgive me if I've left anything out. Eve, nobody falls apart over their entire body." She stops, feeling Eve's hatred emerging from her tightly clenched fists. "I'm not saying that something hasn't happened to your system. You had a miscarriage, you lost a lot of blood. Your whole body rhythm has been upset; there may be a chemical imbalance, I don't know, I'm not a doctor . . ."

"You're damn right . . ."

"But I do know that whatever has happened to your body is not fatal . . ."

"How do you know that?"

"All right, I don't know it. Suppose it *is* fatal. Let's suppose the worst. You have six months to live. What are you going to do about it?"

"What are you talking about? I don't want to die!"

"Of course you don't. And you're not going to. All I'm trying to say is that if there *is* something fatally wrong with you, there's not a whole lot that you can do about it except try to make the most of whatever time you have left. I don't think that you're going to die. *Nobody* thinks you're going to die but you. Would it hurt so much to see a psychiatrist?"

"It would be a waste of time."

"What else have you been doing with your time lately?"

"I am in *physical* pain!"

"Yes, but physical pain can have an emotional source. Nobody can tell the difference."

"I can."

"Then you're the only person in the world with that ability."

"Joanne, I am not the one who's having a mental break-down . . ."

"Nobody said that you were having a breakdown."

"I'm not the one who's imagining weird phone calls."

Joanne takes several seconds to let this statement sink in. "I was wondering when you were going to get around to that," she says, realizing this is true.

"I'm not the one whose husband left her after twenty years and feels she has to make up stories about a bunch of crazy phone calls to get attention."

Joanne's voice is quiet. "Is that really what you think I've been doing?"

Eve suddenly brings her hands to her face and bursts into tears. A second later, she flings her head back in an angry gasp, swallowing the cry, stuffing it back inside.

"Let it out," Joanne urges softly, her own anger vanishing. "There's so much rage in there, Eve. Let some of it out."

Eve leans back against her seat. "Damn," she mutters repeat-edly. "Damn, damn, damn." She looks at Joanne. "Why do you argue with me? You know I always go for the jugular."

"You never have with me before."

"You've never fought back before."

"Maybe the phone calls *are* all in my mind," Joanne admits after a long silence where neither friend looks at the other. "I really don't know anymore. Tell you what," she says, laughing despite herself, "I'll see a psychiatrist if you'll see one. We can even drive in together for our appointments. Make a night of it. Go to dinner and a movie. You might even get me to another horror movie. How does that sound?"

Eve does not laugh or even smile. "I don't need a psychiatrist," she says.

Chapter 21

The phone is ringing.

"Dr. Gold's office," Joanne chirps into the receiver, smiling at a chunky young man who walks through the office door. "Be with you in a minute," she whispers in his direction. "I'm sorry, Dr. Gold is all booked up for the next two months. The earliest appointment I can give you would be September twenty-first. Yes, I realize that doesn't help you much now, but the best I can promise is to call you sooner if we have a cancellation. Yes, there are usually a few. Yes, I'll try. In the meantime, I'll put you down for the twenty-first of September at two-fifteen. May I have your name, please? Marsha Fisher? And your phone number? Yes, okay, I'll call you sooner if anything comes up." Joanne replaces the receiver and looks at the young man standing before her. He seems intimidated by the modest surroundings. "Can I help you?"

"I'm here to see Dr. Gold," he mumbles, his chin against his chest. There is something familiar about his voice.

"Your name?" Joanne asks, feeling vaguely uneasy, glad that the room is full of people.

"Simon Loomis," he tells her, and Joanne checks the appointment calendar.

At first she cannot find the name but then she locates it. "Your appointment isn't until three o'clock," she tells him, glancing at the wall clock behind her. "It's not even two yet. You're very early."

"Nothing else to do," he shrugs, his light brown hair falling into his deep-set eyes.

"Well, if you don't mind waiting . . . there's a restaurant down-stairs if you feel like a cup of coffee."

He lowers his small, tough frame into the room's only empty chair which is located directly across from her desk. Joanne estimates his age at somewhere between eighteen and twenty-five and wonders why he doesn't have a job, thinking that his attitude might have something to do with it. In his obvious uneasiness, he tends to make the people around him equally uneasy. At least, he seems to be having this effect on her. She begins sorting through the payments she has received in the afternoon mail, aware that the young man's eyes are still on her. She looks up at him and smiles. The corners of his wide lips turn upward in a brief twitch. The rest of his unremarkable face remains impassive. "Have you been here before?" she asks, remembering that new patients are supposed to fill out a form. He shakes his head. "Here then." She hands him the necessary paper. "It helps the doctor if you fill this out before he sees you."

"What is it?" Simon Loomis moves warily toward her, his arm outstretched.

"Just some basic information we require. Childhood illnesses, any allergies to medications, things like that. Name, rank, serial number," she adds, but he doesn't laugh. "Here's a pen."

"Got my own," he tells her, sitting back down, pulling a black ballpoint out of his shirt pocket. The young woman in the seat beside him lifts her elbow from the arm of her chair and places it in her lap.

Joanne returns to her work. The phone rings; she picks it up. "Dr. Gold's office." Again she feels the boy's eyes on her. "Yes, Renee. When did that happen? Okay, let me check his appointment book. Okay, how about tomorrow at one o'clock? I'll squeeze you in quickly and he can have a look. Okay, bye-bye." Joanne looks back at Simon Loomis. He is still staring at her. "Do you need help with any of the questions?" she asks. He shakes his head. The pen remains unopened in his hand.

Ronald Gold comes out of his office followed by a young girl of fourteen with tears in her eyes, her face dotted with bits of cotton. "Sorry I hurt you, darling," he is saying, a comforting arm around the girl's shoulder. "You forgive me?" The girl smiles through her tears. "Give Andrea another appointment for six weeks from now. She'll be fine, Mrs. Armstrong," he says to the anxious woman who has risen out of her chair by the window and now stands protectively beside her daughter. "What can I tell you? Puberty! The pits! We all live through it." He points to Joanne. "We went to school together," he says. "Her skin was a mess, you wouldn't have believed. In fact, she was my inspiration to get into this line of work. Now look how beautifully she turned out. That's one reason I hired her. How you doing?" he asks, winking at Joanne.

"Renee Wheeler called. She has some sort of boil . . ."

"Yuchh, boils, I hate 'em," Ronald Gold exclaims and young Andrea Armstrong bursts out laughing.

"I told her to come in tomorrow at around one."

"Not to see me! I don't want to see any yucky boils." Now Andrea's mother is also laughing. "You want to hear a joke?" the doctor asks, seeing the sullen boy across from Joanne and moving to include him in the select group. "A priest, a minister, and a rabbi are discussing when life begins, and the priest says that life begins at the moment of conception. The minister says, I beg your pardon, but life begins at the moment of birth, and the rabbi says, excuse me, but you're both wrong. Life begins when the children leave home and the dog dies." Joanne laughs out loud. "That's the other reason I hired her," Ronald Gold says quickly. "Who's next?"

"Susan Dotson."

"Susan Dotson, my favorite!" the doctor exclaims as a snarling, overweight teenager walks past him, eyes rolling. "She's crazy about me," Ronald Gold whispers and follows the girl into one of the small examination rooms off the main reception area as Andrea Armstrong and her mother depart.

"Is he always like that?" Simon Loomis asks, pushing his chair back against the wall so that its front legs are off the floor.

"Always," Joanne answers as the phone rings again. "Dr. Gold's office. Hi, Eve! How was the test? . . . Oh, God, that sounds awful. Did it make you gag? . . . What did the doctor say? . . . Again? Why? I mean, if he didn't see anything the first time and it made you sick . . . I know, but why put yourself through it again especially if he doesn't think it's necessary? . . . Well, no, of course you have to do what you think is best. Okay, I'll speak to you later. Try and get some rest. I'll call you when I get home." She hangs up the phone, feeling as helpless and depressed as she always does lately when she speaks to Eve, and looks back at where Simon Loomis is sitting.

His chair is empty. Joanne takes a quick glance around the office. The boy is definitely gone. Maybe he decided he didn't want to wait after all, she thinks, glad that he is gone, wondering whether he will return. She didn't like the way he looked at her, and there was something about his voice that spooked her. She is being silly, she immediately chastises herself, trying to concentrate on the invoices in front of her.

It has been a quiet week, she reflects, idly rearranging the papers on her desk. Her brother, Warren, called Sunday to see how she was doing. Paul phoned that same afternoon for the identical reason. He was friendly and warm, making no mention of having seen her the previous night. He also said nothing about seeing her again before visitors' day at camp. This morning she received three letters from Lulu. She has yet to hear anything from Robin, though Lulu reports that her sister seems to be having a good time. Perhaps Paul has received a letter; perhaps she could call him . . .

She puts her hand on the telephone, mentally rehearsing her opening lines—Hi, Paul, I thought you'd be interested to know we finally got some mail—about to lift the receiver when it rings. "Hello, Dr. Gold's office," she says quickly, listening to another request for an appointment. "I'm sorry, but Dr. Gold is fully booked for the next two months. The earliest appointment I could give you would be September twenty-first. Yes, okay then, thank you." She replaces the receiver, deciding against phoning Paul, and tries, once again, to concentrate on the accounts in front of her. But now she sees Paul in the empty chair before her, sees a young blonde lean over to whisper in his ear, hears Warren asking her, as he asked on Sunday, how long does this go on, Joanne?

I don't know how long this goes on, she told him. I guess as long as it takes.

The phone rings again. "Dr. Gold's office."

"Mrs. Hunter . . ."

"My God!" Joanne's head shoots up. She should hang up, she thinks, but her hand is paralyzed and won't budge.

"You're looking good these days, Mrs. Hunter," the raspy voice confides.

"How did you find me?" she whispers, trying to smile at a wide-eyed young girl whose unwanted attention her sudden moves have attracted.

"Oh, you're easy to trace, Mrs. Hunter. The easiest one yet."

"Leave me alone." She moves her other hand to block her mouth.

"I have been leaving you alone. I just didn't want you to think that I'd forgotten you, or lost interest in you . . . like your husband has. Isn't that so, Mrs. Hunter? Hasn't your husband found himself another love?"

Joanne slams the receiver back into its carriage.

"The pressure getting to you?" her boss asks, peeking his head around the corner, eyebrows raised.

"Crank call," she tells him, trying to regain her composure. How has he found her?

"My wife's been getting a bunch of those lately. I guess everybody gets them."

"What kind has your wife been getting?" Joanne asks, curious.

"You want details?" He laughs. "The usual." He bends toward her, his voice a hoarse whisper. "Nothing very original, the standard fuck-suck routine. Very boring. My wife likes kinky. What can I tell you? I'm a lucky man." He looks around. "What happened to Mr. Personality?"

"I don't know. I looked up and he was gone. His appointment isn't for another hour."

"That joke I told probably scared him off. I've got to learn some new ones. Where are the samples of benzoyl peroxide?"

"Second room, bottom shelf."

"I looked there. Nothing."

Joanne pushes back her chair and gets up, following the doctor into the second room off the narrow hallway and crossing past the examining table to the cabinet against the far wall. Kneeling down, her skirt hiking up past her knees, she opens the bottom drawer and rifles around inside for a few seconds. When she brings her hand out, it is filled with small sample packets of benzoyl peroxide.

"How'd I miss them?" he asks as she drops them into his hands.

"You have to open your eyes. Occasionally you even have to lift something up."

"You sound like my wife. And she sounds like my mother." He smiles. "But you have the nicest legs."

"Ron, get back to work," Joanne admonishes playfully. "Susan Dotson is waiting for you."

"Oh yes, Susan Dotson, my favorite! She's crazy about me."

When Joanne returns to her desk, Simon Loomis is standing behind it, rifling through the pages of her appointment calendar.

"What are you doing?" she asks, caught off guard, her voice louder than she has intended.

"Just wanted to see if you were really as booked up as you keep telling everybody." The boy backs away from her desk, his loose grin unapologetic. He takes a long sip from the Styrofoam cup Joanne now notices he is holding in his left hand.

Joanne glances across the top of her desk, trying to determine whether anything is missing. "I'd appreciate it if you'd stay on your side of the desk from now on," she tells him curtly, as he takes another sip from the Styrofoam cup. Suddenly, as she watches, his hand begins to shake, and some coffee spills out onto his wrist.

"Ow, Jesus, that's hot!" he yelps. "Why are you staring at me like that?" he demands, accusingly. "You think I stole something? I told you I was just checking . . ."

"Did you phone me?" she asks, her voice surprisingly steady. Would he be so bold, so cocky?

"Phone you? Of course I phoned you! How else would I get an appointment?"

"I don't mean that. I mean *now*. Did you just phone me now?"

"What are you talking about? How could I phone you? I'm standing right in front of you."

"I mean when you were out. When you went for coffee. You know what I mean."

"I don't know what you're talking about. Why would I phone you? Is everybody crazy in this office? You got a doctor who thinks he's a comedian, a receptionist who thinks people phone her when they're standing right in front of her . . ."

"I asked you a question."

"And I gave you an answer. Just what are you accusing me of?"

Joanne looks helplessly around the room. Everyone is staring at them. What is she doing? She doesn't know this Simon Loomis and he doesn't know her. Why would he be the one phoning her? Where would he get his information? "I'm sorry," she says, lowering her body into her chair. "Have a seat. The doctor will be with you as soon as he can." She looks back at her desk. Was anything missing?

"Think I'll wait outside and come back later," the boy tells her.

"Your appointment's at three," Joanne says without looking up.

"Thank you." The sarcasm remains in the air as Joanne hears the door to the office close after him. She takes a deep breath before checking that he has really left, realizing that the pencil in her right hand is shaking and laying it down.

The phone rings. Again her eyes dart toward the door. Impossible, she thinks, he hasn't had enough time.

"Dr. Gold's office," she says, holding her breath. "Oh, hello, Johnny. Oh, okay. How about . . ." She shuffles through her appointment book. ". . . How about the following week then? That's right. Same time the following week. The thirteenth instead of the sixth. Okay. Have a good trip. 'Bye." She replaces the receiver, aware her hand is still trembling, her heart pounding. She bangs her fist against the side of her desk. "Damn," she whispers. "I will not jump every time the phone rings. I will not."

"Talking to yourself again?" Ron Gold asks, emerging from his examining room behind a still snarling Susan Dotson. "Make another appointment for Susan in eight weeks. My mother always used to talk to herself," he continues. "She used to say that whenever she wanted to talk to an intelligent person . . . you know the rest, your mother must have said it to you."

Joanne laughs agreement.

"Mothers have a book of special sayings. They pass it back and forth. Who's next?"

"Mrs. Pepplar."

"Mrs. Pepplar? My favorite!" A tall, dark-haired woman of around fifty rises from her chair. "Right this way, Mrs. Pepplar." Joanne hands Susan Dotson her new appointment card as Ron Gold and Mrs. Pepplar disappear down the narrow hallway.

"See you in eight weeks," Joanne says to the young girl, who pockets the appointment card and exits. The room seems strangely quiet, although it is still filled with people. But they have gone back to their magazines and their own problems, probably having already forgotten the brief exchange they witnessed between Joanne and Simon Loomis. Would any of them be able to describe him for the police, should such a description be necessary? she wonders.

Joanne opens her purse, which she has stuffed underneath her desk, and finds the letters that Lulu has written, taking them out and reading them through quickly again: "Hi, Mom. Camp's great. The food stinks. Kids in my cabin are okay except for one who thinks she's a princess doing us all a big favor by joining us. Weather is great. Did I tell you the food stinks? SEND FOOD! I ripped my new T-shirt. Robin seems to be having a good time although we don't communicate much. See you on visitors' day. Much love. SEND FOOD!!! Love, Lulu. P.S. How are you? Love to Dad."

"Love to Dad," Joanne reads again, picking up the phone, pressing down quickly on the appropriate numbers before she can change her mind. "Paul Hunter," she says, wondering if the receptionist still recognizes her voice. "Paul, it's Joanne," she says quickly when he comes on the line. She doesn't want to take the chance that he might mistake her for somebody else.

"How are you?" He sounds glad to hear from her. "I was going to call you today."

"Yes?"

"I had a letter from Lulu this morning," he tells her.

"I had one too," she says quickly so as to mask her disappointment that this might be the only reason he was planning to call. "Actually, I had three. They all came at once."

"She seems to be enjoying herself—except for the food."

"You got that message too?"

"We can bring her a few things when we go up, I guess. Nothing from Robin, I take it?"

"No. You neither?"

"No, but Lulu says she seems fine."

"Yes," Joanne smiles, "she wrote the same thing to me." There is a pause.

"Are you at work?" he asks finally.

"Yes. It's been very busy all day."

"Here too. I should go . . ."

"Paul?"

"Yes?"

Joanne hesitates. What is she planning to say? "Would you like to come for dinner this weekend? Either Friday or Saturday night, whichever is more convenient."

Even before she is finished with the sentence, Joanne can feel the discomfort on the other end of the line. "I'm sorry, I can't," he tells her quietly. "I'm going out of town for the weekend."

"Oh." Alone? I bet you aren't going alone.

"But the following Sunday, of course, visitors' day at camp . . ."

"Sure, that's fine."

"I'll call you."

Joanne hangs up before realizing she has forgotten to say good-bye.

Why is she here? Joanne wonders as she pulls her car into a vacant spot in the parking lot of Fresh Meadows Country Club. What is she going to do? She gets out of the car and proceeds around the side of the clubhouse to the tennis courts. It is almost six o'clock in the evening. Will he still be here? Why is she here?

The courts are filled. In the first court, two women are playing with a sureness that amazes Joanne. How do women get to be that sure? she wonders, focusing on their concentration, feeling their knees bend, the effortless strokes, the easy follow-through. "Out!" one of the women calls on a shot that is clearly in.

Joanne says nothing, her eyes traveling to the second court, mixed doubles of mixed ability, a husband chastising his wife over an unforced error. "If you're going to hog every ball," he is telling her, "at least get them over the net!"

Joanne walks behind the wire fence past the third court, where four women are wildly fumbling with the ball. None of the players is any good, she realizes, thinking that she could easily fit into this group. They are laughing and having a good time, merrily missing one shot after another, not even bothering to keep score. "Get serious," one woman keeps shouting, but she is laughing as hard as the rest, and Joanne surmises that this is as serious as it gets.

He is watching her from the last court, his eyes following her as she walks behind the wire fence. The basket of bright green balls rests beside his feet as he lifts one from the pile and hits it across the net at the young man he is coaching. "That's it," he calls out, "keep your eye on the ball. Don't try so hard to hit winners every time. Concentrate on getting the ball over the net." He acknowledges her presence invisibly. I'll be with you in a minute, he tells her without saying a word, wait for me. Sure, Joanne thinks, giving her silent consent. Waiting is what I do best.

She sits down on a nearby bench and lets her eyes drift haphazardly from court to court, her mind a bright green tennis ball bouncing back and forth between now and earlier this afternoon. She hears Paul's voice—I'm busy this weekend—sees Simon Loomis's face— I'm back for my three o'clock appointment—recalls the look of concern that flashes across Ron's face—You feeling okay? You're not getting sick on me, are you? She hears the phone ring. Dr. Gold's office. *Mrs. Hunter.* How did you find me? Oh, you're easy to trace. I'm back for my three o'clock appointment. How did you find me? I'm going out of town for the weekend. You feeling okay? *Mrs. Hunter. Mrs. Hunter.*

"Mrs. Hunter?"

"What?"

"Sorry," Steve Henry is saying, his tanned body directly in front of hers, blocking the sun. "I didn't mean to startle you."

Joanne jumps to her feet. Why is she here? "Am I interrupting your lesson?" she asks.

"It's over. I have a couple of minutes. I'm assuming it's me you're here to see." It is as much a question as a statement.

"I have a job," she tells him. Why is she telling him that? "That's why I haven't been around, why I had to cancel the last few lessons."

"I give lessons until nine o'clock in the evening," he tells her, smiling. Is he aware of her discomfort? "Is that why you're here? Do you want to make an appointment for more lessons?" Joanne says nothing. Why *is* she here? "Mrs. Hunter?"

"Please call me Joanne," she tells him, hearing another voice repeating her name. *Mrs. Hunter. Mrs. Hunter.* "I was wondering if you'd like to come for dinner this weekend," she continues quickly. "Either Friday or Saturday night, if you're free." Joanne feels her heart sink into her feet. Why is she saying these things? Why is she asking him to dinner, for God's sake? What is she doing here?

"I'd love to," he answers. "Saturday night would be great."

"I'm a good cook," she informs him, and he smiles.

"I'd come even if you weren't."

"My address is . . ."

"I know your address."

"You do?"

"It's in the records," he reminds her.

She nods. What is she doing here? Whatever possessed her to invite this man for dinner? Because I already asked my husband and he said he was busy! a little voice answers, and because there's some lunatic out there who's not going to give me a whole lot more time on this earth, and damn it, I'm getting tired of waiting, why shouldn't I invite this man for dinner? "What?" she almost shouts, realizing he has spoken.

"I asked you what time you'd like me?"

"Eight o'clock? Or are you still giving lessons then?"

"Not on Saturdays. Eight o'clock is fine." She turns away, not sure what else to do. "Joanne," he calls after her and she stops immediately. Has he changed his mind? "Your new job must agree with you. You look terrific." She smiles. "See you Saturday."

Joanne Hunter drives back to her home thinking that she must be crazy after all.

Chapter 22

"I'm early," he says as she opens the front door and steps back to let him enter the well-lit foyer.

"Come in," Joanne tells him, forcing the words out of her mouth.

Steve Henry stands before her smiling, his right hand half-hidden behind his back, his blond hair brushed away from his forehead. He looks relaxed and confident in tight white pants and a pale pink polo shirt. "Brought you something," he says, bringing his right hand forward, displaying a bottle of Pouilly-Fuissé. "I didn't know if you preferred red or white, and I didn't know what you'd be serving, but I thought that white was the safer choice."

"That's lovely. Thank you." Joanne takes the bottle, not quite sure what to do with it, what to do with *him,* now that he is actually here. Her fantasies have taken her only this far.

For the past few days, she has pictured this scene in her mind in any of a hundred ways, heard his knock at the door, imagined what he will be wearing, seen his hair parted in every conceivable fashion, listened to his opening words. She has allowed her imagination to progress no further. And now Steve Henry is standing in the middle of her well-lit foyer—has she overdone the lights?—having just handed her a bottle of expensive white wine, and she sees that his hair is combed away from his handsomely sweet—yes, sweet!—face, that he is wearing tight white pants (which she thought he might) and a pale pink shirt (which she usually pictured as blue), and he obviously thinks he's staying for dinner (Isn't he? Didn't she spend all morning and most of the afternoon cooking her little heart out?), and she doesn't know what to do with him. (Thank you for the wine; it's been a lovely evening?)

"Would you like to sit down?" she hears herself ask, the hand that is not holding the expensive bottle of white wine motioning toward the living room.

"You have a lovely home," he says, moving easily inside and

comfortably settling into one of the cream-colored swivel chairs, ironically, she thinks, Paul's favorite.

Joanne remains in the foyer, not sure whether to follow Steve Henry into the brightly lit living room or to take the wine into the kitchen, wondering what Mary Tyler Moore would do. "Did you have any trouble finding the house?" she asks, deciding to put the wine in the fridge.

"No, I've been here before," he answers as she disappears into the kitchen.

"You have?" Joanne deposits the wine in the fridge, then stands rooted to the tile floor.

"Well, not here exactly. My parents have friends who live over on Chestnut. Can I help you with anything?"

"No, not a thing. I'll be right there." She doesn't move.

"I love your art," he is saying. "When did you start collecting?"

Joanne has no idea what he is talking about. What art? Her mind is a blank. At this moment, she has absolutely no idea what her living room even looks like. She can see nothing on the walls.

"Joanne?"

"Sorry. What did you ask me?" She has to go into the living room —she can't spend all night in the kitchen. She is being silly. She's acting like an idiot. Still, maybe if she stands here long enough, he'll take the hint and leave. She should never have invited him over in the first place. She can always bring his bottle of wine back to the club later in the week, with a clever little note of apology attached, something that will explain her rude behavior in twenty-five words or less, endearing her to him without encouraging him further. The last thing she needs is another enemy, she thinks, automatically glancing at the phone.

"I asked you about your art," he is saying from the kitchen doorway. "How long have you been collecting?" he repeats, smiling.

"We started a few years back," she tells him, unconsciously switching to the plural pronoun.

"I like your taste." He takes several steps into the kitchen.

"It's Paul's taste mostly," she explains, and he stops. "Dinner's not quite ready. Would you like a drink?"

"Yes," he says. "Scotch and water, please."

"Scotch and water," Joanne repeats, wondering whether or not there is any Scotch in the house, trying to think where it might be.

"If you don't have any . . ."

"I think we do." She hurries past him into the dining room, to the buffet against the tan-colored wall where Paul keeps the liquor. This has always been Paul's department—she has never been much of a drinker. Down on her knees, she rifles through the various bottles in the cabinet. She never realized before just how much liquor they kept.

"Here," he says, his arm brushing against her shoulder as he bends over her to extricate the correct bottle. "All I need now is a glass." Joanne moves immediately to the breakfront on the other wall and retrieves a suitable glass. "And a smile," he tells her as she places the empty glass in his outstretched hand. She finds herself staring into his eyes, her mouth trying to form the requested shape. "That's better," he says. "I think that's the first time you've really looked at me since I walked in the front door."

Joanne is about to protest when she realizes that this is probably true. She immediately looks away.

"No, don't do that. Look at me," he instructs her. Reluctantly, her eyes lift back to his. "You look lovely," he is saying. "I've been wanting to tell you that since I arrived, but we always seemed to be in different rooms." She finds that she is smiling in spite of herself. "You've done something different to your hair."

Joanne's hand lifts automatically to her head. "I had a few streaks put in it," she tells him, feeling instantly self-conscious. "Too much? I told him to just put in a few."

"It's beautiful. Just the right amount. I like it."

"Thank you."

"I also like what you're wearing."

Joanne's eyes drop to her body. She is wearing a pair of narrow, gray silk trousers and a wide-shouldered yellow cotton blouse, a yellow and gray silk scarf belted around her hips the way the sales-lady showed her, all of which are new, as is her cream-colored satin and lace underwear. Joanne blushes at the thought.

"Why are you so nervous?" he asks.

Joanne tries to dismiss the question, to laugh it away—Who me? Nervous? Don't be silly. Instead she replies, "You make me nervous."

"I do? Why?"

"I don't know why, you just do." She abruptly turns and walks back into the kitchen. He is right behind her. "I don't know anything about mixing drinks," she says somewhat defensively. "I'm afraid that you'll have to mix it yourself."

He does so wordlessly, the only sound that of the tap water running. Joanne keeps her eyes on the glass in Steve Henry's hand, eventually following it out of the kitchen and back into the living room as if she is under a hypnotic spell.

"You're sure I can't get you anything?" he asks after they have resumed their former positions, he leaning well back in Paul's favorite chair, she perched on the very edge of the sofa.

"No, thank you. I'm not much of a drinker."

"You still haven't told me why I make you nervous." He is holding his glass in front of his mouth, forcing her to raise her eyes. She notices that he is smiling. "You think I'm going to pounce?"

"Are you?"

"I don't know. Do you want me to?"

"I don't know."

Who are these people? she wonders momentarily. What are they talking about?

"Why did you ask me for dinner?" he is asking.

"I'm not sure."

"Is that an improvement over 'I don't know'?"

What is going on here?

"I'm sorry, I must seem like a real idiot to you," Joanne exclaims, not sure whether to laugh or cry. "I mean, I'm forty-one years old and I'm acting younger than most of the girls I'm sure you date . . ."

"I don't date girls," he corrects. "I date women."

"What does that mean?"

He laughs. "It means that I think most women don't get really interesting until they reach thirty."

Joanne stares into her lap. "And men? When do they get interesting?"

"You'll have to tell me."

Joanne's head moves restlessly from side to side. "I hope you like chicken," she says when she can think of nothing else to say.

"I love chicken."

"I'm a good cook."

"So you told me."

Her head returns to her lap. "This was a mistake," she says finally. "I should never have asked you here."

"Do you want me to leave?"

Yes. "No . . . yes!" No.

"Which is it?"

"No," Joanne whispers after a pause, realizing it is true. "I want you to stay." She tries to laugh. "I spent all day cooking."

"All day?"

"Well, almost all day. I took a few hours off this afternoon to visit my grandfather." Steve Henry looks interested. "He's ninety-five," she continues, not sure why except that it feels good to take the focus off herself. "He lives in a nursing home. Baycrest Nursing Home over on . . ."

"I know where it is."

"You do?"

He nods and takes a sip of his drink.

"I visit him every Saturday afternoon," Joanne continues, reassured by the sound of her own voice. "Most of the time he doesn't know who I am. He thinks I'm my mother . . . she's dead . . . she died three years ago . . . so did my father . . . anyway, I visit my grandfather every Saturday afternoon. I tell him everything that's been happening, try to keep him up on things. Everybody thinks that must be very hard on me but the fact is that I enjoy it. He's kind of like a father confessor, I guess. I tell him everything; it makes me feel better." Why is she going on about this? What does Steve Henry care about her relationship with her grandfather? "Are your grandparents still alive?" she asks.

"Both sets," he smiles.

"You're lucky."

"Yes, I am. We're a very close family."

"You've never been married?" Why is she asking that? Why is she bringing the conversation back into this room?

He shakes his head. "Came close once, but it didn't work out. We were too young." He finishes his drink. "How old were you when you got married?"

"Twenty-one," she says. "I guess that was pretty young, but it just seemed right." Her voice lapses into silence. "I think maybe I will have a drink," she says suddenly.

"What'll it be?" He is already on his feet.

"Is there any Dubonnet?" She feels instantly foolish. The man has never been in her house before tonight, and she is asking him what liquor she keeps.

He disappears into the dining room. She can hear bottles being moved about, soon the sound of liquid being poured into a glass, followed by footsteps, and the sound of water running in the kitchen.

She watches as Steve Henry returns several minutes later with a freshly filled glass in each hand, handing her one. "Are these your daughters?" he asks, pointing to a framed photograph of Robin and Lulu on the mantel over the fireplace. The picture is two years old; the girls have their arms entwined around each other's waists and are mugging broadly for the camera.

"Yes," Joanne tells him. "The one on the left is Robin, she's fifteen now, almost sixteen . . . she'll be sixteen in September, and the other one is Lulu . . . Lana, actually, her real name is Lana, but we've always called her Lulu. She's eleven."

"They look very sweet."

Joanne laughs. "Well, I'm not sure sweet is a word I would use to describe them." She shakes her head, recalling some of the events of the last few months. "There are some days when they're wonderful, when I wouldn't trade them for all the money in the world. Then there are other days, I'd sell them both for a wooden nickel. They're at camp for the summer," she continues. "I got a letter from Lulu the other day . . . she seems to be having a great time. Robin, I'm afraid, isn't much of a letter writer . . ." She stops abruptly. "Why am I telling you this? You can't be very interested."

"Why can't I be?"

"Why should you be?"

"Because things that interest you, interest me."

"Why?"

"Because *you* interest me."

"Why?"

"Why not?"

Joanne lifts her glass to her mouth and takes a long swallow, trying to organize her thoughts into something vaguely coherent. "For one thing, I'm twelve years older than you are. I know that you think that women don't get interesting until they hit thirty," she continues quickly, "but the fact remains that I was a teenager while you were still in diapers."

He laughs. "I'm out of diapers now."

"What do you want from me?" she asks.

"Dinner?" he ventures shyly, watching with a smile as Joanne downs the remaining contents of her glass.

"That's the best lemon meringue pie I've ever tasted," he is telling her as he finishes his second piece and pushes his plate into the center of the long, rectangular, oak table. "I'd ask for a third, but I'm afraid I might never walk again, let alone live to dazzle on the courts."

Joanne smiles, grateful that the dinner is over and that it has been a success. Steve Henry is sitting at her right elbow, having moved his placemat from the far end of the table to the place beside hers. He has said all the right things, made none of the wrong moves. He has complimented her on the decor, the food, and even the coffee. They have discussed tennis, her toes, and the state of world politics. He has been pleasant and attentive and generally nice to be around. Why then does she so desperately wish that he would leave?

"How about a liqueur?" he asks, pushing his chair back and moving swiftly to the liquor cabinet, fully at ease now and obviously not in any hurry to rush out.

"No thanks." She shakes her head for emphasis.

"Drambuie, Benedictine, Grand Marnier," he reads, reciting the various labels. "I think I'll have a little Tia Maria. You're sure I can't persuade you to join me?"

Joanne hesitates. She has always found the taste of liqueur too sweet. "Maybe just a bit of Benedictine . . ." she ventures. Benedictine has always been Paul's choice.

"A bit of Benedictine it is."

In the next minute, they are toasting each other with delicate glasses of amber liquid. "To tonight," he says.

Joanne nods without speaking and takes a tiny sip from her glass. The thick syrup warms her insides immediately, tasting sweet and curiously pungent at the same time. "It's good," she has to admit, savoring its conflicting nature.

"Tell me about your husband," Steve Henry says, surprising her. She feels the small glass almost tumble out of her hand, catching it by its rim just before it slips through her fingers. Has he noticed?

"What can I say?" she asks, careful not to look at him. "He's a lawyer, very smart, very successful . . ."

"Very successful maybe. Not very smart."

"Why do you say that?"

"If he had any brains, I wouldn't be here."

"I wish you wouldn't say things like that."

"Why?"

"Because they make me uncomfortable," she tells him, fidgeting in her chair and taking another sip of her Benedictine, feeling her throat warm instantly, as if someone had lit a match.

"Why should compliments make you uncomfortable?"

"Because they're too facile," she says strongly. "I'm sorry. I don't mean to be unpleasant, but I've never been very good at any of this . . ."

"Any of what?"

"Any of . . . this! The games. Dating. I wasn't very good at it twenty years ago and I'm worse at it now."

"Am I the first man you've dated since your separation?"

Joanne nods, feeling her cheeks redden.

"I'm flattered."

"I'm scared to death."

"Of me?"

"You'll do."

He laughs. "Is that why you have every light in the house on?"

It is her turn to laugh. "Subtlety has never been my strong suit."

"What is?"

"You just ate it."

"There's more to you than lemon meringue pies." He smiles.

"What makes you so sure?"

"I'm a good judge of character."

She laughs. "I'm a lousy judge of character," she says.

"Describe yourself in three words."

"Oh, come on . . ."

"No, I'm serious. Indulge me. Three words."

She rests her head in the palm of her left hand, positioning her face away from his penetrating eyes. "Scared," she whispers finally. "Confused." She lets out a deep breath of air. "Lonely," she says finally. "How's that for an uplifting appraisal?" Her eyes return reluctantly to his.

"Lousy," he says and suddenly he is kissing her, his lips softly pressing against her own. The subtle scent of Tia Maria enters her nostrils; she tastes it on the tip of her tongue. "Now how do you feel?" he asks.

"Scared," she replies evenly. "Confused." She laughs. "Not quite so lonely."

He leans forward to kiss her again.

Immediately she brings her small glass to her lips.

"What's the matter?"

"I don't think I'm ready for this."

"Ready for what?"

"For whatever this is leading up to."

"Which is?"

She shakes her head. "I feel so foolish."

"Why? Why do you feel foolish?"

"Please don't play with me. I told you I wasn't very good at these games."

"You don't like games? Okay, I'll tell you straight out where I'd like this to lead," Steve Henry says. "I'd like it to lead upstairs. I'd like it to lead to your bed. I want to make love to you. Is that straightforward enough?"

"Can we talk about something else?" Joanne pleads, standing up and starting to clear away the dishes.

"Sure. We can talk about anything you'd like. Here, let me help you." He picks up his empty plate.

"I'll do that," she tells him.

"Let me help you," he repeats.

"Oh, put the goddamn dish down!" she shouts, then immediately buries her face in her hands.

Suddenly he is beside her and his arms are around her, his mouth buried against the soft curls of her hair. "Let me help you," he says again, his lips finding hers, his body pressing tightly against her own.

"You don't understand," she tries to tell him.

"I do understand."

"I'm afraid . . ."

"I know."

"No," she says, pulling back, feeling his arms reluctantly letting her go. "You don't know." She is aware of tears falling the length of her cheek. "You think that I'm afraid because you're the first man I've dated since my separation, but it's more than that." She looks helplessly around the room. "I got married when I was twenty-one. My husband was the first real boyfriend I ever had. Do you understand what I am saying? Paul is the only lover I've ever had, the only man I've ever known. I'm forty-one years old and I've only known one man my entire life. And he left me! Somehow I let him down. And now you come along, with your perfect twenty-nine-year-old body, and I don't know what you think I can give you but . . ."

"How about what I can give you?"

"I'll disappoint you . . ."

He pulls her into the hall. "Let's go upstairs," he says.

"I can't."

Once again his arms are around her waist as he presses her back against the hardness of the wall, her body beginning to respond to urges she has felt in the past only when she was with Paul. She sees Steve Henry lift his arm toward the light switch, watches as the hall goes suddenly dark, feels his lips brush against the sides of her own. And then suddenly, he is backing away. Her eyes search out his in the surrounding shadows.

"I'm not going to force you to do something you don't want to do," he is saying. "If you want me to go, then say so. Tell me to go."

Her eyes remain locked on his. Slowly, her lips move to form the appropriate word. "Stay," she says.

Chapter 23

Joanne cannot believe what is happening. She is trying her best to pretend that it isn't.

They are in her bedroom. She has a vague recollection of having been half-carried up the stairs, her arms draped around unfamiliar young shoulders, her mouth fastened to lips that are somewhat fuller than she is used to, two mismatched bodies curiously joined at the hip as they tumble toward the bedroom. Now they are beside the bedroom window, and she has barely enough time to pull the drapes closed before this stranger surrounds her again, his strong hands delicately caressing her outstretched arms as he draws them around his narrow waist, his mouth searching out hers, his legs burrowing in between her own. She feels strangely giddy and light-headed and has to resist the ill-timed impulse to laugh. Sex is funny after all, she thinks, but knows that he will not understand. The young take sex so seriously. They have yet to discover the humor in it. She feels confident hands at her breasts and closes her eyes tightly, pretending they are Paul's hands. Her breath comes in short, frightened gasps, as if he is holding a pillow over her head. She tries to pull away, to throw off the suffocating pillow, but he refuses to release her.

"Easy," he cautions, drawing her toward the bed, his fingers tugging at the buttons of her blouse.

She is momentarily distracted by the mechanics of disrobing. This is a new blouse, she thinks. She has just paid almost a hundred dollars for it. The buttons are unique, flower-shaped, which is probably why he is having such difficulty with them. She feels the impatience in his fingers, and hopes that he doesn't get tired and just rip the buttons off. They would be difficult to replace; the blouse is new; it would be a shame to ruin it after only one wearing.

Somehow he has the buttons undone and he is slowly pulling the blouse off her shoulders. She fights the urge to catch it before it falls to the floor, recognizing that they will probably step all over it in the next few minutes, and that she will have to wash and iron it the next day. Perhaps she should take it to the cleaners. She'll have to check the label in the morning.

His hands are tracing the soft lace around her new bra. Can he see it in the dark? Has he any idea how much these things cost today? Oh God, what is he doing? she wonders as he easily locates the front clasp and pushes the soft fabric away from her now bare breasts. "You're beautiful," she hears him mutter as he moves his mouth down her neck. She covers her eyes with her hands, her arms blocking her exposed breasts from his view, her elbows knocking against the bones of his cheeks.

"Sorry," she apologizes quickly, but her arms refuse to budge from their protective position.

He says nothing, gently prying her arms apart, holding them firmly behind her back as his lips return to her breasts, tracing the outlines of her nipples.

Joanne looks helplessly around the room, searching for someone to rescue her. In the darkness, she locates the image of Eve watching her from the doorway. Not bad, Eve is saying. Relax. Enjoy yourself.

Help me, Joanne pleads, but Eve only smiles, making herself at home in the comfortable blue chair at the foot of Joanne's bed. Relax, silly. This is opportunity knocking. Enjoy it.

Steve Henry's hands are at the side button of her trousers, Joanne realizes, wishing they could just forget about all this nonsense and go back to kissing. That was fun, not nearly so demanding. It didn't require as much concentration, being relatively easy to close her eyes and imagine the lips she was kissing were Paul's. It is harder to make substitutions when entire bodies are involved, when she is dealing with altogether different techniques.

As if he understands what she is thinking, his mouth is suddenly back on hers, his tongue growing more insistent. Paul would not be so relentless, she thinks as her slacks fall to the floor. She hears the soft fabric being kicked aside, wonders if he has taken off his shoes. Silk is so expensive to clean, she thinks in dismay, wondering where she acquired this streak of practicality, wishing that she could lose herself in the fantasy of what is happening.

Which is precisely the problem, she realizes—that it *is* happening. This is not a fantasy. This is reality. And the reality of the situation is that she is on her way to bed with a man she doesn't love and barely knows except that she knows he is not Paul, no matter how tightly she closes her eyes and tries to imagine otherwise.

Whatever it is, she hears Eve protest, it's not half bad. Get with it, my girl. Reality or illusion—who cares? Enjoy.

I can't, Joanne cries silently as Steve Henry pushes her across her bed, leaning her head gently against her pillows, his hands skimming over the bare surface of her exposed stomach. This is not the way I'm used to being touched, she tries to tell him, though she says nothing. It tickles and I'm very ticklish. Paul understands this. He knows just how to touch me. He knows how to make me relax, how to dispel my self-consciousness, not heighten it.

His fingers are pulling at her panties, pushing them down over her thighs. I'm so embarrassed I could die, Joanne thinks, burying her face into the side of the pillow, trying to pretend she is somewhere else as his hands pry her legs apart.

"You're going to like this," he is whispering softly as she feels his tongue teasing the insides of her thighs.

It is typical of the younger generation, she decides in this moment, that they think they have invented oral sex. All the various rock singers writhing on the concert stages of the world, miming fellatio to the shocked squeals of their pubescent audience and horrified parents. What would really shock them, she thinks, is the discovery that their parents—and just about everybody else—were doing it for years before they were born, and that the only thing shocking about any of it is their collective naiveté in imagining that theirs is the first generation to have come up with this idea.

She pulls at his hair, forcing his head up. He mistakes this for passion, interprets her discomfort as excitement, impatience to move on. She hears the rustle of clothes, knows that he is pulling off his shirt, feels Eve lean forward in the blue chair to have a better look. Joanne's eyes remain closed tight. She refuses to open them as he takes her hand in his and guides it toward the front of his pants.

"I know where it is," she says suddenly, her voice cutting through the stillness of the room like a knife through a perfect arch of meringue.

"What?" he asks, his voice hoarse, as if she has just jolted him awake, which perhaps she has.

Her hand grips the bulge at the front of his pants. "I said I know where it is," she repeats. "You don't have to show me."

He sits up abruptly, dislodging her hand. His tone is sad, curious. "What's the matter?"

She shakes her head, pulling her body into a sitting position.

"There's nothing the matter."

"You sound angry."

"I'm not angry."

That's exactly what I am, she thinks. I'm angry. Angry at me for putting myself in this position; angry at you because you're not the man I want you to be, because you can't be the man I want you to be, because the man I want doesn't want me anymore, because I'm stupid and old and useless and ugly . . .

"If you're not angry," he is saying, oblivious to these inner ravings, "then lie back down beside me." He pulls her back across the bed, his fingers returning to her nipples. "Relax," he says.

"I can't relax," she says impatiently, brushing his hand aside.

"Why not?"

"Because I find what you're doing very distracting," she tells him.

"Distracting?"

"I can't concentrate when you do that."

"You're not supposed to be concentrating on anything *but* that," he tells her. "What's the matter, Joanne? What's happening that I'm not aware of?"

She pulls at the covers of the bed and brings them up protectively around her naked body. "It's not your fault. It's not you."

"Who else is it?" he demands. "Who else is here?"

"Too many ghosts," she replies helplessly, after a pause.

Eve pushes herself off the blue chair at the foot of Joanne's bed. She shakes her head in dismay, lifts her palms into the air in a gesture of defeat, and promptly disappears.

"I'm sorry," Joanne is saying as Steve Henry pulls his pale pink polo shirt over his head, struggling momentarily with one of the sleeves. "I wanted to. I thought I could."

"Maybe you thought you could," he corrects her, looking around in the dark for his shoes, "but you certainly didn't want to. Do you mind if I turn on some lights?" he asks. "I can't see anything."

Joanne pulls the covers higher so that they reach her chin. "Go ahead."

He doesn't move. "Where are they?" he asks finally, sounding like a lost little boy afraid of the dark.

"I'll do it," Joanne says, reaching over to the end table beside her and switching on the lamp, wincing as the room comes into bright, sharp focus.

Steve Henry quickly locates his shoes as Joanne glances at the clock radio. It is only half past ten.

"Are you angry?" she asks.

"Yes," he tells her truthfully, "but I'll get over it."

"It really has nothing to do with you."

"So you've said." Fully dressed now, he turns to face her. "I'm not sure quite how to take that, to be honest. What exactly does it mean?"

"That I love my husband," she says quietly. "That it may be stupid and old-fashioned and even pathetic, I don't know, but something inside me is telling me that there's still hope for Paul and me, and that if I give in to . . . this, then I'm somehow giving up on us, that I'm setting myself down a different path, starting down some irreversible course, and I'm not ready to do that. Not yet anyway. I don't know if I'm making any sense . . ."

He shakes his head. "I'm a tennis pro," he says, "what do I know of sense?"

She smiles. "I like you," she says, meaning it sincerely, hoping he understands this.

"I like you too."

They laugh.

"You're a nice boy," she tells him.

"Man," he corrects.

She nods.

"I'll show myself out." Joanne can see the question in his eyes. He is wondering whether he should kiss her good night. "Goodbye," he says finally, having decided against it, disappearing through the doorway. Joanne listens to his footsteps on the stairs, hears the front door open and close, listens as the house lapses into silence. Drawing her knees up against her chest, she lowers her face into her hands and pulls at the sides of her hair in frustration.

The phone rings.

"No!" she yells, jumping out of bed, running into the bathroom and slamming the door behind her. The phone's persistent ring follows her to the bathtub as she frantically turns on the faucets full blast, trying to block out the unwanted sound. "Stop it!" she screams through the closed door. "Stop it. I can't take it anymore!" The phone ignores her. It continues to ring, mocking her pleas.

Joanne suddenly pulls open the bathroom door and glares at the telephone. "Come and get me already!" she yells. "Just stop playing with me!" He is out there somewhere watching me, she thinks, twirling around. He is hiding out there, has been hiding out there all evening waiting for Steve Henry to leave. He is out there now—right this minute. He knows what I've been doing. He knows I've been a bad girl. Soon he will punish me for it.

She runs to the phone and yanks the receiver from its hook. She says nothing, only waits.

"Joanne?"

"Eve?" Joanne collapses on the bed, tears springing to her eyes.

"What took you so long to answer the phone? What's going on there? Where did Steve Henry go?"

"I was in the bathtub," Joanne replies, stretching the truth in order to simplify it, answering Eve's questions one at a time. "Nothing's going on. He went home."

"What do you mean he went home? Is he coming back?"

"No, he's not coming back."

"You're finished already?"

"Nothing happened, Eve."

"Please don't tell me that, Joanne, you'll ruin my night. What do you mean, nothing happened?"

Joanne shrugs, grateful for the sound of Eve's voice though she is reluctant to go into details, wanting to forget the evening as quickly as possible.

"You mean he just ate dinner and left? No pitch? Nothing?"

"Nothing," Joanne confirms.

"Nothing? I can't believe that! You're not telling me something, Joanne. I can feel it."

"He made his pitch," Joanne says, giving in part way. "I said no."

"You said no? Are you crazy?"

"Maybe. I don't know anymore."

"If you don't know, I'll tell you. You're crazy! I can't believe that you actually let that magnificent hunk get away. I said to myself as I saw his car pull out, she can't be letting him leave. Maybe he's going out for some cigarettes, maybe he forgot his toothbrush and he's going home to get it, but surely to God, *surely* she didn't tell him to leave!"

"What were you doing watching my house?" Joanne asks suddenly.

"I wasn't watching your house," Eve replies defensively. "I happened to look out my window and saw his car pulling away. How is that watching your house? What are you talking about?"

"Nothing," Joanne says quickly. What *is* she talking about? "Where's Brian?"

"Asleep."

"Why aren't you?"

"I can't. I'm too nervous."

"About what?"

"About that CAT scan on Monday morning."

"Well, try not to think about it. Why don't you come by the office on Monday after it's over and we'll have lunch together."

"I can't."

"Why not?"

"I just can't. Look, I'll speak to you tomorrow. Get back in your bath and contemplate what a jerk you are!"

Joanne stares into the receiver as the line goes dead in her hands.

What is she doing here? Joanne wonders as the outside air brushes against her bare legs like a cat. How did she get here?

She is standing in her backyard by the deep end of her empty, aborted swimming pool, staring through the darkness at what looks like a giant open grave. My grave, she thinks, for when he comes for me.

There is something in her right hand. Joanne lifts her arm into the air. The tennis racquet slices silently through the night sky. Follow through, she hears Steve Henry say. "Damn!" she curses into the surrounding stillness. "Damn!" She lets the tennis racquet fall to her side, feels its weight heavy in her hand.

What is she doing here? Why is she standing in the middle of her backyard in the middle of the night with nothing on but her panties and a hot pink T-shirt with the name Picasso scrawled across its front —a remnant of the 1980 exhibit at the Museum of Modern Art— clutching her tennis racquet tightly in her right hand? Why isn't she asleep?

She isn't asleep because she couldn't sleep. After a scalding hot bath that she hoped would relax her—but that only succeeded in making her more restless—and an hour spent tossing and turning in her bed to no avail, she finally abandoned any hope of sleep and came downstairs, where she first cleared the dining room table, then stacked the dirty dishes in the dishwasher, and finally made herself a fresh cup of coffee, all the while replaying the night's events in her mind like a series of bad television reruns.

"You're an idiot," she whispers, feeling her toes overlapping the side of the pool, wincing as she recalls her little speech to Steve Henry just before his departure. I can't give up hope, she hears herself say, or whatever dumb phrase she used. "What hope?" she asks out loud. The hope that your husband will come back? Your husband is going forward, not coming back! He's away for the weekend, out for the duration. You can bet that he isn't standing beside the deep end of some empty summer cottage without the traffic worrying about his soon-to-be ex-wife. What's to worry about? He knows she's there waiting should he ever decide he's had enough of the little Judys of this world and want to come home.

Eve is right—I *am* a jerk. Joanne thinks. A middle-aged jerk who doesn't even have enough brains to let a beautiful young man give her one night of pleasure. Jerk! she hears Eve chide. Follow through, Steve Henry urges.

Lifting the tennis racquet, which she only vaguely remembers having retrieved from the front hall closet, Joanne hurls it with all her strength into the deep end of the pool. It crashes against the side of the concrete and bounces several times along the pool's bottom before finally spinning to a lonely stop. She can't make out where it has finally come to rest. She doesn't care. She has no more use for tennis racquets. Standing alone in the darkness, Joanne thinks that this empty, concrete hole is the perfect symbol for her life. Nature (or Rogers Pools anyway) imitating the thoughts of man.

It is several minutes before she is aware of other sounds, a crackling of branches, a subtle rustling of grass. Movement unconnected with the natural sounds of night. She turns quickly, but sees nothing, hears nothing. But something is there. She can feel a new presence, knows instinctively that she is not alone.

So he has come, she thinks, feeling her heart beginning to race. He has been waiting for just this opportunity and now she has handed it to him without even a struggle. She pictures the headlines in the morning paper, wonders where the police will discover her body, tries to imagine her final seconds of life. Can you imagine what must have been going through her mind those last minutes? she remembers Karen Palmer asking.

"Mrs. Hunter," the voice wafts eerily through the stillness.

Joanne gasps, closing her eyes against the sound of the recognizable dull rasp. "What do you want from me?" she cries.

"You know what I want," the voice replies.

Where is he? Joanne wonders, opening her eyes to strain through the darkness, trying to figure out from which direction the voice is coming. Somewhere to her left she hears movement, feels someone walking toward her.

"Mrs. Hunter," the voice calls from almost at her side.

Joanne spins around to see a tall figure emerging from the blackness. Gradually she discerns the familiar outline of a long, angular face framed by hair that falls in even waves around its narrow chin. "Eve!" she cries as the figure comes fully into view.

Eve's laugh is almost a shriek. "You should see your face!" She hoots. "Even in the dark, you look like you're going to shit your pants!"

"What the *fuck* are you doing?" Joanne screams, not aware of the profanity until she hears it echo against the silence of the night.

Eve is nearly hysterical with laughter. "You should have heard your voice—'What do you want from me?' " she mimics. "I love it! You were wonderful."

"What are you talking about? What are you doing here?" Joanne repeats, her knees giving out as she collapses to the ground, sobbing. "You scared me half to death!"

"Oh, come on," Eve retorts, managing to sound like the injured party, "where's your sense of humor?" The laughter has left her voice. "I was looking out my bedroom window and I saw you come out here. I thought you might like some company."

"Are you crazy?" Joanne can see Eve clearly now, as if someone had suddenly turned on all the lights. She sees the smile on Eve's face turn sour, her expression freeze. "Why should you try to scare me like that?"

"I didn't think you'd take it so seriously," Eve replies, again sounding as if she, and not Joanne, is the one aggrieved. "I forgot how obsessed you are about all this."

"Obsessed?"

"Yes, obsessed. You should hear yourself sometimes on the subject, you sound positively Looney Tunes." Her voice slips back into its former eery rasp. " 'Mrs. Hunter,' " Eve mimics, "I'm coming to get you, Mrs. Hunter . . .' "

"Stop it!"

"Look, Joanne, I'm sorry I scared you. I really didn't think you'd turn it into such a big deal."

Joanne says nothing. She is suddenly overwhelmed by exhaustion and cannot find her voice.

"Are you going to sulk?" Eve demands.

Joanne shakes her head. "I'm not sure what I'm going to do," she whispers finally.

"Well, I'm going home to bed," Eve informs her, making no move to go anywhere. "Serves you right for letting Steve Henry get away," she adds, trying to joke.

"Eve," Joanne begins, her voice rising with each successive word as she pushes herself up off the flagstone. "Get out of here before I push you into the goddamn pool!"

A masculine voice cuts through the darkness. "What the hell's going on down there?"

Both women turn toward the sound, looking up, seeing nothing but the outline of Eve's house next door. Joanne recognizes Brian's voice, is grateful for it.

"Joanne, are you all right? Is that Eve with you?"

Joanne swallows hard. She feels dizzy and light-headed and wonders if she is going to faint.

"We're fine," Eve answers for her.

"Well, what the hell are you doing? This is hardly the time for a hen party. It's after midnight. Is something wrong?"

"Everything's fine," Eve says wearily. "Stop yelling before you wake up the whole neighborhood. I'll be right up." She turns to Joanne. "You're not still angry, are you?" she asks plaintively.

"Yes, I'm still angry," Joanne responds, her voice a frustrated, disbelieving whisper.

Eve's eyebrows arch and her jaw stiffens. She says nothing as she spins around and vanishes into the night.

Chapter 24

"Are you tired?" he is asking.

Joanne closes her eyes against the bright morning sunlight—she has forgotten her sunglasses on the kitchen table—and leans her head against the deep tan leather of the car's interior, realizing that it has been a long time since she has occupied the passenger seat of her husband's car. It feels good, she thinks, glancing over at him. "A little," she confesses. "I didn't sleep much last night. I guess I'm a bit nervous."

"Don't be," Paul tells her. "Everything will be fine."

"I hope you're right."

"You brought the food they asked for, didn't you?"

"Every piece of junk they requested."

"Then they'll be happy."

Joanne smiles, trying to look reassured. Will the girls be glad to see her? She pictures Lulu running full throttle toward the car, sees Robin linger behind in the shadows, her eyes as unforgiving as they were a month ago, her posture as unapproachable.

"It's hard to believe the summer's half over," Paul is saying.

Joanne nods. Time goes by quickly when you're having fun, she thinks, checking her watch. It is almost eight o'clock. They have been driving for an hour, making good time despite the steady stream of traffic. Barring any unforeseen accidents, they should arrive in Massachusetts in another two hours, arriving at Camp Danbee when the gates open at 10 A.M. Will Robin be waiting at the gate to greet them?

She has received only one letter from her older daughter in the month she has been away, as compared to Lulu's five. The letter was brief, mildly informative, and decidedly formal: "Dear Mom, how are you? I am fine. The weather is good. I am participating in all the sports. My swimming has improved. The girls in my cabin are nice enough. The counsellors are okay; the food is not. Your new job sounds interesting." Signed, simply, "Robin."

At least it was something, Joanne supposes, studying the scenery along the highway. How green everything is, how beautiful in the early morning sunlight, although the weatherman on the car radio is gloomily predicting rain for later in the afternoon.

"Did you see your grandfather yesterday?" Paul is asking.

Joanne nods. "He slept the whole time."

"And Eve? How is she?"

Joanne feels her body tense; her fingers curl forward into tight little fists, her nails digging into the palms of her hands. "I haven't spoken to her all week," she tells him, catching the look of surprise that fills his face.

"You're kidding! How come? She and Brian finally get away somewhere?"

"No," Joanne says, wanting to provide him with the details of what has been going on, but not sure what useful purpose this would serve. "We've both been very busy this week."

"Your job keeping you pretty occupied?"

"Never a dull moment," she comments wryly, thinking how wonderful Paul looks. His face is deeply tanned against the open neck of his white shirt. His legs look lean and muscular as they stretch out from beneath white jeans that have been cut off above the knees. He has always looked good in shorts. "Are you still working out every day?" she asks.

A brief chuckle escapes his lips. "Not quite every day," he admits sheepishly. "I tried. I was pretty good for a few weeks there, but I don't know, I guess it's true what they say about old dogs and new tricks. I just can't seem to get into it the same way these younger guys can. Hell, that stuff hurts! I wake up in the morning, my legs are stiff, my arms are sore, my back is killing me, and I think, who needs it? Not that I've dropped the exercise program completely," he adds, "but I find my enthusiasm is definitely on the wane. It's too much work to have muscles. I've managed without them up to now." He smiles. "Besides, my arms will never develop fully anyway . . . all those accidents as a kid . . ." He looks over at her slyly and they both laugh. "You look wonderful," he tells her sincerely. "What have you done to yourself?"

"I put some streaks in my hair."

He shakes his head. "It's more than that."

"I lost a few pounds. I've been running around a lot lately . . ."

She feels his eyes on her legs. "And the tennis lessons?"

"I've stopped those." She clears her throat nervously.

"Oh?"

"Too hard on the toes," she tells him, her eyes following his as they travel the length of her bare legs to the tips of her sandaled feet. "I think the nails are about ready to fall off."

He winces. "And then what happens?"

"Ron says that there are probably new ones under there already."

"Ron?"

"Ron Gold, the doctor I work for. I told you. We went to school together."

Paul shrugs, his eyes returning to the road ahead, but not before Joanne has caught a strange look passing across them. "Have I ever met him?" Paul asks, and Joanne recognizes in his tone the familiar sound of someone straining to sound casual. Familiar because it is a quality she associates with her own voice.

"I don't think so," she tells him.

"The name sounds familiar. What does he look like?"

Joanne has to suppress a smile. She can actually feel Paul's discomfort. Is he jealous? "He's not too tall," she begins. "He has reddish-blond hair. Actually he looks the same as he did twenty-five years ago. He's a nice-looking man," she adds, not sure why.

"Married?"

"Yes."

"You still planning to stop work at the end of the summer?"

"Yes," Joanne replies after a pause.

"You don't sound sure."

"Ron doesn't want me to leave. He says he'll be lost without me." She laughs. "I think he's right."

"So you're thinking of staying on?"

Joanne takes a minute to ponder the question seriously. "No, not really," she says finally.

They drift into silence, the remainder of the journey passing with only a minimum of words between them, the easy-listening music on the radio providing a soothing backdrop for their individual reveries.

What is he thinking? Joanne wonders, curiously relaxed, the early morning tension dissipated. Or is it that it has been transferred from her body to his? Can it be that Paul is jealous? Probably not jealous, she corrects herself, but certainly curious, maybe a touch anxious. The thought that there could be another man in her life is something that has obviously not occurred to him. Up until this minute, he has been sure that she will do nothing to disturb the status quo, that she will remain available until he has decided her fate, confident that he has all the time in the world to reach a decision. Now he is not so sure. Are you thinking about me? she asks him silently, her eyes sneaking toward his.

He looks at her and smiles warmly. Surprisingly, she is the first to turn away, laying her head against the headrest, gradually allowing her heavy lids to close. Something is happening, she feels, though she is not sure what it is.

When she opens her eyes, their car is off the main highway, traveling slowly down a different road.

"We're almost there," he tells her, and she sits up, searching for the camp gates. "Just another couple of miles," he says. "How was your sleep?"

"Terrific," she says, amazed that she dropped off so easily. Last night she was sure she'd never get through the day, and now she's already slept through part of it. It should all be this easy, she thinks as the gates of Camp Danbee come into view. "What time is it?" she asks, noticing for the first time that they are in a long lineup of cars.

"Just after ten. We're right on time."

"Do you see them?" she asks, looking through the crowd gathered just inside the camp gate.

"Not yet."

Paul maneuvers the car into the campgrounds to the designated parking area. Joanne looks eagerly around for a glimpse of her daughters, her previous anxieties returning full force. Will Robin be here to greet them? Will she be receptive or standoffish? What will the day be like? What will the drive home be like? Will they ever be a real family again?

The car comes to a stop and Paul pulls the keys out of the ignition. With deliberate slowness, he reaches over and takes her hand in his.

"It'll be all right," he tells her softly, reading her thoughts, his fingers lingering on hers. Then quietly he adds, "I love you, Joanne."

Joanne's heart lurches. The lushness of the surrounding scenery vanishes; the noisy crowd of some three hundred girls grows silent. Joanne is aware only of Paul, of the touch of his fingers, the sound of his voice.

"Mom!" she hears from somewhere outside the car window and turns to see Lulu banging rapturously at the glass beside her head. How long has she been standing there?

"Sweetie!" Joanne cries, opening the car door and immediately encircling her younger daughter in her arms. "Let me look at you. I think you've grown a foot since you left." She pushes the hair out of her daughter's eyes. "And your eyes have gotten bigger!" She laughs.

"It just looks that way because the rest of me is wasting away," Lulu says. "Did you bring food?"

"Yes, we brought food," Paul laughs, joining them. "You look wonderful. Are you having a good time?"

"It's great. Only this one kid in the cabin is a real pain, but everybody else is great, and the counsellors are terrific. You'll meet them." She throws her arms around their waists, pulling them toward one another with surprising force. "I missed you. You both look terrific." Reluctantly she releases her grip and pulls back, her eyes darting back and forth between them.

"Where's Robin?" Paul asks, a question Joanne has been afraid to voice.

"She's at the waterfront," Lulu tells them. "She's in the sailing exhibition. It starts in a couple of minutes. I'm supposed to take you there if you want to watch her sail."

"Of course we want to watch her sail," Joanne says, her arm tightly around her daughter. "Point us in the right direction."

"What about the food?"

"We'll get it later," Paul tells her, moving to Lulu's other side.

They proceed to the waterfront, arms tightly interlocked. Joanne feels happy, confident, even peaceful. Something has changed between herself and Paul. They will be a family again, she thinks as the water comes into view and a panorama of white sails greets their smiling eyes.

"So then I go, just trying to be nice, I go, 'Do you know you have your sweatshirt on inside out?' and she goes, real snooty, 'Of course I know it's inside out. It's supposed to be inside out. That's how everybody wears them,' and I go, 'I've never seen anybody wear them inside out before,' and she goes, '*Everybody* at Brown wears them that way,' like *she* goes to Brown University, not her older brother. And I go, 'Oh, really. Tell me about it.' "

Joanne is listening to Lulu but watching Robin, who has said very little all morning. The family of four is sitting on a large red-and-blue quilt that once belonged to Joanne's mother, eating the barbequed hamburgers and drinking the soft drinks that are the regular staples of the camp's annual outdoor picnic. The parents have been privy to a sailing exhibition, an archery display, and a baseball game. They are now being treated to lunch and a chance to get reacquainted with their children. Lulu has been chattering nonstop since they sat down; Robin has volunteered almost no information since their polite, but reserved, greeting at the waterfront. Her letter was more effusive, Joanne thinks, not sure how to handle the situation, deciding between mouthfuls of well-done chopped chuck not to handle it at all. Things have a way of working out, she hears her mother say.

"Anybody for another hamburger?" Paul asks.

"Me!" Lulu shouts immediately.

"Anybody else?"

"No thanks," Joanne tells him. Robin shakes her head.

"Mustard and relish and a pickle on mine," Lulu orders quickly as her father stands up. "And a tomato," she adds as he is about to turn away.

"Maybe you'd better come with me," Paul says, his eyes on Joanne as Lulu grabs hold of his outstretched hand.

He's giving us this time alone together, Joanne understands, acknowledging his gesture with a nod of her head. She looks at Robin, who looks back at her expectantly. Clearly, Joanne thinks, she is waiting for me to say something.

"So," she begins reluctantly, "are you having a good time?"

"It's all right," Robin shrugs.

"We were very impressed with your sailing."

Robin acknowledges the compliment but says nothing.

"Your counsellors seem very nice."

"They are."

The conversation grinds to a halt. Joanne searches through the large crowd of picnickers hoping to overhear snatches of dialogue that will provide her with a new topic for discussion. She hears nothing.

"What are the boys at Mackanac like this year?" she asks finally, hoping that this is a safe enough topic, that she doesn't appear to be prying.

"They're okay."

"Just okay?" Joanne immediately regrets this additional query, wishes she could take it back. She's gone too far—her question will be misinterpreted.

Robin looks into her lap. "There's one guy who's kind of cute," she says.

Joanne says nothing.

"His name's Ron," her daughter continues.

"Oh? The same as my boss."

Something almost approaching a smile appears on Robin's lips, then disappears. "How's your job?" she asks.

"Great," Joanne replies enthusiastically.

Robin stares off in the direction of the waterfront though the water is not visible from the picnic area. "How are things between you and Dad?" she asks quietly.

"Better," Joanne answers.

Robin brushes an imaginary bug off the red-and-blue quilt. "Camp is good," she says softly, nodding her head, looking back in the direction of the water, careful to avoid her mother's eyes. "It was good that I came. You were right," she adds, almost inaudibly. "Not just about camp . . ."

Should I take her in my arms? Joanne wonders, wanting to, afraid to. This is my child, and I'm afraid to put my arms around her, afraid to overstep my bounds, to misread the signals. What happens to children when they reach a certain age? she wonders, then answers her own question—they become adults.

"Joanne!" comes the voice from somewhere up above.

Joanne lifts her hand to her forehead, shielding her eyes from the sun, noticing the clouds that are gathering overhead. "I thought it was you," the woman is saying as Joanne strains to make out who she is. "Ellie," the woman tells her, "Ellie Carlson. You probably don't recognize me because I've lost so much weight," she adds hopefully.

"My God, you're right," Joanne admits, getting to her feet. "You must have lost fifty pounds."

"Sixty," Ellie Carlson says proudly. "Then I went into the hospital," she whispers, "and had a tummy tuck."

"Well, you look wonderful." Joanne is not sure what else to say. She knows nothing about this woman except that their daughters were once bunkmates. "How many kids do you have here now?" she asks when she can think of nothing else.

"Just one, my baby." Ellie Carlson's entire face frowns. "We're

having trouble with the two older ones," she confides. "They refused
to go to camp this summer. They're hanging out at the local shopping
mall wearing Salvation Army rejects and shaved heads. It seems that
they want the one thing we can't give them."

"Which is?"

"Poverty."

Joanne laughs out loud as the woman gives her a reassuring pat
on the shoulder and makes her way through the crowd to the hamburger table.

"That's Carol Carlson's mother?" Robin asks in disbelief as Joanne sits back down beside her.

"She's lost sixty pounds and had a tummy tuck," Joanne tells her,
fighting the strange urge to laugh. "I often wonder," she hears herself
say, "what happens to these women who have tightened themselves
all up if they put the weight back on. Do you think they explode?"

"Mom!" Robin gasps, then starts to laugh. "That's really gross."

There is a sudden loud noise from somewhere on the campgrounds, a car backfiring perhaps, or a balloon popping. "Listen,"
Joanne squeals, "there goes one of them now."

"Mom!"

"What's going on here?" Paul asks as he and Lulu sit back down
on the quilt, eager to join in the gaiety, aware that something has
changed.

"I think Mom's been out in the sun too long," Robin remarks, but
the words are full of affection and not scorn. Joanne reaches over and
takes Robin's hand in her own. Robin doesn't pull away.

"So, what do you think?" he is asking after they have bid their
daughters a tearful goodbye.

Joanne wipes a few leftover tears from her eyes and smiles. "I
think it went well."

"So do I. Robin seems to have come around."

"She told me she was miserable for the first week, that she was
determined not to have a good time, but that everyone was so nice to
her, and there was so much to do, she couldn't help herself. Plus, I
think meeting that boy, Ron, funny his name is Ron," she adds,
noticing Paul wince, "he probably had something to do with her
change of mood."

"I never quite understood the point of having an all-girls' camp if you're going to have an all-boys' camp right beside it," Paul says, flipping on the windshield wipers.

"It was nice that the rain held off."

"It's going to be god-awful driving home though," he tells her. "We're driving into a real storm."

"Are you hungry?" she asks him minutes later, the rain now pounding against the front window.

"Not really," Paul answers. "I ate three hamburgers at lunch."

"I was thinking that maybe we could stop at one of these lodges along the way for something to eat and wait until the rain lets up a bit." She looks over at Paul, aware that he is staring at her, feeling her body starting to tremble. "We could have dinner . . . or something," she adds, her voice breaking.

He pulls the car into the parking lot of the next motel. "Or something," he says.

This is what she has been imagining these past few months, praying silently that she is not dreaming now. He is on her and over her and inside her and everywhere around her, filling her and loving her and telling her that he needs her, and she is telling him the same things.

They have been here in this room, with its awful red broadloom and tacky deep purple bedspread, for several hours. The rain has stopped, but if Paul has noticed he has ignored it.

At first she was afraid, afraid he might find her ridiculous or pathetic, perhaps a combination of both, afraid how her body might look and feel to him after months of little Judy's, but soon he was whispering how beautiful she was, and his hands were soft and reassuring and familiar, and they had forgotten nothing of what they had learned over the course of their twenty years together. They still knew where to touch her and how. Techniques of the heart, she thinks, something Steve Henry couldn't understand. And soon any embarrassment or fears she might have had passed, and she was lost in the act of love she had been raised to believe it should be. After they were finished the first time, when she initially became aware that the rain had stopped and was fearful he might suggest that they leave, he had simply reached over and brought her to him once again, and they had made love a second time, and Joanne thought that this was the best time in all their years together.

And now he is inside her again, inside her and all around her, as they roll over, exchanging positions, laughing when they find themselves uncomfortably intertwined, finally lying sweat-drenched and exhausted in each other's arms, his body arranging itself around hers for sleep. Joanne feels her own body slowly relax though she knows sleep will be impossible. But it doesn't matter. They are sharing the same bed. And when he wakes up, she will be beside him.

"Do you have a nine o'clock appointment?" she asks as he pulls his car into their driveway the next morning. It is almost nine o'clock already and he has to drive all the way back into the city.

"No, I told them on Friday not to expect me until after ten."

Joanne feels a strange stab of anxiety. He told his office on Friday that he wouldn't be in until ten on Monday? Had he known then what would happen between them? Had he been so sure? She dismisses the uncomfortable thought. It is irrelevant, after all. He obviously planned that they would reconcile this weekend; this is what he means. Why then does she feel so unsettled? Why has she felt this way since he pulled himself out of bed this morning and hurriedly showered and dressed, saying little on the drive back into New York, smiling guiltily in her direction only when he could no longer avoid her gaze.

Paul walks her to the front door, carrying the bags of items that the girls have sent back with them. Things they no longer need, Joanne thinks as Paul rests the bags on the doorstep.

"Do you have time for some coffee?" Joanne asks. Should she ask him now when he plans to move back in?

"I better not. I still have to change, shave," he tells her.

"Will I see you tonight?" she ventures, the words sticking in her throat. Why is she hedging?

"Joanne . . ."

"What's happening, Paul?" she asks when she can no longer bear the suspense.

"I hoped you'd understand about last night," he begins.

"Understand what? I understand that we made love, that you told me that you loved me . . ."

"I do love you."

"What else is there to understand?"

"That it doesn't change anything," he is saying and Joanne finds that she is backing into the doorway, trying to get away from his words. "Maybe I shouldn't have let last night happen," he continues, "but I wanted it to happen, and face it, Joanne, *you* wanted it to happen. We're consenting adults . . ."

"What are you trying to tell me?"

"That what happened last night doesn't change anything," he repeats. "That I'm not ready to come home."

"Last night . . ."

"Doesn't change anything."

Joanne begins fishing wildly in her purse. "I can't find my keys."

"I didn't mean to mislead you."

"Then why didn't you tell me these things *before* we made love?" She flings her purse to the ground. It lands beside the bags of returned goods. Appropriate, Joanne thinks, hearing her voice rising in anger. "I can't find my goddamn keys!" She buries her face in her hands.

"Joanne . . ."

"Just leave me alone."

"I can't leave you outside on the steps crying, for God's sake."

"Then find my keys and I'll cry inside. You won't have to watch."

"Joanne . . ."

"Find my keys!" she screams.

Paul scoops up Joanne's purse and rifles through it. Seconds later, he finds the house keys and hands them to Joanne. "I see you found your old set," he comments absently.

Joanne grabs them from his hand, glancing at the keys she thought she misplaced long ago.

"It's a wonder you can find anything in there," he says, trying to joke.

Joanne fumbles helplessly at the front lock, unable to make the proper connection. Suddenly she feels Paul's hand on hers, twisting the key in the lock for her. She hears it click, feels the door fall open. She stands in the doorway, unable to move as his hand withdraws. Mission accomplished, she thinks, time to make a clean getaway.

"Don't you have to shut the alarm off?" he asks.

Joanne moves like an automaton to the alarm box as Paul lifts the various bags inside.

"I'm sorry, Joanne," he offers when it becomes obvious that she will say nothing to make his departure an easy one. "I'll call you," he adds weakly.

Joanne says nothing. She waits until she hears his car pull away before stretching back with her foot and kicking the front door closed.

Chapter 25

He is sleeping when Joanne enters the room.

Joanne stares at the old face, the withered body completely hidden by the gray-white sheets, the New York Yankees baseball cap temporarily dislodged and lying next to him on his pillow, revealing an egg-shaped head from which escape only a few stray gray-white hairs. She has never known him with hair, she thinks, recalling that even as a child, she can remember hair only at the sides of his head. This always felt right, natural. Grandfathers should be bald, she decides. Bald and overweight and jolly. How comforting our stereotypes are, she thinks, sitting down beside the sleeping old man and resting her hand across the stiff mountain of sheets. How much more pleasant than reality.

She is not used to Mondays. For the past three years, she has visited this room every Saturday when the halls are busy with family members paying their weekly respects to their not-so-distant pasts. She didn't realize how still everything became during the week. It seems especially quiet here today. Except for nurses' footsteps and the occasional confused cry emanating from a patient's open door, there is little sound. Like her grandfather, most of the elderly residents are asleep, though it is not yet one o'clock in the afternoon. She has come on her lunch hour. Ron told her to take the rest of the day off, to take all the time she needs.

He had only to take one look at her red, swollen eyes to know that she had been crying. Talk to me, he said, leading her out of the crowded reception room, away from the curious eyes of his waiting patients, and into the one examining room that was still empty. He said nothing about the fact that she was late, asked her only what was the matter. She broke down again—has she ever stopped?—and told him everything that happened between herself and Paul, waiting for him to pass judgment. Instead, he took her in his arms and held her. Take the rest of the day off, he urged, I can manage. And they had both laughed. All right, he quickly amended, I *can't* manage—take a long lunch. Take as long as you need, he repeated gently.

But she couldn't eat lunch, couldn't swallow, couldn't stop the newly reactivated, seemingly endless stream of tears. And so she got into her car and drove, not sure where she was going until she saw the familiar institution, strolled the uncompromisingly institutional halls.

And now she is here, sitting beside an old man who has given her a wealth of memories, but who no longer remembers who she is. She isn't sure herself anymore who she is, she realizes, looking around the room. What is she doing in a room with two sleeping old men, neither one of them aware of her presence? Joanne stares at the figure of Sam Hensley, thinking how exposed he appears without the combined presence of his daughter and grandson. She is used to sharing her space with them. Another signpost vanished.

The old man's eyes flicker open. As he stares at her, the many lines that fill his ancient face crease upward into a series of small smiles. "Joanne?"

"Grandpa!" The tears, which Joanne has been barely managing to keep in check, return and spill down her cheeks. "You know me?"

He looks puzzled, straining to sit up.

"Here, I'll help you," she says quickly, moving behind him to prop up his pillows and free his arms from their starchy constraints.

"I think there's something at the foot of the bed that you can turn," he says clearly.

Joanne is instantly at the foot of the bed, cranking the handle to raise the bed so that her grandfather can comfortably assume a sitting position. The baseball cap on his pillow falls into his lap. He grabs it and places it on top of his head, his eyes merry, twinkling.

"We're going to take the series this year," he smiles, and Joanne realizes that his teeth are missing. He doesn't seem to notice, and if he does, he doesn't care. He looks like a dolphin, she thinks wondrously, her own smile stretching widely, some tears falling into her open mouth. "Why are you crying?" he asks.

"Because I'm happy," Joanne tells him, realizing that this is true. He knows who she is. "I'm so glad to see you," she says.

"You should come more often. Your mother comes every week."

"I know. I'm sorry. I'll try to . . ."

"I'm thirsty."

"Would you like some water?"

"There's a glass on the table." He points to the bedside table on which rests a glass with a straw. The glass is half-filled with water.

"I'll get you some fresh water," Joanne offers, the glass already in her hand.

"No, this will be fine. I just want to wet my lips." He sucks on the curved straw before returning the glass to Joanne. "They get dry. They never get the humidity right in this place. I've been telling them for years. Look at you," he says suddenly, watching as she returns the glass to the small table. "You've gotten so grown up." Joanne laughs, wiping more tears from her face. "How old are you now?" he asks.

"Forty-one," Joanne answers.

"Forty-one?" He shakes his head. "That must make your mother . . . what?"

"Sixty-seven," Joanne says quickly.

"Sixty-seven! My little Linda is sixty-seven. I can't believe it. How's your husband?" The questions come rapid-fire now, as if he knows he has only a short time to get them all in.

"Fine," Joanne responds automatically. "He's good."

"And your children? You have how many?"

"Two."

"Two. Forgive me, I sometimes forget. Their names . . . ?"

"Robin and Lulu. Lana, really, but we've always called her Lulu."

"Little Lulu, I remember. Do you have pictures?"

Joanne searches through her purse. "Just these." She locates an old leather photo holder. "They're a few years old." She dusts off the plastic which covers the two photographs. "They're bigger now. Robin, especially, has changed quite a bit." She pauses, checking to see whether her grandfather is still listening. "They're at camp for the summer," she continues when she sees that he is. "We were up to see them yesterday. They're having a wonderful time. They send you their love," she adds, and his smile broadens. "I'll bring them up for a visit as soon as they get home. Would you like that?"

He nods, and the rim of his baseball cap slips down over his eyes. Joanne quickly adjusts it.

"Minnie bought me this hat," he tells Joanne proudly, referring to Joanne's grandmother. "Even though she was always a Dodger fan herself." He closes his eyes and Joanne fears for an instant that she has lost him, that he has returned to his more comfortable world, but when he opens them again, they are still focused, almost mischievous. "Do you have time to play a few hands of gin?" he asks.

Joanne gasps loudly with delight.

"Is everything all right in here?" comes a voice from the doorway. "Oh, hello, Mrs. Hunter," the nurse continues, recognizing her. "Didn't expect to see you today. Your granddaddy okay?"

"Do you have any playing cards?" Joanne asks quickly.

"Playing cards?"

"You know, for gin rummy. Cards," Joanne repeats.

"I think your granddaddy has some right in his drawer," the nurse answers after a second's thought. "I remember seeing some around somewhere. Check in the drawer. If there aren't any, I'll see if I can get you some."

"They're here," Joanne exclaims triumphantly, pulling out an old deck of well-worn cards. "I found them." She slides them out of their faded pink-and-white package.

"You're looking very fit today, Mr. Orr," the nurse says, entering the room and lifting the old man's hand into her own, feeling for his pulse. "Sounds good," she says, winking at Joanne. "Have a good time, you two. Don't you beat her too bad now, Mr. Orr."

She is gone before Joanne has finished dealing the cards onto the stiff gray-white sheets. Her hands shaking, Joanne arranges her cards into proper order, too excited to concentrate.

All she can think about is that she is actually playing cards with her grandfather. And suddenly, she is ten years old again and they are sitting at the round table in the living room of her grandparents' cottage, listening to the sound of the rain outside. The table is covered with a heavy green felt cloth, trimmed with long white tassels. It is located in the far right corner of the square-shaped room. On the opposite wall are hung a series of small paintings (prints, she realizes now) by such artists as Van Gogh, Gauguin, and Degas. Interrupting this wall are the doorways to the two bedrooms, one room for her parents and younger brother, and the other, which she shares with her grandparents. Her small single bed faces their larger double bed, and she can lie there and watch the leaves shaking on the tall tree just beyond the window. When the window is open, as it usually is, she can hear the sound of the leaves through the screen as they rustle in the breezes. She can smell the grass, hear the distant wail of a passing train whose lonely sound, even now, makes her feel secure whenever she hears it.

On the weekends, when the men have returned from the city, the smells of summer are joined by another odor—the intrusion of rubbing alcohol, which her grandfather laboriously slaps on his face after he has shaved. It is this smell, more than the sunlight or the noises of the day, that awakens her on Saturday and Sunday mornings, a sort of aural alarm clock. This smell is what makes Joanne, unlike most people, unlike Eve, so comfortable in doctors' offices, in hospital corridors.

The haunting sound of a train's whistle and the abrasive smell of rubbing alcohol—her security blankets. She thinks of Paul—skinny arms and allergies. Funny the things we fall in love with.

"You taking that card?" her grandfather is asking impatiently.

Joanne realizes that she has been staring at the two of hearts for several seconds without absorbing which card it is. "No," she says, deciding, too late, that she should have picked it up. Her grandfather quickly tucks the two of hearts into his hand and discards a seven of diamonds. Joanne checks her hand carefully to make sure she has no use for this card before she draws one from the deck. It is the ten of spades, which she takes, putting it between the eight and the jack of the same suit. She needs the nine.

Her grandfather's eyes narrow in concentration. He draws a card from the deck and quickly discards it, watching as Joanne does the same, grabbing the next card that she throws out, watching as she picks up his discard. Joanne looks at her hand. She is only one card away from gin—the nine of spades. She debates throwing away a needed card, eager to prolong the game, to let her grandfather win, to further buoy his spirits. And her own.

"Gin," her grandfather suddenly exclaims, proudly displaying his cards. Joanne stares at him in disbelief. "You thought I was going to give you this one?" he asks slyly, turning over his gin card, the nine of spades.

"I don't believe it," Joanne states incredulously, then eagerly, "Think you can do it again?"

"I'll try," he ventures.

The results of the next hand are the same as the first. "Gin!" he cries with a child's delight. The third and fourth hands proceed in almost identical fashion, though these take longer to play. Each is punctuated by the same satisfied yelp. "Gin!" her grandfather exclaims, though his voice is starting to fade.

"One more hand, Grampa?" Joanne asks.

"Deal the cards," he tells her softly.

"We can stop now if you want to rest for a while."

"Deal the cards," he says again.

Joanne gives them each ten cards and quickly sorts hers out, noticing that her grandfather doesn't bother, doesn't need to. "The four of clubs, Grampa," she tells him, looking up from the exposed card. "Do you want it?" He shakes his head. "Then I'll take it," she smiles, and he nods. She throws off an eight of hearts. "An eight, Grampa, do you want the eight?" He shakes his head. "Pick a card," she instructs him gently, understanding that something has happened, that they are playing a different game.

She watches as his heavily veined hand reaches out and picks a card from the top of the deck. He holds it in front of his eyes and studies it as if it were a foreign object. "Do you want that card, Grampa?" she asks, refusing to acknowledge that he no longer sees it. He shrugs. "Lay it on the pile then," she tells him, and he does so. "That's the three of spades, Grampa. You're sure you don't need that?"

He shakes his head, regards her with bewilderment.

"Well, I'll take it then," she proceeds stubbornly, lifting it into her hand. "And I'll give you the king of hearts. Grampa, do you want the king?"

She stares at him. The dolphin has become the giant turtle, the smiling eyes vanishing as the long neck stretches back against his pillow, his eyes closing in sleep. "Grampa!" she cries and his eyes snap open before closing once again. "Please don't leave me, Grampa. Please don't go. I need you!"

Her trembling hands reach out and gather the cards together, collecting them into their worn box, dropping some on the floor, bending to scoop them up, forcing them inside the package before returning them to the side table. She stands at the foot of his bed for several seconds before turning the crank, lowering the bed to its original position. Then she returns to her grandfather's side, taking his arm in her hand, surprised by how light it feels.

"Please wake up, Grampa," she pleads, knowing he will not. "I'm so lost. I don't know what to do anymore. I lied to you. You asked me how Paul is and I said he was fine. Well, he is fine . . . it's just that he's gone. I told you that before. I told you that he left me. . . . But I always felt that he'd come back. I thought all I had to do was wait, give him enough time. I love him so much, Grampa. He's been my life for twenty years. Now he wants a different life, and I don't know what to do. I don't know who I am anymore. Can you understand that? Everything is falling apart. I'm losing my children—they're growing up. They're growing away from me. And Eve . . . you remember Eve? The one who never knew her left hand from her right?"

Joanne searches her grandfather's face for a flicker of recognition, but finds none. She continues. "Well, something is happening to Eve, Grampa. Something strange. She's convinced that she's dying. She's been to thousands of doctors. Everybody tells her that there's nothing wrong with her, all the tests are negative, but she won't accept what anybody says. She's acting very peculiar. I can't explain it. She's been my best friend for thirty years and all of a sudden, I don't know who she is—I don't trust her anymore. I'm afraid of her!" Joanne stops, startled by her admission. "I haven't said that out loud before. I don't think I've even thought it. But it's true. I'm afraid of her." Joanne pauses to let this thought sink in. "I've been getting these phone calls, Grampa. Scary, sick phone calls. A voice threatening to kill me. And one night last week, it was late and I went outside to the backyard—it was around midnight—and I was standing there staring at the stupid hole in the ground, and I heard that voice from the telephone calling my name, and I got so scared, I thought he had come to kill me . . . but it was Eve! It was her voice! And, in a way, that was worse than anything I'd been expecting. I can't get the way she looked out of my mind. I'm afraid, Grampa, afraid that Eve is the one who's been phoning me. I'm afraid that she wants to hurt me. I can't believe it, even as I'm telling you this, but then I can't believe any of the things that have been happening to me these past few months. I'm so confused. I don't know what to do with myself anymore. Please help me, Grampa. I don't know what to do."

Slowly, her grandfather's eyes open. "Would you like to trade places?" he asks gently.

Joanne collapses into the chair beside his bed, his words echoing in her ear. His hand reaches out to hers, bringing her fingers to his dry lips.

The room is suddenly filled with sound. "It's a long way to Tipperary!" Sam Hensley is bellowing loudly.

Joanne sits by her grandfather's side, unable to move. She feels that she is in the middle of a surreal painting, something by Dali or Magritte.

"It's a long way to Tipperary . . ."

Would you like to trade places?

"To the sweetest girl I know . . ."

"Linda?" her grandfather asks, startled by the sudden noise.

"It's a long way to go . . ."

"Linda?"

Joanne stands up, bends forward, and kisses her grandfather's cheek. "No, Grampa," she whispers as his eyes close in sleep. "It's Joanne."

As she pulls the car into her driveway, Joanne thinks she sees Eve staring down at her from the small bedroom window at the front of Eve's house. Joanne climbs out of her car, checking her watch. It is after five o'clock. She has been driving all afternoon, her head an echo chamber in which both spoken words and unspoken thoughts steadily collide, one-legged runners on America's highways. Now she wants only to take a bath and get into bed, to give the runners a rest, yet something is pulling her toward Eve's house.

As she crosses her front lawn, she again looks to the window of the small front bedroom, the room Eve had been saving for the expected baby that never arrived, but the window is empty. No one is watching her. Has Eve seen her approaching? Is she on her way down the stairs to answer the front door?

Joanne knocks several times and then rings the bell. No one comes, though she can hear voices arguing. "Eve," she calls. "I know you're there. Are you all right?"

She hears footsteps approach the door and backs away as the door opens. Eve's mother stands before her. "Eve doesn't want to see you," she says simply.

"Why not?" Joanne has trouble digesting this new information.

"She says she's tired of having to defend herself to everyone, that if you were really her friend she wouldn't have to."

"I *am* her friend."

"I know that," Mrs. Cameron nods sadly. "And deep down, I think she knows that too, but . . ."

"I'm tired, Mrs. Cameron," Joanne hears herself say, "too tired to argue. I've had kind of a rough day myself. I'm going home; I'm going to take a bath and get into bed. Tell Eve I was here and . . . tell her that I love her." She tries to smile but fails and quickly abandons the attempt.

"I'll get her to call you."

Joanne runs down the steps and cuts across her front lawn, taking the stairs to her front door two at a time, turning the key in the lock, pushing open the door and stretching out her hand to shut off the alarm. Except that it isn't on.

Joanne takes an involuntary step backward. The green light isn't on, and if the green light isn't on, that means the alarm isn't on. Can it be that she has forgotten to set it?

Her mind returns to the morning. She was upset when she left the house, tired, depressed. She was thinking about yesterday, about last night, about Paul's latest abandonment. This doesn't change anything, he said. She hears his words now as she heard them on her way out the door. She sees herself grabbing her purse and closing the front door behind her. It is entirely possible that she has forgotten to set the alarm. Stupid! she thinks, deciding she'd better check the doors and windows to make sure they are secure. It's possible that someone might have tried to get in, she thinks, realizing that, despite Brian's earlier assurances that he would have someone watch the house, she has never seen any police cars even casually patrolling the area.

Thoughts of Brian lead to thoughts of Eve. What is happening to her friend? she wonders as she proceeds cautiously into her kitchen to the sliding glass door. The lock is securely fastened. No one has tampered with it. Joanne feels herself relax, thinks that she is being silly, but feels her feet leading her into the living room and then the dining room. Nothing has been disturbed. The windows are tightly closed.

Almost reluctantly, she moves down the stairs to the bottom floor, where she quickly checks out the sliding glass door in the family room. Again, it is securely fastened. No one has been here.

The bedrooms are the same—still, empty, as she left them. After satisfying herself that no one has tried to open any of the upstairs windows, Joanne collapses on her bed. Maybe she won't bother with a bath after all. Maybe she'll just crawl under the covers and try to sleep.

The phone rings just as she is starting to doze.

Joanne picks up the phone on its first ring. "Hello, Eve?"

"Bad girl," the voice chides her. "Slut! Whore!"

Joanne slams the phone into the receiver and buries her head in her hands. In the next instant, she is racing down the stairs to the kitchen, rummaging through her address book, finding Brian's phone number at work. Her hands shaking, she dials the number, misdialing the last digit and having to dial again.

"Sergeant Brian Stanley, please," she says to the policeman who answers the phone.

"He's not here right now. Can I help you?"

"Who is this?"

"Officer Wilson."

"I need to speak to Sergeant Stanley or his superior," Joanne announces.

"That would be Lieutenant Fox."

"Fine, can I speak to him please?"

"Just one minute."

A new voice comes on the line, deeper than the first though no more authoritative. "Lieutenant Fox here. Can I help you?"

"This is Joanne Hunter, Lieutenant Fox. I live next door to Brian Stanley."

"Yes?" He is waiting for her to continue.

"I've been getting these threatening phone calls and Brian, Sergeant Stanley, said that he was going to speak to you about having a patrol car keep an eye on my house. I haven't seen any police cars and I just got another call and I know it's probably nothing to worry about, but I just wondered when was the last time the police went by here . . ."

"Slow down a minute, please. You say that Sergeant Stanley told you he asked me to have a patrol car keep an eye on your house?"

"Well, he said he was going to, but that was a while ago . . . maybe he forgot . . . or maybe he hasn't had time." Her voice drifts to a stop. "He never mentioned anything to you?" she asks, already knowing the answer.

"What was your name again?" the lieutenant is asking as Joanne replaces the receiver.

"It's Joanne," she says.

Chapter 26

"This is delicious, Joanne. Thank you."

Brian Stanley, looking five pounds slimmer and ten years older than the last time Joanne was here, smiles at her from across his kitchen table. He is finishing the last of a large piece of fresh raspberry pie that Joanne has prepared this afternoon and brought over.

"Just what you need," Eve smiles, her voice decidedly cool. "Cholesterol."

"I used whole wheat flour in the crust," Joanne says. "And only half the sugar the recipe calls for."

"Aren't you the considerate one?" Eve asks sarcastically.

"Cut it out, Eve," Brian says flatly.

"Oh, the big, tough cop act. I love it. Don't you, Joanne?" Eve asks pointedly.

Joanne stares into her plate. The small piece of pie she has cut for herself remains untouched. She has no appetite for it. Why did she come here tonight? Why did she put herself in this position?

"It was very nice of you to think of us," Brian says, as if aware of what she is thinking. "I love raspberries."

"You like anything that reminds you of the sight of blood," Eve interjects.

"I love them too," Joanne says, determined to carry on a normal conversation. "They've always been my favorite fruit. Just that they're so expensive . . ."

"Do you want us to pay you for the pie?" Eve asks.

"Eve, for God's sake . . ."

"Go ahead, Brian," Eve continues. "Ask my mother for some money."

"Jesus, Eve!" Brian exclaims, banging his fork against the side of his plate.

"Maybe I should leave . . ." Joanne starts.

"Please stay," Brian urges.

"Yes, please stay," Eve mimics. "We need you. Don't we, Brian?"

Joanne stares at her friend, scarcely recognizing the woman she has known and loved for most of her life. Like Brian, Eve has lost weight, and the angular features, once so attractive, are now pointed and severe. The red hair, long grown out of its stylish cut, seems curiously inappropriate and the green eyes have lost their former natural vitality. Eve looks as harsh and as mean as she sounds. She is no longer who she was. The trusted friend has become a feared stranger.

"Did you have any more tests this week?" Joanne asks, forcing the words out of her mouth.

"Did I have any more tests this week?" Eve repeats cruelly. "What do you care? You're too busy these days with your own doctor to worry about me."

"I do worry about you."

"Not enough to call or come over."

"I *have* called. I *have* come over. I'm here now."

"When did you call?"

"I called several times this week. Your mother said you didn't want to speak to me. I came by on Monday; you wouldn't see me."

"Why should I?" Eve exclaims. "All I ever hear from you is that I'm crazy."

"I never said you were crazy."

"You say it every time you open your mouth." Eve's eyes dart from Joanne to Brian. "He has you completely brainwashed, doesn't he? How many times have you been meeting secretly behind my back?"

"Eve, shut up!" Brian Stanley says forcefully.

"Oh, that's good, big man. Talk dirty to me. I love it when you talk dirty."

"Eve, you don't mean what you're saying," Joanne begins.

"Why don't I? There's nothing wrong with my eyes—at least not so far anyway. I can see the way you two look at each other. I can see how you're blossoming, how you've fixed yourself up . . ."

"Eve, you're the one who's been telling me for years to put streaks in my hair."

"But you waited till now. Why?"

Joanne hesitates. "I don't know," she answers honestly. "I don't know much about anything anymore."

"Welcome to the club," Eve states, then bursts into tears. "Jesus, I hate this." She struggles to regain her composure.

"Cry, Eve," Joanne urges. "Let it out. It's good for you."

"How do you know what's good for me?" Eve demands viciously. "Why do you want to watch me break down? Do you enjoy seeing me like this? Does it give you a sense of power?"

"Of course not. It hurts me to see you like this. I only want to help you."

"How? By bringing over rich desserts that you know will upset my stomach? By trying to steal my husband because you couldn't hold on to your own?"

"Eve!" Brian Stanley jumps to his feet. "Joanne, I'm sorry."

"Don't you dare apologize for me!" Eve yells. "You have no right." She buries her head in her hands.

"Eve . . ." Joanne's hand reaches out to her friend: she rests her fingers gently on Eve's arm.

"Do you know what he did, Joanne?" Eve asks, her voice suddenly that of a child. "He sent my mother away. Yesterday. He made her go home."

"The woman was falling apart," Brian starts to explain.

"I'm the one who's falling apart."

"You won't let anybody help you."

"He won't let me have an operation that could save my life," Eve wails, surprising Joanne, who looks to Brian for an explanation.

"She saw some quack this week . . ."

"He's not a quack."

"He's the tenth gynecologist you've seen and he's the only one to recommend a hysterectomy."

"He's the only one who knows what he's talking about."

"What exactly did he say?" Joanne asks, puzzled by this new development.

Eve grips tightly onto Joanne's hand. "He says I have a badly tipped uterus and a fibroid . . ."

"A small fibroid, we've known about it for years," Brian interrupts.

"And he says that that could be what's causing the terrible pains in my groin."

"What about the pains in your chest, in your back, in your stomach?" Brian questions.

"Not to mention the giant pain in my ass!" Eve states caustically, looking straight into her husband's eyes.

Normally, Joanne would be reassured by such a remark. But it is too late for reassurance. "What does he say about the other pains?" Joanne asks.

"He doesn't say anything about the other pains," Eve tells her, impatience creeping into her voice. "He's a gynecologist. He knows uteruses and ovaries. He doesn't claim to know anything else."

"He's recommended a hysterectomy? Isn't that a little drastic?"

"What should I do, Joanne?" Eve pleads. "You think I'd even consider such a thing if I weren't in such dire pain? You know how much I hate hospitals."

Joanne shakes her head. "I don't know what to tell you," she admits honestly.

"Tell her that this doctor is as nutty as she is," Brian states flatly. "Tell her that if she goes to enough doctors, she's bound to find a few who are willing to tell her what she wants to hear. A surgeon likes to operate, for Christ's sake. That's what he's there for. You have a pain in your groin, fine. We'll give you a hysterectomy. What, your stomach hurts? Well, we'll just take it out. You're experiencing a shortness of breath? Well, who needs two lungs anyway?"

"Shut up, Brian," Eve orders. "You're making a fool of yourself."

"*I'm* making a fool of myself?"

"It appears you don't need any help."

"Eve, take it easy," Joanne cautions.

"Why did you come here?" Eve demands suddenly. "Isn't Saturday your day to visit your grandfather?"

"I was there this afternoon." Joanne lowers her head. "He was asleep. He didn't wake up."

"That's what I'm so afraid of," Eve whispers. Joanne regards her quizzically. "I'm afraid that if I close my eyes and go to sleep, I'll never wake up again."

"Of course you'll wake up."

"I'm afraid to go to sleep at night," Eve repeats.

"You need to sleep, Eve."

"I'm afraid I'm going to die."

"You're not going to die."

"I don't want to die, Joanne."

"You're not going to die."

"Then what's the matter with me? Why can't anybody tell me what's the matter with me?"

"Because there isn't anything the matter with you, goddamn it!" Brian shouts from across the room.

"Brian . . ." Joanne begins.

"No, Joanne. Stop coddling her. She's manipulating you. She manipulates you, her mother, me, everybody who cares about her."

"You don't care about me," Eve screams.

"And it's got to stop," Brian continues, ignoring his wife's outburst. "Because the more we give in to this craziness, the more we listen to it, the more credence we give to it. That's why I sent her mother away, that's why I'm telling you to stop coddling her. Eve needs help . . ."

"What for? You're the one who's crazy."

"I'll *be* crazy if I let this go on for much longer."

"Why don't you just leave?" Eve taunts. "It's what you want to do, isn't it?"

"It's not what I want."

"It's what all this is leading up to, isn't it? Go ahead, leave. You're never here anyway. Go. Go on over to Joanne's house. She has a freezer full of home-baked pies and a nice big bed with lots of extra room in it . . ."

"Eve, calm down," Joanne urges.

"He's very good in bed, you know," Eve tells her. "He has this neat little trick he does with his tongue . . ."

"For God's sake, Eve . . ."

"And he's got a long prick, Joanne. Not too thick. But nice and long."

"Shut up!" Brian rages, advancing toward his wife, his fists clenched.

"And a nice tight little bum. Sometimes he likes you to stick your finger . . ."

The next instant is a blur: Brian's fist unclenching, his open hand extending into the air, catching the side of Eve's face, Eve's head snapping back, her red hair spilling across her newly reddened cheek, her body tottering off the side of her chair into Joanne's arms.

"Brian, stop it!" Joanne screams, struggling to steady Eve's chair so that it doesn't fall over, her eyes registering fear and disbelief at the violence she has witnessed.

Brian's hands remain poised in midair. He sways back and forth

unsteadily. For an instant, Joanne wonders if he is going to faint, but
he only looks around him questioningly, as if someone has said something he doesn't understand, before spinning around on his heel and
wordlessly fleeing the room.

Joanne turns back to her friend.

Eve is staring at her with undisguised hatred. "Go home," she
says.

Joanne is in her kitchen when she hears the knock on the door.
She has been sitting at the wooden table for almost an hour, not
moving. She has been witnessing the same scene over and over in her
mind: Brian's fist clenching and unclenching; his large bulk moving
inexorably toward his wife; his hand shooting into the space between
them, catching Eve's face with the palm of his hand; Eve's head
ricocheting back, her hair sweeping up past her cheek, mimicking
the line of his blow; her chair tottering, almost falling; the blankness
in Brian's eyes; the hatred in Eve's. Go home, Joanne hears Eve say
again. Go home.

The persistent knock at the door continues, followed by a ringing of the bell. Joanne forces herself out of the chair and over to the
intercom. She presses the appropriate button. "Who is it?" she asks,
knowing that her voice is being carried down the street.

"It's Brian, Joanne," comes the response.

Joanne lifts her finger from the intercom and stares at the floor.
What does he want? What is there left to say? She starts toward the
door and suddenly stops. Why hasn't he spoken to Lieutenant Fox the
way he said he would?

His large bulk fills the door frame.

"I brought your pie plate back," he says, handing it over. "I
washed it."

"Thank you."

"Can I come in?"

"Should Eve be alone?"

"Eve's locked herself in the bathroom."

"Do you think she'll hurt herself?"

Brian almost laughs. "Are you kidding? Not before she's buried
the rest of us." He catches the look of dismay that passes across
Joanne's face. "Please, Joanne, can I come inside?"

Joanne backs in to let him enter. He closes the door behind him

and follows her into the kitchen. "Do you want some coffee?" Joanne
offers, hoping he'll say no.

He shakes his head. "I'll be up all night as it is." He stares out the
sliding glass door into the night. "I've never hit a woman before," he
says finally. Joanne says nothing. "I don't know what happened," he
continues, trying to explain the events to himself, almost ignoring
Joanne's presence. "I just went blank there for a few minutes. I kept
hearing this strange voice saying those awful things, and bingo, something snapped. The next thing I knew, my fingers were stinging, the
palm of my hand hurt . . . I didn't mean to hit her, Joanne. I don't
know what happened."

"What can I say?" Joanne asks. "I don't know what to tell you."

"Maybe I should do what Eve says. Maybe I should leave."

"You can't do that."

"I can't beat her up every time she goes off the deep end."

Joanne nods. "No, you can't. But you can't leave her. What would
she do? How would she manage?"

"Her mother would come back."

"Do you think that's wise?"

"I don't know. I *do* know that I can't stand much more of this.
I'm being honest. I'm pretty close to cracking myself these days. I
mean, I just slugged my wife. I might have killed her if you hadn't
been there." He laughs, and the incongruous sound fills the space
between them. "Who am I kidding? *She* might have killed me."

"Maybe she should have the hysterectomy," Joanne ventures.

"What? Why?"

"Maybe it's what she needs."

"Nobody needs unnecessary surgery."

"Maybe once you get her into the hospital, you can persuade her
to see the staff psychiatrist . . ." Joanne is aware that she is thinking
out loud. "And if the miscarriage *is* the source of her anxieties, well
then, maybe once the problem area is removed, the rest of her
problems will disappear as well."

"That's taking a pretty big risk, don't you think?"

"I don't know what to think."

"Maybe I will have that cup of coffee, if you don't mind," Brian
tells her. Joanne moves to the coffee machine, hoping that her face
doesn't register the annoyance she feels at his request.

What does he want coffee for anyway? she grouses. He already
had two cups with his pie. Why did he come here? Why doesn't he go

home? She is worried about Eve, about all of them. How easy it is to lose control, she thinks, recalling her discussion with the frightened young mother at the hospital. How little control we actually have.

"Have you seen Paul lately?" Brian asks as she brings his mug of hot coffee to the table.

"Last weekend," she tells him, her voice flat, her eyes downcast. "We visited the girls at camp."

"Sounds promising."

Joanne says nothing.

"Any progress?" Brian asks.

"Not really." She doesn't want to talk about this. She wants him to finish his coffee quickly and go back to his own house.

"I can't believe Paul would be foolish enough to let you get away," Brian is telling her.

"I'm not going anywhere." Where is this conversation headed?

"Are you dating?" he asks.

Joanne stares at him in surprise. She has never known Brian to be so loquacious. What is he getting at? "No," she says quickly.

"What about that tennis instructor?"

"What about him?"

"I thought . . ."

"He was here for dinner one night," Joanne replies testily. "He left early."

"Not of his own volition, I'm sure."

Joanne's eyes narrow. What is Brian trying to say?

"Eve's right about one thing," he says. "You're looking wonderful these days."

"I feel like shit," Joanne says simply, the words fitting her tongue exactly. "Nothing like a good dose of misery, I guess, to make you look your best."

"How are you managing?" He has put down his mug, is walking around the table to where she is sitting.

"Well, I've learned where the fuse box is located. I can change a light bulb all by myself. And I canceled our subscription to *Sports Illustrated.*"

His arms are on her shoulders.

"I guess I'm managing okay," she continues, feeling the warmth of his fingers through her thin sweater.

"Are you?" he asks again. "It must be hard alone after all these years . . ."

Joanne pushes her chair back, forcing Brian to release his grip on her shoulders. She rises to her feet. "Men aren't all they're cracked up to be," she tells him. "Do you want more coffee?"

"No," he says, moving toward her.

Joanne feels the counter top at her back. "Brian," she begins, but it is too late. He is only inches from her mouth, his arms around her waist, pulling her close to him, his lips pressing down on hers. What the hell is she supposed to do now? Joanne wonders. Why are all these things happening to her? A tennis instructor twelve years her junior, her crazy friend's husband, some lunatic who wants to spank her before he kills her . . . what is the secret of her strange appeal?

She glares at the phone as Brian's mouth crushes down on her own. Why don't you call me now, you bastard? she screams silently as Brian's tongue searches for hers.

"Brian . . ."

"Don't stop me, Joanne. I need you."

"Brian . . ."

"You need me."

Joanne manages to extricate herself from his arms. "I don't need any of this!" she yells. "What I need is a little sanity in my life. What I need is to be left alone." Whenever I want to talk to an intelligent person . . . "Why didn't you ask Lieutenant Fox to have a patrol car watch my house?" she demands suddenly, surprising them both.

"What?"

"You said you would."

"Joanne, what are you talking about?"

"You said that you'd ask your lieutenant to have a patrol car watch my house."

His eyes register remembrance. "I did ask him," he tells her.

"No you didn't. I've spoken to your Lieutenant Fox. He didn't know what the hell I was talking about."

"Joanne . . ."

She is moving angrily away from him, relieved she has something to throw between them. "Why didn't you ask him?"

There is a long pause. "I couldn't," he finally admits.

"Why? Don't you believe me either? Do you think I'm imagining the phone calls?"

"No."

"Then why? You don't think my concerns are legitimate? You were just trying to humor me?"

"No."

"Then why?"

"Because I'm afraid," Brian mumbles, turning away from her angry eyes.

The word is not one Joanne is expecting.

"Afraid? Afraid of what?"

There is another long pause. "Afraid that Eve might be the one who's been phoning you," he confesses, his voice barely audible.

Joanne says nothing. His words are only an echo of her own thoughts, after all.

"You're not saying that you think that Eve might be the Suburban Strangler, are you?" Joanne whispers incredulously, after all the ramifications of his words have sunk in.

He shakes his head vigorously, his incongruous laugh once again filling the air. "Oh God, no!" He obviously finds this thought very amusing. His laugh takes a long while to fade. "But then I don't think that whoever's been phoning you is the killer either. I don't think one thing has anything to do with the other." He smiles at Joanne sadly. "I think we should pull back a bit. We all seem to be going a little crazy." He lifts the palms of his hands into the air. "What can I say? I'm sorry, Joanne. About everything. About not talking to Fox, about what happened over at my house earlier, about what happened here a few minutes ago . . ."

The phone rings.

"Do you want me to answer it?" Brian offers. "I'd recognize Eve's voice no matter how hard she tried to disguise it. You must have a phone in your bedroom," he continues before Joanne has a chance to respond, already on his way up the stairs. "Give me a minute before you answer it. Let it ring three more times. Pick it up after the third ring from now."

The ringing continues as Joanne hears Brian's footsteps overhead. At the end of the third ring, she slowly reaches over and picks up the receiver, listening dully as the voice on the other end makes its terse announcement.

Brian returns instantly to her side. "I'm sorry, Joanne," he says, his hands gesturing helplessly between them, having forfeited their power to comfort.

"It had to happen sooner or later," Joanne tells him. "He was ninety-five."

Chapter 27

Joanne stares around the room at the small collection of mourners. Counting herself, there are six people present. Her brother, Warren, and his wife, Gloria, flew in from California two days earlier, and are now sitting on either side of her, their hands intertwined. Directly behind her is her boss, Dr. Ronald Gold. Across the aisle, on the other side of the small chapel, sit Joanne's husband, Paul, and Eve's mother. Eve is not here, being too sick; nor is Brian, being too busy. Joanne was surprised when she first saw Eve's mother; now she is grateful. She smiles in the older woman's direction. Paul smiles back.

Their daughters are not here. Joanne decided that there was no point in making the two girls return from camp, even though Paul offered to drive up and get them. She is not being protective, she realizes, satisfied with the decision she has made. She is being practical. And, to a certain degree, selfish. Right now, she neither wants nor needs the responsibility of two more mouths to feed, two more egos to cater to. She wants to think of no one but herself, to hear no one's voice but her own. She wants, as Greta Garbo is often reported to have said, to be alone, and she is strangely grateful that her brother and sister-in-law will be departing for California shortly after the funeral. She feels comfortable with her solitude. At least she knows what to expect.

Gloria squeezes Joanne's hand. "That's the sad thing about living so long," she says quietly. "You outlive all your friends. And most of your family," she adds, leaning her head against Joanne's.

Joanne nods. She had forgotten how pretty Gloria is. A typical California girl, her hair blond, her skin bronzed, she appears younger than her thirty-five years. Only her voice is old. It has a vaguely guttural, almost masculine, quality, a quality which serves her well in the voice work she does for radio and television commercials. Like most of her friends, Gloria once confessed, all she ever wanted from life was to be an actress and marry a doctor. Unlike most of her friends, however, she actually managed to carve out something of a career for herself in the peripheries of show business, and her marriage had proved both durable and successful. Her daughters are healthy, beautiful, and a reflection of the times: they want to be models and marry rock stars. Living in California, they fully expect to get what they want. Which they probably will, Joanne thinks.

"It's so hard to believe he's really dead," Warren says, staring at the open coffin at the front of the chapel. "I always thought that he'd be around forever."

"He was," Gloria reminds him gently.

"He looks so small," Warren marvels. "He was always such a big man. I don't know if you remember him, Gloria . . ."

"How could I forget him?" Gloria's husky voice fills the small room. "He was master of ceremonies at our wedding, for God's sake. When he introduced me as your 'lover,' I thought my parents were going to expire on the spot."

"I think he'd had a few drinks," Joanne chuckles, remembering the scene.

"And then he couldn't get my name straight. He kept calling me Glynis."

"He always liked the name Glynis," Warren remarks, and suddenly both Warren and Joanne are laughing.

"Sounds like *my* grandfather," Ron Gold interjects, leaning forward to rest his elbows on the back of their bench. "He was nearly blind and quite senile by the time I got married. As my future wife and I were approaching the judge, my grandfather, who was sitting in the front row, yelled out, 'Who is that nice-looking young couple?'" He joins in the laughter.

"Your grandfather always said exactly what was on his mind," Eve's mother says to Joanne, moving from Paul's side to sit next to Ron Gold. "I phoned your house one night, interrupting a big family dinner, to ask where Eve was, and your grandfather answered the phone and told me to mind my own business. I told him that Eve *was* my business, and he said, 'Quite right. But she's not ours, and she's not here.' And he hung up on me!" She, too, starts to laugh.

Joanne remembers the occasion, recalls the look of bemused horror that crossed her mother's face. How could you say that to her, Pa? she can hear her mother asking, watching her grandfather shrug his massive shoulders mischievously in reply.

Joanne's eyes steal over in Paul's direction. He sits alone, his

posture indicative of an internal debate about whether to stay where
he is or to join the rest of the small group. For an instant, Joanne is
tempted to make the decision for him, to walk over and lead him
back to the others. A familiar song drifts into her mind: We-are-a-
family, it sings. No, she decides, cutting the silent impromptu concert
short, We-*were*-a-family! The past tense was Paul's decision. The man
has legs of his own. They have led him to exactly where he wants to
be—apart. Her eyes return to the front of the chapel.

The ceremony is brief. A psalm is recited, a few necessary words
are spoken. It is over.

"I won't come to the cemetery," Eve's mother is saying, reaching over to take Joanne's hands in her own.

"It was so thoughtful of you to come to the ceremony," Joanne
says sincerely.

"I always admired your grandfather. I wanted you to know that."

"Thank you."

"Eve would have been here except . . ."

"I know . . ."

"I tried to persuade her to come with me . . ."

"Really, it's all right . . ."

"She was in so much pain . . ."

"Please, Mrs. Cameron, it's all right. I understand."

"Do you?"

"I'm trying."

"Stand by her, Joanne," Eve's mother urges. "Don't give up on
her. She needs you. You're the only one she's ever listened to."

"You have things backward, Mrs. Cameron," Joanne tells her
gently. "I'm the one who always did everything Eve said, not the
other way around. Eve was the strong one."

"No," Eve's mother forcefully corrects her. "Eve was the *noisy*
one. *You* were the strong one."

"What was all that about?" Gloria asks, touching Joanne's elbow.

"I'm not sure," Joanne admits.

"Are you ready to go to the cemetery?"

"I'd like a few minutes alone with my grandfather," Joanne says,
looking toward the coffin.

"We'll be outside," Warren tells her. Joanne watches as her
brother and his wife disappear up the center aisle behind Paul and
Ron, who exchange curt nods in one another's direction.

Slowly, Joanne advances toward the front of the chapel.

They have selected a plain pine box. Her grandfather's body lies inside it, dressed in a dark blue suit, his eyes closed, his cheeks slightly rouged. "You were right, Grampa," Joanne whispers, confident her grandfather will hear her. "Thank you."

Joanne reaches into her purse and slowly pulls out the crumpled Sherlock Holmes hat she had given him on his eighty-fifth birthday.

"You've got to take a hat with you," she smiles, puffing up the cap with surprisingly steady fists and laying it gently on top of her grandfather's folded hands. "That's better," she says, feeling her grandfather agree, almost seeing the still lips smile. Joanne bends forward and kisses the kind old face, the touch of his skin cold against her lips. "I love you, Grampa," she whispers for the last time.

"I just wish we didn't have to rush off so quickly," Warren is saying as Gloria clears the kitchen table of dishes.

They have returned from the cemetery and are sitting at Joanne's kitchen table, drinking coffee and eating a store-bought rhubarb pie, which Paul has noted with disappointment isn't nearly as good as the ones Joanne bakes herself.

"Don't be silly," Joanne tells her brother. "Of course you have to go back. You're going to be a movie star. This is your big chance."

"There was no way I could get them to reschedule . . ."

"You don't have to explain or apologize," Joanne tells him. "I'll be fine. Really." How can she explain that she is actually eager for them to leave?

"Why don't you come back with us?" Gloria asks suddenly.

"I can't," Joanne answers quickly.

"Why not?" Warren demands, warming to his wife's suggestion. "You have another two weeks before the girls get home from camp."

"And I have a job," Joanne tells her brother, glancing at Ron Gold, who looks instantly relieved.

"I'm lost without her, I swear," Ron Gold laughs. "I mean, I'd like to be noble and all that, but I really need her. If she were to leave me for two weeks, my entire practice, not to mention my life, would fall apart."

Paul glares at the doctor across the kitchen table. "I was under the impression that Joanne was leaving at the end of the month anyway," he says.

"I've decided to stay on," Joanne tells him, clearly catching him by surprise.

"Praise the Lord," smiles Ron Gold.

"I didn't realize," Paul begins, then breaks off. "When did you reach this decision?"

"In the past week," Joanne tells him. "Actually my grandfather had a lot to do with it."

It's Warren's turn to look surprised. "Grampa? How?"

"It gets complicated," Joanne answers. "He just made me realize certain things." She looks at her watch. "Shouldn't you be leaving for the airport pretty soon?"

"I'd be happy to drive you there," Paul volunteers.

"That's not necessary."

"I'd like to."

"All right," Warren agrees, glancing at his sister.

"You're sure we can't persuade you to come back with us?" Gloria asks, although both women recognize this is just a matter of form.

"How about at Christmas?" Joanne asks.

"Wonderful," Gloria exclaims. "I know just the man . . ." She breaks off awkwardly, her eyes carefully avoiding Paul's. "We'll have a great time. Leave everything to me."

"I'll look forward to it."

The small group proceeds to the front door. "Say hello to Eve for me," Warren says. "Tell her that I'm sorry I missed her, and that I hope she feels better soon."

"I will."

"Is this all your luggage?" Paul asks, looking at the small carry-on bag that sits on the floor next to the hall closet.

"That's it," Gloria answers.

There is an awkward pause in which no one seems sure of what to do with their hands or feet.

"Take care of yourself," Warren finally says, drawing his sister into his arms. "If you need anything . . ."

"I'll call."

"I feel so guilty," he whispers helplessly.

Joanne pulls back so that she can stare directly into his troubled eyes. "Guilt is a waste of valuable time."

He smiles. "How'd you get to be so smart?" His lips brush against her cheek.

"I'm not smart," she whispers in his ear. "Just not as stupid as I used to be."

"You were never stupid."

"I love you."

"I love you, too. Say hello to my beautiful nieces."

"Ditto," she laughs.

"Goodbye, Joanne," Gloria says, hugging her sister-in-law close against her. "If things aren't straightened out by Christmas," she confides, her deep voice descending to yet another level, her words remaining clear, "I know the perfect man."

"I'll look forward to him."

Paul glances around the small hallway impatiently. "Ready?" he asks, opening the front door. "Are you leaving now?" he asks Ron Gold casually as Warren and Gloria step outside.

"I think I'll stay around a while and keep Joanne company," Ron says easily. If he is aware of any tension, he ignores it.

Paul nods, the beginnings of a smile freezing on his lips. He looks at Joanne. "I think we should talk," he tells her.

"I think that's a good idea."

"Maybe I could drop over tonight."

"That would be fine."

He stands awkwardly in the doorway. "What time is good?" he finally asks.

Should she ask him for dinner? Joanne wonders, then decides that she doesn't feel like making dinner. "Eight-thirty," she tells him.

"See you then." Paul takes a final look at Ron Gold before following Warren and Gloria down the front steps.

"Do you think he'll try to talk you out of keeping your job?" Ron Gold asks after Joanne closes the door.

Joanne shrugs, patting her boss reassuringly on the shoulder as she walks past him back into the kitchen. He follows her.

"Your brother's a nice guy," Ron says. "I don't remember him from school at all."

"He was a few years behind us."

"You're sure you don't want to go to California with them?" he asks. "Please say you're sure."

Joanne laughs. "I'm sure."

"I must say you surprised me today."

"How do you mean?"

"I thought you might . . ."

"You thought I'd fall apart."

"I thought you'd fall apart," he repeats.

Joanne stares at him thoughtfully. "How many times can you fall apart?" she asks. "Eventually you either pull yourself together or you find there's nothing left."

"And you've pulled yourself together?"

"Let's say that I'm in the process of," Joanne explains.

"I'm glad to hear it. Paul's dropping by later won't upset you?"

"It probably will," Joanne admits.

"Think you're up to coming back to work tomorrow?"

"Face it, Ron," Joanne deadpans. "Without me, you can't function."

"I knew that the minute you found my pen," he says.

Paul steps nervously into the front foyer at just after eight-thirty that night. Joanne notices that he has changed his clothes, is more casually attired in light brown pants and a pale beige shirt that accentuates the deep chocolate brown of his eyes. "How are you?" he asks, following her to the living room, where Joanne quickly sits down in the swivel chair Paul has always staked out for himself. Has she done so deliberately? she wonders as Paul tries to make himself comfortable on the sofa. "The place looks good," he comments, absently looking around.

Joanne nods. "Would you like a drink?"

Paul is immediately on his feet. "Yes, as a matter of fact. Can I get you something?"

"No, thank you." She notices a certain hesitancy in his gait despite the seeming self-assurance in his voice. He is aware of a subtle change in what he always considered his home, and though everything looks the same, he has been thrown slightly off-balance, unsure of where things are, if they still occupy the same positions in which he left them.

She hears him pouring himself a drink, feels his hesitation at the doorway before he reenters the room.

"It was nice to see Warren again," he says, sitting down and taking a sip of his drink.

"He looks good," Joanne agrees.

"Can't say I'm overly fond of his wife."

"You never were."

"Something about her that I don't trust."

"She's all right. I think she means well."

"I guess I just don't like women whose voices are deeper than mine."

Joanne smiles.

"It's too bad they had to rush off so quickly."

"Well, I'm a big girl now," Joanne says, impatient with the conversation, which she has already had once today. "I have to learn to take care of myself."

Paul seems puzzled by this assertion. "Were you serious about visiting them at Christmas?"

"I thought I might. Why?"

"Just curious."

"I haven't been to California in a long time."

"You're sure Ron will give you the time off?" The question is delivered with a light cadence, hiding the more serious question underneath. "You're sure that it's a good idea, your continuing to work?" he continues, staring into his glass to avoid her eyes.

"I'm very sure," she answers simply.

"What about the girls?"

"What about them?"

"They're used to having you at home."

"They'll get used to having me work."

"It'll be difficult to work a full-time job and run a household."

"So we'll eat out more, order in more, and the girls will have to learn to help out more than they're used to. I think it'll be good for them. I think it'll be good for me," she adds, her voice strong.

Paul finishes his drink and returns his empty glass to the coffee table between them. "You've changed," he says after a long pause.

"You didn't leave me much choice."

Her answer clearly upsets him. "There's no need for you to work, Joanne. I promised that I would support you. You don't have to worry about money."

"It's not the money," she says quickly, then backtracks. "Well, no, that's not entirely true. It's partly the money. I *like* earning my own money. It gives me . . . a little bit of power, I guess. It gives me some independence. I'm not saying that I don't expect you to contribute. My salary is no great shakes, and I have a house to look after. You have two daughters you have to support . . ."

"You're talking as if I'm never coming back," he says quietly.

"Are you?" Joanne asks directly.

"I asked you to give me time."

"I've given you time." Joanne's steady gaze forces Paul's eyes back to her own. "Time's up."

"I don't understand. A few weeks ago . . ."

"A few weeks ago my husband and I made love, and I thought everything was all right again. I woke up the next morning to the news that nothing had changed, and to the realization that, as long as I'm prepared to put up with it, nothing ever will."

"Has Ron Gold had something to do with this sudden epiphany?" Paul asks pointedly.

Joanne almost laughs at his choice of words. She feels herself rise out of her chair, is aware that she is pacing back and forth across the hardwood floor. "Ron Gold is a lovely, generous man who gave me back a little of what I'd lost over the years—what I'd given away—my self-respect. For that, I will always love him and be grateful. But we're not having an affair, if that's what you're implying."

Paul seems relieved. "Then why the sudden deadline? Why the rush?"

"It's been almost four months, Paul," she informs him. "I can't waste any more time waiting for you to decide what you want to do with your life. I have my own life to get on with. My grandfather told me that." Paul looks appropriately confused. "I went to see him after we came home from camp. I was very upset. I was pouring my heart out as usual, complaining about all the awful things that were happening to me, when he suddenly opened his eyes and asked me if I'd like to change places with him." She pauses, hearing her grandfather's words still echoing. "I don't know what happened. I guess something suddenly snapped, and I realized that, no, I didn't want to change places with a dying old man. I'm young—or at least, I'm not old—and there's still lots that I want to do." She takes a deep breath, watching Paul do the same. "I love you, Paul. I love you very much. You are the only man that I have ever loved. I want you to come home. But I won't be manipulated any longer, and I'm not prepared to wait anymore for you to come to your senses and see that I am worth a truckload of little Judys . . ."

A look of surprise passes across Paul's face.

". . . and if you haven't discovered that fact for yourself by now, then that's your problem. Not mine. Not anymore." She swallows hard before continuing. "The girls come home in less than two weeks. We're either a family by then or we're not. I'll wait till then before calling a lawyer."

"Joanne . . ."

"I don't want to see you again, Paul," Joanne says steadily, "unless it's the sight of you pulling your suitcases up the front steps." She walks to the door. "Please go."

A loud knocking wakes her up at just before seven the following morning. Confused, Joanne reaches for the alarm clock, which suddenly goes off in her hands. "Jesus!" Joanne exclaims, jolted instantly awake, pushing herself out of bed. Realizing someone is at the front door, she proceeds to the intercom on the bedroom wall. "Hello?" she asks, sleep still clinging to her voice. "Is someone there?"

There is no reply.

Joanne stands absolutely still in front of the intercom. She understands that the knocking was not part of any dream. She knows that there is something—or someone—downstairs waiting for her.

With deliberate slowness, she proceeds to her closet and throws on a robe. Her feet are bare against the carpet of the stairs.

She reaches the front hallway, pressing her body against the heavy oak door to stare through the small peephole. She sees nothing. Carefully, she reaches over to shut off the alarm, her fingers drawing back abruptly when she realizes that the alarm light is not on. Staring at the front door as if she can see through it, Joanne quickly runs over the events of the previous evening. She sees Paul step out into the warm night air, watches him pull his car out of their driveway, feels the weight of the door against her shoulder as she closes it behind him. Joanne follows the memory of herself as she proceeds into the kitchen to make herself a cup of tea, feels the soothing heat as it travels down her parched throat, reexperiences a sudden wave of fatigue as her image disrobes and crawls into bed for what proves to be a long, dreamless sleep. A loud knock at her front door awakens her just before her alarm clock is scheduled to go off at seven o'clock this morning.

There is no memory of having set the burglar alarm. She has forgotten—again. You'd forget your head if it wasn't attached, she hears her mother chastise gently. "Way to go, Joanne!" she exclaims loudly, pulling open the front door.

It is lying at her feet, beside the morning paper, large and black and eerily appropriate.

Joanne bends down and gingerly scoops the funeral wreath into her arms. She brings it into the house, slowly extricating the small

white envelope that has been wedged between the wreath's delicate
branches. Her fingers curiously calm, she tears open the tiny envelope and pulls out the note inside. Across it is scrawled one word in
large black letters: SOON.

Chapter 28

Joanne is putting her house in order.

It is Saturday night. She has spent the day going from room to room, straightening up, deodorizing, reorganizing—spring cleaning, though it will soon be fall. For the last several hours she has been going through her daughters' rooms, throwing out papers they no longer need, sorting through their closets to see which clothes are too small, too old, or too worn out to be used again. She is careful not to discard old favorites, careful not to impose her own preferences on her daughters. They have their own decisions to make. She is only trying to make things easier for them when they return from camp next week. It will be difficult enough for them to come home to the news that their mother is gone. Not that she intends to go anywhere without a fight.

There is still time, time to pick up the phone and call California, tell her brother that she has changed her mind, that she is flying out on the next plane. But that would only delay the inevitable, she knows, and she is tired of delays, tired of waiting. Waiting will only put her daughters' lives in jeopardy, and it will not save her own. She can't stay in Los Angeles forever. One day she will have to come back and he will be waiting for her when she does. Let's get on with it, she decides, returning the last of Robin's freshly dusted books to her bookshelf.

Everything is in order now. The house is clean. There are fresh fall clothes hanging in the closets; the freezer is stacked with food. She is ready for September though she is not sure that she will be around to enjoy it. Instinctively she understands that her tormentor will strike this week. Before her daughters come home. Before neighbors who have gone away for the summer begin filtering back.

Joanne crosses the upstairs hall to her bedroom, heading directly for the bedside phone. She has several calls to make. Balancing herself on the edge of the king-size bed, she picks the receiver off its carriage and dials.

Surprisingly, Paul answers the phone on the first ring. "I was just thinking about you," he says.

When he doesn't elaborate, Joanne speaks. "I wanted to make sure about next week," she begins crisply. "That you'll pick the girls up at the bus station."

"A week today," he confirms. "One o'clock."

"You have it written down?" she presses. "You won't forget?"

"Joanne, is everything all right?"

"Everything's fine," she tells him, her voice steady. "I just wanted to make sure. Paul . . ." She stops. How can she tell him to take good care of the girls should something happen to her without alarming him? She can't. She can only trust that he will. She *knows* that he will.

"Yes?"

"Don't be late," she says. "You know how upset they get when they're kept waiting."

She says goodbye before he has the chance to add anything further, her fingers returning to the phone, dialing her brother in California.

"Warren?"

"Joanne? Is everything all right?"

"Everything's fine. I just wanted to say hello, see how you made out with your movie."

"I was brilliant. A star was born, what can I say? How is everything?"

"Nothing's changed," Joanne tells him, sensing that this is the real question he is asking. Nothing's changed except me, she thinks but doesn't say. "So what now?"

"Back to the same silicone-filled breasts and tucked-in tushes that I see every day," he laughs. "Tits and ass. This is California— what can I tell you?"

"I love you, Warren."

"I love you too."

Joanne checks her watch as she replaces the receiver. It is almost nine o'clock in the evening. She has one more call to make, but she'll have to go downstairs to look up the number.

Quickly, she makes her way to the kitchen, flipping through her telephone-address book until she locates the name she is looking for.

"Camp Danbee," the woman announces minutes later.

"I'd like to speak to my daughters," Joanne informs her. "I know it's against camp policy, but this is very important."

"Your daughters' names, please?" the woman asks, sensing that it would be pointless to argue.

"Robin and Lulu . . . Lana . . . Hunter."

There is a brief pause, the sound of pages being turned.

"They're in the recreation center watching a movie."

"Could you get them please?"

"It'll take a few minutes. Why don't I have them call you back?"

"How long?"

The woman is clearly flustered. "Well, it'll take me a couple of minutes to walk over there and a few more minutes to bring them back. It shouldn't take longer than five minutes altogether. Is this an emergency, Mrs. Hunter? Something I should prepare the girls for?"

"No," Joanne tells her. "It's not that kind of emergency. I just need to speak to them."

"I'll have them call you in a few minutes."

"Thank you." Joanne hangs up the phone and stands with her hand still on the receiver, waiting for it to ring.

It does.

"Hello, Robin?"

The voice on the other end of the line is shrill and bordering on hysteria. "Joanne," it manages to spit out, "it's Eve's mother."

"Mrs. Cameron," Joanne says dully, concerned, yet not wanting to tie up the line. The girls will be trying to call. "What's the matter? Has something happened to Eve?"

The words that follow proceed in short, staccato bursts, making them difficult for Joanne to follow.

"I don't know. I called to check on her, and she started shouting, calling me names, screaming that I'm a witch, that I ruined her life, that she wishes I were dead!"

"Mrs. Cameron, please try to calm down. I'm sure that Eve doesn't mean those things. You *know* she doesn't mean them."

"I don't know anything anymore," the older woman sobs. "You had to hear her, Joanne. It didn't even sound like her. She sounded like something inhuman. It wasn't her voice. She says she's my Evie, but Joanne, it isn't her. It's someone who's using her body. It's not my baby. A baby would never wish its mother dead."

"What can I do?" Joanne asks helplessly, looking at her watch, already knowing the answer.

"Go to her, Joanne," Eve's mother tells her. "Please. Brian isn't home. She's all alone. I told her that I'd come over but she said she'd kill me if I tried to come near her. I don't know what to do. You're right next door. She'd never hurt you. Please, go to her. Make sure she's all right."

Joanne stares out the sliding glass door into the darkness. "Okay," she says after a slight pause.

"Call me back," Eve's mother instructs as Joanne is about to hang up.

"What's your number?" Joanne frantically searches the small desk for a sharpened pencil, finally locating one with just enough of a point to write and scribbling down the number that Eve's mother dictates.

"Call me," she hears again as she is replacing the receiver.

Her hand is still on the phone when it rings again.

"Hello, Robin?" she asks immediately.

"Mom?" Robin's voice is frightened but clear. "Is everything all right?"

Everyone keeps asking me that, Joanne thinks, relieved to hear her daughter's voice. "Everything's fine, darling."

"Then why are you calling?" Robin is clearly puzzled.

"I miss you," Joanne shrugs. "I just wanted to speak to you for a couple of minutes."

Robin's voice becomes very soft, very low. Joanne can visualize the teenager shifting position, cupping her hand over the receiver so that no one else in the vicinity can hear what she is going to say. "Mom, you know it's against the rules to do that," she says. "Everybody's looking at me like they expect somebody to be dead or something. What am I going to tell them?"

"Tell them that you're sorry to disappoint them, but as of this moment anyway, I'm still alive and kicking."

"Mo-ther!" There is a long pause. Then, "Have you been drinking?"

Joanne laughs out loud. "No. Do I have to be drunk to want to speak to my daughters, whom I love very much?"

"Well," Robin stumbles, "it *is* against the rules."

"Tell them that there's been a change in the arrangements for picking you up and I had to phone because I wasn't sure that a letter I wrote would reach you in time."

"Pretty lame, Mom," Robin comments.

"Well then, you think of something better."

There is another, longer pause. "How about I tell them that you called to tell us that you and Dad got back together?"

Joanne says nothing.

"Have you, Mom? Is that the reason you're calling?"

Silence, then, "No." Another silence.

"I love you, Mom."

"I love you too, sweetie."

"Lulu's standing here griping because she's missing the movie. You'd better speak to her."

"Goodbye, doll," Joanne says as Robin transfers the phone to her younger sister.

"What's going on?" Lulu whines. Perversely, the sound is reassuring.

"Nothing, honey, I just missed you and wanted to say hello."

"You're not supposed to do that."

"Yes, I know."

"I'm missing the movie, Mom. Mrs. Saunders came and got us right at the most exciting part."

"So, it's been a good summer?"

"Yeah, it's been great." Joanne can see the look of confused impatience in her daughter's eyes.

"Think you'll be ready for school in a few weeks?"

"I guess so. Mom, can't we talk about this when we get home?"

"Of course we can," Joanne says quickly. "I'm sorry, sweetie. Go back to your movie."

"Is Daddy okay?"

"He's fine."

"Your grandfather?"

Joanne is caught off guard by the question, which she was not expecting. "He died," she says finally, not knowing how else to answer.

"What? Why didn't you say so?" Joanne can see Lulu turning toward her sister and whoever else is present beside them. "Mom's grandfather died," she is telling them.

"What?" Robin's voice exclaims in the background. Joanne is aware of a slight shuffle as Robin comes back on the line. "Great-grampa died?" Robin repeats, relating Joanne's grandfather to herself for the first time. "When?"

"A week . . . maybe ten days ago. I'm all right," Joanne adds hastily. "Now you can tell them that somebody died," she says, and has to fight an urge to giggle.

"Mo-ther!"

"Go back to your movie, darling. Your father will pick you up at the bus station next week. I love you."

"I love you too," Robin says clearly.

"I love you," she hears Lulu shout.

"I love you, angel," Joanne whispers.

"Mrs. Hunter?" Another, older voice.

"Yes?"

"It's Mrs. Saunders here. I just wanted to say that I'm very sorry about your grandfather."

"Thank you," Joanne replies before hanging up.

She walks to the sliding glass door and stands staring out at the night. Slowly, with no conscious plan in mind, she unfastens both locks and slides the door open, the warm night air immediately surrounding her, pulling her onto the patio, like a lover's arms leading her into a hidden corner for a furtive kiss.

She stares into the open pit that is most of her backyard. A perfect night for a swim, she thinks, slowly making her way down the stairs, which still await their final coat of varnish. She pictures herself gliding gracefully across the pool. It is long enough for a decent swim, not just adequate for splashing around. Still, splashing around is what she does best. She makes a mental note that if she survives the summer, she will take swimming lessons. Maybe she'll even resume her tennis, she thinks, approaching the edge of the pool and searching through the darkness for the tennis racquet she threw away, unable to locate it. Hell, she decides suddenly, if she survives the summer, she'll buy herself that new tennis racquet that Steve Henry suggested.

It's quiet. She is aware of a warm breeze against her bare arms. She hears the familiar shuffling of leaves in the trees, returning her momentarily to her grandparents' cottage. She feels herself snugly tucked into her small bed, staring through the screen of the open window at the trees beyond. She closes her eyes, catching the lowered voices of her parents and grandparents from the next room. In her mind, she hears the distant wail of a passing train. She feels peaceful, even serene.

The sound of the phone ringing in the kitchen pushes Joanne abruptly back into the present. She pivots toward the sound, catching sight of Eve glaring down at her from her bedroom window next door.

Joanne runs quickly up the patio steps and back inside, leaving the sliding door open behind her. "Hello?" she says into the phone, realizing she is out of breath.

"Did you speak to Eve?" the voice asks without further introduction.

"Mrs. Cameron . . ."

"Did you see her?"

"I haven't had a chance yet . . ."

"What do you mean you haven't had a chance?"

"I'm going to phone her now, Mrs. Cameron. I'll call you after I speak to her."

"Don't phone. Just go over there."

"I'll call you later," Joanne states flatly, and hangs up. Her entire life, it seems lately, revolves around the telephone. Hesitantly, she presses the appropriate numbers to connect her to the house next door. The phone rings five, six times, before it is picked up. Then there is no sound on the other end.

"Eve?" Joanne asks. "Eve, are you there?"

The voice that responds is remote, as if the call were long-distance. "What do you want?" it asks.

"I want to know what's going on," Joanne replies. "Your mother called. She was very upset."

"Just like the old days," the voice cackles.

"Where's Brian?"

"Who?"

"Are you alone?"

"Just me and my pains," Eve laughs, sounding like herself for the first time in the conversation. "Want to join us?"

"Do you *want* me to come over?" Joanne asks in return.

"I'm dying, Joanne," Eve suddenly cries.

"You're not dying."

"Yes, I am," Eve screams. "I'm dying and I can't get anybody to believe me."

"I'll come over."

"Now!"

"Right now."

"I'm dying, Joanne."

"Hold on till I get there."

"I don't know if I can."

"You can. You can," Joanne repeats. "Hold on, I'm coming right over."

"Hurry."

"I'm coming now." Joanne throws the receiver back into its carriage and races toward the front door, almost forgetting her house keys, returning to the kitchen to fish them out of her purse, returning to the front door, suddenly aware that she has left the sliding glass door in the kitchen wide open. "Stupid," she mutters, hurrying back into the kitchen to close it, quickly securing the locks. "You'd forget your head if it wasn't attached," she says out loud.

The phone rings as she is scurrying past it. Her hand shoots out automatically to pick it up.

"I'm leaving right now," Joanne promises quickly.

"Mrs. Hunter . . ." the voice begins, and Joanne feels her heart stop. She says nothing. "Did you like my flowers, Mrs. Hunter?"

Joanne squeezes the keys in her hand, feels them digging into her palm.

"I was sorry to hear about your grandfather," the voice continues. "Still, I bet you're glad. One less obligation to meet. Gives you more time to have fun."

"Who are you?" Joanne asks steadily.

"Well now, if I told you that, it would spoil the surprise, wouldn't it, Mrs. Hunter? And we wouldn't want to do that, would we? Especially since I'll be there so soon, and you'll be able to see for yourself. I'm coming for you, Mrs. Hunter."

Joanne feels an involuntary sigh escape her throat.

"Oh, I like that, Mrs. Hunter. That was sexy. Sexy with fear. My favorite combination."

"You're crazy!"

The voice loses its tease. "And you're dead." There is a second's pause before the soft lilt returns. "I'm coming for you, Linda," it repeats, capturing its former rhythm.

"Wait a minute—my name's not . . . You have the wrong . . ."

What was she about to say? she wonders as the line goes dead in her hands. You have the wrong number? It's another Mrs. Hunter you want? What difference does it make if she's the Mrs. Hunter who's going to wind up dead? "And you're dead," she hears the ugly voice repeat.

Racing toward the front door, her keys firmly in her hand, she sets her alarm and rushes out of the house.

Chapter 29

Joanne cuts across the two front lawns, stealing a hurried glance down the street as she tucks her keys into the back pocket of her jeans. There is a phone booth at the corner. From this distance, in the dark, it is impossible to make out whether or not someone is inside it. The street lights clarify little, only serving to define and accentuate shadows. Is there someone there?

I'm coming for you, Linda.

Just her luck, she thinks sardonically, running up Eve's front steps and knocking loudly at the door. She's not the woman he really wants. The story of my life, she decides. The story of my death.

No one answers her knock.

"Eve!" she calls, pressing down on the bell and then knocking again. "Eve, it's me, Joanne. Let me in."

I'm coming for you, Linda.

Joanne's head spins. "Eve, open up. Come on. I'm not going to stand out here forever."

"I can't answer the door, Joanne," she hears faintly from inside the house.

"Why not?"

"I'll die if I answer the door."

And I'll die if you don't, Joanne thinks. "Eve, for Christ's sake, open the door."

I'm coming for you, Linda.

"I can't."

"Open the goddamned door!" Joanne screams, and immediately the front door falls open. Joanne pushes her way roughly inside and slams it behind her. "What is this nonsense about dying if you answer the door?" Joanne demands angrily, relieved at finding herself safely inside.

"I'm so scared," Eve whines, backing toward the stairs and falling into a semifetal position on the bottom step.

Joanne stares at her friend, her hair pinned erratically back from her gaunt face by a series of oversized bobby pins, her cotton housecoat stained and smelling of perspiration, her feet bare beneath old, shabby slippers.

"Of what?"

"I don't want to die."

"You're not going to die."

"I want to live, Joanne. What's happening to me? Help me."

Joanne joins Eve at the foot of the stairs. "Listen to me, Eve," she begins. "Hear me out." Eve nods. Joanne feels Eve's body give an involuntary shudder as she puts her arms around Eve's shoulders. "You probably won't like what I'm going to say . . ."

"Say it," Eve urges, surprisingly docile.

"You're having a nervous breakdown," Joanne tells her as gently as she can. "You're *not* dying. I know that's how you feel, but you are *not* dying."

Surprisingly again, Eve does not argue. Instead she stares questioningly into Joanne's eyes. "How do you define a nervous breakdown?" she asks quietly, clinically.

Joanne almost laughs, thinking that she could well be having one herself. A classic example of the blind leading the blind. "I'm not sure," she begins honestly. "I'm not sure how a psychiatrist would define it, but I would say that someone who's having a breakdown is someone who has ceased to function."

"And you think that's me?"

"Isn't it?"

Eve says nothing.

"Four months ago," Joanne explains, "you were an active, vital woman, a psychology professor taking extra courses at night toward a Ph.D., a powerhouse who crammed thirty hours into every day, who took tennis lessons and went to exercise classes and was always busy. I'd look at you in awe. I couldn't believe one person could do so much."

Joanne is aware of a stiffening in Eve's shoulders. "And now?" she asks dully.

"And now you do nothing," Joanne states simply. "Your whole identity is wrapped up in being sick."

"I'm in pain!" Eve retorts, pulling out of her friend's grasp. "What do you want from me? You think that I enjoy being an invalid?"

"I don't think you have any control . . ."

"What am I supposed to do, Joanne? What am I supposed to do about the pain?" Eve struggles to her feet and begins pacing the front hall like an animal in a cramped cage. "I know you don't believe me about the pain . . ."

"I *do* believe you . . ."

"But you think that my mind is creating it."

"Yes," Joanne says directly, watching Eve roll her eyes in frustration. "But let's say that I'm all wet," Joanne continues, getting up, trying to keep time with Eve's frantic pacing. "Let's say there *is* a physical source to your pain that all the doctors have missed. Eve, thousands of people across this country suffer from chronic pain that doctors are unable to diagnose or treat. Ultimately, these people have to make a choice. They can either make the pain the center of their lives, which is what you've been doing, or they can accept that the pain is there, that it's going to stay there, and that there's not a whole lot that they can do about it except *get on* with their lives."

"I'm supposed to ignore the pain . . ."

"As best you can. I know you think that's very easy for me to say . . ."

"Only because it *is* very easy for you to say . . ."

"No," Joanne argues. "No, it isn't. It isn't because I've been going through the same sort of thing for the past few months."

Eve stops pacing. "What are you talking about?"

Joanne hesitates. "The phone calls," she says finally.

It takes Eve a few seconds to understand Joanne's reference. "The phone calls," she repeats with disdain. "You're convinced that you're the strangler's next victim and *I'm* the one who's crazy?!"

"All right," Joanne concedes, "maybe *I'm* the one who's crazy. I honestly don't know anymore. The point is that it doesn't really matter. *I* think I'm getting these phone calls from someone who says he's going to kill me. He called me tonight, in fact, just before I came over. He says he's coming very soon."

Eve laughs out loud.

"The point is," Joanne repeats, "that this has been going on for months now and nobody believes me, or if they do believe me, they say there's nothing they can do about it. And the thing I finally realized is that there isn't a whole lot that *I* can do about it either. I've done everything I can—I've informed the police, I've changed my phone number twice, I've put in new locks and installed an alarm system. So now I have a choice. I can either lock myself up in my house forever, or I can make the most of what's left of my life, and just *get on* with it." She searches Eve's eyes for a glimmer of understanding, but they remain blank, reveal nothing. "I don't want to die," Joanne admits. "My grandfather made me see that. But there are certain things that are beyond my control, and I guess that part of being an adult is learning to accept which things those are. I don't like it. It scares the shit out of me, to be perfectly frank. But what choice do I have? I can either make my fear the center of my life or I can . . ."

"*Get on* with it," Eve interrupts, her voice heavy with sarcasm.

"Okay, I'll stop. I'm starting to repeat myself."

"Our situations aren't at all comparable," Eve informs her decisively.

"I think they are."

"Who gives a shit what you think?" Eve demands angrily, suddenly pushing past Joanne and running up the stairs.

"Eve!"

"Go home, Joanne."

"Let me help you," Joanne urges, following Eve up the stairs and into the larger of the front bedrooms, the room Brian uses as an office. "My God, what happened in here?"

Joanne stares in bafflement at the once tidy room, which now bears all the earmarks of a bungled burglary attempt. Books lie scattered across the floor; the chair behind the desk has been overturned; the large Oriental rug is carpeted with papers and file folders, their contents spilled indiscriminately about and trampled on. "What happened in here?" Joanne repeats in a whisper.

"Hurricane Eve," Eve tells her and smiles, her hand reaching over and swiping at the few papers that are still clinging to the top of Brian's desk, sending them scattering to the floor.

"But why?"

"He said he was going to have me committed," Eve sneers, sitting down in the center of the mess, scooping a fistful of papers into her hand. "He uses a bottle, you know," she adds cryptically.

"Who? What are you talking about?" Joanne is already on her knees, gathering papers.

"The Suburban Strangler," Eve whispers, her voice a singsong. "It seems he can't do the job on his own." She holds up a few random papers, as if they somehow back up her words. "I've been doing some reading. They say it could even be a woman." Her voice has an eerie, nasty undertone. Joanne stops what she is doing, finds herself staring at the woman who has been her closest friend for thirty years. "It could even be me," Eve smiles, obviously enjoying herself.

"Don't talk nonsense," Joanne says curtly.

"How do you know it's not me? You already think I'm crazy. Why couldn't it be me?"

"Because I know you. Because I know that you couldn't hurt anyone except . . ." Joanne breaks off.

"What?" Eve asks quickly. "You stopped. Finish what you were going to say."

"You couldn't hurt anyone," Joanne continues softly, "except yourself." She lets the papers she has gathered into her hands slide back onto the floor. "Eve, you had a miscarriage," she says quietly, staring deep into her friend's eyes. "That doesn't make you a bad person. It doesn't mean that you failed. It means that something was wrong that was beyond your control. How long are you going to punish yourself for it?"

"For as long as you continue practicing psychiatry without a license," Eve quips humorlessly, kicking at some file folders with her feet.

"All right then, since I've come this far, I'm going to go all the way . . ."

"I look forward to it."

"I don't think you're afraid of death," Joanne states. "I think you're afraid of life."

"Interesting theory," Eve says, her right foot beginning to twitch nervously.

"I think that you set impossible goals for yourself. You're not the only one. I'm as guilty as you are. Somewhere we got the notion that it's not enough to be wives and mothers, we have to be *perfect* wives and mothers. And while we're running our perfect little households, we're also expected to be perfectly successful businesswomen. Oh, it also helps to stay young and beautiful while we're doing these things. Well, the hell with it! We get old. We put on weight. We get veins and lines and, goddamn it, we get tired. We are not perfect. But that doesn't make us failures either. Eve, do you understand what I'm trying to say? It wasn't your fault that you had a miscarriage . . ."

"I know that."

"Do you?"

Eve lowers her head into her lap, rocking back and forth. When she speaks, her voice is a low moan. "Any idiot can have a baby, Joanne. Why couldn't I?"

Joanne says nothing. She moves slowly to her friend's side and puts a comforting arm around her. "Our mothers had it easier in a perverse kind of way," she whispers absently as Eve begins to sob. "They had rules to follow, roles to play. And not *all* the roles either. They . . . my God!" Joanne drops her hands to her sides.

Eve is momentarily startled by the sudden cessation of soft soothing words. "What's the matter?" she asks through her tears.

"Our mothers . . ."

"What about them?"

"My mother's name was Linda."

"Joanne, are you all right?"

Joanne is suddenly on her feet. "He called me Linda. It wasn't a mistake."

"What are you talking about?"

"It wasn't a mistake. He called me Linda because he thinks that's my name. And why wouldn't he? It's the only name he ever heard my grandfather call me."

"What are you talking about?" Eve repeats.

"It all makes sense. Where he got his information, how he knew everything. He was there the whole time listening to me pouring my guts out every Saturday afternoon. My God, Eve, I know who it is!"

"Joanne, you're scaring me."

"I have to use your phone." Joanne begins moving toward the desk. "Where's the goddamned phone?" she asks, finally locating it, on its side and disconnected on the floor.

"You can't use it!" Eve shrieks suddenly.

"Eve, I have to call the police."

"No! I know what you really want to do. You want to call the hospital. You think I'm crazy. You want them to come for me. Brian put you up to this."

"No, Eve, I swear . . ."

"I want you to get out of here."

"Eve, I know who's been calling me, threatening to kill me. It's that boy from the nursing home. He might even be the Suburban Strangler. I have to call the police."

"No!"

Eve is at Joanne's side, her hands flailing wildly, ripping the phone from Joanne's hands and hurling it across the room, crying triumphantly as it crashes against the far wall, chipping the paint and leaving a large blood-colored stain.

"Get out of here," Eve is shouting. "Get out of here before I kill you myself!"

"Eve, please . . ."

"Get out of here."

"Call Brian," Joanne begs, fleeing Eve's fists and rushing to the bedroom door. "Please, tell him I know who's been phoning me, that I know who the killer is. Tell him to call me . . ."

"Get out!"

Eve bends over and scoops up a book from the floor. Joanne sees it hurtling toward her, but is unable to duck out of its way in time to fully escape the impact of its blow as it crashes painfully into her back. Tears stinging her eyes, she races down the stairs, Eve still screaming behind her. She reaches the front door, opens it, and escapes into the night.

Seconds later, she is at her front door, hearing Eve's door slam closed behind her, fumbling inside the pockets of her jeans for her keys. She hears something at her shoulder and spins quickly around. There is nothing there. "Calm down," she says to herself. "Just take things slowly. Don't panic. Your keys are here somewhere. You put them in your pocket," she reminds herself, silently praying that they didn't drop out during the melee at Eve's. "They have to be here," she cries, finally locating them in her back pocket, hidden underneath an old tissue. "Thank God," she mutters, turning the key in the lock and pushing the door open, shutting it swiftly behind her, moving in one fluid motion to the alarm.

The alarm light is not on.

"Oh no, not again," she moans. "How could I be so stupid? What is the point of having an alarm system if I'm going to keep forgetting to turn the damn thing on?" She reaches over angrily and presses the button that activates the system. Then she takes a deep breath and heads toward the phone. She dials emergency—911.

After three rings, the phone is answered. "Hello," Joanne starts, "I'd like a policeman . . ."

"This is police emergency," a voice begins.

"Yes, I'd like a . . ."

"This is a recording. All our lines are busy at present . . ."

"Oh, God."

"If you need police assistance, please hold on; someone will take your call as soon as possible. If you wish a police car to come to your house, leave your name and address after the tone . . ."

Joanne hangs up, rubbing the palms of her hands against her forehead. What is the point in leaving her name and address? Immediately she picks up the phone again and redials emergency. The point is survival, she tells herself, listening as the recorded message drones on, once again instructing her to leave her name and address after the tone. "Joanne Hunter," she says clearly, then enunciates carefully her full address. "Please hurry," she adds, deciding to stay on the line in case someone human answers her cry for help.

It is exactly thirty minutes later that Joanne hears a car pull up in front of the house. She waits for the familiar sound of footsteps on the outside stairs, for a loud knocking at the door, but she hears nothing except the unending stream of recorded music coming from the telephone receiver in her hand.

She transfers the phone from one hand to the other, feeling her joints stiff from the strain of holding the receiver against her ear. She stretches her head back against the nape of her neck, hearing the crack, aware of a cramping in her shoulder muscles. Slowly, carefully, she raises her head, her eyes falling absently across the sliding back door.

She sees him standing in the darkness, his face pressed against the glass, peering inside. Before she has time to think, to recognize the uniform, she is screaming wildly.

"Police officer," the figure announces, displaying something in his right hand. Joanne understands that it is a badge.

At the same moment there is a loud banging at the front door. Joanne drops the phone, which she has been screaming into, and listens to it knock against the side of the counter, echoing the banging from outside the front of the house.

She runs to the door. "Who is it?" she yells, staring through the peephole at the uniformed officer.

"Police," the voice curtly informs her. "We received a report of an emergency at this address."

"Yes, I phoned," Joanne exclaims, about to open the door, remembering that the alarm is on, pressing the button to turn it off, pulling open the door. The young, slender policeman, who seems barely older than Robin, looks nervously around.

"What's the problem?" he asks, moving into the kitchen. "May I?" he asks, indicating his partner positioned outside the sliding door.

Joanne watches him unlatch the side lock. "There's one at the bottom, too," she informs him. In the next second, his partner, perhaps an inch taller and maybe a few years older, is standing beside him.

"I'm Officer Whitaker," the first policeman introduces himself, "and this is Officer Statler. What exactly is the problem?"

Joanne is about to answer when she hears a small voice. The officers become aware of it at the same time, and all three turn toward the phone, which is still dangling off the hook against the counter. Joanne runs over and picks it up. "Hello," she says.

"Police emergency," a human voice answers. "Can we help you?"

"Police emergency," Joanne explains to the two officers. "I've been holding on."

Officer Statler takes the phone from her hand. "Officer Statler here. We're on the scene now. Yes. Thank you." He returns the phone to its receiver. "Just what *is* the problem?" he asks, his eyes searching the room. "Did you see a prowler? Are you hurt?"

"No." Joanne shakes her head, catching the look of surprise in each man's face. "I know who the Suburban Strangler is," she announces, trying not to recognize the look of impatient scepticism which passes between the two men.

"This is police emergency, ma'am," Officer Whitaker reminds her.

"And this *is* a police emergency," Joanne states vehemently.

"I see. Is this person here with you now?"

Joanne shakes her head. "No . . . But he called earlier. He said that he was coming."

"Nice of him to let you know," Officer Statler remarks, suppressing a grin.

"Listen, I am not some crackpot," Joanne tells them, knowing this is exactly how she sounds. "Sergeant Brian Stanley lives next door. He knows me. He'll tell you that I'm not some crackpot."

"Okay, okay, Mrs. Hunter," Officer Whitaker says, checking his notes for her name. "You called and reported a police emergency. You requested a police car to come to your home. We're here now. Why don't you tell us whatever you think you know and we'll do our best to follow up on it as soon as we can."

"As soon as you can? What does that mean?"

"Tell us what you think you know," he states again, and Joanne tries not to bridle at the implicit condescension of his words. Tell us what you *think* you know! As if she knows nothing, only *thinks* she does. Why did she bother to call? What did she hope to accomplish? What did she *think* would happen? "He's been calling me for months," Joanne tells them anyway, "telling me that I'm next . . ."

"You've reported these calls to the police?"

Joanne nods. "I didn't know who it was. The voice sounded familiar, but it was a very strange voice, hard to pinpoint. Now I realize that he was mimicking his grandfather's voice, not exactly of course, but that rasp that old people sometimes get . . ."

"I'm not following . . ."

"You see, every Saturday I visit my grandfather, or I did until he died about ten days ago, and every Saturday this boy was there at the same time visiting his grandfather. He was always with his mother, but his mother couldn't be the killer because she wasn't always in the room when I'd be talking to my grandfather. Sometimes she'd go out for a cigarette, and it would look like the boy was sleeping, but I guess he was only pretending to be asleep. He was really listening. Listening to everything that I was telling my grandfather. That's how he knew that the girls would be away at camp, that my husband had left me . . ."

"You're divorced?" Officer Statler interrupts.

"Separated," Joanne tells him. Does this make her less relevant? she wonders, again catching the look on his face as he jots down this new information. "Anyway, it was only after Sam Hensley was transferred to my grandfather's room that I started getting the phone calls. Eve asked me once when I started getting these calls and I couldn't remember exactly . . ."

"Sam Hensley? Eve?" Officer Whitaker asks.

"Sam Hensley is the boy's grandfather. Eve is my friend. She's Brian Stanley's wife, Sergeant Stanley's wife," she emphasizes. "You see, everything falls into place. How he got my phone number, how he knew when I changed it. I mean, it's very easy for anybody to check the records. They're kept at the nursing station."

"The boy's name is Hensley?" Officer Statler asks, the laughter in his eyes belying the seriousness of his tone. "Could you spell that?"

"The old man's name is Hensley," Joanne corrects. "The boy's name is something different." She searches her memory for the name. "God, what is it?" She sees the image of the young man before her, but his features are indistinct, blurred. She never really noticed what he looked like. He was just always there, blending into the furniture. Nice-looking, she thinks, but not memorable.

The image of his mother pushes the boy roughly out of the way. She is the easier of the two to describe. She has substance, weight, a voice that carries, that sticks in the memory. Alan, Joanne hears the woman call, summoning the reluctant boy away from the small black-and-white television in the nursing home's waiting room. "Alan," Joanne repeats aloud. "God, what was his last name? Alan . . . Alan something . . . Alan Crosby!" she exclaims triumphantly. "That's it. Alan Crosby. He's about nineteen or twenty. That's all I can remember about him. I never really took any notice of him."

"Thank you, Mrs. Hunter. We'll check this out," Officer Statler tells her, snapping his notebook closed.

"When?" Joanne demands.

"We'll get started on it right away," Officer Whitaker says before his partner can answer. "It's Saturday night, but we'll do what we can." He studies the phone. "Is this still your number?" he asks, reopening his notepad and copying the numbers from the face of the phone.

Joanne nods.

"Try not to worry, Mrs. Hunter," Officer Statler says, opening the front door. "We picked up some guy last night we're pretty sure is our strangler. We're just running a few final checks on him before we make a public announcement. Keep this locked anyway," he advises, stepping outside. "There's a lot of screws loose out there. If this Alan Crosby has been threatening you, we'll put a stop to it soon enough. I don't think you have anything to worry about, but if it'll help you sleep any easier, we'll drive by the house as much as we can tonight."

"I'd appreciate that. Thank you." Joanne shuts the door after him, double locks it, and reactivates the alarm system in one continuing gesture. "So," she says aloud, "it appears I'm safe after all." She flips off the hall light and makes her way up the stairs to her bedroom.

Chapter 30

Joanne is exhausted. It has been a long day and a longer night. But the nightmare is over, and as Joanne stares across the room at her empty king-size bed, she thinks only of how good it will feel when her head hits the pillow. She is even getting used to sleeping alone. It is like any other space, she thinks as she undresses, tossing her clothes across the blue chair at the foot of her bed. You grow into it.

Sliding her bare feet across the thick carpet, hearing her mother's voice tell her, pick your feet up when you walk, she enters her bathroom and begins filling the tub. Her body is sore; her muscles ache; she needs the help of a soothing tub of hot water to ensure a good night's sleep.

Thoughts of Eve, of the police, of Alan Crosby, crowd into her head. She doesn't want to think, she decides, pushing the thoughts rudely back out.

Catching sight of her naked body in the full-length mirror, she does not turn away. Rather, she walks steadily toward her image, allowing her eyes all the time they require to take the necessary stock.

"I'm over forty," she says aloud. "I'm middle-aged." She looks deep into her own eyes. "I'm a grown-up." Her eyes fall to her breasts, then continue down past her rounded belly to the thatch of pubic hair below. "I am woman."

On impulse, she suddenly sits down on the small, rectangular mat in front of the mirror, arranging her body in the pose she remembers seeing in Paul's magazine months ago. Shoulders back, knees up and well apart, she silently challenges her reflection. "You still look ridiculous," she laughs, watching her image laugh with her. "Maybe we should pose for one of those magazines," she tells it, laughing louder. Show the world some real tits and ass, not these inflated imitations they're trying to pass off as the real thing, perfectly round aberrations that never move or age. Remind people what women looked like before silicone and surgery tried to fool them into thinking that they could be young forever.

Joanne stands up quickly and bends forward, touching her fingers to her toes and staring back at herself from between parted thighs. "Well, hello there, Joanne Hunter, I'd know you anywhere." She sticks out her tongue. "Same to you, buddy," she says, straightening up and swiveling in a full circle, surprisingly satisfied with what she sees. "Not half bad for a woman over forty," she congratulates her image.

Joanne returns to the bathtub and shuts off the water. It is very hot, perhaps a touch too hot, she thinks as she lowers her body. She presses her shoulders against the white porcelain, feeling the water ripple underneath her chin. Beads of perspiration immediately form on her forehead and upper lip. She closes her eyes, stretching her arms and legs out before her. I could fall asleep right now, she thinks. Just let myself drift off and fall asleep.

She hears a noise, feels her body instantly tense. Straightening her shoulders, sitting up, drawing her knees to her chest, Joanne waits to hear the noise again. But there is nothing, and after a few minutes of listening she relaxes back against the tub. There is nothing to worry about. The alarm is on; the Suburban Strangler has been apprehended; the police are keeping an eye on the house anyway. The nightmare is over. Almost, she hears a little voice whisper. Don't close your eyes. Don't fall asleep.

She closes her eyes despite the silent admonition, but it is already too late. She is no longer alone in the tub. Eve has joined her, and the two officers who were here what already feels like a lifetime ago, and Alan Crosby, his features indistinct behind an odious smile. They are leaving her no room to relax, no room to stretch out. Joanne reopens her eyes and grabs the bar of soap from its dish, quickly sudsing herself and then rinsing the soap off, standing up and stepping out onto the floor. Her bathtub has become a public pool. It is too crowded. She wants solitude.

Back in her room, Joanne pulls a T-shirt out of a drawer and pokes her head through its neck, her arms through its short sleeves. She is getting into bed when something makes her turn, forces her to alter her course. Almost against her will, she finds that she is tiptoeing across the upstairs hall, peeking first into Robin's room and then Lulu's, satisfied that both rooms are empty, thinking briefly how nice it will be when they are occupied again next week. She finds herself looking forward to her daughters' return, to the coming year. Her first, she thinks, as a full-fledged adult.

Passing by the top of the stairs, she decides to make a final check on the alarm. She remembers having turned it on after the police left, but her memory has not been serving her well lately, and she wants to be sure.

Seconds later, she finds herself in the downstairs hall. The green light shines brightly from the small box on the wall, telling her that the alarm is on. She is safe.

Proceeding next into her dining room, she stares out the front window at the street, is further reassured that all is well when, in the next minute, she sees a police car drive by, slowing down to take a good look at her house. She waves, but it is dark in the room and the police cannot see her. Still, she feels better knowing that they are there.

She is tired, so tired that her head is beginning to throb. Climbing in between the bedsheets, Joanne immediately lets her eyes shut. Don't close your eyes, the little voice warns. Don't fall asleep. "Go away," she tells it impatiently, watching a young Kevin McCarthy embrace the beautiful Dana Wynter for the last time. Joanne is asleep almost before her head reaches the pillow.

Joanne is playing cards with her grandfather.

He is winning, which does not surprise her. What does surprise her is the number of people who are gathered inside his room at the Baycrest Nursing Home to watch them play. At first their faces are indistinguishable, one blending into another, impressionistic sketches only, their boundaries not clearly defined, a few simple strokes of color and light. As Joanne searches these faces, she sees familiar features intermingle, combine, disappear. Her mother's eyes watch her from beneath Eve's startling red hair. Lulu's arms reach out to her from Robin's shoulders, her father's full-throated laugh emanates from Paul's open mouth.

Go away, she tells them silently. I can't concentrate when you're so busy moving around. Stay still or go away. Instead, the strange audience remains; the cards disappear. She finds herself in a soundproof booth; her grandfather, an aging master of ceremonies, is asking her a question. She is on a quiz show, she realizes, straightening her shoulders and tucking in her stomach for the camera. If she answers the question correctly, someone is saying, she will win a giant egg roll. But the sound in the booth is faulty; sentences are begun only to disappear. How can she be expected to answer the question when she can't hear it? she demands, catching snatches of good wishes from the excited crowd.

We're rooting for you, her mother enunciates clearly, though Joanne cannot hear the words. She nods, but she is worried. She doesn't want to disappoint her mother. She has been a good girl; she has studied hard. All her friends are here; she doesn't want to let them down.

You can't disappoint us, her father says clearly, and then the sound is gone. We love you, he mouths silently.

We should go now, Eve says. Let you concentrate.

I love you, Paul tells her.

I need you, Ron Gold reminds her.

And then they are gone. She is alone. The sound in the booth crackles ominously as if the booth has been electrified.

Are you . . . your question? her grandfather asks, his voice fading in and out.

I can't hear you. Joanne gesticulates wildly, but either he cannot see her or she is being deliberately ignored.

Here is . . . question, the voice says.

I can't hear you. I missed . . .

When is . . . date . . . start of . . . ?

I'm sorry, I can't hear you. I keep missing words. I don't know the question.

Joanne feels the initial stirrings of panic in her chest, knows that her glass booth has become an airless prison. She wants to get out. But she must answer the question correctly before they will release her. Frantically, she searches out the faces that suddenly surround her. But she is in a roomful of strangers whose faces blend into their surroundings, whose bodies are inseparable from the walls they lean against. Her breath catching in her throat, she realizes that she is in a room full of Alan Crosbys.

The glass booth is not a prison, she realizes in sudden desperation as she watches it disappear. It is what has been keeping her alive. Now she stands alone and unprotected in a room full of killers.

When is the date of the start of the Boer War? their collective voices taunt her, their bodies drawing closer.

I don't know, Joanne pleads.

Sure you do, the voices insist. Just ask Lulu. She told us she'd never forget it.

What are you talking about?

"Linda . . ."

We were there when you told your grandfather.

"Linda . . ."

We know the combination to your alarm.

"Linda . . ."

Eve's voice suddenly pierces through the others. I'm dying, Joanne, she cries. Help me!

I'll be right there, Joanne calls to her, pushing through the tight circle of Alan Crosbys into her front hall, her keys clutched firmly in her hand. She pauses for an instant to press the numbers on her alarm system before racing out the door.

When is the date of the start of the Boer War?

I turned on the alarm.

"Linda . . ."

I turned it on when I went out but it was off when I came back in.

"Linda . . ."

I turned it on. Someone turned it off.

He's in the house.

He's been here all along.

Joanne bolts upright in bed, her eyes open wide in terror.

"Linda . . ."

The voice fills the room.

"Linda . . ."

Joanne's eyes move to the intercom on her bedroom wall. She is not asleep. She is wide awake. The voice she has been hearing is not part of any dream. The voice is real. It is part of her nightmare. And it is real.

Alan Crosby is in the house.

"Wake up, Linda," the voice sings eerily, like a child. "I'm coming to get you."

Joanne feels her hands start to tremble, her body start to shake. She feels sick to her stomach. Where is he? What room is he speaking to her from? Where can she hide? Where can she run?

Why didn't she install panic buttons? she berates herself. Karen Palmer told her to install panic buttons.

"Linda . . . I know you're awake now. I can feel it. I can feel your fear. I'm coming."

It wouldn't have made any difference, she realizes. He would have found a way around them, just as he found his way here tonight. He must have taken her keys from her purse and returned them after he'd had copies made. They disappeared after she'd been to visit her grandfather; they were returned after another such visit. Why hadn't she thought to put it all together?

"Ready or not, Linda . . . here I come."

He is playing games with her. Silly, childish games. Murderous games. Hide-and-go-seek. The cat and the mouse.

Joanne looks around wildly as total silence suddenly surrounds her. The voice is gone. The house is completely still except for the sound of her own shallow breathing. Somewhere in the house, he is moving. He is coming for her.

Are you just going to sit here in bed and wait for him? a little voice demands angrily. Move!

Joanne remains rooted to her bed.

Move, you motherfucker!

Joanne scrambles to her feet. Where do I go, big shot? she implores, her knees knocking painfully together. Now that I'm up, what the hell do I do?

She grabs at the phone, balancing the receiver against her ear with her shoulder as she tries to dial. But her fingers jam in the small plastic circles, and she has to start again. Her eyes fastened on the doorway, she tears at the three digits which will connect her to police emergency.

"You have reached police emergency," the familiar taped message informs her seconds later. "All our lines are busy . . ."

Joanne hears another click. A different voice comes on the line. "Can I help you, Linda?" it asks, less human than the tape. Joanne drops the receiver back into its carriage, holding her breath, too terrified to move.

She can lock herself in the bathroom, she thinks, then immediately decides against it. Like her imagined counterpart in the glass booth, she will only trap herself inside. A simple bobby pin is all it takes to open the lock, and there is nothing in the bathroom that she can use to defend herself. Paul took his razor blades with him when he left.

Her only hope is to get outside.

Joanne looks at the bedroom windows. But she is two floors up— three off the ground—and even if she can succeed in breaking one of the windows, the fall will undoubtedly injure her severely, enough to let him find her and finish the job.

She has to get outside. Perhaps the police are still circling the block. She checks the time. It is after two o'clock. Are they still out there? Can she get outside?

Where is Alan Crosby? In what room is he waiting for her? Is he still by the phone in the kitchen or has he snuck upstairs?

She continues holding her breath, listening for the slightest sound, hearing nothing. She looks frantically around the bedroom. What can she use to defend herself? A hanger? A shoe? Her eyes return to the phone. Well, why the hell not? she thinks, pulling the cord from the wall, brandishing the phone wire like a whip in front of her.

Slowly she moves toward her bedroom door.

Her eyes stare down the upstairs hallway through the darkness, seeing nothing. Is he hiding in Lulu's room? In Robin's? Was he there, under the bed, when she checked their rooms earlier? Was he watching her in morbid anticipation while she slept? Her heart wedged firmly in the middle of her throat, the butterflies in her stomach multiplying and invading every inch of her body, Joanne pushes her reluctant feet out of the room. If she can just get down the stairs . . .

Her bare toes slide along the carpet, inching their way toward the top step. Where is he? Will he let her get down the stairs?

Cautiously her right foot lowers itself down the first step. Joanne sees the fleeting image of a young girl with a rectangular face and flat chest. She hears Eve's voice. You know she's the survivor because she has no boyfriend and no boobs, she says. Well . . . Joanne thinks, looking down at herself—close enough. How did the girl escape? Joanne wonders, searching her memory and finding nothing. Great, she thinks. Alzheimer's disease now too, on top of everything else.

She is on the last step. If she can only get to the front door . . .

She sees the movement before she hears the sound, hears his piercing scream before she hears her own, feels his hands reaching for her throat. In a total panic, she drops the phone she has been carrying to defend herself, feeling its weight crash close beside her, hearing another sharp cry, this time of pain, the word "shit!" as it escapes his mouth, feeling his hands retreat, everything happening so fast that she is halfway out the front door before she realizes that she has dropped the phone on his foot and that their screams are now mingling with the shrill shriek of her alarm.

She is outside and the alarm siren is racing boldly through the neighborhood.

She sees Eve peering down at her from one of her bedroom windows.

"Eve!" she screams, running across the grass toward the house next door, watching as Eve disappears from view. "Open the door!" she screams, stopping midway between the two houses, waiting for Eve to open her door, turning her head to catch Alan Crosby smiling sickly at her from beneath her front porchlight. He is holding something in his hand. As she watches, a long silver blade snaps menacingly into view.

Move! her inner voice commands, and instantly she obeys, her bare feet carrying her through the grassy lane between the two houses into her backyard.

Now what? she screams silently, staring into the large, concrete-lined hole. My grave, she thinks, racing toward the shallow end and tripping down the three steps into the empty pool.

There is no moon and only a few stars. Maybe he won't see her. Maybe he won't see the hole. Maybe he'll fall in and break his neck.

Sure, she thinks immediately, hearing the loud pounding of her heart against her chest. As if he hasn't carefully gone over every inch of her backyard. Her fingers tracing the sides of the pool, Joanne creeps toward the deep end, the continuing sound of the alarm siren screaming into the night. Where are the police? If she can just keep out of the boy's way until they arrive.

Maybe he has already left. Maybe the sound of the alarm scared him away. Maybe she is safe . . .

She hears him. He is somewhere above her, moving across the flagstone. Can he see her? Has he seen her already?

Joanne lowers her chin into her chest, trying to muffle the sound of her breathing. She feels the concrete rough against the back of her bare legs. What is she wearing? Looking down, her hands tracing the outlines of her breasts, she sees the bold white letters jump up toward her as if they are printed in three-dimensional ink. I SPENT THE NIGHT WITH BURT REYNOLDS . . . they proudly proclaim. Goddamn, she shouts to herself, crouching forward, blocking the letters with her hands. Of all the T-shirts to put on, why did she have to pick this one?

I can't believe that I'm worrying about what I'm wearing, Joanne suddenly berates herself, recalling Karen Palmer's observations. What are people supposed to think about when they are faced with almost certain death? My thoughts were never that deep in life, she apologizes to Karen's image. I can't be expected to turn into Kant or Hegel because I only have a few minutes left to live.

"Linda . . ."

The voice twists through the darkness like a snake through grass. He is somewhere above her head, across from where she is crouching. Is he staring at her? She is afraid to look up, afraid the movement will draw his attention. It is possible that he hasn't seen her. Perhaps he is hoping that the sound of his voice will frighten her into betraying her hiding place. It is important that she stay very still.

"Linda . . ." the voice calls again, this time closer.

Where are the goddamn police? Why aren't they here? What is the point of having an alarm system if nobody is going to pay any attention to it when it goes off?

The girl who cried wolf, she thinks, recalling the earlier false alarms. Where are Officers Whitaker and Statler? They said they'd keep an eye on her house. But that was hours ago. It's after two in the morning. They're probably in bed by now, long since sound asleep.

There is a slight movement above her head, which Joanne realizes a second too late is a hand moving toward her. Instantly her hair is scooped into a tight ball, the force of her assailant's fingers lifting her to her feet. She twists her head back to see a knife flashing through the air, a horrifying shriek escaping her lungs as the knife slices across the top of her hair.

"Cowboys and Indians!" the boy whoops, as Joanne trips over her feet to the other side of the boomerang at the deep end of the pool.

"Leave me alone!" she yells, her eyes reaching his through the darkness.

"I'm not finished with you yet," he laughs, waiting to see which way she will move.

"The police will be here . . ."

"I have lots of time," he says confidently.

"Please . . ."

"But maybe you're right. Maybe I shouldn't get too cocky. Maybe I should start showing you that good time I promised you . . ."

Joanne starts inching along the side of the pool back toward the shallow end.

He moves with her. "That's a girl," he says. "Come to Poppa."

Joanne watches in horror as Alan Crosby leaps easily into the shallow end of the pool after her.

In a mad scramble, Joanne dashes toward the steps, feeling something slam against her toes and then snap up painfully against her shins, causing her to lose her balance. She stumbles, feeling her body crumble, her fingers curling into the familiar strings of her tennis racquet, as her hands reflexively reach out to block her fall. Her feet somehow miraculously maintaining their balance, she scoops up the racquet and scrambles up the steps, hostile hands reaching out from behind her to grab hold of her T-shirt.

She struggles to slip out of the boy's tight grasp, but his grip on her T-shirt is solid and he begins reeling her toward him like a prize fish on a line. Again she hears the ominous click of a switchblade.

"You promised me a good time," she suddenly snaps, catching them both by surprise with the vehemence in her voice. "I am *not* having a good time!"

What the hell is she talking about? Joanne wonders, feeling his grip relax and taking advantage of the confusion of the moment to propel herself out of his reach.

She tries to run but he is only inches behind her. Once more she feels him at her back, hears the knife cutting through the space between them. As the blade slices through the back of her T-shirt, a series of snapshots, tiny black-and-white photographs of the Strangler's victims, flashes before her eyes. "No!" she hollers defiantly, her left hand joining her right on the handle of her tennis racquet. Watching herself as she spins around, almost in slow motion, Joanne Hunter bends her knees, her back foot planted firmly on the ground, and, starting low, swings the racquet, full force, up and through.

Chapter 31

Joanne hears the car pull up as she is finishing her third cup of morning coffee. Laying down her cup, she waits for the familiar chimes to ring. Shooting the intercom a nasty look, she walks briskly to the door and peers through the peephole.

"Hi," she says, pulling open the door.

"Hi," he says in return, and husband and wife stare awkwardly at each other from opposite sides of their threshold. "Can I come in?"

Joanne says nothing, simply backs away from the door to allow Paul to come inside. He closes the door behind him. "You look tired," Joanne observes. "Would you like a cup of coffee?"

"I'm exhausted," he replies, "and yes, I'd love a cup of coffee."

He follows her into the kitchen, walking to the sliding glass door to stare into the backyard.

"It's been quite a week," he says, almost absently, as if he is barely aware that he is talking out loud.

Joanne makes a sound halfway between a laugh and a cry and places his cup of coffee on the table.

"I tried to reach you," Paul continues. "As soon as I heard about what happened, I called . . . I came over. Eve's mother finally told me that you'd gone to California."

"I needed a couple of days away," Joanne explains. "I'm sorry. I should have phoned you. I wasn't thinking too clearly. Everything happened so fast." She looks around distractedly. "It's not every day I almost kill someone," she says quietly.

"Couldn't have happened to a nicer guy. That's quite a swing you've got," Paul jokes. "I understand that he broke his arm and leg when he fell into the pool. I guess it was a good thing that it wasn't filled after all."

"Things have a way of working out," Joanne smiles. "Your coffee will get cold."

Paul sits down at the kitchen table in what was traditionally his seat. Joanne pulls out the chair across from him and wonders why he is here. The girls will be returning from camp in less than an hour.

"I feel so guilty," he says at last.

Joanne shrugs, saying nothing. What is there to say?

"I should have been here," he continues, unprompted. "I should have been here for you. None of this would have happened if I'd been here."

"That's not so," Joanne tells him. "And I'm not saying that to make you feel better. I'm saying it because it's the truth." Paul regards her quizzically. "Those women that the Suburban Strangler murdered had husbands around to protect them. They died anyway; I didn't. Maybe the fact that you weren't around, that I had only myself to depend on, maybe that's what saved my life. I don't know. It's a nice theory. Besides, it's over now, and I'm okay. So unless you enjoy the feeling, I'd suggest that there's nothing for you to feel guilty about."

Paul looks at Joanne with more than a trace of surprise. "You shouldn't have had to go through it," he says quietly, not quite ready to relinquish his guilt.

"No, I shouldn't have," Joanne agrees. "But there you go." Her head pivots toward the pool. She sees the darkness, feels the knife slice through the soft fabric of her T-shirt, hears the swoosh of her tennis racquet as it crashes against the boy's head, watches as he plummets into the concrete hole. "I'd like to sell the house," she announces evenly.

"I can understand that," Paul tells her.

Joanne nods. She is grateful that he doesn't feel the need for a major discussion. "Find something without a pool," she adds.

"Agreed," he says easily, taking a long sip of his coffee. "How was California?"

Joanne laughs. "Actually, compared to here, it was kind of quiet."

"How's your brother?"

"Good. He's been trying to convince me to move out there."

"Are you considering it?" Paul asks, his shoulders arching stiffly though his voice remains steady.

"Not really," Joanne answers. "It would mean uprooting the girls, putting them into new schools, taking them away from their friends. Besides, I have my job . . . ."

"Still planning to keep working?"

"Yes."

Paul's shoulders relax. "I think that's a good idea."

"I thought I'd take the girls with me to the office tomorrow," Joanne tells him. "Show them where I work. Show them what I do."

"I think they'd enjoy that."

"I think it's important that they see that their mother is more than just a doormat with a welcome sign across her back."

"I'm sure that's not how they see you."

"How could they help but see me that way?" Joanne asks. "I've been so busy submerging myself in everybody else's expectations that I disappeared. I'm not blaming you," she adds quickly. "It wasn't your fault. You didn't do it to me. I did it. Somewhere along the way, I forgot how to be me. I don't blame you for leaving, I really don't. How can you live with a shadow?"

"I wasn't any great shakes myself."

"Well, at least you were honest."

"Honest, hell!" Paul exclaims. "I was a self-indulgent, stupid son of a bitch." He stands up, taking his empty coffee cup to the sink and rinsing it out. "I mean, what did I think was going to be out there? Adventure? Youth?" He laughs bitterly. "There's nothing sadder than a middle-aged man trying to find his lost youth. So what if I'm not Clarence Darrow? I'm still a damn good lawyer. I've finally discovered that there's really nothing else that I want to be when I grow up."

He stares at her, waiting for her to speak, but Joanne says nothing, simply returning his steady gaze.

He is the first to break away, looking toward the doorway. "How's Eve?" he asks, seeking safer ground.

"She's in the hospital. She agreed to let Brian take her. I think that maybe what happened that night finally shook a little sense into her. She's the one who called the police, you know, got hold of Brian, made sure they got there in time. She probably saved my life."

"Some summer."

"It hasn't exactly been a summer I'd care to repeat," Joanne admits, running a hand across the top of her head. "He gave me a punk haircut," she laughs. "Think the girls will like it?"

"Why don't you ask them when we pick them up?" he suggests.

"I don't think that would be a good idea," Joanne answers slowly, finding the words difficult to speak.

"Why not?" Paul asks.

"Because I think that if the girls see us together at the bus station, that will only get their hopes up, and then we'd have to let them down again."

"Would we?"

Joanne stares at her husband. "What are you trying to say, Paul?"

There is a slight pause. "That I'd like to come home," he says.

"Why?"

The question is startling in its simplicity. "Because I love you," he answers. "Because I realized in the four months that I've been gone that there's nothing out there . . ."

"There's everything out there," Joanne interrupts quietly.

Paul smiles sadly.

Joanne stares out the sliding glass door. "So much has happened. So much has changed. I've changed."

"I like the changes."

"That's the problem." Joanne turns back to confront her husband. "I won't always have a psychotic killer around to bring out the best in me!"

They are suddenly both laughing. "We should get going," Joanne says finally.

"There's something I have to do first," Paul tells her, walking steadily to the front door. Following behind him, Joanne watches as he heads down the front stairs to his car, quickly extricating two suitcases from the back seat.

Smiling confidently, Joanne watches as her husband of twenty years pulls his suitcases up the front steps.